WAR OF THE WORLDS: FRONTLINES

*To Carrie,
As close to an alien invasion as I ever want to get!*

Aug 18/2010.

Also Available from Northern Frights Publishing

Shadows of the Emerald City
Timelines: Stories Inspired by HG Wells' *The Time Machine*

Watch for these titles coming soon from NFP!

Fallen: An Anthology of Demonic Horror
Things Falling Apart by JW Schnarr

WAR OF THE WORLDS: FRONTLINES

EDITED BY
JW SCHNARR

Northern Frights Publishing
In the Great White North, Blood Runs Colder...
www.northernfrightspublishing.webs.com

War of the Worlds: Frontlines © 2010 by JW Schnarr
This edition of
War of the Worlds: Frontlines © 2010 by Northern Frights Publishing

War of the Worlds: Frontlines
Edited by JW Schnarr

Cover Art and Design © 2010 Gavro Krackovic
Internal Layout and Design © 2010 JW Schnarr

All rights of all stories © Their Respective authors.
Northern Frights Publishing reserves the rights to publish
War of the Worlds: Frontlines in Perpetuity.

Northern Frights Publishing is Proudly Canadian.

This book is a collection of stories inspired by the Herbert George Wells novel *The War of the Worlds*. No animals were harmed in the making of this anthology, but many aliens and fictional people were beaten, maimed, burnt, tortured, or otherwise mistreated. Or killed.
War is Hell!

This collection of short fiction is based on the Public Domain work of Herbert George Wells and his novel *The War of the Worlds*. The characters, names, and places in some of these stories are derivatives of the original work.

FIRST PRINTING

ISBN: 978-0-9734837-2-7

For Poppa John,
who pointed up at the sky one night and asked a little boy what he thought he saw.

ACKNOWLEDGEMENTS

In no order, thanks to my sister Janice for her continued support and insight as NFP rolls along. Many thanks and lots of love to my daughter Aurora for her continued inspiration, and thank you to my parents for their help during the difficult periods that life brings. I also want to thank my good friend Sam El Rifai, for letting me invade her house and use her internet when I was in dire need.

Of course, this collection would be nothing without the artists and authors that contributed to make it so special, and to you, the reader, goes the biggest thanks of all.

—JWS.

TABLE OF CONTENTS

FORWARD by Eric S. Brown 1
AFTER WELLES by Michael Scott Bricker 5
WEIRD FRUITS by Camille Alexa 17
KILLERS by Vincent L. Scarsella 24
THE DODO DRAGON by Sheila Crosby 43
THE VIRUS OF MEMORY
    by Gerard Daniel Houarner 48
WHAT MAKES YOU TICK by David Steffen 63
THE BROKEN HAND MIRROR OF VENUS
    by Mark Onspaugh 65
COMMON TIME by Bruce Golden 80
STEVE'S REALLY COOL MOVIE BLOG
    by RJ Sevin 94
MOTH TAMUTH ROBOTICA
    by Kristen Lee Knapp 100
EMPIRE OF THE MOON by Harper Hull 108
THE SPACER AND THE CABBAGES
    by Auston Habershaw 125
JOHN'S LIST by Brent Knowles 139
TEQUILA SUNSET by Michele Garber 150
GAUSS'S INVITATION by Gary Cuba 158
ANOTHER END OF THE WORLD
    by Michael Penkas 170
A SWEETHEART DEAL
    by JW Schnarr and John Sunseri 182
THE RAINMAKER by Mike Barretta 195
NEWS ON THE MARCH by Edward Morris 204
MY BEAUTIFUL BOY by Jodi Lee 207
TO LOVE A MONSTER by Victorya 218
THE CANDLE ROOM by James S. Dorr 225
USHER by Davin Ireland 236

But who shall dwell in these worlds if they be inhabited?

...Are we or they Lords of the World?

...And how are all things made for man?

—KEPLER

(quoted in The Anatomy of Melancholy)

"I go to London and see the busy multitudes in Fleet Street and the Strand, and it comes across my mind that they are but the ghosts of the past, haunting the streets that I have seen silent and wretched, going to and fro, phantasms in a dead city, the mockery of life in a galvanised body. And strange, too, it is to stand on Primrose Hill, as I did but a day before writing this last chapter, to see the great province of houses, dim and blue through the haze of the smoke and mist, vanishing at last into the vague lower sky, to see the people walking to and fro among the flower beds on the hill, to see the sight-seers about the Martian machine that stands there still, to hear the tumult of playing children, and to recall the time when I saw it all bright and clear-cut, hard and silent, under the dawn of that last great day...

"And strangest of all is it to hold my wife's hand again, and to think that I have counted her, and that she has counted me, among the dead."

Herbert George Wells, *The War of the Worlds*

FORWARD

by Eric S. Brown

H.G. Wells is considered by many to be the father of the science fiction genre and for good reason. Wells was a visionary far ahead of his time as a writer. His body of work includes such classics as *The Island of Doctor Moreau*, *The Time Machine*, *The Invisible Man*, *The Food of the Gods*, and *The War of the Worlds*.

The War of the Worlds is one of the definitive tales of extraterrestrial life invading our planet. It tells the story of an army from our neighboring planet, Mars, sent to our world to enslave it and use us as food using technology far ahead of our own. Anyone acquainted with the genre instantly recognizes the Martian tripods from Wells' novel. Twice, mainstream Hollywood has adapted this legendary novel to the silver screen. The first time with hovering, atomic age tripods and the second with the walkers much closer to what they were in the novel. However these two films are far from being the only takes on Wells' work. There are countless rip offs and B movie adaptations such as *The War of the Worlds II* film that aired on Sy-Fy. Earlier this year, I even got to try my hand at Wells' novel, being hired by Coscom Entertainment to give it a "living dead" overhaul with my book- *War of the Worlds Plus Blood Guts and Zombies*, adding zombies to a world already under the heel of Martian invaders. The main thing about *The War of the Worlds* is that it is both a war story and tale of human survival in the face of an alien invasion.

Aliens come in all shapes and forms from James Cameron's chest bursting, perfect predator monsters in *Aliens* to the more subtle and manipulative Visitors from *V*. The joy of a well told alien invasion tale is much like that of a zombie story in some ways. The tale speaks of humanity's courage in the face of overwhelming odds and the struggle to stay alive and save our world and its culture. It opens the door to exploring the human condition in the context of fighting an inhuman foe. It's also an adventure story with heavy elements of war (or at the very least action) whether it's a war of the mind or one fought with tanks and guns. Where an alien invasion tale goes beyond a zombie story is the technology and science that fills its pages. Beyond being a simple survival tale of horror, an alien invasion tale adds the coolness of things like blasters, spaceships, ray guns, and all the toys the science fiction genre has to offer. It can allow science and reasoning to be the heroes that save the day or doom us all by showing that there are forces and species far more powerful than that of mankind in the cosmos. Stories and novels like Wells' *The War of the Worlds* open our minds to the fact they we may not be alone and that a threat to our very existence could already be watching and preparing to come for us from the very stars themselves.

This amazing anthology of original fiction set in Wells' *The War of the Worlds*' universe is full of almost every type of tale you could hope for in such a collection. The book opens with a tale of love, prejudice, and fear by Micheal Scott Bricker entitled *After Welles* that will leave you thinking about what the story has to say long after you read the last sentence.

What makes you Tick by David Steffen is a darkly disturbing and sickly humorous tale of human scientists studying a Martian prisoner, only are they really studying it or is it studying them? Steffen's take on the Martian psyche is brilliant and his use of their telepathy in this story will leave you in awe of his ability to evoke emotions from his readers.

My personal favorite tale in the book however was *The Broken Hand Mirror of Venus* by Mark Onpaugh. As with many stories in this collection, humanity level of technology is far beyond what our race had to face the Martians with in the original War of the Worlds and it's fun to see the tech of the modern world challenging the invaders. What makes this story so great however is that it's truly a post-apocalyptic tale of the highest order. After the Martians return to Earth with bigger, stronger, and more deadly machines now designed to withstand even most of Earth's viruses and bacteria, we humans create a virus of our own to take them down with. Of course, the virus mutates and things get worse for everyone. I cannot sing the praises of this tale enough as it captures everything so wonderful about the "after the end of the world" genre and crams it into a few pages of absolute fun.

But if you bought this book looking for a good war tale like I would have done, no worries. There are some of those too such as Harper Hull's *Empire of the Moon*, which has the British Royal Navy and Spitfires going head to head with the invaders in all out, edge of your seat action.

The book concludes with a mind-bending future tale of the human

FORWARD

race post the Martian invasion that contains everything from "portal travel" to androids by Davin Ireland, simply titled *Usher*. This tale is one of the most unique in the book and the originality screams at you loud and clear.

So as you read this anthology, I hope its tales thrill you and perhaps even terrify you, but most of all cause you to look at the stars and know that there may indeed be life out there beyond this world we inhabit. . . And it may be watching us.

Eric S. Brown, 2010

AFTER WELLES
by Michael Scott Bricker

The odd had become commonplace, the ordinary, all too rare. While driving home through downtown Grover's Mill, New Jersey, I was slowed by a passing military convoy, and was reminded of the war in Europe. Jeeps and big, heavy trucks secreted what I assumed to be Martian goods along the eastern road. Spindly mechanical legs, blackened, muddied, poked out from under a massive tarp on one of the larger trucks, and I wondered if another ruined Martian machine had been uncovered. Somewhere under that tarp was a heat ray, I assumed, and I imagined scientists and military men examining their find in locked rooms, drawing diagrams, blueprints, building prototype machines, Martian weapons, splashed with air force insignia. I imagined U.S. machines crawling into Europe, going up against Nazi war machines, cities obliterated in the flash of a heat ray. The United States would become involved, it was inevitable, and in human hands, the new weapons could finish the mission that the Martians had failed to complete. By handing us the tools of our own destruction, I thought, the Martians may have won, after all.

I wondered if Ruthie would be offended, if she would find a gift of Martian origin to be distasteful, or worse, offensive. It was a handmade silver brooch, a product of black market artisans, more beautiful than any I had ever seen. Spun silver, little intertwined bows fashioned into the image of a rose, and at the center, a polished Martian mirror. I rubbed my thumb across the surface of the mirror and thought of the girl who had sold it to me, her gentle face (so beautiful, I imagined, before a heat ray had bubbled her skin), and I wondered why she would sell artifacts that would certainly hold painful memories.

The centerpiece of the brooch, that fantastic, reflective mirror, had been crafted from a shattered heat ray assembly, taken from a Martian Cylinder which had been discovered only a month ago by a worker with the New Works Progress Administration. That was what she told me, and I had no reason to doubt her, because as I held the brooch in the sunlight, rotated it in my palm, the mirror changed color, red then yellow then blue, and I felt that nothing of earthly origins could be so beautiful, so frightening.

They had nearly destroyed us all.

The New Jersey State Militia was out in force, uniformed men wandering along crumbling walks, stopping people, searching through packages, and as I drove slowly down Main Street, I took the brooch from my coat pocket, reached down, hid it beneath the seat. Grover's Mill was slowly coming back to life. A new building was going up where the old Owl Drugs had been, a cold, formidable structure in brick and steel. All of the new buildings were like that, built for strength and utility, void of ornament, as if to show the world, the universe, that we were not to be provoked. I missed Owl Drugs. It had been in an old brownstone with apartments above, and I would have lunch there almost every day. I had eaten lunch there on the afternoon of October 30th, 1939. Hours later, the first cylinder had impacted.

The Militia was stopping automobiles ahead, asking questions. I thought about Ruthie, hoped that she would still be waiting for me if I were late. It took twenty minutes for my Plymouth to make it to the front of the line, and as it did, I remembered the photograph on the seat next to me.

"Where are you coming from?" The uniformed man leaned over, reached in, put his hand over the steering wheel.

If he saw the photograph, what would he do? He might search the automobile, find the brooch, fine me or put me in jail for possessing Martian goods.

"What's wrong? Didn't mean to startle you."

I was staring at the photograph, hadn't realized it until the man spoke. "Sorry. On my way out of town. Business..."

"You all right?"

I turned, looked at the man, was relieved to find that I knew him. His name was Jim Breckenridge, and he used to live in Morristown before the invasion. "Jim, it is you, isn't it?"

"Sure. Haven't seen you in some time." He paused. "I've stayed away from New Jersey during the last year. Now I'm in the Militia. Too much free time. Had to do something, you know?"

Although it had only been a year since I had last seen Jim and his wife, he looked years older, and he carried himself awkwardly. I wondered what could have happened to change him so, and then I remembered the Morristown Cylinder. It had given birth to three of the most destructive Martian Crawlers of the invasion. After choking the countryside within a fog of poisonous black smoke, the machines had joined three more then moved towards New York City. Jim, who had been away on business at the time, lived through the invasion. His wife and two children had not.

Jim paused, stared at the seat next to me. I knew he had seen the photograph, watched his face grow pale. He took his hand from the wheel, backed up, said "Move along."

I sensed no emotion in his voice, and it was obvious that I was no longer welcome, an invader like those leathery creatures that had taken his family. As I drove off, I wondered why Jim hadn't taken me into custody, and I imagined that he no longer had any fight left, that the Martians had taken his spirit as well. The photograph kept me company as I left the repopulated main drag of Grover's Mill behind and headed for the ruins of the Wilmuth Farm. I held the photograph as I drove, stared at the beautiful image of Ruthie and I holding hands, and I wandered from the dirt road now and then as I thought about how severely the local laws might punish a white man like myself who had been photographed while holding hands with a Negro woman.

Ruthie waited at the Wilmuth Farm. I found her standing near the edge of the crater where the first cylinder had impacted. When I touched her shoulders, she barely reacted. "All dead."

"What?"

She turned, embraced me. "All dead."

"I know." Who were dead? I wondered. Certainly not the Martians. We were still being watched, scrutinized. That was what journalists like Edward R. Murrow and Orson Welles had reported, and even the noted astronomer Professor Pierson reasoned that one day the Martians would learn to combat the earthly bacteria which had ended their lives, and they would try again.

The roof of the farmhouse had burned and fallen in, and not far away, blackened wood littered the ground where a heat ray had struck the silo. I wondered why the Wilmuth farm had not burned to the ground, and I remembered hearing that Martian heat rays burned only those areas that they were focused upon, that they rarely ignited larger fires. Their destruction was very precise and complete, just as the Martian invasion might have been had the bacteria not stopped them.

Ruthie gently pushed me away and said "Someone might come. They might see us."

"Nobody comes here anymore," I said, and I wondered how much longer that would be true. The first Martian machine had risen out of this crater, over the rim where Ruthie and I stood, and its heat ray had burned forty people in a matter of seconds. It took several days to recover the bodies.

"There are ghosts here." Ruthie held my hand and guided me towards the farmhouse. "They talk to me sometimes."

I picked up a blackened stake from the weed-choked garden and knocked off shards of glass from the frame of a broken window. We crawled in and found ourselves in the Wilmuth's kitchen. I was surprised by how modern the kitchen looked, not at all like what one might expect from the owners of a small farm. Along the wall, pots, pans and burnt timbers were scattered on the floor near a new white enameled kerosene range and a porcelain cabinet. I saw an electric refrigerator near the opposite wall, and wondered how the Wilmuths had afforded it. Electric refrigerators cost at least one hundred dollars, while an ice unit could be had for less than twenty. I felt a chill; the touch of Ruthie's ghosts, of autumn. It was two days until Halloween, and tomorrow would be the first anniversary of the invasion.

I hoped that the Wilmuths had enjoyed their farm before the Martians had taken their lives. Bob Wilmuth, his wife, their two children; all killed in one, terrible blast of a heat ray.

"I've brought you something," I said, then reached into my coat pocket and handed the brooch to Ruthie. I gently closed her fingers around it. "A year. Nearly a year."

"Our first anniversary." Ruthie smiled, opened her hand, and sunlight reflected from the mirror into her deep brown eyes, against her smooth, dark skin. She was so young, so beautiful, and at twenty-six, she reminded me of a girl of eighteen. Again I thought of the girl who had sold the brooch to me, of how a heat ray had disfigured her so, of how grateful I was that Ruthie had escaped a similar fate. "I'm sorry," I said. "I didn't know what to get for you. It's a terrible gift." I felt foolish for giving the brooch to Ruthie. It was irresponsible, even cruel. If the militia found her with it, she would be arrested.

"It's beautiful," Ruthie said. "Don't worry. I'll be fine."

"Will you?"

She hugged me, laughed uncomfortably. I could feel tremors moving throughout her body. "It's not nearly as bad anymore. It's been weeks since anyone has thrown rocks. Maybe they've decided that I'm not a Martian."

"It's stupid, ridiculous." I said. Ruthie looked beautiful and I told her so, told her that people who refused to acknowledge her beauty were blinded by ignorance. I embraced her, wrapped her in my pale arms, and then I saw a Forager peeking through the window.

He was perhaps fifteen years old, and he had wild, matted hair and a feral look about him. Like many Foragers, he had painted his face in the Martian Style, had streaked soot along the edges of his lips so his mouth formed an inverse "V." I remembered the reporter's radio broadcast during the evening of the invasion. He had stood on the edge of the Wilmuth Crater as a Martian emerged from that first Cylinder. It was horrible, he had said, the most terrifying thing he had ever witnessed. "Tentacles, wet leather, V-shaped mouth dripping with saliva, large as a bear."

"Don't worry," I said. "Foragers work on the wrong side of the law. He won't tell anyone." I had no sympathy for Foragers, and had Ruthie not been with me, I might have gone after him, turned him in. It was rumored that the Nazis had harnessed heat ray technology, and Foragers were precisely the sort of people who were responsible. They were scavengers of the worst sort, selling Martian artifacts to whoever would pay, no questions asked. The United States Government considered Grover's Mill to be an important strategic area, and weird bits of Martian machinery were still being found in abandoned fields or on the bottom of shallow lakes. It was technology that we wanted to keep in the United States, technology that could win a war, or prolong one.

"I worry about you. You're not safe with me." Ruthie paused, and after an awkward silence, said "You should find a white woman. It would better for you."

Her comment angered me, and I pulled back. "I don't care what color you are, white, yellow, green... I really don't think about that sort of thing. I'm not some backwards paranoid idiot..."

Ruthie began to cry, and I held her close, hated myself for my outburst.

"I'm sorry," I said. Ever since the invasion, racism had been on the rise. This was particularly true in Grover's Mill. Ignorant locals had accused a Negro family of helping the Martians, had developed the moronic theory that Negroes had Martian Blood. I watched as friends were jailed on trumped up charges, was sickened by it, wanted to leave Grover's Mill behind, but Ruthie's father insisted on remaining in town. He said that things would get better, and so I stayed as well. Ruthie's father was named Nathan, and he was a widower, an accomplished surgeon, and I had found it shocking to learn that a man who had helped to save the lives of so many invasion victims was being terrorized almost nightly by supporters of the Purity Movement. They claimed that they were defending the American Way of Life. If this was America, I wondered if Mars might be better.

We explored the rest of the farm, spoke about us, our love, avoided talk about the grim world. We found joy in the rubble, and it was an odd thing, this juxtaposition between our feelings of destruction and renewal, and I wondered if it was because we were angry at Grover's Mill, if we wanted to see the entire town obliterated. The rubble reminded us of our beginnings as well. Ruthie's father saved my life. He found me lying on a downtown walk, gasping for breath as a cloud of greasy Martian smoke floated through the air. He covered his mouth, moved into the cloud, pulled me away, offered me life-giving breath from his own mouth. It was something I had never seen before, "resuscitation," he called it, and he told me that it was simple, a technique that every person could learn. The doctor's house was located a mile from the Wilmuth Farm, yet it had been overlooked by the Martians, and the doctor was good enough to let me recover in his home. That was where I met Ruthie, and I believe that I fell in love with her the moment that I met on her.

We sat on the rim of the crater until the sun set, then watched the stars, in silence, for a long while. A meteor flashed across the sky, and I made a wish upon it, wondered if Ruthie had done the same. I saw her lips moving, her eyes close, and then I knew that she, too, was praying that the arc of light had been a meteor, and nothing more.

I returned home and found a human skeleton hanging from the colonnade over my front porch. The morning light played upon bare bone, glowing yellow-red, deep shadows shrouded empty eye sockets. It was a teaching skeleton, I assumed, not the remains of an invasion victim, although to me, it was just as terrifying. This was a sign, a warning, similar in nature those which Ruthie and her father had been tormented with. Last week, Ruthie had found a human skull in her garden, in the midst of her poisoned roses. It was a symbol of the invasion, a way of saying that she was responsible. I always worried about Ruthie, had felt angry, frightened, disgusted every time she was terrorized, but until that moment, she had never been threatened directly.

"Are you afraid?"

A Forager had spoken to me, and I had not been aware of his presence until I turned and saw him standing a few feet away. His appearance shocked me, and I wondered if he was the same Forager I had seen at the Wilmuth Farm. "Are you responsible for this?" I heard anger in my voice, which surprised me, because I felt only fear, felt violated by that swaying skeleton.

"No. I didn't do that. I'm a friend."

I laughed, and again, my reaction surprised me. My emotions were boiling over. "Go away. You won't find any cylinders here. No heat rays." I thought about the brooch I had given Ruthie, and it occurred to me that he might have been there to sell me Martian goods. He was just as young as the Forager I had seen at the Wilmuth Farm, just as frail, and I found myself feeling sorry for him. I had heard that many Foragers were orphans, children of victims who roamed the streets after the invasion without direction. "Whatever you want, I'm not interested." I stared at him and found no reaction in those dark eyes of his. "Do you know who hung that skeleton?"

"Yes." He waited.

"Tell me." I paused. "Please."

"They know about the baby."

"What are you talking about?"

The Forager smiled. His expression looked maniacal. "Maybe she didn't tell you."

"What? Stop playing with me." I grew more terrified, weak, as I thought about Ruthie. "Tell me."

"Your girl. The Martian…"

"What did you say?" I balled my fists, felt anger flush my cheeks.

The Forager backed up. His smile faded. "It's okay. We know about you. The baby will be half Martian. The first one…"

I lost control, hit him in the face. "I'm sorry," I said, and I watched him fall to the ground. I am thirty-two years old, and the Forager was easily half my age, half my weight. Hitting him had been an act of cowardice, of uncontrolled anger. I dropped to my knees, held my stomach, felt as though I was about to vomit. *Please, God, no*, I thought, *if Ruthie is pregnant…*

Tears stained with Martian makeup ran down the Forager's cheeks. He stood, looked at me, said "They know already. Everybody knows already."

I looked at the skeleton again, and then I became more frightened as I thought about Ruthie's safety, about what the Purity Movement might do if they found out about our relationship, our *physical* relationship. Two minutes later, I was in my automobile, heading for Ruthie's home.

There were no skeletons on her porch, no skulls in the roses. When I arrived at Ruthie's home, Nathan was standing near the garden in his bathrobe. I once informed Ruthie that I wanted to tell her father about our mutual love, but Ruthie refused, told me that it would jeopardize our relationship. I said that she was wrong, and then all she told me was "I know my father better than you do," and that was it.

"Hello," I said, and I realized only then that my early morning appearance must have seemed odd.

"No bones."

"What?"

"There aren't any bones here. I never know what I'm going to find."

I noted that his demeanor seemed strange. He was usually cheerful, but I felt as though he was masking some great pain, that he was a man who had secrets. Ruthie had told me that her mother had died at a young age, that Nathan had felt guilty for not being able to stop the cancer that eventually consumed her. "I'm sorry." I felt stupid.

"Not your fault." Nathan looked at me suspiciously. "How are you doing?"

"Fine. Just wanted to make sure everything was going well." I stared at his house, noted that everything looked in order. "Just passing by."

"You're up early." He put his hand on my shoulder, squeezed it in an unfriendly manner, said "Are you going to celebrate the invasion?"

I looked into his eyes, at his hair that had gone gray during the last year. "It's nothing that should be celebrated." Something was wrong. I felt a remarkable tension between us.

He took his hand from my shoulder, said nothing.

I wondered if Ruthie had made it home before her father awoke. We had stayed at the Wilmuth Farm until an hour before dawn. I knew that Nathan would worry if Ruthie were gone for the entire night, and when I asked her about it, she said that she had lied to him. She had told her father that she was planning to walk into town in order to see the "The Thief of Baghdad" at the Metropolis, that she was meeting a friend, that she wanted to stay at her friend's house after the movie. I didn't believe that Ruthie had lied to her father. She simply wasn't good at it, hated the idea of lying, although I wondered why she would lie to me. The Metropolis hadn't admitted Negroes in months. Nathan knew that, so did I. If she had lied to her father, it was a very poor lie, one that he would have seen through. It occurred to me then that he had found out about our meeting, that he had known about our relationship for some time.

Ruthie's father moved closer, and to my astonishment, I smelled alcohol on his breath. "Be here tonight," he said.

"What?"

"Be here tonight." He backed up, smiled. "Don't you remember? The president will be speaking tonight. I thought that you might come and listen to the radio with us."

I had forgotten about Roosevelt's fireside chat. This evening, it would be devoted to the victims of the invasion. I had heard a rumor that the president had planned a visit to Grover's Mill today, the first anniversary of the Martian invasion, but it was canceled due to his declining health. "I'll be here," I said, and I felt uneasy. I watched Ruthie's father go back into his house, got into my automobile, and drove away.

The thought of Ruthie's pregnancy terrified me.

Flags flew at half-mast. As I drove through town, men hung black crepe from window ledges. Large signs bearing the message "We Shall Never Forget" had been placed within store display windows. I had grown accustomed to that message. It was everywhere, even in the pages of *Collier's* and *The Saturday Evening Post*, alongside the redesigned blue eagle of the new NRA. All businesses were closed for the day in honor of those who had lost their lives during the invasion, and as I looked at those motionless flags hanging in the still morning air, I felt as though I were driving through a tomb.

After I returned home, I walked around the house, then went inside. I expected to find something out of order, a broken window pane, mud tracked on the floor, but everything seemed right with the exception of the skeleton on the front porch. Exhaustion weighed me down, so I cut the skeleton down, threw it in the garbage, washed, went to bed. I doubted that I could sleep. Thoughts of Ruthie's safety, of my own, disturbed me, made me nervous and frightened, yet I fell asleep in moments, and did not wake until dusk.

President Roosevelt's speech would commence at seven o'clock, and I arrived at Ruthie's home by six. Nathan was civil, and when I arrived, a place had been set for me at the dinner table. We ate shortly after I arrived so that we would finish in time to sit by the radio and listen to the entire speech. Ruthie prepared a wonderful dinner, tender chicken with boiled potatoes, but for the most part, we ate in silence. I complimented Ruthie on her cooking. She smiled, nodded. Her father ate, never spoke, rarely looked at either one of us. Ruthie and I were left alone in the kitchen as I helped her with the dishes, and I decided to move beyond the polite conversation that had held me back during the course of the evening.

"Something is bothering you," I said.

"No. It's nothing." Ruthie forced a smile.

"I need to know."

"Know what?"

I was growing tired of her polite banter, knew that she was holding something back. "Somebody threatened me yesterday." I hadn't intended to tell Ruthie about the skeleton, knew that it would worry her, but I was tired of deception.

Ruthie's smile faded. She put down the dish she was washing, turned off the water. "What are you talking about?"

"After we left the farm, I went home and found a skeleton hanging over my front porch." I looked into her eyes, saw that she was frightened. "I'm sorry. I shouldn't have told you."

"You don't have to protect me. I've seen so much of that. More than you. You're a white man..." She stopped herself, then said "Was anybody waiting for you? Did they hurt you?"

I felt angry, insulted. "Negroes aren't the only people who are threatened." We stared at one another, embraced, apologized for our comments. "It's been hard," I said.

"For both of us."

"Nobody threatened me."

"What?"

"When I came home, I found the skeleton, but nobody threatened me. There was a Forager..." I regretted bringing him up.

"What did he want? Do you think that he hung the skeleton? My God, what if they know about us? What if he hung the skeleton in order to threaten us both?"

"The thought hadn't occurred to me." I lied. "I imagine that somebody targeted my house by mistake." I wanted to tell her about my conversation with the Forager, ask her if she was pregnant, but I couldn't do it. We held each other until seven o'clock approached, then moved from the kitchen to the sitting room where the radio was located. Ruthie's father was standing outside the kitchen, and I knew that he had been listening to our conversation.

At that point, I no longer cared.

It was a nice Zenith floor radio, inlaid with burled wood, with a green eye that had little dark bands around a silver iris that grew larger or smaller according to the strength of the station. It reminded me of a Martian Crawler, of the hooded, green-eyed heat ray assemblies that had snaked up from the weird, shelled machines. Ruthie and I sat on the floor like children, waited for the radio to warm up, while Nathan watched and listened from an overstuffed sofa on the other side of the room. I tuned the radio dial, and after we listened to an advertisement for Barbasol and a lengthy introduction to the President's fireside chat, we heard Roosevelt's familiar voice.

"On October Thirtieth, Nineteen-Hundred and Thirty-Nine, forces from the Planet Mars did willfully, and with malice, attack the United States of America. It is a day which shall not be forgotten..."

As I listened to the President's speech, I wondered how different things might have turned out if the Martians had invaded Germany rather than the East Coast of the United States, if the bacteria hadn't done them in, if the invasion had taken place on a worldwide scale. I wondered if they had touched down in Grover's Mill by chance, or if they intended to weaken the United States on the eve of another Great War.

"...nameless, unreasoning, unjustified terror. We shall not fear..."

Ruthie stared at the radio dial, listened to the President's words as static cut in and out, and then she looked at me with tears in her eyes, took my hand as Nathan watched.

We heard something hit the roof. Nathan stood, moved towards a window. Ruthie and I followed, and as we stood before the window, we watched firelight play upon their hoods and robes. A dozen people stood near the house, torches in hand. Balls of flame arched across the night sky as a few of the men threw torches towards the house. One landed on the porch. Another thudded down the roof.

We stood, stared, calmly walked towards the back door. It was an odd reaction, completely logical, void of emotion. We might have screamed, I thought, tried to hide. Ruthie once told me that her father disliked guns, that he had been physically threatened so often that he would die rather than inflict violence upon another. We opened the back door, walked out, calm, orderly, accepting of fate.

They waited, rifles in hand, and we watched as one of them gestured with his weapon, told us with that long, dark barrel, that we should move to the front of the house. We obeyed, said nothing, and as we walked, we joined hands.

They surrounded us on the lawn, and under the smoky flames I looked at Ruthie's ruined garden, at their robes, and then I closed my eyes, tilted my head back. When I opened my eyes again, I saw the meteors. They streaked across the night sky, dozens of them, and I found myself smiling. I looked at Nathan and Ruthie, saw that they had followed my gaze, that they were smiling as well. We watched as a fireball arched across the sky, brilliant, sharp against the darkness, and with a blue flash it struck no more than five miles away, somewhere, I imagined, beyond the Wilmuth Farm. If these people were going to kill us, then that was how it would be. The Martians would kill them in time, complete their task, wipe Grover's Mill from the map. There was an odd, perverted justice to it. Nathan released my hand, pointed towards the sky, said, "See that one? That Orange speck near that group of stars? That's Mars."

I doubted that the star or planet that Nathan pointed at was Mars, didn't remember whether the planet was visible during this time of the year, but it didn't matter. Any one of those lights in the sky might have been Mars, but they all meant nothing to me. Grover's Mill had become Mars for us.

They lowered their rifles, moved towards their trucks and cars, then one of them stopped, turned, removed his hood. His sweaty skin seemed to change color under his sputtering torch, and then I saw the gummy streams of makeup that ran from the corners of his eyes and mouth. The rest of them removed their hoods then, and I wondered how a real Martian would respond to those painted Martian faces of theirs, if they would think twice before burning those robed men to cinders. I doubted it. Orson Welles had told us that "intellect, vest, cool and unsympathetic, regarded this Earth with envious eyes..." They drove away, towards the dull blue glow in the distance, and I knew that those men would not have a chance.

My mind filled with questions. I had assumed that the hooded men had been members of the Purity Movement, but as I thought about their faces, I wondered if they represented some odd faction of the Foragers, if they had not intended to kill us all along. I felt Nathan's hand upon my shoulder, Ruthie's arm around my waist, and my questions melted away. We turned, watched the house as fire licked through shattered windows, as the porch collapsed, as the second story spilled into the first. Sirens blared in the distance, towards that odd glow, and the house was left to burn. We made no attempt to save anything, and Nathan smiled as he watched, and I could feel his freedom. Ruthie and her father would leave now. Their was nothing left to hold them to Grover's Mill, and I would go with them.

I handed Nathan the keys to my Plymouth, then Ruthie and I sat in the back seat as Nathan drove away, leaving the burning house behind. We looked through the windows, watched as fireballs rained through the darkness, heard the distant hum of a heat ray. None of us said anything, and I wondered if Nathan had a destination in mind. It didn't matter. Ruthie slid across the seat, moved close, placed my hand over her stomach. I broke the silence, said "Will it be..."

"A Martian?" Ruthie hugged me.

"Of course." I kissed her, said "We're all Martians," and we drove through the night of the new world.

WEIRD FRUITS

by Camilla Alexa

When the largest volcano on Mars erupted, people of every nation on Earth watched the live satellite feed as plumes of fire and dust and the very stuff of the planet itself roiled into the Martian sky and filled its heavens. Tiny machines, which had roved the rocky red surface of Earth's neighboring planet and faithfully transmitted back through intervening space images of unfathomably deep craters, majestic mesas, and countless photos of seemingly endless rubbled terrain, recorded and relayed the massive eruption in all its beauty and terribleness. The little mechanical rovers and wanderers and data gatherers recorded and sent, recorded and sent; the Martian skies grew brighter and brighter, then darker and darker, as ash and particulate matter boiled into the atmosphere, filled it, and finally choked it.

For a brief time Earth's scientists were united in speculation and observation. They shared data and collaborated on notes, thrilled to have been able to witness, even remotely, an event of such magnitude. Especially exciting was the thought that it may have mirrored Earth's own geologic history; if Mars had had any dinosaurs, it was observed, they certainly would have gone the way of the dinosaur.

But that brief time of peace and undivided interest ended. Earth's customary bickering and squabbling ensued. Movie rights were scrambled for, transmitted footage from Mars was bought, borrowed, stolen. Theories flew across oceans like missiles, and scientists the world over had to be separated like bickering schoolchildren when their arguments came to blows. Only one thing was agreed upon by all: the force of the Martian eruption, certain unexplained atmospheric phenomena, and the mysterious makeup of the erupted matter had combined to cause an enormous cloud of uncertain composition to separate from Mars's orbit, and it was headed directly for Earth.

Nobody was frightened. This was, after all, just a cloud. A big cloud, true; a strange cloud, which seemed to be traveling through space with inexplicable, increasing speed. But not a frightening cloud; not an *alarming* cloud. It was, agreed most scientists, merely a Gaseous Spaceborne Event.

Events, like rodeos and rock concerts, are successful only as long as hype is sustained. If the Gaseous Spaceborne Event had managed to reach Earth in a timely fashion—say, the first few weeks or months after it had caught public attention—its arrival might have been the Event of the year, the decade; even of the century. As it was, by the time it reached the planet, three years after it had faded from the front pages of Earth's virtual newspapers, Earth's citizenry had already seen the movie, read the subsequent book, and bought and discarded all the Mars-inspired Spring fashions. In fact, by the time the Gaseous Spaceborne Event reached Earth it was *last-year's* last-year's news, and interesting to hardly anybody at all.

It reemerged as briefly interesting when, upon hitting Earth's upper atmospheric strata, the cloud dissipated, spreading evenly enough to cover nearly the entire planet with a thin veil of tiny Martian particles. For a day and two nights, by North American reckoning, the sky glittered and twinkled as billions of tiny bits of that alien world traveled the last small portion of their interplanetary journey. Everywhere but the icy poles, people around the world glanced up for a moment or two to appreciate the sight of a sky sparkling as though sprinkled with fairy dust. It was generally admitted to be very pretty, but also generally said to be not quite as spectacular as the movie detailing the same event, released the previous summer to great acclaim and massive box office profits. No one, not even the scientists, thought any of the billions of little grains of Mars, shot deep from the bowels of that planet and propelled across the empty nothing of space, would survive intact to actually land upon Earthen soil.

Jennifer Jay Johnson, aged thirteen and three-quarters, was the first to find a doppel seed.

Jenny, as her parents insisted on calling her over her increasingly strong objections, actually saw the doppel seed fall. Unlike her older brothers, she was outside watching the glittering Martian dust in the evening sky; watching the glorious dancing of a million pinprick embers sparkling against deepening violet twilight. One seemed to glow brighter than the rest, then a little brighter, then much brighter. She followed its path, openmouthed and silent, as it fell to Earth. Directly into the earth at her feet, to be precise.

It made a slight *plop* when it hit, as though it fell into water rather than dirt, and then a hiss. Jenny squatted on her haunches beside it. She didn't touch it. Even in the gloaming she could see faint wisps of smoke or steam rising out of the little hole it had made in the ground. Smoke or steam: either way it would be too hot to touch, Jenny decided. She leaned over the hole and blew gently into it, closing her eyes and breathing deep the burnt spice and hot salt scents which rose from the hole to greet her. *This is how Mars smells*, she thought.

She pushed a little dirt with her finger until it fell into the hole and filled it up.

At dinner, Jenny tried to tell her parents about the tiny piece of Mars which had buried itself in the dirt at her feet. Her brothers heckled. Her mother sighed. Her father laughed and said she'd be the next great scriptwriter for movies about things from outer space, only she'd have to pick a planet other than Mars because everybody was tired of it. Nobody believed her until after her father answered the knock on the front door. *Damned Green Peacers,* he'd muttered as he passed under the large archway which was the only demarcation between the dining and living rooms; *Damned religious nuts, or people wanting to mow the goddamn yard, or whoever that is asking for goddamn money in the middle of goddamn dinner.*

But it was none of those things. When Jenny's father opened the door, an unclothed Jenny stepped in from the front porch.

Nobody said a word. Even Jenny's brothers fell silent, though there was a naked girl in the living room. Jenny, sitting at the table, was grateful for the thick ropy vine which coiled its way, leafy and slick, from the navel of the naked girl. It twisted down between her legs and disappeared into the darkness behind her, enough leafy growth sprouting from it to cover at least the lower portion of the naked Jenny's torso.

Jenny's mother got up from the dining table, took the blanket that was always draped over the back of the living room sofa, and went to wrap it around the shoulders of the naked Jenny. The naked girl looked up into Jenny's mother's face, then grasped with both hands the thick ropy vine attached at her navel and gave it a two-handed wrench. It fell to the hardwood floor with a loud wet smack, and the girl turned to push it with her bare foot until it was on the other side of the threshold. When it lay just outside the open door on the painted boards of the porch like a huge dead snake, she closed the door behind it with a solid slam. Jenny's father, standing stock still and gaping, turned slowly and stumbled to the living room sofa.

Nobody finished dinner that night.

By the time the sun rose over New York, ten million Americans had doppelgangers: by noon, thirty million. And twenty-six million people living in South America, and forty-two million in Africa and eighteen million citizens of the European Union and sixty-seven million from Asia. New Zealand and Australia had an undisclosed number of doppelgangers, but Canada had virtually none, outside a smattering on the west coast. The doppel seeds didn't seem to like cooler temperatures.

Twenty-four hours after Jenny Jay Johnson's copy invited itself to dinner, nearly half the population of the United States of America had doppelgangers.

They did not seem to eat. They did not seem to produce waste. The thick twisted vines which bore them pushed up out of the ground like enormous blind eels. They unfurled large hairy leaves veined in orangey red, and sprouted small gourd-like growths at their ends, with little nubby warts which rapidly swelled and grew into arms, legs, fingers and toes. As soon as the weird fruits were as large as the nearest uncopied human they reached down, detached themselves from their parent vines, and sought out the human they resembled. Scientists called this, for lack of a better word, *imprinting*. All over the world, families went about their daily business—working, eating, defecating, sleeping—with a host of doppels silently observing, like mute out-of-town relatives come for an unexpected visit of no certain duration.

No one ever had two doppels at once. The only difference between the copies and the originals, other than the eerie silence of the former, was in their eyes, which instead of containing whites and irises all the colors of all Earth's people were nothing but a field of pale gritty orange-red, the color of Martian dust.

Doppels could not be cut or abraded, crushed or sliced. As governments around the world discovered in their secret laboratories and out of the sight of their own peoples, no technology or material or weapon at human disposal could rend or damage any portion of the doppels' bodies. The vines and leaves from which the doppels grew withered to dust as soon as their produce matured and disengaged.

Communities around the globe reacted differently, based on any number of cultural and personal preferences, tempered or inflamed by local attitudes and beliefs. In some places the doppels were greeted and treated as lost children, or unfortunate but not unwelcome relatives. In others, doppels were attacked on sight, though they never made any move or retaliation against the ineffectual efforts of their human counterparts, other than to stare unblinking as people tried without effect to run them over, shoot them or set them ablaze. In some places people did their best to ignore their doppels, which seemed compelled to remain near the people they specifically resembled. In a few places the mute, red-eyed beings were honored and treated as ambassadors, as kings; even as gods.

But other than physical space, they took nothing. Once people grew accustomed to their silent, staring presence and complete indestructibility, most of them simply continued the routines of their daily lives. In more than one household, after just a matter of days, doppels of multiple family members were ensconced in darkened dens, propped on faded cushions in front of eternal television reruns as though they had always been there. More than one household took to standing their doppelgangers in broom closets, out of the way along with skis and mops and unused toys. That was why, when the deaths began, they were already there.

Jenny's mother was one of the first to die. Throughout the day at the hospital, test after test came back as *inconclusive*, as her mother's body shriveled and dried, the creeping orange tint visible in her veins through the sallow paper of her skin. The vivid streaks covered more and more of her wasting body as it sank into itself and dried up, until all that remained was a small mound of rust-colored dust.

It happened so quickly; the unnatural orange tint of the veins showing like blood poisoning but running its course to death and dust in just over a single day. By dinnertime, ten million North Americans had begun to die, and Africans and South Americans and people all over Asia and Europe. Even Canada had its share of deaths.

Jenny and Jenny's brothers and Jenny's doppelganger sat at the dining room table. Mr. Johnson was still at the hospital while doctors ran tests on the dust of his wife, and Mrs. Johnson's doppel stood in the kitchen, silent and inelegant in its parka and apron. Unlike with some families, the Johnson doppels, though there were only two of them, wore clothing at all times. The very first night, Jenny's father had laid down the law. He'd said: *No-goddamn-body's going to see my wife and daughter walking around in the goddamn nude.* After the first awkward dressing, it was easy. The doppels were perfectly capable of mimicking simple behaviors. By the second morning, they helped themselves to clothes whenever the ones they wore became soiled or torn. Their choices were erratic and without human logic, but at least they allowed for what Jenny's mother would have called *minimum decency*.

Jenny rose from the table and went to her mother's doppelganger. Meeting its strange red gaze, she reached past it to the cupboard. She pulled out a box of macaroni and cheese. She filled a pan with water and placed the water on the stove and turned on the burner. Every move she made was watched in silence by her brothers and the two doppels. When the macaroni and cheese was ready, Jenny divided it into three bowls, and she and her brothers ate in silence as the two sets of odd red eyes watched, unblinking.

The next day at school, Michael Turner's doppel came to class without him. It was waiting in his seat when the bell rang, its hair combed, its books piled on the corner of Michael's desk. Mrs. Frample only stared at it a moment before proceeding with the day's lessons. When class was over, it rose and left the room along with the other children. The next day, three more of Jenny's classmates didn't show up, and by the end of the week a quarter of the class was made up of doppels. Class time had become very quiet and productive, but in between classes the remaining human children became riotous, uncontrollable, as though to counterbalance the silence and stillness of their red-eyed classmates.

That Friday, Jenny walked home by herself. She usually walked home with Laura Sheffield, but Laura hadn't come to school that day. Laura's doppelganger looked like her. It wore her clothes, and her mother had sent it to school with Laura's lunch money, though everyone knew doppels didn't eat. It carried Laura's books and wore Laura's shoes. But it didn't come to meet Jenny at the bench by the flagpole after school let out. So after waiting for a short time, Jenny had headed home alone.

That night, Mrs. Johnson's doppelganger made the same macaroni and cheese it had made each preceding night that week. After the second night, when Mr. Johnson had lurched up from the table and vomited orange shell pasta all over the combined living and dining room hardwood floor, dinner had gone quietly and smoothly every evening. Shown once, Jenny's mother's doppel had known how to load the dishwasher and put away the milk. If it still wore mismatched shoes and bikini bottoms with pajama tops, at least Jenny took some small comfort in having a mother which was indestructible.

When Jenny finished dinner, her mother's doppel cleared away her dishes and began to load them into the dishwasher. More tired than usual, Jenny rose and clumped heavily up the stairs to her bedroom. She switched on the light, and turned to shut the door behind her doppelganger, which had followed her up the stairs silent and close as a shadow.

"First," she said, taking her doppel by the hand and leading it to the edge of the bed where she pushed it gently until it sat, "you've got to stop dressing like an idiot. Nobody wears underwear on the outside of their clothes, and nobody—I mean it—wears one hiking boot and one slipper at the same time."

She went to her closet, flinging the door wide and glancing back to make sure her doppel watched. She pulled out a nice sweater and her favorite jeans. "This is what you should wear Monday. And this . . ." she rummaged through the pile of clean clothes on the closet floor for a cool tee shirt and her good corduroys with the embroidery on the hip ". . . would make a nice outfit for Tuesday. If it's cold on Tuesday you can wear this green jacket with it."

She lined up three more outfits, pointing to each and saying *Wednesday, Thursday, Friday*. "Weekends you can wear whatever you want so long as you don't leave the house. And so long as the shoes match, I guess you can wear whatever you want on your feet."

Leaving the outfits lined up on the floor like a policeman's suspects, Jenny went to her bedside table and fished a few objects from the tumbled chaos in the drawer. She sat on the bed next to her doppel, and its shoulder brushed hers with the motion of the mattress dipping under her weight. "This is my grandmother's locket, which I wear to school every day, and this is the book I'm reading right now. It's kind of stupid but it's pretty good, especially page one-forty-two with the makeout scene. And here's some money I've been saving up just in case. I've got about forty dollars."

She put the book in the doppel's lap, and placed the money and the locket in its cupped hand. "I sit third row from the back in Mrs. Frample's homeroom class, and I don't like Jimmy Kemper, who sits on my left. David Mapps sits behind me, and I do like him. I like him a lot. I don't think he knows. And . . .

and my name's not Jenny. It's Jennifer."

The doppel looked down at the things in its hand, then up at Jenny's face. In its customary silence it stared into her brown eyes with its strange solid red ones. It reached the hand not holding Jenny's grandmother's locket and Jenny's forty dollars and placed it on her arm, partially covering the sharp orange veins which crept, stark and visible, beneath her pale skin.

KILLERS

by Vincent L. Scarsella

Out of a clear blue sky, we were dropped into a nest of humans. Sent them scattering, screaming.

We slashed through the bramble and bush in no particular hurry, stalking and blasting our prey, picking them off one by one. Not the entire tribe, mind you, but an easy fifty, sixty. A good kill. Just like that. The mission took maybe five minutes.

Back at the regroup point, some new kid fresh out of killer school; a strapping, blue-eyed, Aryan blond, came panting and laughing between Larmer and me and slapped us across the shoulders.

"Great kill, hey comrades ?" he said, panting, grinning.

I spied Larmer's glare, felt the same way. There was no joy in killing, never was, had been, or should be. Only a sick ass like this new kid could feel pleasure killing his own kind.

Sure, in killer school, you were brainwashed to feel good about it. You killed thousands of your fellow men in simulators; you were constantly reminded that nest humans were low-life scum unworthy of existence. Pukes, they were called. Useless, mindless pukes. Pretty soon, they were pukes to you, too. Toward the end of school, there were real kills in a fenced-in chunk of forest just outside the school, where some hapless puke captives were set loose, chased, cornered and killed. Still, even that was nothing compared with killing nest humans in the wild, real people. Unlike the sick-ass kid, after my first patrol, I threw up.

Ignoring the kid, I hitched the blaster into my belt holster. Looking up, I followed our silver, cigar-shaped transport as it made a wide, soundless loop above towering evergreens before swooping down to the clearing where we were to be picked up. As the rest of the platoon gathering around us, the Sarge started his usual grousing that we had let too many pukes get away.

"You bastards are too fucking slow," he growled.

He was constantly carping at us like that, doing his job, I guess. Like the rest of us, doing what he had to do to stay alive, though sometimes he seemed to enjoy it a tad too much.

This time, Sarge glanced my way. "How many you get, Spence?"

I frowned. I hadn't counted. I had to squint at the read-out on my blaster which gave a fairly accurate count how many of my fellow human beings I had murdered on this particular hunt.

"Eight," I told him.

That was pretty good on any hunt. Tribe humans were crafty, tenacious pests who slithered and hid like mice in the deep forest brush. Sarge nodded, pleased, knowing that I was a wily veteran and a good shot.

He went around the platoon and grilled some of the others. When old man Lewis said: "Four," Sarge burst out laughing.

"You got *nada*, old man," he said. "Zip."

The Sarge snatched the old man's blaster from his trembling hands and squinted at the read out box. After a moment, he looked up with a forced grin on his wide, hard face chipped from granite. But he did not look happy.

"You keep this up your fucking days are numbered," he snorted and tossed the blaster back into the old man's gut. He'd been riding Lewis hard lately for his nonexistent kill numbers. "You hear me, old man?"

Lewis nodded glumly. He was keenly aware that his days were numbered. But there was nothing he could do about it. He was either going senile or just couldn't kill anymore. Either way, he'd be toast if he kept failing to get his quota.

We had to wait in the stifling hold of the transport while a scavenger team collected the dead or injured puke bodies and tossed them into a pile of human meat. Babies, children. Husbands and wives. Doused with gasoline and flamed, dead or alive.

We cheered as the fire roared up into the stench of a high summer wind. Had to. Meant we'd live another day.

There was no sense of acceleration as the transport rose into the cloudless sky and proceeded back to camp that bright blue summer afternoon. It was as if the thing had not even left the ground. No lift, no decline, no landing thump. But it got us to our destination somehow, by some marvelous technology years ahead of what we humans had come up with by the time the ETs came.

During the trip back, while our comrades, including the bright-eyed, blond haired new kid dozed or simply stared ahead mindlessly, Larmer turned and whispered into my ear, "Word is, they're bringing girls tonight."

I grunted, still thinking of the scrawny, desperate face of teenage girl whose head I had seared clean off only minutes ago.

"It's been what, three weeks," Larmer went on. "I could use a hump."

I shrugged. To be honest, so could I. But still it made me sick like everything else to think of the poor little girls, some of them just beyond puberty, sent to please us.

"You sure ain't saying much today, *hombre*," Larmer commented.

Suddenly, the transport door opened. We had already returned to the small pad at the edge of our camp.

I shrugged.

"What's to say?" I stood with the rest of the killers and waited at the uplifted wing-door. When it was my turn, I hopped out ahead of Larmer into the afternoon glare. Squinting back at him, I hissed, "What we outta do, if we had any balls, is turn the goddamn blasters on them."

If I had been talking to anyone else, I wouldn't have said that. As it were, Larmer stopped me with a cold stare.

"Don't involve me in that kind of crap talk, hombre," he said as we started double-timing it with the rest of the platoon towards the barracks. Then he smiled, and as my friend, turned to me with a quick wink. "Partner, just do what you gotta do. Okay?"

That was our mantra, our battle cry: "Do what you gotta do." But after almost two years, and roughly five hundred kills, it was growing thin on me.

"I'm gonna run someday," I went on anyway, panting, as we squeezed into the long dirt path that led from the transport landing pads to the barracks. "One of these goddamn days, I'm gonna run and let the collar choke the life outta me. Sear my fucking head off."

"Now, that is silly shit talk, hombre," Larmer huffed behind me.

He was a massive black man with a gorilla chest, thick arms and skin dark as fudge. In his former life, he had played defensive end in the National Football League. How bizarre it was to think that he was making millions tackling quarterbacks only two years ago, before the ET motherfuckers came and blew mankind away. Just like in the movies, except this time there was no Hollywood box-office happy ending.

"That…hombre," Larmer went on in between huffs and puffs as we finally neared the barracks, and grabbing at the glimmering silver ring around his own thick neck, "is … one … gross … way … to … die." He puffed out again: "Ever .. seen … it?"

I'd seen it. A false hit. During a routine march behind this guy, his collar had malfunctioned - the computer chip or whatever that controlled it activated, thinking that its wearer was trying to escape.

What I saw after that wasn't pretty. Zap, just like that, the poor bastard fell in a lump to the ground, writhing and screaming, cursing, slithering and grabbing at his neck, as the collar lit up like a red-hot poker. Until he couldn't fight it anymore, only scream, vomit last night's dinner, piss and shit his pants, as the fucking thing got hotter and hotter and hotter around the quivering muscle and bone of his neck. Blood started oozing out of the wound, gurgling, spurting non-stop, until finally, and quite literally, his head seared off. His fucking head seared off! The poor fuck didn't look too good after that, with his head detached from his torso, his body still twitching, his eyes bulging, his swelled tongue long and purple, licking dust off the ground.

"Yeah," I told Larmer, "I seen it."

I often thought that maybe it hadn't been a malfunction. Maybe the ETs occasionally picked a killer at random, and used the collar to sear his head off, just for show. To scare us shitless into obedience like nothing else could.

Larmer let go an exaggerated shiver.

"Then how could you say you'd choose to go like that?"

I shrugged.

"There's gotta be a way out of this crazy fucking life," I said. "There has to fucking be."

We finally arrived at the dirt clearing in front of the barracks, our home, a corrugated Quonset hut just like in the Marines.

"Ain't," Larmer answered.

And he was right. Something turned off the blaster mechanism so you couldn't even shoot yourself. Would work the same way if you tried to kill a sarge or a fellow killer, followed by the collar going red hot, and searing your head off. Thus, no suicides, no mutiny.

Just kill, kill, kill.....

Sarge barked that after chow, there'd be another blaster inspection. Our kill ratio was down, way below quota, he yapped, worst in the battalion (though that was probably bullshit). And if it continued like that it would not only be his ass, but ours, too.

"No ladies either!" he screamed, "until you puke bastards shape up."

Larmer swore under his breath as the Sarge stormed out of the barracks.

"Fuckin' eh," he moaned, as he took out his blaster and started taking it apart.

The whistle blew for chow and we quickly finished reassembling our blasters before rushing outside and getting into formation. As usual, old man Lewis marched us, though it was funny to watch him limp alongside the platoon, desperately trying to keep up and look snappy. Another reason his time was definitely short for this world. The lucky bastard, I thought, though I didn't envy how he'd be pulverized in a puff of ash and smoke.

The mess hall was buzzing by the time we got there. Word was that Bravo Company had just returned from a patrol in which they'd bagged two hundred. Two fucking hundred. Some kind of killer record, must have been.

This caused Sarge to waltz up to our table and piss and moan over our measly take that afternoon.

"A lousy fifty," he spat, and looked over at Bravo Company's table.

They were in a swagger over the accomplishment, which made me even sicker. Sick fucks, all of them. Don't you realize what you're really doing? Killing not them, but us! I wanted to stand up and shout it out for everyone to hear and realize. But I knew that after barely a sentence of such mutinous talk, I'd be blasted by one of the sarges, pulverized. Then, quickly forgotten.

"Yeah," continued Sarge, "go ahead, eat, fill your big fat bellies. Bravo is numero uno right now, best in the battalion, now and probably forever, and don't you forget it!"

When I saw veins popping out of his neck, and across his stone forehead, I realized how pissed off he really was.

After glaring at us awhile longer, with our mush of food growing colder and more tasteless than it already was, Sarge about-faced and like the kiss ass that he was, strode over to the Bravo Company table. Smiling no less, he congratulated their sarge with the sharpest salute he could muster.

"Big friggin deal," spat Curly Joe from the other end of the table. He was a tall, gangly Texan with a slow drawl. "Two hundred. Dropped into a lucky zone, is what I say. A fucking puke anthill."

"We just let too many get away," that new kid piped up disagreeably. He glared across the long table at Curly Joe. "It had nothing to do luck. We just got too many bad shots, or killers without the stomach for the job."

It wasn't right for a goddamned rookie to speak up that way. Like he owned the place.

"Shut the fuck up, Rook," Curly-Joe drawled, returning the glare. "You speak when you're spoken to."

Sarge returned to interrupt the feud.

"Hurry up, fuck-ups," he bellowed. "We got an inspection waiting."

Somebody made a gink noise from the other end, causing Sarge to bang the table, sending plates and mush and cups flying.

"Look you fucking useless bungholes," he snarled, "I got no time for your funny bullshit. We got numbers to reach and you ain't holding up your end of the bargain. This keeps up and I promise I'll be sending you away like I did the Harley Man and the Injun Chief last month. You know I can do that and I did and I will." He drew in a breath. "So quit the bullshit horsecrap."

The whistle blew and we re-assembled outside the mess hall. First thing I noticed was that old man Lewis was no longer our platoon leader.

In fact, he was quite gone.

After the inspection, which fortunately went well, Sarge actually seemed to soften. It had been a mere ploy anyway, a motivational trick learned in "sarge" school.

Strutting with a pleased expression for a time, he suddenly announced that we'd have the girls after all that night. We hoorah-ed for joy. Even me. The ultimate joy the thought of sex can bring, when for at least a few minutes, we could forget this nightmare.

In the deep darkness of the barracks later that night, the sudden clatter of high-heels on our shiny, spic-n-span floor, and giggling voices, announced the arrival of the girls. They were marched in, led like cattle to their respective bulls. Once in bed, they knew what to do. It was their method of survival.

A girl, smelling of cheap perfume, a skinny, breathless thing with straight dirty blond hair down the length of her back, slid between the covers and snuggled next to me. The lights were off, so her face was barely visible, but I could make out small, bony almost boyish features and the scared look of a fourteen year old. She had probably been caught in a raid, similar to the one we had pulled last week, when Sarge hollered for us not to kill the little girls but grab them before blasting their moms and dads and little brothers to death.

My "date" that night didn't smile. She didn't protest either, as I ran my right hand up the length of her thigh, across her stomach (which tensed), then up again, and around, small, firm breasts, and finally back down her belly until I was fingering a dry snatch.

While rubbing her there awhile, I said, "Gotta name."

From the other bunks, I could hear the grunts of guys already getting off on little girls.

"Sue," she tweaked.

Across the way, the mattresses were squeaking. Some guys were already shouting out in orgasmic delight. The ETs, our keepers, must have been laughing at the silly, barbaric apes they ruled.

"Aren't you gonna do me?" the little girl asked, almost begging for it.

I thought of abandoning the effort, of letting her go unused. But I feared that would cause me a problem with Sarge, be considered an act of civil disobedience.

So I "did" her, and the way she went with the flow, I knew this wasn't her first time. I finished soon enough, too fast actually, and for at time, we just laid there in each other's arms. Most of the other killers in the bunks around us had finished as well and were enjoying a few intimate moments in the arms of their "woman," even though she was barely a teen.

I found myself thinking of my wife, Karen, who'd been shipped off in a saucer as long as a football field with our two little girls and about a thousand other scared faces shortly after the ETs had arrived. Sniveling humans had acted as guards, shoving them at the point of a blaster into the saucers for transit to some kind of concentration camp destined for certain extermination. They had plucked me out of line at the last minute and sent me to killer school.

"You awake?" asked the little girl.

But before I could answer, whistles shrieked, sounding like a squad of frenzied referees, as sarge and some guards burst in to retrieve the girls so they could be carted off to another barracks.

What a life.

Not five minutes after they had retrieved the girls, just as I was falling into a deep, dreamless sleep, Sarge was bleating his silver whistle again, calling us to action.

"Up!" he shouted between bleats. "Up sluggards!"

We were scrambling out of bed falling over each other, slipping into our camouflage jumpsuits, reaching for our blasters. In seconds, we had fallen into formation outside with Sarge shouting at us sluggards from the barracks steps to hurry it goddamn up. Then he shouted the order and we were double-timing it to the transport. A scout ship must have spotted a nest and we were next in line for the mission. Lucky us.

A sleek transport brooded on the landing pad. We quickly entered by one of two winged doors, and sat along the benches on either side. After the doors closed with a dull thud, the transport lifted without the slightest tug of gravity.

Within five minutes, fifty or so miles from the killer camp, we were lowered into a clearing. Before the doors opened, Sarge gave us a quick rundown: A good size tribe of a humans, five hundred, maybe more, had bedded down for the night along the ridge a hundred yards across the field where we had just landed. All we had to do was keep quiet as we climbed the hill on the other side. There, we could set up a mega-blaster and slam a fifteen g-force into their midsection, killing a few of them and disorienting the rest. With his meanest scowl, Sarge growled that he fully expected us to wipe out the fucking puke survivors.

"This is your chance," he told us as a kind of pep talk, "to top Bravo Company!"

"Yeah!" That stupid ass kid shouted. "Let's get em'"

As the wing doors lifted, finally giving us a whiff of the damp early morning dew on the brush and grass, I wondered how these humans had been so stupid as to have let us sneak up on them.

Part of me was desperately hoping for a trap.

But there was no trap.

Fifteen minutes later, his arms crossed mightily, Sarge stood at the regroup point with an elated glare, watching the dead bodies burning in a mound perhaps a thirty feet high.

After reassembling, out of breathe and sweaty from the orgy of easy killing, I looked down at my blaster and noticed a count of thirty-seven. A personal best. It took everything I had to stop from puking as I recalled the desperate look in the face of that woman just before I blasted her with the baby in her arms.

Back at the camp, we whooped it up, proud that we had surpassed Bravo Company's efforts of the previous afternoon. Proud that now we would be the talk of our fellow killers on that day and for a long time to come, or at least until some other platoon beat our record.

Sarge was in his glory now, patting backs and telling us what a great job we did. Watching him cavort, I was thinking how wonderful it would be to pull out my blaster and fry him. The look of total surprise as thick face went up in flames would do me a world of good.

As the celebrating flagged, Sarge blew his whistle. "Alright, you pukes," he shouted. "Enough! Time to bed down. We got more killing to do later, after a good rest."

We all let out a roar, happy to be killers, happy to be alive.

Beat tired from a most memorable night, we hunkered off to sleep.

Waking, I felt that there was something definitely wrong. For one thing, the barracks was empty and I was alone. Not a single killer in sight. And except for the buzz of flies, not a sound.

Sitting up, I took it all in, struck by something I had not felt in over two years - privacy. Where the fuck was everyone?

I crept out of my bunk and slinked over to the front door. Outside, the sun was fairly high up already, telling me that I had slept through reveille, and was missing breakfast. How and why I could have been left behind was a complete mystery.

The collar should have shot an electric buzz through my brain to wake me up.

The collar.

Here, alone, it should have killed me, seared my head right off.

Then all at once, I knew: The collar was dead.

I had no time to think. The Sarge might have already noticed that I was AWOL. He'd send a couple killers to find me and blow me away. What else could he do?

Before I had another moment to think this out, my platoon was hustling back to gather their gear for another surprise raid. As Larmer rushed in, his eyes widened at the sight of me.

"Where you been?" he asked. "I thought you tried to run and the collar got you."

"I - I overslept," I said, still in a daze.

"Overslept?" he laughed wide-eyed. "The collar - "

Then his face filled with recognition.

"You lucky motherfucker." His voice was low, full of admiration.

"What?"

"Your collar is dead, man." Larmer grabbed hold of me and whispered straight into my ear: "Dead."

We had heard about that, a happy myth among the killers that no one really believed. Some lucky bastard's collar going dead, like winning the lottery, freeing him from the killer's life, freeing him to escape and lead the blessed life of human prey.

"Your collar goes dead," the Sarge had been heard to say, "all you become is human. Puke meat."

The others were scrambling out ahead of us, falling over each other, mindful of Sarge's unholy intolerance for stragglers. Somehow the Sarge, perhaps still elated over last night's huge success, hadn't noticed that I was missing.

"C'mon, you guys," urged the asshole kid. He glared at me standing there.

"Gotta run, friend," Larmer said to me, and started trotting out of the barracks.

At the door, he turned to me and said, "Run, man. Run like hell." Then he shook his head one last time. "You one lucky bastard, Spence." His eyes glazed over. "Getting to be human one last time."

Just like that, he was gone, outside into formation, waiting for Sarge's order to move out on another kill.

I had no time to waste. Somehow, I was free! After two long years, I was no longer a slave. But the thought of my collar being dead, of being free, made my legs go numb. I seemed stuck in molasses. I couldn't move.

Plus, I couldn't quite believe that the collar was really dead. What if it was a trick, some kind of test? The only way to find out was to leave the camp perimeter. But if I was wrong, there'd be no turning back. Once the collar activated, my head would be seared right off.

I finally managed to walk backwards a couple steps, almost stumbling over my bunk, until I was in the long row separating all the other bunks. I continued backwards like that towards the back exit, holding my breath for something bad to happen.

At the back door, I hesitated, momentarily reluctant to give up the perverse security of the killer's life, helping the bastard ETs eradicate our pesky brethren still roaming the hills.

At last, I backtracked into the morning sunlight, and drew in a mouthful of crisp air. The fresh pleasure overwhelmed me, and I reeled back a moment. Recovering, I turned around and saw our transport silently lift off straight up for a time, hover momentarily, and suddenly head south.

Around me, the camp seemed deserted, vacant. I hunkered low, clinging to the side of the barracks. About fifty yards away, the forest and beyond that, the hills, beckoned. Perfect cover. Where I was going, what I would find, I had no idea.

Finally, after another moment of uncertainty, I bolted. Ran so fast, I almost fell forward head over heels. At last, I made it to a stand of trees and leaned against a thick trunk. Looking back, I was relieved to see that no one was coming after me. Nothing stirred from the camp. My escape had apparently gone unnoticed.

I felt for the collar, tugged at it and held my breath. But nothing happened. After another moment, thanking God and my lucky stars, I headed into the woods.

The first night was bad.

After running until I literally dropped, I burrowed a hole of dead, slimy leaves under a rotting thick trunk of a tree that had fallen ages ago. Trembling like a frightened rabbit, I ended my first day of freedom hungry, exhausted and cold.

I woke shivering at the first gray haze of morning. Starving and alone, I gave half a thought of heading back into the killers' camp and surrendering, hoping that they'd simply fix my collar, feed me, and make me a killer again. For all the other bullshit, the ETs had kept us lean and healthy and strong with their tasteless nutrient gruel. In fact, in the best shape and health I had ever been in. But out here, alone, how would I survive? I had to find shelter and warmth and food. After a few minutes of panic, I decided it would be pure folly to go back. I would certainly be killed; pulverized into smoke and ash. I was also ashamed for even thinking of going back to the killers' life, and of again killing my fellow man – mothers and babies – merely to save myself.

I took some deep breaths. I tried to remember back to my Boy Scout days and the basic survival techniques I had learned to earn badges. Finding water was the first thing. One of my first scoutmasters had constantly reminded his troop that a person couldn't live very long without water. It should be easy to find a little brook or creek in these woods.

And it was! I picked myself up, started walking, and within five minutes I came upon a narrow stream. As I bent down and slurped from the gurgling, clear water, my spirits lifted Soared in fact.

Over the next few days, I surprised myself how resourcefulness I could be. I remembered how to start a fire without matches, using the bow and string method, although my patience did run out occasionally and I cursed and yelled up into the tall pines surrounding me.

For shelter, I constructed crude lean-tos between trees out of branches and brush and rested comfortably, warm and dry, as I headed ever deeper into the forest and farther away from the killer camp.

Food was an obvious concern and at first, I satisfied myself with grubs, worms, grasshoppers and other assorted crunchy bugs. I also came upon sweet berries from the various wild bushes, though some of them gave me diarrhea.

Into my second week, I started hunting wild game, content at first with rabbit and squirrel. After only a month of freedom, I even bagged a ten-point buck with a crude bow and arrow that I had patiently fashioned out of some thick branches and twine from some fruit bushes. I gutted the animal and skinned it without a thought as if I had been in the wild all my life, and proudly ate a feast of roast venison that night and for several days thereafter. I even constructed a crude fishing pole and caught trout and bass in the small creeks and streams that coursed through the dark forest.

Of course, I was ever alert for scout drones sent out from killer camps, though traveling alone reduced the risk of being spotted. I made sure my fires didn't make a lot of smoke. At night, I kept them low and hot.

After awhile, despite my ability to stay reasonably comfortable alone in the wild, despite my freedom, the complete solitude came to bother me, frighten me actually. I craved human contact, companionship. The lonely silence and darkness of the forest began to have a profoundly disquieting effect upon my soul.

At times as I marched onward without a clear idea where I was going, remorse and shame took hold of me for having become a killer. A better, more courageous man would have refused to become a killing agent for the ETs and a traitor to his species. I should have spat on the ground and let the collar work it's awful torture.

I was also gripped by the awful guilt that came with having been responsible for the murder of over five hundred human beings. I was haunted by their ghosts in the deep, dark woods - the faces of the men, women, and children - whom I had massacred in order to save myself. I was, in fact, no better than the humans who had herded my wife and little girls into a cattle car to be exterminated in some nameless ET concentration camp.

One afternoon, out of nowhere, overwhelmed by such incalculable guilt, I fell to my knees and wept. Then, for some minutes, I held a sharp flint arrowhead to my neck with both hands, trying to find the courage and will to run myself through with it.

"Do it!" I shouted. "Do it, you bastard killer! Do it!."

But, alas, I could not bring myself to do it. Finally, I tossed the arrow to the ground and, looking up, begged forgiveness from God, and every human I had ever killed.

After an indeterminable time, I took a deep breath, got to my feet. It came to me that forgiveness would come only with the fulfillment of this penance:

First, to survive, to live. Second, to find a nest of humans and, with my unique knowledge of killer ways, help them survive. Perhaps, even to fight, and kill killers.

By the end of that summer, nearly four months after the collar had failed and I had escaped the killers' life, I felt confident that I had accomplished my first goal - that is, simply to survive. In fact, I was certain that I could last a long lifetime this way, avoiding killers to the end of my days.

But I still craved the company of humans. I missed Larmer, and some of the other guys from my killer unit (but certainly not that asshole kid), even the misplaced spirit of our Sarge. But killers weren't really human any more, just slaves forced to perform a terrible function, too scared to resist. What I needed was the company of real humans, nest humans, and the kind of companionship I remembered from that seemingly ancient time before the ETs came.

Then, with a chance turn one afternoon, I spotted them in the distance:

A human tribe.

It was a small tribe, less than a hundred. They were on the march in a narrow valley within earshot of a shallow creek.

My heart raced at the sight of them. Ever since my escape, I had thought of this moment, of meeting up with prey humans, free men. I thought of running down the steep ridge and engaging them at a bend in the creek which twisted around and disappeared into a thicket of forest. But I quickly dismissed the idea, knowing that it would be a mistake to startle them. They were edgy nomads, constantly on the alert for killers. And, despite my beard and worn appearance, I still wore the collar and camouflage gray uniform of a killer. If I came out into the open, I might be mistaken for an enemy scout and killed before I ever got the chance to explain.

Of course, I worried that they might kill me anyway, execute me for the terrible crimes I had committed in my former life. Despite this, I resolved that this opportunity could not be missed. From the ridge where I now stood defiantly in the open, I took a breath and shouted out to them: "Hey! Over here! Hey!"

That stopped them cold. But only for an instant. In the next, they were scattering into the trees and brush. After a time, one of them cautiously stepped forward, squinting in my direction.

He was a tall man, dressed in black, wearing a white collar. Not a slave's collar, a priest's.

Waving my arms, I walked down the ridge into a small clearing between us and stopped.

"I'm a friend!" I shouted. With my arms still up, I stood there, praying that I'd be given a chance to explain. That hearing what I had to say, they'd forgive my sins and let me live with them. That a priest seemed to be their leader was reassuring. But as I approached, I saw from his fierce, skeptical gaze that he was no fool. He had held this little band of humans together through many difficult times, and meant to keep them safe. Despite his theological background, I knew that he would not necessarily turn the other cheek. He would not hesitate to have me killed if he felt it was in the best interests of his people.

We were no more than thirty yards from each other when he stopped and pointed his long, boney hand at me.

"The collar," he squinted, surprised. "*You're* - you're a killer."

I swallowed, knowing that this was my moment of truth. I would either be forgiven or killed.

Nodding, I shouted: " "

He frowned, considering this. Could I be trusted? Or was it merely a clever killers' ploy?

"Malfunctioned," I quickly added, tugging at the collar, then shrugged. "Turned off."

I stared straight into the priest's eyes, hoping for compassion.

"So I ran."

Scowling, the priest deliberated. It was impossible to tell whether there was forgiveness or hatred in his eyes.

With a sudden nod, it seemed decided.

"Come closer," he said, gesturing. I walked forward a few steps until he stopped me with his hand. After regarding me for what seemed an eternity, he nodded decisively. Then, with a wave of an arm, he announced to my relief:

"Join us."

The priest, Father Alec, gave me a new name - Lazarus, because, he said, I surely had come back from the dead.

As I learned only a few days later, the reason I was spared had nothing to do with Christian virtue. Father Alec had simply decided the tribe could use my knowledge of killer strategies. I might teach them how killers found human nests, how they tracked, how they killed.

The first day or two, he pumped me for every shred of information about the killers' life until I begged him to change the subject. I wanted to forget what I had done, the awful murdering.

"Think of this as your penance," he said. "By revealing everything there is to tell, you will be cleansing your soul, releasing your guilt."

Nodding, I wondered why he never took my confession to save my eternal soul.

So I told him everything. Our training in the killer schools where they taught us to kill and to like killing; the daily grind of a killer's life, what we ate, where we slept, a rundown of every kill mission I could remember; sex with little girls.

With each revelation, he nodded glumly. Sometimes, he grunted. Always, he listened.

But he never asked me to explain why, as a killer, I had so easily betrayed our race. I sensed that long ago, he had realized that humans will do anything to stay alive - even kill their mothers.

The day came when I had nothing left to tell him, but still Father Alec continued walking by my side, seeming to favor my company above all others, even his hardened lieutenants, Carlos and Nathan. Scowling behind us as we marched, they must have regarded Father Alec's new affection for me - a former killer - with a mixture of bafflement and disdain. Of course, they dared not question him about it.

From these walks, I soon learned that Father Alec and I were, in many ways, kindred spirits. When not discussing killers, we talked about our former lives, who we had been before the ETs came.

"I was a prick," I admitted with a laugh. "A bully. Everyone hated me in the end. My wife, my co-workers, even my children. I was a miserable SOB who hated life for the smallest difficulties. Like a rainstorm on a summer's day because it washed out a game of golf. Instead of appreciating the beauty of summer rain - the green smell of it - I cursed God for the little inconvenience it had caused.

"At first, I was even glad the ETs came. Glad to see our messed up world, with its messed up relationships and politics, torn apart. I was glad to have an excuse, finally, to be rid of my life.

"Boy, how wrong I was."

Father Alec had a similar story. When the ETs arrived, he had long ago lost his faith in Christ, perhaps as far back as the seminary, and his career in the church had been stuck in neutral for many years. His superiors, some of them men of real faith, had long recognized his lack of ambition. A year before the ETs came, he had been demoted again to a small parish in a ghetto neighborhood. Without the right connections, and no flair for politics, he would likely remain there a very long time.

"In the end," he confessed as we walked in the fog one cold October morning, "I was having an affair with one of my parishioners. A Puerto Rican beauty." He stopped a moment to think of her.

"Dark," he went on. "full of lust." He looked at me with a wave of his hand and apologetic shrug. "And, married."

Father Alec sighed and let a shadow come over his eyes.

"I, too, was glad the ETs came," he said. "It provided a convenient excuse for ending the lie about my faith in Christ." Then, he laughed. "But even here, the lie continues, and I dare not confess it to them."

The tribe trudged on behind us, oblivious to his lie.

We spent hours trying to figure out why the ETs had come, and equally important, what they looked like. In all the wandering of Father Alec's tribe, they had not come across a single alien settlement. No cities, no camps. Not even a landing field.

"Have you ever seen one?" he asked. "In the killers' camp?"

I shook my head. They had never shown themselves to us; we had only dealt with sarges.

No human being had ever seen an ET, not a single one, or even heard the voice of one. They were the silent, mysterious authority behind the fantastic machines and technology which had, for the most part, conquered us. Humans who had survived their vicious initial onslaught had been forced into slavery. They trained the sarges and the killers to wipe out their fellow man. But through all this, they remained invisible puppet-masters.

What could be so horrible, so mysterious to make them hide from us? When would they come out of their motherships and transports, march upon the earth and reveal themselves as the masters that they were? We wondered, too, how it was that as advanced as they must have been to have traveled such an immense distance in space and time to have found our planet, that they could so cruelly destroy a sentient race.

"It is said," Father Alec once preached to me as we walked, "that we humans were created in the Lord's image. But what does that mean? Are the ETs likewise creatures of the Lord? I think not. The way they commit murder shows such a cruel level of intolerance that they cannot be spiritual in any way."

Then he sighed, seeming weary of his own sermon.

"Yet," he went on, "we humans have done the same thing, haven't we, the way we treated primitives in the course of history. You will note an equal level of cruelty and intolerance, for instance, in the way the American Indians, the African primitives were treated. So, really, what the ETs have done to us shouldn't surprise us.

"Maybe because of their advanced culture, they are simply embarrassed to show themselves. Maybe they want to walk upon the planet only after they have exterminated us completely, so that they won't have to look us in the eyes."

I nodded, and watched as Father Alec glumly pondered these questions while we walked deeper into the woods, no longer speaking, listening instead to the call of birds and hum of insects.

Walking, ever alert.

The next morning, killers zoomed down amongst us like lightening from a crystal blue sky. Following my lead, the tribe scattered in a way which would best give us cover and evade the patrol. After only minutes, we regrouped.

There were surprisingly few kills up to that point, making me wonder if we hadn't lucked out and were being pursued by fresh killer recruits, or a platoon of old, tired, incompetents.

On Father Alec's command, we pulled out our shotguns and rifles and readied ourselves for the platoon of killers, wondering how we had slipped away from them in the first place.

"Here they come," somebody whispered.

Tense, we listened to the rush and crack of brush as they cut through to our position.

At Father Alec's command, we pointed the rifles and shotguns toward the noise, anxious to shoot.

"Hold it," he whispered sharply. "Hold it."

Then we saw them, blasters cocked and ready. Killer eyes darting, still wondering how they had missed us. How what should have been an easy kill had gone so foolishly wrong. Knowing that if they didn't find us, there'd be trouble, hell to pay.

"There!" one of them called out. "There!"

"FIRE!" shouted Father Alec.

And we did. The blast was deafening, bouncing like thunder off trees in the dark forest.

The salvo had the desired effect. With the call to fire, a collective groan had ushered from our attackers, and with the blast of gunfire, the killers fell fast. The second round killed a few more of them. What was left of the platoon turned and ran.

For a change, free humans had won.

We went to inspect the dead. I cringed momentarily as I came upon the bodies.

Seeing my expression, Father Alec touched my shoulder.

"What is it, my son?"

I knew the faces. There was Ike Kelly, Salverson, Gruber. And then I saw the gangly Texan, Curly-Joe, so likable with his even-handed way and soft drawl. A few feet further down, I almost stumbled over Sarge, the old Sarge.

"My son?"

I looked up at Father Alec.

"This is my old platoon," I said with a laugh. "These are all my – my - friends."

I hurried to another clump of bodies.

There, I found my old friend, Larmer. Fallen next to him was that fool kid. I knelt at Larmer's bloodied, hulking frame, lifted a limp arm, and felt for a pulse. Nothing. At least his eyes were shut. He looked asleep, and I felt strangely glad for him, now that he was at peace.

Father Alec had come over. He stood next to me for a time without a word. "We have to go," he finally urged.

With a nod, I dropped Larmer's arm and stood over his body.

"It's better now," I said, standing one last moment over his body. "You are free."

The tribe had suffered only six killed. As soon as Father Alec was sure that everyone had been accounted for, dead or alive, we began a fast trot out of there, heading toward the sun, west. And he did not let us slow our pace for at least ten miles before the swoosh of a transport cut a wide swoop over the trees, stopping us cold.

Father Alec had us hunker down and dig foxholes and rig some camouflage. The tribe worked fever pitch. In less than five minutes, all of us were covered and secure. Only infra-red heat sensors could locate us now, but that would be difficult with us deep in the foxholes and covered by damp dirt and brush per my instructions.

The transport made several wide loops before, with one razor-sharp turn, it headed back to the killer camp. None came that night, or the next, and finally Father Alec felt secure enough to let us come out of our foxholes into the light of morning.

After that, we continued deeper into the trees, without an apparent destination.

After a week, Father Alec finally concluded that they had lost our scent. The tribe breathed a collective sigh of relief and a sense of joviality returned. The boys and girls ran and frolicked again. The mothers cooed to their babies. And the fathers joked about each other's manhood.

I had never been so glad to be alive.

Until out of nowhere one bright November afternoon, we saw the odd craft - a gigantic, smooth silver cylinder - going soundlessly down into a clump of low hills a couple miles straight ahead of us. There was a thud, then a thunderous explosion that shook the ground.

"It's one of their mother ships!" someone exclaimed.

Father Alec gave me a knowing look. He formed a search party, seven of us. I thanked him for picking me.

"I thought you'd want to see your former masters," he said with a grin.

We hurried through the underbrush at the side of a steep hill into which the ship had fallen. Despite our haste, we took it slow, alert for an ET rescue mission.

Within a hundred yards from where the cylinder went down, a stiff hot wind from the fires it had ignited in the dry bush pushed us back. We went around the heat until we were literally on top of the hill, above where the alien craft had crashed.

"What do you think happened?" I asked Father Alec, as we stood on the edge of a cliff observing the destruction. Twenty yards below, the cylinder smoldered in the ruins of a charred stretch of trees and blackened brush.

"Looks like a transport," he speculated. "Bringing supplies somewhere." Shrugging, he added: "Something malfunctioned and she went down." Father Alec gave me a cold stare.

"Like us," he said, "they aren't perfect." He looked around and gestured for us to get going. In a couple hours, our light would be gone.

"They're be a rescue party sent up here right away," he said to me. "Let's go down and take a look while we have some time."

We quickly descended into the burnt out clearing, with fires still raging in spots around us.

The cylinder had been sheered in half where it smashed into the trees and ground. One part of it lie imbedded in the soil, smoldering. The other half had exploded, sending shards of twisted metal in every direction, parts of which we had found during our long approach.

"Is it safe?" I wondered.

Father Alec shrugged. He didn't seem to care. The danger was worth the chance of finally seeing what a real ET looked like, or capturing one alive.

He ordered two of our party to stay outside the hulking carcass of the smoldering cylinder while the rest of us, five in all, followed him single file into the hot core of the remaining half of it. We came into a kind of control room, cluttered with debris, hazy with smoke. The smell of burnt wires hung in the stifling air.

"There!" one of our party shouted. I turned and saw that he was pointing to the bodies of three creatures – ETs - strewn across what was left of the crushed, steaming control room of the transport.

After a pause, we followed Father Alec as he edged closer to the bodies. Within moments, we were on top of them. We stopped and held our positions, pointing rifles at the bodies, frozen with indecision and fear.

The ET bodies were obscured by the darkness and smoke. All I could tell was that there were three of them side by side, each about six feet long. Bipeds. I was struck by the fact that there was nothing inhuman about their shape or size.

Finally, Father Alec knelt. With a breath, he turned over one of the scorched ET bodies.

"What is it?" someone asked, from the rear.

At last my eyes focused upon the dead ET corpse. And my mouth fell open.

"Human," gasped Father Alec. He backed straight up on his knees. His face cringed with revulsion. "It's- *it's human.*"

That made us all fall silent and for a long time, we gazed at the alien, human bodies in the haze and darkness of the burnt out control room of alien transport. Except it made no sense. They weren't aliens after all, but human beings, like ourselves.

At last, we dragged the bodies out of the craft. Now, in the afternoon sun, their unmistakable humanity only made it all seem even more absurd. Based upon their brutality, we had expected lizards or something.

Someone speculated that maybe these pilots were really humans in cahoots with the ETs. Like sarges or killers.

"No," said Father Alec with glum certainty. "No collars."

After staring for a time at the dead ETs, Father Alec made a chopping gesture commanding us to leave this place. An ET search and rescue craft would soon be up here.

As we silently scurried down the hill, I couldn't help but smile. It was funny somehow, ridiculous, that there was really no difference between us and the ETs.

We are all human.

THE DODO DRAGON

by Sheila Crosby

I am the last and I am lonely.
Last night I saw three of the large moons hanging together, with the sea sparkling and dancing below.
It gave me no pleasure. There was no-one to share it.

For a full year before my first mating, the males gave me no peace. I miss them now. They thronged the air round me, begging me to fly with them until the air shimmered.

They were all surprised when I chose Uao for my mate. True, he was rather small, even for a male. He wasn't properly transparent either; he looked more like smoke than water so that he cast a faint shadow and his lunch sometimes saw him coming.

"It's not really a problem," he said. "I hunt with the sun in my eyes so my shadow's behind me. I have to squint a bit, that's all"

Uao's slight smokiness dimmed the brilliant tracery of his veins, but it set off the pale rainbow sheen on his skin to perfection. To me he was even more beautiful than a perfectly transparent dragon.

Besides, he made me laugh. Often I came back to my perch to find that he had left me some fish, and arranged them into the shape of one giant fish, or a dragon, or a heart. He did that sort of thing all year round, not just a few days before mating. And he looked into my eyes, not under my tail all the time.

Oh there was no-one like Uao! I knew he'd make a wonderful father too. I could hardly wait for spring and the mating flight.

One winter's night, a ball of fire streaked across the sky. It caused a great deal of comment. Some said that it was a very large shooting star; others said that one of the mountains must be spitting fire again. I wanted to see for myself, so a group of us set off in great excitement. We visited twenty or so islands, but four days later we returned disappointed. Every island was boringly normal.

One of the elders called a meeting, and said he'd seen one of these fireballs before. It was just a shooting star, and it happened perhaps once in a dragon's lifetime, if the dragon was lucky. He had seen one himself, many years ago. Nothing for us youngsters to worry about.

"Pompous old ass!" said Uao that night. We were lying side by side as usual, with our tails entwined, and Uao's wing over my back. It was too small to keep out the cold, but it gave me a cosy feeling anyway.

"Who?" I asked.

"Eo the Elder," said Uao. "He doesn't know any more about that fireball than we do."

"But he said he'd seen one," I objected sleepily.

"Only after we went and found there were no fire mountains. If he'd really seen one before, you'd think he'd remember straight away. It was pretty memorable."

"True." Uao had a way of being right.

"One thing," Uao continued. "If we ever do find out what it was, I'm sure there'll be plenty of dragons pretending that they knew all along, or at least that they had a feeling about it."

He was right about that too. Eventually almost everyone claimed to have known that it was an omen. They just didn't feel the need to mention it for the first three years, that's all.

Perhaps forty nights later we saw another twelve fireballs, all in V formation like migrating dragons.

"Once in a lifetime?" murmured Uao. "My, my. Aren't we doing well."

There were no more fireballs, or at least we saw no more, and the memory began to fade. We never did find out whether the fire balls had anything to do with the disaster.

We were fishing. It was a beautiful day, and the sky was a lovely deep rose. I flew with the sun behind me, but Uao was flying into the sun as usual. I turned, and saw him with a huge fish in his talons, struggling to gain height. I went to help. I knew straight away that there was something odd about that fish, but we had no breath for talking. We just hefted it back to our perch, and sat gasping.

The fish made no attempt to escape. In fact it lay strangely still, except for its tail which was spinning madly. As soon as we got our breath back, we examined our prize. It was half as long as Uao, narrow, and very black.

Uao tried scratching it with a claw. "It's as hard as an *iay*. I wonder if the insides taste as good?"

"Lets crack it open and find out," I said.

So we grabbed it with our claws, flew up about a dragon's length, and dropped it.

It smashed into the rocks with a peculiar "CLANG" and split open.

"Yuck!" I said. "It's got parasites."

There were about a dozen little white things wriggling around inside it, squawking and screaming.

They were about as big as my feet, and they ran about on two legs, waving two other leg-like appendages near the top. Some scrabbled into corners of the strange fish. Others were squashed, and these were red instead of white. A few looked as though they were helping the squashed ones, for all the world as though they were intelligent.

"Somehow I don't fancy eating - Ow!" Uao broke off suddenly.

"What's the mat - Ow!" I said. The horrid maggots had stings. My eyes must have been playing tricks, because it looked like they picked up black rods from somewhere, and pointed them at us. But whoever heard of an animal that could take its sting off?

"Let's go and catch something else," said Uao.

We fished, and took our catch back to another part of the island - "In case those stingy maggots are still there," said Uao - and ate. Then we settled down for a nap.

We discussed names for the maggot-things. Uao made up the name "*humans*". It was perfect. Just the right touch of casual contempt.

"I wonder where those *humans* came from," I mused. "I've never seen one before."

"They probably came on those fireballs," said Uao, completely straight-faced. "We'd never seen those before either."

I laughed so hard that I fell off the ledge. It took me a while to fly back, because all my breath went on laughing.

"All the same, Uao, I think perhaps we should have squashed them. Suppose they go and infest the whole island?"

But they didn't. They did something much worse.

Spring fever is contagious. I ached and shivered and couldn't sleep. Uao caught it from me. He rubbed his head back and forth along my neck and crooned. He traced swirls and curlicues along my flank with his claw in a whisper of touch. I nuzzled under his wing, giving him tiny, delicate nibbles. Our tails writhed together in the starlight. We carried on for days. Not a single dragon thought of food. The only flights we made were barely more than hops, male and female leaping up a dragon's length, and fluttering back down together. Over and over we leapt and hovered. The tension grew and grew until it became unbearable, and still it grew.

Time.

As one, the dragons rose into the red dawn, even the yearlings who were too young to mate. We circled the island, spiralled up and up into the pink heaven. When the island was no more than a dot below us, we streamed away from the rising sun in a giant V of dragons. I flew half-way down one arm, with Uao just behind and to my left. We quivered with anticipation.

We flew on and on as the sun rose, and still we flew. When the sun was high in a pale heaven, I saw many more flights of dragons coming from other islands. We met over the ocean, and formed a giant swirl of hundreds of dragons, circling and waiting.

Years later, I thought how beautiful we must have looked.

Uao flew above me, and stroked me with his tail as we flew. We circled, waiting.

We dived. Half a thousand dragons poured into the ocean like a waterfall. I took a deep breath just before we hit the water.

It was cold. The fish fled from us, but we ignored them. We flew down through the water, down and down towards our special undersea mountain. The warm crater on the mountain top was the only place to spawn.

It had gone.

The entire crater of the mountain was covered by a clear dome, many dragon-lengths across, and surrounded by unnatural lights. Inside we could see scores of *humans* moving around. They lined the sides of the dome, staring at us.

I ached to breed, but there was nowhere to lay my eggs. I raked a claw across the dome, but it was as hard as the strange fish. There was no way to break it. We could only circle the dome in frustration.

Uao nudged me, and pointed a claw upwards. Suddenly I realised that my lungs were bursting.

We headed upwards, following a few others. It was a long way. I flew up though the water, with my lungs burning. The water above me got slowly lighter. My sight grew rapidly dimmer. I had left it too late to head for the surface, and I was dying. Then I felt air on my nose, and sucked for my life.

I looked round for Uao, and didn't see him. I took one last gulp of precious air, and dived again. I found him only a little way under, but floating slowly down, unconscious.

I swam under him, and tried to push him up. I was tired, and he was too heavy for me. In despair, I dropped my eggs, and for a long moment I watched them slowly fall into the darkness below, unfertilized. Then I heaved with my wings, and we slowly started to rise.

I heard Uao gasp, and knew that he had made it. I broke the surface beside him. We wallowed in the troughs between the waves, our ribs heaving. Slowly, dimly, I became aware just how few dragons there were around us. The sun set.

The night was cold, and the waves dashed into our faces and kept us awake.
Towards dawn I found the strength to cry.

Few of us survived, and none of the yearlings. We searched for somewhere else to lay eggs, but all the other undersea mountains were cold and the eggs died. We tried sitting on them on a perch, but they dried out. It was useless. No baby dragon ever hatched again.

We grew old. One by one, the others died. Losing Uao was terrible.

I am the last.

Now the *humans* infest all the islands. They follow me around. The point black things and strange lights at me. Every time I move, they all make "Ooooh!" and "Ahhhhh!" noises. They give me no peace.

And I am lonely.

THE VIRUS OF MEMORY

by Gerard Daniel Houarner

Clarence woke to his wife Sylvie shaking him. He blinked, shaded his eyes against the light from the hurricane lamp behind her on the side table. "What?" he said, his throat raw.

"You were talking in your sleep," she answered. She wiped her eyes, brushed back grey-streaked hair. "'Something's going to happen,' you kept saying." She glanced at the ticking clock beside the lamp. "It's four-thirty in the morning."

Clarence grunted as he sat up and shook his head. "Dreaming..."

Sylvie froze. A tremor started in her hand and spread rapidly down her arm. By the time Clarence grabbed her shoulders, her entire body was shaking. She cried out as his grasp tightened. Her eyes opened wider, as if to take in something vast and terrible coming at her out of the shadows behind him.

"Not that, not that," he said, voice growling. "It was— I can't remember now, but it wasn't that."

Sylvie wept, and Clarence cradled her face in his big, rough hands. Tears flooded the wrinkles around her eyes, dribbled around the black mole at the corner of her mouth.

"Something already happened," he told her, searching for the words to reassure her. "It's over. We're fine."

"No, we're not," she said, tearing her self away from him and throwing herself back on to the bed. She curled up, honey brown knees peeking out of her night shirt as she drew them up to her chin. "More's coming. I can feel it. I can't stand no more."

"Stop it," he barked. He had no comforting words for her when she let herself fall apart. All he had was strength. That had been enough for him, for his family, for all these years. His strength had carried them through the worst of it over the past year. There had to be enough for the rest of the way. Wherever the rest of the way was taking them.

Clarence reached over and turned down the flame. He rolled over to give her his back, closed his eyes, and eventually went back to sleep.

Sylvie woke him up again, this time standing beside the bed and waving a piece of paper in his face.

"She's gone," said his wife. "She left this. You were right, something did happen. This is just the start of something else, isn't it? More's going to happen."

The world shifted in Clarence's mind, leaving a desert where once there had been life. Connie missing. Another piece of the life he had built for himself taken away.

Be strong. Like with everything else that had happened, he had to fight for what was his. And if he lost the fight, adapt, as he had done all his life. And particularly since the Swarms had come. Clarence swallowed, roused himself to the task at hand.

"I'll go look for her," he said, sliding out of bed. He had ideas where his daughter Connie might have gone. Sixteen was a tough age. It wasn't natural for a girl that young to be cut off, away from others her own age. Clarence remembered his own loneliness from that time. Of course, it was different for a girl. Boys could pass for all right being big and strong, even if they didn't move too fast or didn't have much to say, and had to work with all their heart just to get passing grades. Boys didn't need so much attention. Not really. Girls, they needed people. Just didn't have the strength to be alone. He could see it in Sylvie: the weakness, the ache for her long dead family, for her sons, even for neighbors and people with whom she had once worked. Same for poor little Connie, crying for school mates and even teachers.

"She's not coming back," Sylvie said. "She was dreaming, she says here. Remembering things. You know, from the other life."

"No such thing," Clarence answered. He got into his coveralls as quickly as he could, anxious to get out. He didn't want to have to tell Sylvie to shut up. "You go ahead and have breakfast. I'm going now, try to catch up with her." He raised the flame in the hurricane lamp and looked over her. The flesh of her cheeks had sunk into the hollows of her skull. "You need to eat. There's plenty of stuff in the storeroom. I'll get us all steaks out of the freezer when I get back with Connie."

Sylvie held the paper out to him. "You should read your own daughter's note."

"Does it say where she's going?"

"No."

Clarence left her in the bedroom, lit a candle outside and made his way across the bunker he had carved out from a corner in one of the hospital's sub-basements. He passed the sealed rooms of his two sons, Mark and Damon, without a glance at the locked metal doors. They hadn't even had the chance to come down. The Swarms had taken them topside, along with almost everyone else. He had managed to seal off enough space below to give them their own, empty tombs. It made him happy to think at least their spirits had a place to rest.

He walked, holding the candle before him, past the storerooms and lockers, the main lock, the old, tiny morgue powered by a small generator that served as their freezer for as long as the gasoline from the abandoned cars jamming the streets held out. When he reached his daughter's room, the one she'd picked out for privacy, the door was open. The smell of sweet incense hung in the air. He poked around. Her down winter coat was missing, though it was only early Fall. So were a new pair of Timberland boots, socks, jeans, a couple of sweaters. And her favorite Sandman T-shirts and shorts, for the summer. Knife, machete, her Glock and M-16. Her journals were still on the make-shift bookshelf above her metal desk. Her dolls, pictures of friends and family, her radio and CDs were all over the room. Only one picture, with herself and Damon and Mark, was missing. A framed picture of Connie with Sylvie and Clarence was on the floor, its glass broken.

Clarence went back to the main lock and took out an environment suit, noting Connie had taken her own and one of the reserves. Smart girl. With a bag for clothes, another for food and supplies, she'd be able to travel far and light on one of the mountain bikes he had upstairs. If she was as serious as her preparations showed her to be, he would never catch her. If she was as strong as he had been at her age, inside, she would make it. But she wasn't. There had to be a friend, even a group, she'd planned to meet. There would be problems. Jealousies. Conflicts. It would all end badly. Her only hope was a moment of weakness, a need to say goodbye to old things. He could catch up to her, then. He was sure he would catch up to her.

Clarence zipped the plastic environment suit he had taken from the Army depot, checked the seals and filters, and picked the Sten gun and clip bag from the weapons locker. The suit smelled of sweat, and the filters replaced the closed, stale bunker odor with a chemical taint. But a Swarm couldn't touch him in the suit. He was safe for topside.

He reached for the lock door, stopped. The latches were sealed from the inside. She hadn't left this way. He glanced up at the air duct. No, not that way either. She would have wanted to leave quietly. The emergency exit.

He moved carefully back through the bunker so as not to tear the baggy suit. He took a side passage that led away from the main living area. He came up on the old service door he had rigged as an emergency exit in case the bunker was discovered or its seals breached by a Swarm. The door was open.

Stupid girl.

He lifted the suit's face plate and called for Sylvie. When she didn't answer, he went back to the bedroom. She was sitting on the bed looking at the letter.

"She went out the back and didn't lock the door," he said.

Sylvie ignored him.

"I'm going out that way after her. Close the escape door after me. Leave the latches on the main lock open so I can get back in. And fog the bunker out, in case something got in."

Still, Sylvie didn't answer. He went down on one knee, took the note from her and let if fall to the floor. He took her hand in his plastic glove, squeezed. "Go to the main lock first, get into a suit. Just in case. They don't come out at night. They wouldn't have gotten down here so quick in the morning. We would have heard them."

Clarence lifted Sylvie's head by the chin and tried to meet her gaze. She stared through him. He slapped her once, and her eyes closed, opened, focused on him.

"You have to be strong, Sylvie. I can't take care of you and Connie at the same time. You got to hold down the place 'til I get back. You'll do that, won't you? Come on, Sylvie. You will."

Sylvie smiled, shook her head, reached with her fingers through the suit opening and stroked Clarence's cheek. "You were right, honey," she said softly. "Something happened."

"You'll do it, won't you?" He took her hand away from his face.

"Yes."

He stood up and went to the door, waited until she was standing, then left.

As he thought, Connie had taken one of the mountain bikes he had hidden in the dumpster that partially hid the stairs leading down to the bunker's emergency exit. He took another and went to Khalid's shack under the highway by the river.

The evacuation sirens had stopped a few days ago, and Clarence was glad for the quiet. There was nothing as peaceful as an abandoned city. He threaded his way through the jumble of cars with nothing but the sound of his own breathing and a faint squeak from the bicycle. It was only when he reached Khalid's shack that he felt the morning's wrongness.

The outer door of the lock to young vet's shack was open. Clarence dismounted, slung his weapon off his shoulder. Sun light angled in between the low skyline across the river and the road bed overhead, casting bright morning light on the back of the structure pieced together from loose tin sheets, car and truck panels, doors and cement blocks. Tar and cement seals were still in place, as were the filters over jury-rigged vents. There was no scorch marks or bullet holes that would have indicated an assault by night raiders.

Clarence moved sideways to get a better look into the boxy extension that served as Khalid's lock. The inner door open.

It was daylight. Khalid's home was open to Swarms.

Clarence reached the door, peered in. Called Khalid's name through the suit. No one answered.

Suddenly, rage spiked through Clarence. Khalid. Connie. Could he have been so blind?

Connie came to talk with the vet all the time, just as Clarence did while he did his food and fuel rounds. Khalid had warned them about the night raiders, the survivors without environment suits who hid from the Swarms during the day and came out at night for salvage and to take from the day travellers, who had the benefit of light in which to loot the city. They had traded, and steered each other to valuable resources. Clarence had even invited Khalid to the hospital, offering to help secure space next to their own bunker. But Khalid preferred topside. There were too many hospitals in his past, he claimed, for him to ever feel comfortable living in one.

Most of all, Khalid had made Clarence talk. Not with questions, or a patter of conversation that tempted Clarence to join in, but with a comforting silence. A readiness to accept anything and everything. A fragility within his wiry, dangerous frame that Clarence understood as clearly as his own vulnerabilities. It was a shame the world had to end, Clarence always told Khalid, before he found someone to talk to.

Clarence moved into the shack, Sten gun in shaking hands, hurt blossoming in his chest. Khalid was too old for his daughter, even if it was the end of the world. Khalid talked to the ghosts of men he had killed during his time in the service. Khalid's strength failed too often, and he would keep himself locked in the shack for days, frightened of what the world had become. He was not strong enough for Connie, and had always let Clarence know he knew this about himself.

Clarence kicked over a chair, knocked down a shelf, spilling photos and medals on the filthy floor. He looked for matches or a lighter, to set the shack on fire. To consume the pain of betrayals. Then he froze.

Khalid's environment suit - a black and red rubber body suit with hood and gas mask pieced together from a fetishist sex store's inventory - lay across his cot. The machete he had brought back from his South American forays still hung beside the door. The mountain bike hung on a wall, the cabinets were full of canned goods, and the rack was filled with rifles and shotguns.

Clarence sat down on the cot. Rage drained away, leaving him weak and feeling foolish. Feeling as if he had betrayed Khalid.

The world shifted, and another piece of life inside him died. Khalid was gone. Infected somehow with the virus carried by the Swarms of strange insects clouding the land.

Madness replaced by memories of places that could never be. Delusions eclipsed, as Khalid used to say during his contemplative periods, by the virus of memories.

THE VIRUS OF MEMORY

An overwhelming urge to take off the suit came over Clarence. He put his hand to the helmet visor, stopped when he caught sight of the open door. He tightened his hand into a fist. All he wanted was to get comfortable, drink one of Khalid's warm beers, listen to one of Khalid's black op jungle stories, and perhaps add, in a receptive silence, a story from his own dull time in the Army, or the tale of his discovering Sylvie's sweet attention focused on him, her basking in his strength. Or stories of his sons and daughter coming into the world, growing, exploring. Falling. Getting up, because they were strong. Crying, because they were stronger than Clarence, and able to let out what was inside of them while they went on to walk the path they wished to walk.

Clarence let the Sten gun fall. No, nothing about Connie, not now. Something simpler. The story of his discharge from the Army, perhaps, putting an end to his wandering days for Sylvie's sake. Passing civil service exams with her help, moving from porter to maintenance worker to shop manager in the hospital over the years. Khalid had heard the tale many times in the near year they had known each other, but in nurturing silence, Clarence always discovered new details, a moment forgotten, a sensation he had barely felt when first living the experience.

But there was no welcoming silence for him to speak into.

He searched the shack for hope. The open doors mocked his desperation. He turned to the wall beside the cot, where Khalid had taped pieces of the past year's history: the Time cover with the headline "Vector" splashed across the bulbous and spiked face of an insect; yellowed newspaper photos of riots in other countries; a medical fax alert on an unknown viral infection with sections on genetic damage, brain growths, and thought disorders highlighted; military recon photos lifted from abandoned files depicting the massing behavior of whole town and city populations in the virus' grip; a single 8 by 10 black and white, shot from a building close by, of a stadium filled, like an over-flowing bowl of candy, with the bodies of infected men, women and children. Lines of the living stood in front of the gates, waiting to file into the stadium and find their place atop the mound of flesh. There were polaroids, as well, which Clarence had managed to avoid looking at too closely during past visits. Drawn to them now, he noted the city's familiar landmarks in the background while soldiers in environment suits sprayed chemical fogs at Swarms; or burned piles of bodies; or shot down entire families drawn to the massing sites like salmon to spawning grounds by the false memories, or psychotic hallucinations, planted in the brain by the virus. Half-hidden under a sweat shirt hanging on a nail, a partially burnt, crudely hand-lettered hand-out announced the discovery of an alien organism, a new type of macrophage, capable of genetic alteration and of producing viral organisms targeted to specific genetic sites. A hazy photograph was included, and on a secondary sheet, lists of statistics and test results in fine-print, as well as the beginning of a fact sheet on hybridization. The rest of the report was missing. Clarence tore the papers down, balled them up and threw them in a corner. It was the kind of thing Khalid sometimes tried to talk to him about. But for Clarence, the scientific babble only gave reasons for people to give up fighting and run away. He had no use for nonsense that sapped his strength.

Sweat crawled down Clarence's forehead. He turned on the suit's small, battery operated vent fans. Simpler to take it all off, he thought.

Strength. He focused on the concept. He had the strength to keep going, to keep the suit on and keep looking for Connie. He was not weak, he did not want to surrender, did not want to hear the clicking of the hive mates, or smell the sulphur stench of regeneration, or taste the enzymes breaking down matter to leach out essential minerals, or feel the sun's warm radiance on a spread of wing panels—

Fragments of the previous night's dreams burst into Clarence's consciousness. Towers, rising from mounds of bodies. A hazy orange sky. A squirming sea of hatchlings. An urge to walk, to meet others, to merge body and soul and mind into a whole, to sacrifice self for the communal good.

A sensual moment of bathing in decaying bodies, knowing the flesh is only changing state, contributing vital elements to the process of creating new life—

The sharp pain of birth—

Clarence stood up suddenly. He tore down the pictures from Khalid's wall, ripped files Khalid had said explained the mechanics of the virus' re-engineering of human chemistry to produce new drives, new memories. He knocked down cabinets, the weapon rack, piled clothes in the center of the shack, doused everything with fuel from a canister. After retrieving the Sten gun, Clarence backed out of Khalid's old home, lit the book of matches he had found, and started the fire.

He did not look behind at the cleansing fire as he bicycled away. He was stronger than the need to do so.

Coming up on the library, using the broad path cleared by the military through the stalled traffic and window glass shards on Fifth, Clarence wondered if Connie had discovered Khalid's disappearance. Perhaps that was what had finally driven her away. With Khalid gone, there was no one left except her parents. The hunger she felt must have been terrible. To be alone, cut-off from the—

Clarence shook his head. She was weak, that was all. And if she was weak enough, he would find her.

But not at where she often came, not at the library saying good-bye to the old books she loved to browse through. She would never have gotten through all the rats.

They were standing up on their haunches by the tens of thousands, carpeting the street, the wreckage of cars, the steps leading up to the library as well as the library's walls, statues, terrace. Their noses pointed into the air as if they had caught the scent of some hypnotic fragrance that commanded them to be stand and be still. Forepaws trembling, bodies quivering, they remained frozen even as Clarence gingerly approached the edge of the massing. Quite a few had already collapsed, others fell as Clarence watched. More rats climbed out of sewer holes to make their final stand atop the fallen.

The stench of death and decay that had been so thick in the air during the first months of Swarms' appearance was rising again. Clarence backed away, then turned and fled on the bicycle. The Swarms, or the virus they carried, had found a way to reach the rats and other creatures who had found a haven deep underground.

Clarence told himself to be strong in the face of this new manifestation of the madness that had seized the world.

A Swarm fluttered out of a side street as Clarence circled the boneyard that had once been a small park. He stopped, dismounted, stood still. The Swarm's colors sparkled in the sun as the small, winged creatures that comprised the Swarm turned one way, then another, searching for prey.

Several military foggers clicked ineffectually as their sensing mechanisms triggered the firing of empty chemical tanks. The Swarm continued, spilling over the boneyard like a multi-colored wave, until they came into the range of a bank of foggers which had not been depleted. A cloud of grey mist shot into the air, billowed through the Swarm. Colors blinked. A fine snow of wings fell to the ground.

But the Swarm cloud rolled on, colors drained from its thinned mass. Clarence turned, drawn by the strange new sight. A dream of outlasting the Swarms, emerging out of the ruins to bring new life to a dead world, shuddered inside of him.

The Swarm veered towards him. Engulfed him. The whine of their wings vibrated inside his head.

Clarence shut off suit fans and sealed the vents. The Swarm's surviving insects seemed bigger, harder. The butterfly mimics had fallen, leaving creatures shaped like enormous hornets and even bigger dragonflies flitting around him. Their bodies battered the plastic suit skin. Their impact felt like baby fingers trying to grasp him. Streams of smaller insects, like mites and mosquitoes, streamed past his visor like ghost snakes. Clarence worried about stingers piercing the suit, and tiny insect bodies slipping through seals to bite and infect him with the virus they carried.

Buzzing, clicking sounds echoed inside of him. The suit seemed to fill with a sickly sweet stench that made his gorge rise, until he found it familiar and oddly comforting. His skin prickled.

He felt a call pass through him, inviting him home. He shivered and wept quietly, fighting with all his strength the urge to open his suit up.

The Swarm passed away.

When it had moved on up a street, Clarence frantically checked the suit's integrity. Relieved to find no breaches, Clarence got up on the bike and headed East, where he thought Connie might have headed.

She had not come by the school she had attended before the Swarms, where she might have stopped to say good-bye to some friends who had become night raiders and hid in the building. She would not have left Khalid still alive, hanging from a lamppost in a rough harness, bound but not gagged so he could continue raving of double-sun skies, gleaming mountains covered by hosts of spiked and chitinous warriors, and the soft caress of a Queen's translucent wings.

Clarence felt a guilty sense of relief knowing Khalid had not stolen away his daughter.

As he checked the Sten and sighted, he felt as well a twinge of fear hearing his only friend hallucinate. He did not believe a space-borne virus, dormant for thousands of years, could reconstruct memories of other lives and worlds after being freed from a tundra grave. A virus was tiny, simple, occasionally deadly but for the most part only an annoyance. A virus could not transform itself and its insect hosts, building more complex organisms from whatever organic matter it found, then metamorphose once again in animals and humans. A virus was not a little machine capable of re-arranging gene structures according to some master blueprint, Clarence had heard some scientists say before the TV broadcasts stopped. A virus, or whatever it created, could not take over a human mind, re-program its drives, instincts and memories, and use a man's flesh as the raw material for the creation of new life. Of course, those scientists were dead now, and Clarence had not heard the alternative theories they no doubt had worked out.

And Clarence was certain that no explanation would have helped quiet his fear as he stared at Khalid dangling in the air, mouth foaming, pleading to be released so he could join the work of the Fathers and Mothers. There was no explanation possible for his secret wish to set Khalid free, and join him in a pilgrimage to a place of new birthing.

He squeezed off a round and Khalid was silent. He fired twice more, to make certain his mercy was absolute. He emptied the clip into the other bodies hanging from lamp posts and windows on both side of the street.

Adolescent laughter echoed through the street. Clarence checked his ammo bag, loaded another clip, and emptied it into the school windows. He used two more clips to make sure the job was complete. When he was finished, the laughter had stopped. He imagined young teenagers scurrying deeper into the shelter of their fortress, fleeing the threat of Swarms bursting through broken windows to give them a taste of the suffering they had so enjoyed watching.

He rode away feeling stronger than he had ever felt before.

The West Side docks were his last chance, but he was too late. The mid-morning sun looked down on empty berths. The cruise liners, freighters, Navy escorts and tankers were gone. Checkpoints were abandoned, and no one patrolled the huge mountains of cars and trucks that had been moved aside to make way for the refugee huts. Banks of well-charged foggers remained, as well as solar powered electronic signs giving the date and time, and announcing a weekly pick up boat for stragglers.

He had hoped to catch her before the ships left. Ask her why she had no faith in him, why she wanted to abandon the world Man had made for the uncertainties of the evacuation convoy. As if the virus could not have infected the sea and transformed the life beneath the surface into horrors more dangerous than the Swarms.

Clarence bicycled up a ramp to the upper story of a dock marked by a military green and white sign: REGISTRY. Inside, in the middle of a vast hall he found a row of computer terminals, with cables running to a central box and others going outside to a massive solar power array. He sat at a terminal and touched a key. The screen came alive, listing a set of instructions. He followed them, winding his way through records until he found Connie's name.

The loss settled on his shoulders and his heart. His eyes burned; tears etched paths of pain into his face. The world shifted again, fragmented, turned to dust. Blacked out. He roused himself as his gloved hand clawed at the helmet visor, as if independently trying to wipe the tears from his face.

Clarence straightened. Be strong. There was still Sylvie left. He had to bring something back for her. Connie had been found, she was fine. She was not infected, she was not dreaming alien dreams. She was with Earth's last survivors, at sea. Meeting a fine young boy. Not hiding in some corner hanging on with all the grim strength he always demanded of her to the delusion of sanity. Not leaping into the ocean, driven to madness by the virus. Something had happened, as Sylvie had dreamed, and life had changed again. Connie had moved on, he would tell Sylvie, like all children do when they become adults. It was natural. The something that had happened was not so terrible.

He found the option to print the record copy of Connie's departure on the screen. Further down the hall a machine came alive. Clarence got up.

His gait felt light, and the motion of walking awkward, as if he inhabited a stranger's body. Before he reached the printer, a shot echoed through the building.

Clarence flattened himself on the ground. Another shot, from a different gun, answered the first. Then two more rounds, followed by a rapid burst. Cries. Curses.

Silence.

Clarence turned slowly but saw no one on the floor. He slipped the Sten from his shoulder, got up into a crouch and trotted to the printer. He shoved Connie's departure record in his ammo bag and started back to the entrance and the bike.

Faint smoke drifted up from a staircase.

Clarence approached the stairs, checking corners, doorways, the occasional table or chairs. Finger by the trigger, ready to fire. Old Korean War training, instincts and memories firing up, making him cold and hot at the same time. Clarence smiled, welcoming the surge of familiar sensations. Feeling strong again. In control.

At the foot of the stairs, half-way past a rubber-edged door, lay a body dressed in a tight, pink rubber suit with black gloves and thigh-high form-fitting boots. A hood encased the head, and a military-issue gas mask covered the head. Crotch and breast showed the figure to be a woman's. Her torso was torn open by bullets. A revolver lay on the floor not far from her open hand.

Clarence turned off his suit fans, listened for noise, went down the stairs. Another body, a man's, in a looser black rubber suit with combat boots and a gas mask, lay sprawled across a table. The back of his head was blown open. On the floor lay two more men in military issue environment suits like Clarence's. One's visor was bloody. The other moaned, tried to sit up, waved a hand at Clarence.

He checked the small room filled with dead TV monitors, a few filing cabinets, cartons, and scattered books and papers across the floor. There was no one left standing. He went to the wounded man, kneeled, held him up.

"Missed the boat, sir," said the young soldier behind the visor. He laughed, bubbled. Shells had torn through his chest.

Clarence did not bother to tell him he was no officer, that he had gotten military issue suits and weapons while serving in the Army-run Survivor Corps after the fogger chemical sprays had slowed the Swarms' growth. He did not bother telling the young soldier he had withdrawn to the hospital bunker, where he had already hidden his family, once the evacuation talk had turned serious. He did not think the boy would really care.

"Reported back too late...recon sweep...Jersey...waiting here for pick-up boat...assholes jumped us...asking us for...warehouses...supply depots...Glenn got shots off...got them, didn't we?"

"Yes," Clarence answered. "They're dead."

"Assholes..."

Clarence held the soldier for a while, wishing for a way to feel his skin, to give him warmth. Strength.

The young man began to shiver.

"What did you find? On recon?" Clarence asked.

"Hell..."

"What?"

"They're building a world out there. Million of them...in the dead places. Making towers...hives...pits...people still coming to them...Swarms coming out...of the piles...and other things, too. Goddam photosynthetic. Eat stone. Something to see...but they're alive...that's our future..."

Clarence put the man down, placed his hands on top of his thighs. "No, it's not."

The soldier focused on Clarence, laughed again. Coughed up blood. "Shit...you remember...like them...don't you? Virus...I can tell... see...what was...will be..."

"Shut up."

"Sorry...I'm so sorry..." The soldier grabbed Clarence's forearm, squeezed.

Clarence pulled away, snatched up his Sten gun, held it up, butt first, ready to smash the soldier's head.

The young man's eyes widened. He held one arm up, fingers outstretched, as if the catch the blow.

Clarence hesitated. Stay strong, he told himself. Memories of war rose in his mind, and he welcomed them. Dark figures locked in combat, limned by the bright flash of...lightning, volcanic eruptions. Pincers scrapping over jeweled sensors, spikes tearing into joints, poisoned fangs breaking against armor plating. The screeching of death, the clicking of victory. The hot earth below, boiling sky above. The stench of sulfur, acid, poison.

Clarence let his arms drop.

Stay strong. Stay human.

He ran away and left the soldier to his death.

Clarence tried the outer door to the main lock again, but it was shut. He rang the buzzer, but Sylvie did not answer. He leaned against the metal door he had put in place himself during the days of madness, when the first Swarms had hit the city.

Working in the hospital as a maintenance supervisor had allowed him access to materials he needed, and knowing the place as well as he did had given him the advantage he needed to work in secret during the chaos, even move in his family as doctors and nurses above succumbed to the infection of false memories.

He felt as tired now as he did then, after he had finished sealing off the part of the sub-basement he wanted, after he had rigged the ventilation system and freezer, and stocked the place with food from abandoned supermarkets and military supply convoys. As tired as when he had lost his sons. He needed a new purpose to renew his strength, another Survivor Corps to bolster his spirits and bring his existence into focus.

He pushed away from the door. A wave of nausea passed through him, and the narrow hallway spun around his head for a moment. He fought for control. A purpose.

He went back up the stairs, heading for the hospital lobby to wait while Sylvie finished her bathing, or nap, or whatever she was doing. The military was gone, Khalid, even his children. But there were other survivors in the city. People who did not want to give up. Children who, with a wise and guiding hand, might regain their humanity and create a new world when the Swarms and their madness finally died away.

His steps grew more certain as he walked through the first floor wreckage. He would create a new family, his own Survivor Corps, dedicated to bringing back life, filling the air with brood scents, marking fresh territories and re-claiming old hives, rending enemies—

Clarence stopped, shook his head. Fever, he told himself. Voices carried through the wide hall from the emergency room. Carts crashed over, glass broke. Clarence froze, trying to separate what was real from the strange fever dreams seizing him.

A figure walked past the door to the emergency room. Clarence raised the Sten gun into firing position, crept up the door. Looked in.

A dozen figures were ransacking storage and treatment rooms, supply closets, cabinets. They moved with deliberate speed, loading garbage sacks with goods. Some wore military issue environment suits in a wide range of conditions, others a ragtag collection of protective clothing including one who had visited the same kind of fetishist store as had Khalid and the dock raiders. All were heavily armed.

The figure who had passed by the door moments before returned. Turned, sensing Clarence. Started, cursed. The others looked up at their companion, then at Clarence. As if with one mind, they reached for or raised their weapons.

Clarence emptied a clip in a burst that sent the group scurrying for cover. The figure by the door caught enough rounds to fall back in a bloody heap and remain unmoving on the ground. Others, Clarence knew by flashes of blood and cries of pain, had been hit. He snapped in another clip, fired, caught two more figures rising to return fire. As he locked in a third clip, bullets chewed into the wall across from the opening to the emergency room. Clarence poked the gun into the doorway and fired blindly into the room, loaded another clip, pulled back. He ran, breathing hard, sharp pain cutting between his ribs and into his bowels. It had been a long time since his last firefight, his last flight for life.

The sounds of voices cursing and bodies moving followed him. He ducked through side hallways, crashed through locked doors, climbed gingerly out a side window on to the street, careful not to tear the suit. He left the raiders firing randomly at shadows and each other in the hospital as he rounded the block, came up on the hidden emergency exit, and went down the stairs.

He banged on the door, hoping to rouse Sylvie. The door creaked open, unlocked since he had last closed it.

Sten gun ready, he eased through past the door and entered his domain, closing and locking the door behind him.

He walked slowly, listening for a Swarm or other intruders. He did not dare light a candle, but instead made his way by memory through the hall and living area. He found nothing but darkness until he came to the bedroom. The oil lamp flickered with life on the side table he could see through the open door. Connie's letter lay on the floor by his side of the bed. Ready to fire, he approached the door, imagining one of the raiders on top of Sylvie, hand across her mouth, silently raping her.

He caught sight of Sylvie's night gown, leg, and bare foot. Her stillness startled him. Her foot dangling inches from the ground chilled him.

He entered the room and let the gun slide out of his hands. Sylvie hung from a noose around her neck tied to one of the many pipes running across the ceiling. Her eyes bulged, her tongue protruded from her mouth like a partially swallowed black bug. Through the vents, Clarence could smell the feces and urine soiling her gown and the ground below her.

Clarence sat down on his side of the bed, weighed down by a razor-edged emptiness in his chest. Connie's letter lay at his feet, mocking him with her scrawl. Hurt welled up inside of him, but tears would not come. Not even a cry of anguish for relief. As if his body had forgotten how to vent the heart's grief. Clarence closed his eyes, wondering what else was lost. Tried to remember Connie's face, the faces of his sons. Without looking back at Sylvie, he summoned the memory of her expression when he asked her to marry her, when their first son was born, when she saw each of her children for the first time. He searched for a clear picture of her visage as he had left her that morning.

He found only odd-shaped heads with plates and spikes and mandibles, with multiple hair-like feelers and protruding bulbs filled with poison.

When he tried to recall the last conversation he had had with his daughter, he heard only clicking and humming. The smell of her room from that morning eluded him, lost in the thick, acrid smells of a brood nest. The touch of Sylvie's hand on the back of his neck became the thousand-pointed thrust of a mate's sex into the yielding softness of an egg pouch.

Clarence shuddered. Told himself over and over to be strong as he sat in the dimness of the bedroom. Time passed, and a kind of peace settled over him. The emptiness lost its edges, the hurt its particular twisting ache. It was not so bad, forgetting his own life. With his memories lost, their pain hardly touched him at all. Soon, Clarence was certain, even the memory of the pain would be gone.

Pain made the spirit weak, and when the spirit weakened flesh followed. Death was the inevitable conclusion. He wanted to live.

A new landscape was rising out of ruins of his old world, and he could either adapt and change, or perish. He had gone through eruptions of madness before and survived. He could do so again. If not with his family, if not with the other survivors lurking in the abandoned city, them by himself.

He took off the suit's hood and took a deep breath. Perhaps not so alone.

Clarence stood, took off the rest of the environment suit. His body felt invigorated with its freedom. He went to the main lock, opened its double doors to the world, and walked out of the bunker to search for the place where memories were not full of pain, and where the desert of his existence might bloom once again with life.

WHAT MAKES YOU TICK

by David Steffen

My holding cell fills with the gas, the sedative they use when they wish to experiment. I play my part, allowing my tentacles to go gradually flaccid, dangling off the table. After months of examination they understand nothing about me. Obsessed by the physical world, these self-proclaimed scientists have placed blinders over their own eyes. I don't eat. I don't excrete. I don't breathe or bleed. Their MRIs and other sensing technologies detect no signs of life, yet I move as though I live. I am a paradox they cannot fathom, so they bring their straps and their knives and explore the frontiers of my body. They will find nothing.

I could heal the wounds in seconds. I could reduce their scalpels to molten puddles, but I choose not to. Every operation is videotaped, and my reactions must be consistent. I am curious how long they will maintain interest in the absence of new discoveries. If they start to lose interest I will vary my reaction to draw them back in.

Dr. Talbot's attention is focused on his incision, the eyes above the gas mask narrowed with his concentration. He cuts deeper than ever into my spherical body, and again to make an "X". When he's finished he pulls the flaps wide, revealing deep into my insides, but he sees nothing of interest, only more of the same gelatinous flesh, a uniform gray. Already the first of these autopsy tapes have circulated the internet, but have been dismissed by even the most fanatic believers as a pathetic hoax.

While the doctor focuses on the task at hand, I feel my way delicately across his mind. He pauses for a moment, but dismisses the tickle as nervousness.

This one is a fresh recruit, younger than the others, hired to replace Dr. Carlson who drowned herself in her toilet. Of course, Dr. Talbot doesn't know about that. Fresh in his mind, just beneath the veil of concentration, Dr. Talbot has been thinking about his girlfriend and the sex they had last night. Her name is Amber. He couldn't tell her where he was going or why, only that he had to go and that he would be back in two weeks.

They always work in shifts, two weeks on, two weeks off. She'd told him she was afraid he would never come back. Their fear drove them to fornication, a sweaty and messy affair. I grasp a thread of the memory, entwining it around an extension of my mind.

In the present, Dr. Talbot has one gloved hand shoved elbow-deep in my newly opened orifice. I draw the memory of his girlfriend up from his subconscious, piercing through the shield of his focus like a needle through cloth.

His hand pauses inside me as lust arises in his mind. His genitals respond to the stimulus. He shakes his head, trying to clear his mind again, but I hold the memory there. Already I can feel the associative threads solidifying between this operating table and his bed, her genitals and the gaping maw of my rent flesh. He continues his work as though nothing were wrong, the only visible signs the bulge in his trousers and the sweat on his brow. His brainstem battles with his conscious mind, and he is both aroused by the operation and frightened by his own arousal.

When he's finished I release the memory. I have learned in my short time here that such associations take minutes to create, but are permanent once formed. Operating tables will make him think of Amber, and naked women will make him think of me.

He washes his hands, shuts off the video camera, and returns to his quarters where he immediately satisfies his urges in a complex wash of pleasure, disgust, worry, and fear. He is already my favorite test subject, his mind so easy to inflame. I hope he lasts longer than the last one.

THE BROKEN HAND MIRROR OF VENUS

by Mark Onspaugh

The tripod at City Hall was the largest Dillon had ever seen.

Easily two hundred feet in height, it leaned against the Los Angeles landmark like a drunk being escorted home by a slightly taller friend.

Like every other Martian device he had ever seen, it showed no sign of rust or corrosion. It gleamed in the afternoon sun as if its operators would return at any moment to finish razing downtown.

Dillon knew what he would find if he went up there. Martians a good three years dead, still managing to produce an ungodly stink, their loathsome triple eyes displaying the same amount of humanity and compassion that they had in life.

Zero. Zilch. Nada.

Dillon took some small satisfaction in the English ivy that was making its way up the legs of the machine. Within a couple of decades those gleaming death machines would be hidden under thick vegetation, serving as housing for various birds and rodents.

His stomach rumbled, and he wondered if there were any food stores in the old government building. Looters had cleaned out a lot of warehouses and markets, but sometimes the vending machines held enough stale or rancid treats to get him through another day.

As Dillon drew nearer, he saw that the top of City Hall was a charred and crumbling ruin on one side. The squids had gotten off a shot or two before the AV-19 had claimed them.

AV-19 had been the savior of the human race; the super-virus that would wipe out the goddamn squids once and for all.

It worked, worked fast.

Too bad AV-19 had mutated a few times after its encounter with the Martians, until it found it also liked killing humans just as quickly, albeit more painfully.

Science freaking marches on.

The first invasion of the Martians would have been a success but for their vulnerability to Earth's bacteria. They died within weeks of landing and humans thought they had seen the last of them. The early tripods were also susceptible to the elements, and had quickly rusted and fallen apart without their Martian caretakers to maintain them.

Almost a hundred years passed, and the human race had nearly forgotten the invasion, regarding it with the same nostalgic distance as World War I.

Probes sent to Mars showed no signs of life, and economics and politics prevented manned missions.

A fatal error.

In 1992 the first of the new Martian ships landed, and now the Martians were immune to all the natural pestilence Earth might have to offer. Newer, more resilient tripods and smaller bipods began razing cities.

Dillon was only five when the attacks began, but his family lived in Jasmine, Florida, far from the conflict. By the time he was twelve, everyone was fighting with whatever weapons they had.

The Martian war machines were quicker and far more deadly than ground and air forces, so the scientists of Earth turned to biological warfare. The team consisted of scientists from every country, and was housed in an underground bunker far out in the Australian Outback. Named Project Dreamtime, they worked tirelessly to find a viral or bacteria strain that would kill the Martians.

Thanks to captured specimens, Project Dreamtime perfected the Ares Virus. Strain 19 proved to be the most lethal, and the spin doctors dubbed it "The Fourth Horseman". A quorum of nations elected to release it where wind and water currents would carry it worldwide.

A small minority of scientists pleaded for more testing, but New York, Chicago, Moscow, Tokyo, Paris and London were all in ruins, and the Martians were moving in on every landmass that supported life.

AV-19 was released on Christmas Day, 2003.

And what the Martians had begun, the Fourth Horseman was now finishing.

Dillon found a candy machine near the cafeteria, but it was full of mice nests. He had managed to get along without eating anything living.

THE BROKEN HAND MIRROR OF VENUS 67

It wasn't that he was opposed to eating vermin, hell, the idea of mouse stew made his stomach rumble. He just couldn't take the chance that the creatures were safe to eat.

Like Marie had.

Shaking off such dark thoughts, he found the cafeteria ransacked. It always made him sneer when he saw a cash register emptied. What had those idiots thought that cash could buy? Life was strictly back to bartering. Spam for guns, soup for bullets.

No Good Money. Good Cans = Cash.

It was a bit of graffiti he had seen often since working his way from Tallahassee to Los Angeles. Trouble was, most of the proprietors of those make-shift trading posts were often dead, their bodies swollen like purple sausages, their mottled skin splitting under the ravages of AV-25. Either that, or their corpses lay rotting in the rubble of their enterprise, bodies partially reduced to ash by carelessly aimed death rays, the Martians who had employed them either too sick or too demoralized to aim properly.

Or, maybe the squids had just wanted to hear more screaming. Humans who got lased accurately never had time to do more than sizzle for a second before disintegrating into ash.

Dillon found a dented can of tomato soup in the pantry and a discarded can of beets under the deep fryer. Someone had actually been picky enough to toss it aside. Dillon hated beets, they actually made him gag, but they were loaded with minerals and vitamins. He found a pot and made a fire with some old newspaper and the slats of a fruit crate. He cut up the beets into the soup and used a liberal amount of pepper and garlic salt. The resultant soup tasted like shit, but at least it didn't taste like beets.

He spent the better part of the day going through offices, scoring a couple of Payday candy bars in a baggie, two cans of minestrone soup and some packets of ramen noodles. The noodles never sat well with him, he'd trade them for something better if he could find someone to trade with.

"You're fooling yourself," he thought.

The truth was, he hadn't seen many people left alive since his sister Marie had contracted AV-25. He had promised to stay with her, to be by her side until the end, then give her a decent burial.

While he had been out looking for fresh water, Marie had gone off by herself.

He never found her.

She had been so worried about infecting him that she had gone off to die alone. It was typical behavior for his older sister, and he both admired and hated her for it.

Like their parents, he had never had a chance to say goodbye.

He lost Marie in Texas. In the two years it had taken him to reach California, he had only seen a handful of living humans. One had been an old desert rat in New Mexico.

Dillon had been crossing the desert just after dark, and his only illumination came from starlight. He couldn't risk using a flashlight, and batteries could often be traded for bullets. Besides, his night vision was pretty good.

A trading post loomed ahead like a specter, its chipped and weathered hand-painted signs promising soda, beef jerky and cactus candy. Dillon hadn't eaten in two days, and was hoping to find food and a place to rest out of the sun for a bit.

He was within fifty feet of his goal the old man had popped up out of a hidden burrow like a trapdoor spider and had taken a shot at him, the bullet so close Dillon had heard the whine of it as it passed by his left ear. Fortunately, Dillon was younger and quicker and had put a bullet in the bastard's forehead before he had gotten off a second shot.

It was too bad, because the old bastard showed no signs of infection, and Dillon thought the man might be immune to AV like he was. It would have been nice to have some company, even if just for a little while. He pushed the corpse back down into the rat's hidey-hole and helped himself to the man's supplies, which included a lot of jerky and, wonder of wonders, some stale chocolate cookies. It had been so long since Dillon had had anything like that that he had gorged himself, eating the whole bag at once. This had given him a bad case of the runs the next day, but it was worth it. He also found a paperback copy of The Count of Monte Cristo squirreled away behind some crude Kachina dolls. Paperbacks were a rarity, most of them had been used for fires in the early years. There were still hardcovers in libraries that were still standing, but these were too heavy to carry.

You had to pack light dealing with squids.

His second encounter had been in Las Vegas.

Much of the strip had been demolished by the Martian war machines, but a portion of the Excalibur still stood, its single charred turret looking like an actual remnant of some medieval castle rather than a casino. Dillon had tried to explore there, only to be pelted with silver dollars by a group of four or five laughing children. They were almost feral, hooting and howling at him like wolf children. Dillon wanted desperately to talk to them, to find out if there were other survivors, but they always attacked him with the heavy coins, which they could throw with unerring accuracy. He stayed for nearly a week, trying to coax them to come out, but they called him "Mars man" and "Squid shit" and told him to go away. Finally, he gave up and made his way to Los Angeles, their gibbon-like hooting fading in the distance.

He had quite a scare in Arizona, just a mile from the California border. He had found two toppled tripods that had blundered into deep holes and crashed to the ground. Though there was no one about, he could see the holes had been concealed with a lattice of wood covered with sheet rock and earth. Careful examination of the area showed a line of such holes, nearly fourteen in all.

"I hope you got the bastards," he thought, admiring the work that had gone into so many traps. "I hope you got them before they got you."

He investigated the first tripod and found it devoid of corpses, Martian or otherwise. As usual, it was filled with complex devices that seemed to defy human manipulation. One of the leaders of the human resistance had theorized that Martian machines were attuned to Martian brains, and that no amount of coaxing, fiddling or cursing would get them to respond to humans.

It was just as well. The thought of traveling the country in one of the hated machines made him nauseous. These things had nearly brought the human race to an end.

Human race? Hell, practically all life on Earth had fallen to the Martian war machines, which seemed to fire on anything moving or with a heat signature. It seemed the Martians were only interested in wiping out life on Earth. Whether it was something they considered pre-emptive or they just wanted the real estate, they had very nearly succeeded.

Dillon suspected that there were pockets of wildlife in some of the world's more isolated areas, but it would be long after his lifetime before the Earth was fertile and green again. Something in the Martian arsenal had also rendered the oceans lifeless, or maybe it was another variant of AV-19. Whatever, he wasn't taking a chance of swimming in open water or eating anything that didn't come out of a can or pouch.

He was sure the second tripod would be just as barren, and his mind was elsewhere, wondering if he would find a survivor, perhaps a girl close to his own age.

There were two nude and desiccated human corpses in the second tripod, a middle-aged man and woman. Dillon had just registered that the corpses displayed unusual post-mortem wounds when a tentacle had wrapped around his left ankle. He saw with mind-numbing horror that a Martian had hidden underneath a control panel, and was now drawing him near. It was making that godawful sound they made, which registered on an aural and psychic level, making one's skull vibrate while producing feelings of vertigo and nausea.

The thing's grip was strong, and the natural corrosive in its suckers was eating through his jeans and starting to burn his leg. If he didn't do something, part of his leg would be pre-digested before he crossed another ten feet of floor.

Dillon pulled a hunting knife from his belt, a good solid blade with one serrated edge. With a violence fueled by adrenaline and a life-long hatred he hacked at the tentacle, trying to saw through it before he was in reach of the creature's smaller and more agile tentacles.

It shrieked, and the noise went through his skull like a dental drill, making him cry out in agony. For a moment he nearly lost his grip on the knife, but knew he'd die if he did.

With renewed vigor he stabbed and hacked at the thing, all the while cursing it, its lineage, its planet, its odor and its sexual proclivities.

The mollusk-like body of the Martian raised up a good eighteen inches, and Dillon was horrified to see it possessed a complement of eight crab-like legs on its underside. It began to scuttle closer to him, the better to dine on him and prolong its own hateful existence.

Dillon screamed like a mad man and hacked at the thing, forgetting in his blood rage the pistol in his belt and the rifle in his backpack. He was an atavistic creature, now, like a proto-human facing some terror that had not been dissuaded by his fire.

With a bloodcurdling war cry Dillon cut through the tentacle, taking off the tip of one thumb in the process. The creature shrieked and withdrew the injured stump, and Dillon rolled toward the door, now remembering his firearms.

The shots inside the tripod chamber were deafening, and he did not stop firing until the creature was still and all three eyes had been pulped.

Dillon collapsed just outside the tripod, remembering to crawl into the shade just before losing consciousness.

He awoke around midnight, alternating chills and fever. The burned part of his leg looked inflamed, as did his injured thumb, which was scabbed but swollen.

AV-25 he thought with mounting panic, but calmed himself. It was an infection from the corrosive on the Martian tentacles. If he could weather the fever and stay hydrated, he should be all right.

He had some aspirin in his backpack, and he took these with a generous amount of water. He was loathe to be so free with his meager supplies, but erring on the side of caution might mean his life.

He slipped in and out of consciousness, dreaming uneasy dreams heightened by fever to an almost psychedelic surrealism.

Dillon drifted for three days from his infection. He rallied on the fourth day and made himself a gray sort of stew with jerky and what little water he had left. It was enough to revitalize him and he replenished his supplies in one of the "tiger traps" the locals had dug. He also found a gallon of kerosene. The smart thing would have been to lug it along, hopefully trade it for ammo or a new pistol, but Dillon needed to further punish the Martian who had nearly killed him. He buried the humans he had found in the tripod, marking their graves with simple crosses snapped off from the lattice-work of the traps. He waited until dark, and then had doused the interior of the tripod and the dead Martian with the kerosene. Outside, he used flint and steel to light a piece of kindling, and tossed it inside.

There was a satisfying whumph, and a bright flame he was sure could be seen for miles. The stink of the burning squid was terrible, it made his eyes water and he vomited up his dinner. But he stayed where he was, hoping that stench would carry to any other of the goddamned things left alive.

He found a comfortable couch in one of the offices, and a pre-Invasion copy of Playboy from 1984. It was both maddening and tragic to look at those beautiful, airbrushed bodies and faces. It had been two years since Dillon had been with anyone, and he realized he might very well die alone.

Fine. Everyone he knew was dead, anyway. If he could make sure the Martians were dead, then the Earth would be reclaimed by its own, even if it were just rats and roaches.

Who knows, maybe they would do a better job.

The Playboy featured a pictorial on "The Girls of NU". One of them looked like Kelly Taylor, a girl he had grown up with in Jasmine. She had been his first kiss, a puppy love kind of thing between nine year olds. Kelly's family had moved to Iowa when the Martians began advancing inland from Miami. The two of them had just started getting serious, both fourteen and full of grand plans that now would never happen.

He tore out the photo of the Kelly look-alike and stuck it in his pocket. After that, he locked the office door and tried to bring each photo to life, if only in his mind. Then he slept, the first solid sleep he had had in several months.

He dreamt of a beautiful girl out in the midst of a meadow run riot with flowers. She was naked, but her hair and skin color kept changing, as if she had some internal rheostat which allowed her to alter her appearance.

He ran toward her, but could not gain any distance. It felt like he was running forever when the field began to burn and she was consumed like brittle paper, turning into a light gray ash that fluttered upon the breeze like bitter snow. He still tried to catch her and found himself surrounded by hundreds of tripods. Tentacles from every direction pulled at him, burning him and filling his nostrils with that Martian stench as they tore him apart.

Dillon awoke with a start, the sun low in the west.

He had been asleep nearly five hours.

He was going to chide himself for dropping his guard, then reminded himself the door was locked.

The door was ajar.

Dillon was on his feet in an instant, drawing his pistol as he surveyed the room with quick efficiency.

There was no one in the office but him.

He crept silently toward the door, cursing the failing light. He had both a flashlight and lighter, but both would call attention to him. He had to rely on his sense of hearing and sense of smell.

Dillon moved out into the hallway, praying that, whatever it was, there was only one.

The corridor was undamaged, its bland line of doors on either side a silent testimony to a time gone forever, when people worried about deadlines and layoffs, relationships gone bad and bank accounts emptied. But they had also enjoyed love and vacations, frivolous purchases and fine meals, warm beds and secure, cozy homes.

To Dillon, whose whole life had been framed by the Invasion, the thought of work as a file clerk or office manager was as alien as the Martians themselves.

There was a layer of dust on the floor, and he could see his own progress along the corridor, his handprints on the knob and door of the room he had just vacated. Past this, there was only what seemed to be the passage of several large snakes.

Squid tracks.

Now his adrenaline kicked into high gear, and everything in the corridor seemed preternaturally sharp and well-lit. He moved slowly toward the far end, where the tracks proceeded to a stairwell.

He sniffed the air, trying to locate that odor he knew so well. It seemed absent, which was puzzling. All he was catching was something like flowers.... And... *shampoo?*

The smell made him almost dizzy with nostalgia, and he angrily pushed those thoughts away. He couldn't afford to let his guard down again.

He stopped before the stairwell door, willing himself to breathe slowly and evenly, calming himself. The squid might be just on the other side of the door. The door opened inward, which would tip the creature off that he was coming, if it hadn't already heard or smelled him.

A woman screamed.

He burst through the door to find a young woman halfway down the stairs, her legs wrapped in the tentacles of a Martian that was on the lower landing. The woman looked up at him, and he was shocked to see it was Kelly. How could that be?

"Help me!" she screamed, and now he saw she only resembled Kelly. Her nose was different, as was the small spray of freckles across her nose, a scar on her cheek.

THE BROKEN HAND MIRROR OF VENUS   73

Dillon pivoted and sighted in on the Martian's eyes. He fired three rounds, though he was reasonably sure the first had killed it. His father used to say, "Three rounds for three eyes, cut those squiddies down to size."

Most of its tentacles retracted as it was hit, but one large one was wrapped around the girl's leg. She was dressed in a plaid shirt and jeans, and he could see the corrosive exuded from the thing's suckers had eaten through the fabric.

Dillon holstered his sidearm and hurried down to her. He knelt next to her and removed his knife.

"I'm going to cut this tentacle away, try to stay still."

She regarded him with eyes that were unnervingly blue. He busied himself with cutting the tentacle away, noting she had several burns where the sucker mucus had eaten through her jeans. It must have hurt like hell, but she didn't cry out.

He at last severed the tentacle and flung it down the stairs to the dead squid. Dillon helped the girl up, and together they went up the stairs and back into the corridor. He took her to the office he had vacated, and tried to make her comfortable on the couch.

"Have you ever gotten tentacle burn?"

She shook her head.

"I did, recently. Got a bad fever for several days. If that happens, I'll stay with you until it passes."

"Thank you."

"My name is Dillon, what's yours?"

"Hope."

Dillon looked at her. "Seriously?"

She frowned. "You don't like it?"

"No, it's just... I mean... never mind."

She reached out and touched his hand. "Thank you for saving my life."

He was so lonely for human contact that he nearly pulled her to him in a frantic embrace, but held himself in check.

Don't want her to think you're a head case, he thought.

Hope's bout with the fever nearly mirrored his own, but she passed through it one day faster. He chalked this up to the fact that her wounds were not as severe and she didn't have to sleep in the desert chill.

He watched her while she slept, praying he wasn't imagining her. In her delirium she talked in her sleep, and he gathered she had recently lost someone named Charlie.

The first rays of the morning sun shone through the window and were captured in her hair, bringing out faint reddish highlights against the gold, and her skin seemed flawless except for the scar on her cheek.

For the first time in a couple of years he became concerned about his own appearance. Amazingly enough, there was a mirror intact in the men's room. He was taller than he remembered, and he had bulked up some. His hair was a wild thatch of brown and his face was burned red from wind and sun. He remembered that Kelly had said he was "sweet to look at", and he wondered if Hope would think so. His beard was fairly light but he shaved anyway, using a travel shaving kit from the small convenience store in the lobby. He also brushed his hair and washed his clothes.

When she awoke at the end of the second day he was there with water and some vegetable beef soup he had discovered under a shelving unit in the cafeteria pantry. Compared to what both of them had been eating, it seemed like a feast.

She ate her soup slowly and then took a long drink of water. She smiled at him.

"You cut your hair," Hope said.

"Just combed it."

"Oh. Any special reason?"

He looked at her and she smiled. She was teasing him, and it felt nice.

They stayed there for another five days, the city around them as silent as a grave.

She told him she had been orphaned in Washington during the second wave of attacks that had fanned out from Seattle. She had headed to Los Angeles with her kid brother, Charlie, hoping to find a military presence or some semblance of order. They had only found chaos. Her brother had saved her from a band of men who were using the Invasion as an excuse to rape and loot. One of the men had cut her with a knife, and now she fingered the scar and looked nervously at Dillon.

Dillon took her hand.

"You're the most beautiful girl I've ever seen," he said, and meant it.

She smiled shyly and went on with her story. The men had been dragging her into an burned out dry cleaners when Charlie and their cousin Jack had attacked, killing one with rifle shot and another with a section of pipe. The other men had run off, but the noise had brought a tripod, which had vaporized Charlie and Jack just as they reached the relative safety of City Hall. Hope had hidden inside and stayed quiet. Ironically, the other men who had molested her had run into a bipod, and this caused the tripod to move off. After that, she only left her little suite of offices to forage downstairs for food and water. It was on one of these trips she had run into the Martian in the stairwell.

"I'm lucky you came along," she said.

The smell of the creature was beginning to reach them, now, and Dillon figured they would need to find another sanctuary. He was worried about the band of rapists she had encountered. Were they still in the city? Were they heavily armed.

She was delighted he was so concerned for her, and told him she had seen her attackers killed by the same tripod that killed Charlie. It was the very same tripod now resting against the building like a drunken sailor on leave.

Dillon was relieved her attackers were dead. Although he hoped they might find others who were resistant to the AV strains as he and Hope were (so far), he was glad not to share her company just yet.

"Since the city seems deserted I was going to make my way to the ocean. It would be great if you came with me," he said. That had been his plan, but he was ready to scrap it in a moment if she didn't want to come.

"I want to be with you," Hope said, and he found himself smiling with his whole face. It felt good and strange all at once.

"Great, we can leave at first light," he said.

"No, silly, I mean I want to be with you… *now*," she said, taking his hand and leading him to the couch.

He wanted to say something clever, something sophisticated and grown up, but by then she was unbuttoning his shirt and his throat became too dry to talk.

Dillon had only made love to two other girls in his life. Both had been frantic, hurried episodes before their groups moved out. He knew one had died, crushed under the foot of a tripod. The other girl… Gillian? Her group had headed for Colorado where her brother was supposedly stationed at NORAD. Dillon's Uncle had told them that he had heard NORAD had been one of the first targets of the Martians in America, but they had gone anyway. He never saw her again.

Those experiences were nothing like his encounter with Hope. It was everything he had ever dreamed of, and much more. She was gentle but ardent, patient but desperate to hold him, feel him. By the time the sun had risen over the city, he decided he was in love with her.

They made their way toward the coast, following the path of the freeway system and taking shelter in abandoned offices or shops. It was the hodgepodge of cataclysm that Dillon had seen in other large cities: buildings reduced to rubble by the Martians, others burned by secondary fires or arson, roadways alternating between ash-filled craters and masses of congestion where AV had left scattered cars full of corpses, panicked refugees running from Martians and succumbing to an earthbound bug. The streets were littered with trash and bones, while many vehicles had become hermetically sealed coffins, filled with bloated and liquefying bodies.

Hope was tireless and brave, but she wouldn't go near the tripods. He knew it must be the loss of Charlie and didn't push it. In fact, he wasn't sure why he had been going into them, except for the possibility of finding a live Martian to kill.

Neither one of them talked much as they made their way through the wasteland. Once they reached Fifth and Santa Monica the damage was less severe, this area emptied by plague rather than death rays.

In a small park they actually spotted a live doe with two small fawns, and Dillon kissed Hope and told her it was a good omen.

It took them two weeks to reach Malibu, and it too was deserted. Some had died in their homes from AV-25, but others had left to be cared for in hospitals, leaving their homes pristine and practically sweet-smelling.

They chose a home of redwood and glass perched over the ocean. The pantry was well-stocked with both food and bottled water, and Dillon figured neighboring homes would offer more of the same.

They created a home there before the blue Pacific, sunning on the beach and making love whenever and wherever they felt like it, eating canned delicacies like oyster and lobster bisque, Dillon slowly learning about wines from the home's vast cellar.

"Have some wine with me," he'd say, "I found this Bordeaux from, like, a hundred years ago, and it's really good."

As always, she would make a face. "I hate wine," she said, "besides, you just want me drunk so you can take advantage of me." Then she would stick her tongue out at him and run away, and he would chase her, finally catching her in a cascade of shrieks and giggles that slowly became a passionate embrace and usually more.

At night, staring at the stars or into a campfire on the beach, they made plans for the future. Dillon liked the home they had, but Hope wanted to move far away, somewhere where there was no evidence of the conflict, no trace of either civilization. Dillon broached the subject of children, and she tearfully told him she was unable, a botched medical procedure had resulted in an emergency hysterectomy. He held her and kissed her tears away, and told her children were not necessary, that he was deliriously happy being with her and her alone.

Still, when the moon was low and she was deeply asleep he wondered about the children in the tower of Excalibur, and whether he and Hope might cobble together a family with other feral children.

The summer passed, and the skies over Malibu grew gray with storms out of Hawaii. Dillon wondered if any islands had been left undisturbed. Perhaps there were people in Fiji or Micronesia. Communication had broken down so thoroughly that they might never know how many survivors there were without actually making the journey.

"What... what if it's just us?" Hope asked nervously, watching the rain outside the window with a fascination that seemed a little creepy to him. She explained that her parents had been washed away in a flash flood when she was little, and she had come to think of rainstorms as haunted phenomena, bearing the spirits of any killed by water.

"There were those kids I saw in Vegas. I would think they would have already been dead from the AV if they were susceptible."

"But so many things could happen, even without AV or Martians."

That was true. What if one of the kids accidentally set a fire, or they ate contaminated food?

He pulled her close and kissed her.

"If you are all I have, then I guess I'm the richest man on Earth." It came out both macabre and corny, but she giggled and kissed him back.

They made love, sweetly and with a patience and deliberation born of months of practice. As she slept, he sipped scotch and thought of Marie.

He had lied to Hope. Although he was exceedingly happy with her, he still missed his sister terribly, as well as his parents. He guessed it would be a long time before that ache in his heart eased.

He looked over at Hope, sleeping curled on the floor, and saw her face flicker.

For a split second, her face was Marie's, then flicked back to Hope's.

Dillon dropped his glass and backed away as she sat up with a start.

"Dillon, what's wrong?"

"Your face… it changed."

"Darling, you must have had a nightmare. Come to bed."

"I know what I saw!" he shouted, his mind a jumbled obstacle course of fears and conjecture.

"It's me," she pleaded, "it's just me."

And now, he could smell it, so faintly, that odor he had come to associate with every loss, every shred of misery visited upon his short life.

Martian.

"You… what are you?"

Tears began to spill from her eyes, and it nearly broke his heart. If she had said nothing, he would have decided the alcohol and his own melancholy had played tricks on him, making him see a face he yearned for.

"Please, just love me," she begged, and in her eyes he saw something.

Guilt.

He always kept a gun handy in each room. They hadn't seen a Martian since they had come here, but he vowed never to drop his guard. He trained a chrome .45 on her now, one of the previous owner's many firearms.

"Tell me," he screamed, and she flinched back more from the fury in his voice than the gun in his hand.

"I came to your planet two years ago," she said, looking for all the world like a tearful blonde girl just shy of eighteen. "We're part of a psychic infiltration unit that has been training since the aborted invasion a century ago."

"Psychic?"

"All Martians have powerful minds, it's how we control our machines, how we can sometimes attack you with just a thought. I... I was one of the more gifted ones, but my heart has never been in this war."

Dillon's mind was racing.

"Why pick me? I'm not of any tactical use to you."

"I was lonely," she said. "I found you sleeping and could sense that you were kind, that you had a good heart... but only if I was human."

"So you brainwashed me."

"I gave you what you wanted."

"Then I..." The full realization of what he had been kissing, touching... making love to for the past four months twisted his guts and tore at his heart. His mind was filled with revulsion and loathing, and it was all he could do to keep from vomiting.

"You were lonely, too," she said, her human eyes brimming with tears. Were those dead, triple eyes underneath crying? Did Martians weep?

He thought of how sweet she had been, how it had been so wonderful to laugh with someone, hold them...

But it was all a lie.

"Both our worlds are dead," she said, sobbing. "We received the reports from our world about a year ago. Troops contaminated with AV made it back home. Our resources were stretched to the limit because of the invasion, our scientists had no means to fight the plague. Mars is dead."

"Why didn't you leave me alone?" he cried, the gun wavering in his hand.

"I was lonely," she said, weeping. "My last sweep of the planet showed only one human left... You."

He shook his head. "Las Vegas," he began.

"One of the children ruptured a gas main. They were all killed."

"The Outback... Africa... the Aleutians..."

"The secret installation in Australia was easy to find once we arrived." She sounded almost proud of this. "As for the other continents, your virus was very thorough. There may be some who are immune, but they are nowhere near a major land mass."

Dillon wiped at his eyes and inhaled furiously through his nose to try and clear it.

"I can be anyone," she said. "I will, to stay with you. I love you, Dillon, it may sound insane but it's true. I can even be Marie..."

At the sound of her name his decision was made. The report of the gun was deafening.

"I loved you, too," he whispered.

The rain had stopped, and the house was a blazing inferno by midnight. He had been exhausted, but he couldn't stay.

By the time the sun came up, he was moving north up the coast, and what he had left behind was just another ruin on the ravaged landscape.

COMMON TIME

by Bruce Golden

He stepped through the pandemonium of vines and hulking, water-rich leaves as if walking on shards of glass, planting each step with caution, straining to see beyond the wall of vegetation. Shadows mocked his imagination. Every gargantuan outgrowth became another monster in his path.

Ignoring the pain as another barbed branch reminded him of the wound in his thigh, he scanned the foliage and listened to the distant but crisp sounds of battle. Through a break in the emerald canopy he saw a burst of crimson light streak across the cloud-covered sky like the herald of some great storm.

What was he doing here? He, Willie Solman, who used to go out of his way not to step on even a garden snail. What the hell was he doing here, in the astromarines, trying to kill creatures he'd never even seen, except in some grainy vids? It was crazy. The whole thing was crazy—the hate, the killing, a war over some godforsaken sector of the galaxy. It had nothing to do with him. It was none of his business, at least it hadn't been until the government dusted off an antiquated conscription act and snatched him away from his life. It was lunacy. He didn't belong here. He belonged back home, on stage at *The Bad Penny* playing the blues.

Instead he was . . . well, he didn't know exactly *where* he was—not where in space, not where on this planet. An ambush had separated him from his platoon. The chaotic images still blazed fiercely in his brain. Blood everywhere, weapons fire punctuated by screams, meaningless shouted commands. Gilmore and Fitzgerald and little Jose all fell with the first blasts, holes burned through flesh and bone. He dropped to the ground and covered up at the first sound of attack. Rigid with fear, he didn't move until he had heard an order to withdraw. But withdraw where?

So he crawled, the fighting all around him—crawled over the dead, burnt body of Doc McGee—crawled until he collapsed from exhaustion. He didn't realize he was wounded until later. His first firefight and he hadn't even taken the safety off. For all he knew, everyone else was dead, and he still hadn't seen one of the things he was supposed to be fighting.

He'd heard stories though. Stories like the ones Sergeant Bortman told about killing "slugs" on Vega 7. He called it "exterminating." He described their blue-slime blood and hideous features, and how they would eat their own dead. Willie didn't know how much of what Bortman had told them was true, but the stories alone had been enough to make him want to go AWOL. But where could you go in the dead of space?

The tactical com in his helmet had been spitting nothing but static for a while, so he'd switched it off. His visor display was inoperative, as was his GPS. The heft of the M-90 in his hands didn't make him feel any more secure, but at least he'd taken the safety off now. If only he could be sure which way to go. Toward the sounds of combat? Away from them? He wasn't even sure if he could tell which direction the sounds were coming from. But anything was better than just sitting and waiting–waiting for God-knows-what. Another ragged flicker illuminated the sky and the ground beneath him trembled with a distant rumble. A moldy stench saturated the air and Willie's mouth tasted of his own sweat. The humidity clung to him like a second skin, and with each step green mud clutched at his boots as if to pull him down into the bowels of this alien world.

He pushed aside another elephantine leaf with the barrel of his weapon and stretched to step over a rotting log. His thigh was growing numb. He hoped that was a good sign.

Before he could swing his other leg over the log, something lashed out at him. Only a reflex duck prevented him from getting hit. He swung his weapon around, ready to blast whatever it was, and saw a long, purplish whip recoil like a party favor. The tendril vanished inside a hulking, frog-like creature the size of a cow and as green as its environs. It had no visible eyes or legs, just a bizarre crown of prickly thorns atop what appeared to be its head. Willie wasn't sure if it was animal, vegetable, or enemy booby trap.

He kept his weapon poised as he edged around it, staying what he hoped was out of range of its tentacle tongue. It made no other movement, and though it was soon behind him, he was now wary of running into one of its cousins.

The distant battle sounds had faded, but that only rendered the pounding of his heart that much louder. He found a relatively dry patch of ground and squatted to rest. He even let his eyes close for a few seconds. That's when he heard it. His sense of fatigue vanished and his eyes opened with the alertness fear brings. He didn't move, he just listened. There it was again–music!

A hallucination? Had an alien virus infected his wound? They'd been warned of the high risk of infection and delirium. Willie shook his head and listened again. It was still there—distant but real. The strangest sounding melody he'd ever heard. Light and airy like he imagined the pipes of Pan, yet hauntingly sad. At first it sounded like a flute. Then he could have sworn it was a throaty sax.

It reverberated through the jungle, each note creating its own echo. Willie found it both beautiful and bewitching. He didn't hesitate. He stood and began tracking the sound like he was tracking game back in Louisiana. He was drawn to it—no longer concerned with threat to life and limb. Music was the only thing that still made sense to him, and he didn't care if the devil himself was playing it.

It grew louder, convincing him he was moving in the right direction. When he stepped out of the tangle of thick bush into a small clearing he saw it.

The thing was leaning against a twisted tree and playing a queer looking instrument shaped like a trio of snakes, intertwined at a single mouthpiece but separating into three distinctly different tubular openings. The instrument's oddity, however, couldn't compete with the thing that played it.

It stood on two legs, manlike, and was even dressed in military garb similar to his own. But that's where the similarity ended. Its face was a discolored, gelatinous mass, given life only by the two bulbous eyes which seemed ready to burst from bloated, quivering cheeks. Even several yards away, Willie could see the veins pulsing through its nearly translucent skin. It had no nose to speak of, but three cavernous nostrils where it should have been. The thing was hairless, as far as he could tell, and its mouth was a lipless orifice that wrapped itself obscenely around the base of the instrument.

Willie comprehended all this in the instant he stepped into the clearing— the same instant he froze, paralyzed by fear, enticed by the music—the same moment the alien thing saw him.

Its own shock was evident. It ceased playing, lowered its instrument, and stared. Reality replaced wonderment in a heartbeat, and both soldiers took aim with their weapons.

He was supposed to fire. Willie knew, even as he gripped the weapon, that he should squeeze the trigger, get off the first burst, and dive for cover. It had been drilled into him over weeks of intensive, shove-it-down-your-throat training. He knew he should fire . . . but he didn't. So he waited, waited for death to flash at him. Yet death never came. The creature held its weapon ready to fire, but didn't.

Willie decided to play the moment for all it was worth. Moving as slowly as he could, he shouldered his weapon. Almost simultaneously the thing standing across from him lowered its own. They stood there looking at each other, examining more closely the dissimilarities.

Willie wanted to speak, to say he hadn't fired because he had no stomach for killing, and because . . . because of the music. He wanted to ask the creature why it had not *burned him*, and what was that strange instrument called? Instead he reached carefully into his shirt pocket. When he pulled out his harmonica the thing reacted defensively, raising its weapon once more.

Cautiously, Willie lifted the harmonica to his lips and began playing. At the first note, the alien relaxed. It propped its weapon against the tree and listened.

It was a slow, sad blues number that mingled easily with the dreary rain forest—the small clearing containing it like a living amphitheater. Part way through, Willie stopped, looked at his adversary and grinned. The alien retrieved its own queer instrument and began the same seductively eerie melody it had played before. Willie was amazed at how the creature's flabby puce fingers squirmed up and down the instrument's shafts as if it were playing some three-dimensional game. Watching the performance, he found his eyes as mesmerized as his ears. He listened a while longer, trying to decipher the notes, the melody, then joined in with his harmonica. He played softly and tried to follow along. Just as he seemed to be getting it, the alien stopped. Willie stopped too, and let loose with a big grin. He wasn't sure, but he could have sworn the thing smiled back at him.

The creature took a few plodding steps closer and motioned towards Willie with its triple-pronged instrument. It wanted him to do something. A noise escaped its mouth, but it was gibberish to Willie.

"I haven't a clue what you're saying, bub."

It kept pointing at him as it lumbered closer. Willie realized it wasn't pointing at him, but at his harmonica. It held out its own instrument, and then he understood.

As they made the exchange, Willie's hand brushed the creature's and the clamminess of its skin filled him momentarily with dread. The sensation faded as he ran his fingers over the smooth finish of the alien contraption. He couldn't tell if it was made of highly-polished wood or some synthetic polymer.

Willie raised it to his lips, hesitated before touching it, then shrugged off the thought and tried to play. The noise that squeaked forth was anything but harmonious. After two audibly painful attempts he stopped.

Meanwhile, the alien had fastened its own wide mouth onto the harmonica, but it took several attempts before it made any sound at all. When it finally discovered the proper method, the notes it created made them both laugh. At least it sounded to Willie like the thing was laughing.

Before the echo of their laughter faded, an explosion rocked the jungle clearing and knocked them both to the ground. The alien scrambled to its feet first and headed for its weapon. Stunned, Willie struggled to sit up as an armored juggernaut lumbered through the thick growth and emerged into the clearing. Behind it swarmed a platoon of marines. Like angry insects they opened fire. Blasts of red-yellow heat crackled around the alien in its ungainly dash for cover.

Willie staggered to his feet and looked at his fellow marines through a daze of colliding emotions. Before he could think to call out, the alien disappeared into the bush. Then the jungle exploded in a concussion of shredded leaves and flying mud. The creature's weapon twirled end over end, in dreamlike slow motion through the debris shower.

"Keep moving! Stay alert, stay close!" The platoon leader added a wave of his arm to his commands and moved in behind the treads of still rolling vehicle.

Willie stood mute, a stupefied glaze plastered his face. His arms hung limp, his weapon in one hand, the alien instrument in the other.

"Hey! You okay?" A baby-faced marine tried to get his attention. "I said are you okay?"

Willie nodded in the affirmative and the marine moved on. As quickly as it had stormed the clearing the attack force moved out, the only evidence of its passing the mangled vegetation. Still standing, still staring off towards the jungle where the alien soldier had disappeared, Willie tried to breach the haze clouding his brain. He lifted the strange instrument in his hand, astonished to discover he still had it. His other hand opened, and his M-90 fell to the mud. With both hands he raised the queer mouthpiece to his lips and . . . .

. . . he played. He played it like it was an old friend. His hands were a pair of hummingbirds that fluttered up and down its shafts. The piece was one of his own creation, a fusion of scalding jazz licks that steamed to a crescendo, then cooled and precipitated a more classical interlude. Rising, then falling, then rising again. By the time he had driven the tune to its summit, even the full orchestra backing him had fallen into respectful silence.

He played it like no man had ever played it, because no man ever had. No one else on Earth had an instrument like it. Others had made copies after his fame had grown, but no one had come close to duplicating its unique resonance. He was the one man with the one-and-only sound.

The finale came all too soon for the audience. They stood en masse and applauded with fervor. Willie bowed slightly in recognition of their appreciation and blew them a kiss. After six years he'd become accustomed to the adoration—jaded really. He brushed back his long hair, styled at extravagant prices but graying at the temples, and waved to the audience. Those in the first few rows could see the forced smile he flashed them, but the stage lights washed out the wrinkles.

He backed off stage with the applause still thundering in his ears and wasted no time heading for his dressing room. Close on his heels was a short, heavyset man, who smelled of cigars. He had a hard time keeping pace with Willie.

"Great show, Willie," he huffed, "just fabulous. They're going crazy out there."

Passing through the dressing room door, Willie pulled at the tie around his neck. He plopped down in front of his makeup mirror. An older woman handed him a towel and took his tripet.

"You sounded just lovely tonight, Willie," she said as she helped him off with his coat.

"Thanks, Georgeanne."

Willie wiped the perspiration from his face and began unbuttoning his shirt.

"Yeah, they love you, Willie," said the fat man, having caught his breath from the brisk walk. "Listen, you can still hear them. What about an encore?"

"Not tonight, R.J. I got nothing left."

Georgeanne brought Willie a glass of water and he took a long drink.

There was a knock on the door. A stagehand stuck his head in the room and inquired, "Is he coming out again?"

"No, he's not," Georgeanne told him firmly.

Before retreating the intruder took a quick look at Willie, who offered him no solace.

"That's okay, Willie," said his manager, clapping him on the back, "save it for Sunday. Sunday's the big one. The whole world will be listening. Hell's bells, more than the whole world. You're going to be hooked up to every station and colony in the system. It'll be the biggest show of the decade, or my name isn't Robert Joshua Bottfeld." He pulled out a big cigar, flashed open a platinum-plated lighter, and lit up.

No sooner was the cigar smoking away than Georgeanne snatched it from his mouth and extinguished it in the water. "Not around Willie!" she snapped with a piercing stare.

"Oh, yeah."

Willie ignored the exchange, oblivious to everything but the face that stared back at him from the mirror. Success had put him in that chair, a preposterous kind of success that exceeded his wildest dreams. So why was that face so sullen? How could he spread so much joy with his music, yet find so little himself?

"Guess what, Willie," said R.J., twitching excitedly. "I heard from DreamWorks again today. They still want to do the movie. Did you hear me?"

"Yeah, I heard you. Look, you're a great manager, you've always done me right, but I told you before, I'm a musician, not an actor."

"Hey, for seven mil plus a soundtrack deal you can be ham and eggs on toast!"

"It's not about the money, R.J., it's about the music. You've never understood that."

"I understand all right. I understand you like your limos and your ladies, your house on the Riviera and all your toys. It's always about the money, Willie, and this movie gig will give your lagging music sales the boost they need."

"I'll think about it," replied Willie as if he wouldn't. Before his manager could extend the argument, Willie changed the subject. "How's your boy, Georgeanne?"

Her matronly smile dissolved into worry. "Not too good. He heard they're going to start drafting young people into the military again, and he wants to go to school and study engineering."

"Yeah, looks like the government's gearing up for another fight with them slugs," said Bottfeld.

"But there's been no fighting for years," said Willie. "We've got a treaty and—"

"Treaty-smeaty, those alien bugs are up to no good. Don't you keep up with the news? We should have wiped out every last one of them instead of letting them surrender. Hell's bells, they even let the slimy things on Earth now. Shoot, Willie, you know. You were out there fighting them yourself, back before the treaty."

Willie didn't reply.

"Maybe Georgeanne's boy will go back and finish the job you started. Good riddance I say."

Georgeanne looked even more worried. "Willie, do you think . . . ?" But Willie wasn't listening. He fled to the bathroom, closed the door behind him, and stood over the sink.

Another war? More people dying? For what? For territorial rights? For steaming jungle planets? We were more civilized when we just raised our legs and pissed on trees.

He felt bad about Georgeanne's son. The kid probably didn't have any idea what he was in for. Willie knew though. His own memories were too vivid, too close to the surface.

Still, he couldn't change the past, so why worry about it? Why not enjoy his success? He activated the faucet sensor. He'd made it—he'd made the big time. Did it matter how? He scrubbed his hands with soap and began splashing water on his face. Call it chance, fate, karma, whatever you wanted— it wasn't his fault was it? It was time to move on. Regrets were for chumps.

Willie grabbed a towel and wrapped it around his face. He sat, leaned his head back, and tried to empty his mind. He relaxed, endeavoring to unburden himself of all emotion. He needed a rest. Maybe after this next concert he'd take a vacation, no matter what R.J. had planned.

Then he heard it. That song he'd first heard nearly seven years ago. But he didn't hear it so much as it was in his head. Forlorn and ephemeral, the same tune that had called to him in that faraway jungle. He'd never played it himself—he didn't even want to try. But lately he'd been hearing it more and more, until he wasn't sure what was real and what was only a ghostly recollection.

He yanked off the towel and shook his head. He thought of other songs, other instruments. He hoped it would go away. It wasn't his fault. Why was he . . . ? Then it was gone as suddenly as it began.

Willie exited the bathroom, his hands shaking.

"Are you all right?" asked Georgeanne.

"Yeah, you look a little pale there," added Bottfeld. "Come on, let's get going to the party."

"I'm not feeling much like a party tonight, R.J. I've got a headache. You go ahead without me. I'm going for a walk to get some air."

"But, Willie, there's going to be . . ." Before Bottfeld could even finish, Willie was out the door.

"He's been getting those headaches more and more lately," spoke up Georgeanne, "and nightmares too."

"Nightmares? What kind of nightmares?"

"I don't know. He won't talk about it. I wonder if it has to do with what you were saying. You know, about when he was in the war."

"That was years ago," said Bottfeld, reaching into his pocket for another cigar. "Why would that start bothering him now?" He lit the cigar and exhaled. "Of course those damn slugs would give anybody nightmares. It's not enough they've got to invade our part of the galaxy, now they're messing my golden boy's head."

"There's something else," Georgeanne said hesitantly. "I don't know if I should be saying this, but you being his manager and all."

"What is it?"

"I overheard him once, talking to himself. I think he's hearing things . . . in his head."

Bottfeld exhaled a large blue-gray cloud and replied with a hint of derision, "Let's hope it's material for a new album."

It was cold and damp out, but he didn't care. He had wandered into a familiar neighborhood, but didn't notice a group of derelicts sizing him up. He also paid no attention to some late-night revelers who ridiculed him for sport. He focused on the bottle in his hand and not much else. He knew how to get rid of uncertainty—drown it.

He'd always thought being rich and famous was the end-all, but now, now that he had more than he needed of both, he wasn't so sure. It had been great at first, but what did it all mean now? Was he happy? Was he satisfied? Damn that tripet anyway.

He hadn't asked for it. Now he had it though, and . . . he realized too late that thinking about it had been a mistake. That tune that wouldn't let him forget slipped back into his head. It began softly, like a gentle breeze. Steadily though it grew, until it was a howling gale lashing his tattered brain. That song, that memory. It was so real.

"No!" screamed Willie, flinging the half empty bottle against a wall. The shattering glass and his own rage silenced the haunting melody.

He felt exhausted and drunk, but not drunk enough. He looked around, noticing for the first time where he was. He remembered a dive nearby. A place he used to play, long ago, back before it had all gotten out of control. He could go full circle, finish himself off there. The idea appealed to him.

The rest of the night was a drunken haze. Willie recalled a band playing for a while. He remembered them because one guy, a strange looking dude, was playing the harmonica, and not doing too badly at all. He remembered the guy looking funny, because, in addition to a long overcoat and a big floppy hat, he wore gloves. Musicians don't wear gloves, especially harmonica players. Willie also remembered falling out of his chair and arguing with the waitress over how much more he still had to drink. A tip of significant denomination convinced her he was right, but after she brought the drink he didn't want it.

Sometime after the band stopped for a break, Willie passed out. It wasn't until the music started up again that he came to. There was something familiar about the song which woke him. Something. . . .

A chill ran through him. That song, that curse of a melody. At first he thought he was dreaming, because it wasn't just in his head anymore. It wasn't a tripet he heard, it was the sound of a harmonica.

He opened his bleary eyes. The harmonica player stood alone on stage, performing that tune which had become a tempest in Willie's head. He listened intently to every note, every inflection, and still couldn't believe his ears. It wasn't possible. It was his imagination.

Determined to know for sure, he got to his feet when the song ended. He could barely focus, let alone walk. He took half a dozen erratic steps towards the stage, collided with someone, and went sprawling. Before he knew which way was up, someone had grabbed hold of his shirt and hit him. There was much yelling and confusion. Willie felt himself being pulled away.

"You're out of here, buddy. I don't care how much dough you got."

Willie saw the bartender had come around to help the bouncer restore order. He reached into his pocket and tossed a wad of bills at the bartender, then looked to the stage. It was empty. The harmonica player was gone.

They hustled him outside and pushed him towards the street. He fell and didn't try to get up. He lay there wondering—wondering what was real and what wasn't, and whether it even mattered anymore.

People poured into the concert hall like the streams from a mountain thaw. Even backstage Willie found their discordant murmurings deafening. Tripet in hand, he paced his dressing room like a caged animal. He paused to massage his throbbing temples and paced some more.

"Willie boy, settle down," said Bottfeld when he saw his client's nervous look. "Save it for the show. You know they're going to love you. They always do."

"Yeah, but am *I* going to love me?"

Bottfeld's phone beeped for attention.

"Yeah. What? Well make sure security clears him out. All right."

"Problem?" asked Willie.

"Nothing for you to worry about. Security had to chase off some old guy playing his harmonica out by the rear exit near your limo."

"What?"

"Don't get excited. It's no big—hey! Where you going?"

Willie was out the door already. "I'm going for some air."

"Wait!" called Bottfeld. "Hell's bells, don't be too long, Willie. You go on in 20."

Willie exchanged nods with the security guard at the rear exit and started down the alleyway. There was another guard next to his limo.

"Do you want me to go with you, Mr. Solman?" said the second man.

"No thanks, I'm just stretching my legs a minute."

He didn't walk far before he heard it—the phantom song that wouldn't go away. For some reason, though, the sound didn't terrify him anymore. It had become inevitable. He accepted it calmly, like an old friend who came to visit and wouldn't leave. He continued down the starlit alley, following a tune that wasn't there. Only when it faded away did he stop. He listened, lost because it wasn't there anymore. The silence was filled with uncertainty. Momentarily he was overwhelmed by apprehension. What should he do? Which . . . ? Then he heard something else. The very real, very ordinary sound of someone playing the blues.

He didn't have to go far to find the harmonica player, dressed as he had been two nights before.

Half hidden in the shadows, covered in clothing, Willie couldn't really see the fellow. But he didn't have to. The stranger stopped playing and Willie lifted the tripet to his lips. He began the same, slow, sad song the stranger had been playing, stopping after only a few bars. The harmonica player responded in-kind.

"It's you," said Willie. "You're alive."

The stranger limped stiff-legged a few steps closer.

"Yes, it is me." The voice had a lisp that wasn't quite human.

"I thought you died on Vega 5. There was an explosion and then. . . ." Willie's voice trailed off.

The stranger limped closer as if to demonstrate his disability and removed his hat.

"Only part of me died there."

The creased, rubbery features of the alien startled Willie momentarily, even though he knew exactly what hid beneath the hat. "How did you know where to find me?"

"The great Willie Solman? Who on this planet has not heard of you? Tonight's performance has been well promoted. 'Songs of the Galaxy' I believe they're billing it." The thing made a sound that was part belch, part cough, then continued. "You have mastered the 'tripet,' as you call it, quite well. Much better than I ever did."

Willie lifted the instrument. "I always wondered what it was really called."

The creature made a weird-sounding noise that welled up from deep inside it, "*Hgs-doushk.*"

"I don't think I could pronounce that," said Willie. "You know, you haven't done too badly yourself with that mouth organ. I heard you the other night. Those were some mean blues you belted out. I bet you've got quite a following where you come from."

"I am afraid the victors are more tolerant than the defeated," the alien said, then spit and coughed roughly. "After your military drove us off our settlement on *Klidcki-sh*–Vega 5 you call it–your kind became the scourge of my world's existence." The alien held up the harmonica. "Yes, I learned to play it. I was fascinated with it. But my people hated anything remotely connected to humans with a passion I doubt you could understand. Your race, your technology, your culture, your music even, became an anathema." The creature hesitated, remembering. "The more I played the harmonica, the more of a disgrace I became. I loved the sound, but I had no audience. They tolerated the crazy, wounded 'war hero' only so long, then. . . ."

"How long have you been on Earth?"

"A few years, ever since they began allowing *my kind* here. The reception, for the most part, has not been very warm. But at least here I could play my music. Carnivals, sideshows, roadhouses–I played wherever I could. The locals are never too fond of my staying long, but I have my music, like you have yours . . . or is it the other way around?"

Willie laughed and the creature responded until its own unearthly chuckle ended in a vile cough. When the cough subsided Willie held out the tripet. "I guess this belongs to you."

"Not anymore," the alien said, and held up the harmonica. "After all, it *was* a fair trade." An inhuman smile formed on its quivering face, only to be interrupted by another uncontrollable fit of coughing. It gagged and gasped for air.

"What's wrong? Are you sick?"

"I am dying." It paused for a moment as if composing its inner self and gathering strength. "The greater force of your planet's gravity, its fouled atmosphere, have taken their toll on my life force. That is why I came. I hoped to see you before I–" Another spasm interrupted, and Willie knew it was fighting for control of its own body.

"Look, I've got more money than I know what to do with. There must be a doctor who can–"

"No, there is no doctor on your world or mine who can alter what is to be. My race recognizes the end when it comes. It is instinctive. We prepare for it."

"It's not right–none of it," said Willie angrily. "I'm sorry I . . . ."

"Do not play the blues for me, Willie Solman. I meet death with no regrets. I lived for my music and shall die for it, as shall you some day. But our music will live on. Maybe, one day, our two races will make music together."

Another wheezing attack staggered the creature. Willie caught it before it fell.

"Willie! There you are."

Willie turned to see Bottfeld huffing down the alley like he was three strides from a heart attack.

"For cripes sake, Willie, hurry up. You're on in thirty seconds."

"Guess what, I'm going to be late. Go tell them I'm on my way. Go on," he said, waving his manager away.

The alien being stood on its own, gesturing to Willie that it was okay.

Willie lifted the tripet and tried to sound upbeat. "Come on. I'll show you how to *really* play this thing."

The creature put its floppy hat back on its head, pulled the collar of its overcoat up closer to its face, and said, "Certainly, for *Cripe's* sake."

The crescendo of applause reached new heights as Willie walked on stage. Smiling to the audience, he put his hands up, pretending their adoration was unexpected. He bowed, held out his tripet to the multitude, and encouraged more applause for the instrument. Then, laughing, he raised his other hand to signal for quiet. The ovation died stubbornly.

"I want to . . . ." Willie started, then waited for the noise to fade. "Since this concert is titled 'Songs of the Galaxy,' and is being broadcast system-wide, I want to dedicate tonight's music to galactic peace. Peace among all races, all beings."

The call for peace was met by enthusiastic applause.

"Now I've got a special treat for you. Backstage is the musician who gave me my first lesson on this thing," he said, holding up the tripet once more. "Let's bring him out here and see if he remembers how to play it."

Willie clapped to start a polite round of applause and motioned for the creature to join him. It hesitated, pulling its collar up as high as it would go. With Willie still encouraging, and the audience still clapping, the shrouded alien hobbled on stage. Its weather-beaten wardrobe inspired a few chuckles, and Willie heard someone in the audience call out, "It looks like a slug. I think it is!" He had no doubt the bright lights had revealed his mystery guest's identity to those nearest the stage, and to the cameras feeding the satellite uplinks. He didn't know for sure how they'd react, and he didn't care. He handed the tripet to the alien, and its gloved hands fondled the instrument with familiarity. Willie gave it an encouraging nod and the creature began to play.

It played the same seductive melody that had led Willie through the jungle to his encounter with destiny. The same song which had haunted him since that day. Only now, for the first time since then, it was beautiful again—no longer a specter of guilt.

When it came to a natural pause in the piece, the creature reached into its pocket and handed Willie the harmonica. Then, to the audience's delight, and a smattering of applause, they played together. Two musicians, in a world of their own, oblivious to everything but their music . . . until the sounds of choking brought Willie back to reality.

The alien clutched futilely at its chest, as if trying to rip open its own lungs as it fell to the stage floor. Its hat rolled off and a collective gasp rose from those in the audience who hadn't already noticed its inhuman features.

Willie knelt down and cradled the grotesque head in his lap. The thing sputtered and coughed before it was able to speak.

"They liked my music, did they not?"

"You were sensational. They loved you."

The alien handed the tripet to Willie, then held out its gloved hand in expectation. Willie looked unsure, started to ask, then realized what it wanted. He handed over the harmonica and the creature clasped it close to its chest.

"I don't even know your name," said Willie, fighting unexpected tears.

"You could not pronounce it."

"That's a funny looking case you've got there."

COMMON TIME

"It's custom made."

"What you got in there?"

"Just an old instrument."

"Instrument?"

"I have a reservation in the name of Solman."

"Okay, one moment please." The purser completed his file search, raising his eyebrows in surprise as he did. "You're going all the way to the Outlands?"

"That's right."

"That's dangerous territory, mister, what with them slugs on the warpath. You've got all the necessary permits and travel visas, so I guess you must know what you're getting into. I don't know why you'd want to go way out there though, unless you've got some kind of death wish."

"Not a death wish. Let's just say I want to see how good I really am, and there's only one place to find out. Can I go aboard now?"

"Yes, sir. Your stateroom has been prepared and personally coded for you. Enjoy your trip."

"Thanks, I will."

STEVE'S REALLY COOL MOVIE BLOG

BY RJ SEVIN

November 16, 12:53 a.m.

Hey, gang. Sorry I didn't get the Bluray releases updated as promised—it's been an INSANE week. It's late, I'm a little tired and I'm a lot drunk. I just got back from a party at Troublemaker Studios. Saw stuff I can't tell you about yet. (Oh. My. GOD.)

Gotta get some sleep. Will have something posted tomorrow, before I fly to SF for my first trip to the Ranch.

Yes. THE Ranch.

Tomorrow is going to be the coolest day ever.

November 17, 5:48 p.m.

Yesterday I told myself that I wouldn't bother updating this site again—I mean, who cares anymore? It's over, right? But so many of you wrote and said that you wanted to know what I had to say about this, so here it is. I'm crying and I'm hating myself for what I'm about to write, but it's who I am and I'd be lying to you and to myself if I didn't tell you what I'm feeling.

The Empire State Building. Woody Allen. Martin Scorcese. Times Square, where I saw Fulci's ZOMBI and BEHIND THE GREEN DOOR back to back, maybe the strangest double feature ever. (Did the projectionist think he was running BEYOND THE DOOR?) Stan "The Man" Lee and Marvel friggin Comics.

All gone. I'm sitting in front of my computer, crying and shaking and New York City is a smoldering crater. Millions are dead, thousands more are dying, and I'm thinking about Spider-Man and King Kong and the fact that I'll never attend another New York movie premiere or read another issue of THE UNCANNY X-MEN.

I'm sorry. I'm gone. This is it. It's been fun. Turn off your computer and go hold someone you love.

November 18, 11:26 a.m.
    I'm back.
    I'm numb. I do not believe what I am seeing, but there it is. You've seen it, too. The answer to our greatest and most urgent question (Who the hell did this to us?) is also the answer to our most ancient question: are we alone?
    No, we're not.
    Back when I was a teenager and going through all the crap teens go through, I went on a bit of a Bible kick. I—damn, I have NO idea where I was going. Just sort of started staring into space and, well
    Nope. I've lost my point.
    A few days ago, I was gearing up for every nerd's dream trip to San Francisco. The next day, the Big—
    Oh, the point I was gonna make, I just remembered it. Funny how that happens. The Bible. When I was a teenager, I went on a bit of a Bible kick, reading Revelation and Daniel and listening to prophecy teachers interpret the meaning of the wounded beast's head or the feet of clay in Nebuchadnezzar's dream or whatever. I came to believe that prophecy—the ability to see the future—was not a gift from God but a talent inherent in all truly creative people. Artists and writers throughout history would get these flashes, they'd peer into the future, through the A to Z linear fog of human existence and into the simultaneously existing seconds of eternity. And so we'd get St. John writing of falling torches scorching the earth (nuclear warheads), Nostrodamus warning of Hister (Hitler), and, yes, the visionary predictions of writers like Ray Bradbury and Jules Verne. You can't read THE ISLAND OF DR. MOREAU without seeing in the words of H.G. Wells a chilling pre-echo the horrors of genetic engineering gone mad, and anyone whose read his THINGS TO COME would
    Wow. That's how I sound all the time? It's pretty pathetic. Even now, I'm an effing nerd, crying about Marvel Comics and going on about prophetic sci-fi writers. (And trying, even now, not to go off on a spiel about the glorious disaster that was the '90s film version of DR. MOREAU. Brando and the ice bucket, man.) So, yeah, my point, dammit, is that I'm drunk and New York City has been leveled by aliens and H.G. Wells was right. The invaders may not be from Mars but they're from SOMEwhere and they're here and things were bad enough, what with the disintegrating economy and the threat of terrorists and gas prices soaring and George Lucas once again adding shit to STAR WARS. Dammit.
    We knew it was coming. After 9/11, I thought maybe that our obsessions with seeing New York obliterated on screen—either through alien attack or in a buckshot hail of meteors or a rampaging giant lizard—came from the collective

pre-cognitive awareness of that day rushing to meet us. Then I sobered up and realized that maybe the brainwashed zealots simply knew what we all knew: that a catastrophic blow to New York would be a catastrophic blow to the world.

Now I know better. Blithering no-talent hacks like Dean Devlin and Roland Emmerich weren't channeling 9/11. No. On some level, everyone who ever wrote a story or made a movie about aliens blowing the piss out of the earth knew THIS was coming.

Look to the skies, bitches.

November 19, 12:48 pm

I keep staring out the window. It's a cool day. Not a cloud in the sky. A few folks milling around. Church is packed, according to the local news. Lots of talk about angels and judgment day. I'm getting scared. They haven't attacked us again, yeah, but it's like a powder keg, isn't it? You know what I mean. Folks don't need aliens raining fire from the skies to go crazy and get violent.

3:20 p.m.

I'm looking at the photos. On some level, you'd think an alien would be hard to look at, like maybe you couldn't wrap your mind around what you were seeing, so you'd see an indecipherable blur or you'd go insane or die or something, like someone in a Lovecraft story looking upon the horrifying form of some Elder God, or maybe someone from the Old Testament gazing upon the face of Jehovah, their face going all RAIDERS OF THE LOST ARK and shit.

None of that. Looking at these things isn't really all that different from seeing some really exotic deep-sea creature on the Discovery Channel. It's jarring and shocking and also very, very cool, but it's just another animal, just another living thing. None of them seem all that different from life on Earth—not the multi-limbed slave-laborers or the little bug things scurrying all over the landing site or the humanoid ones that seem to be running the show.

Humanoid, can you believe it? God's fingerprint, or proof that there are monkeys everywhere, and we are all Devo?

November 23, 1:18 p.m.

Papa Steve and Ling Ling are okay, by the way. Dad is nervous but kind of satisfied, in an I-told-you-something-like-this-was-coming kind of way, and my wife is scared. She wants to head for the hills in the van.

I really don't want to leave all my stuff.

We're going to the store. I expect it to be a madhouse.

6:05 p.m.

I just watched someone die.

I was right: the store WAS insane. People crammed shoulder to shoulder, pushing and cursing and getting pissed. The shelves picked clean. One delivery truck out back, people pressing in like something from DAWN OF THE DEAD. We managed to get some bread and a case of water. The guy who ran the store said that they were closing, and that FEMA trucks were supposedly on the way with supplies. Watch as I hold my breath.

The drive home was as you'd expect it to be. Empty streets. Shattered storefronts, the looters long since gone. We didn't say anything, really.

We got home and were getting out of the car when the shooting started. I don't know how many there were or why they were shooting at one another. I rushed to the house, pushing Ling ahead of me. I remember the sound of the case of water hitting the driveway, my dad cursing, running ahead of us, his head low. The sound of his keys rattling in the front door, and then we were inside and locking the door and on the floor. Outside, bullets and curses flew.

It got quiet, and Dad got up and went to the window. He gasped. I comforted Ling. When she quieted down, I went to the window. There was a man lying face up on the sidewalk in front of our house. His gun lay nearby.

We've never owned guns—never believed in them. Dad is a vegetarian, and both of us have a hard time watching THE OMEGA MAN without bitching about Heston and the NRA. But when I looked at my dad, I knew we saw the same thing in each other's eyes: we needed that gun.

I went into my bedroom and returned with my G1 Megatron. Laughing through her tears, Ling asked if I were serious. I transformed Megatron from robot to gun mode. It made a convincing Walther P-38, so much that it's been banned from planes for years, and every Megatron toy since the original have been day-glow colored tanks or dinosaurs.

I have a real gun now. I walked outside, Transformer held high. They guy wasn't dead yet. Most of the left side of his face was gone. His hand crept through the grass like a bloody pink spider, seeking his gun. His remaining eye was glassy and scared. Looking around, I crouched and scooped up his gun. Then I met his gaze and watched him gurgle and rattle and die. Behind me, Dad urged me to come in.

Real death doesn't look like a Savini effect.

November 26, 7:12 a.m.

Martial law. Troops everywhere. Democracy on hold. The President is gonna be on in a few minutes.

Why haven't we gotten more footage of the aliens? The two clips that are out there are getting old, and the lack of new footage doesn't make much sense.

11:41 a.m.

I'm drinking again. Dad is asleep on the couch and Ling is crying in the bedroom. I tried to go in and comfort her, but she told me to get out.

Watching the video again. I hate to admit it, but the humanoid ones are actually kind of beautiful. Not Na'vi hot, but beautiful. Aesthetically pleasing, one might say, if one were drunk and updating his movie blog while the world ended.

What the hell are those things on their backs and neck, anyway? They look like ornamental tumors, or something, but I can't figure out what kind of evolutionary purpose they could possibly serve. They look like the kinds of frills an over-eager character designer would throw in at the last minute, not something any actual living thing would ever need.

Weird, man. I think I'm gonna keep on drinking.

3:39 p.m.

It won't be long before the lights go out and you're killing your mother for the last can of refried beans. Upshot? That new Owen Wilson and Jennifer Aniston romantic comedy will never be released. There's your proof of a just and loving God, Bill Maher.

I'm still alive. You are, too, judging by the talkbacks and by the emails I'm getting. Moscow is gone. Ditto China, Japan, India, the entire Middle East, and, God help us, New Orleans and most of the Gulf Coast.

New York city is still a crater, albeit a very lively one, if the footage we've all watched a trillion times, footage of our bizarre but oddly familiar visitors terra-forming the former Big Apple is to be trusted.

6:47 p.m.

I just listened to Orson Welles's WAR OF THE WORLDS radio drama on vinyl. What we're experiencing is the Mercury Theater all over again, only now it's not the Rockefeller Foundation engaging in a psychological warfare experiment. It's far more dire.

Great cities have been laid to waste.

Billions of people were burned alive.

The aliens are fake.

It took over one hundred viewings of the second video released of the terra-forming on Long Island for me to realize this. Go to the 2:34 mark in the video and watch the two humanoids walking in the background, to the right of the lung-like organism scientists claim is turning our air into theirs. Notice their identical walk cycles.

That's right: WALK CYCLES. They're CG. The best damned CG ever, but there it is. And now that I see it there, I see the tell-tale giveaways everywhere. Take another look—you'll see. You've probably read you fair share of CINEFEX articles, and you know the difference between mo-cap and key-frame.

What does this mean? Are all those places actually gone? I think so, maybe. But they weren't blown up by intergalactic/interdimensional explorers. They were blown up by our government either to cover up some kind of FAILSAFE level screw-up or to simply seize control. How'd they strike so many targets abroad without setting off a nuclear exchange? Did the US hire suicide bombers to drive nuclear warheads into the hearts of Moscow and Beijing and Tel Aviv? And who created these damned brilliant and awful videos? Who designed the creatures? ILM? Weta? Bernie Wrightson? Did they know what they were doing when they got hired to produce these five and a half minutes of alien invasion footage?

Damn it all.

November 27, 7:43 a.m.

I think I'm right. Maybe I'm just seeing what I want to see. That's what Dad says, anyway. A lot of you are saying the same things in Talk Back, so, who knows?

I think I may be done with this blog.

November 28, 7:21 p.m.

They say there's a body on the other end of town. One of the workers with, what is it, eight arms? So hard to tell. Some of them seem to have six. Anyway, someone said that someone shot one, and now a bunch of folks in the neighborhood are talking about going out there to see it.

I don't think anyone is gonna move the dead guy from the sidewalk.

November 28, 11:18 p.m.

The lights are out. I'm in the van. Just pulled over. Posting from my cell. Explosion about a half hour ago on the other side of town. Nevermind the supposed corpse, folks are saying that they're here, that they've seen them in the woods. Folks saying a lot of things. One way to find out. Dad and Ling stayed home. They have the gun. I'm driving against the exodus. I'm driving toward the smoke. It's black.

More later.

MOTH TAMUTH ROBOTICA

by Kristen Lee Knapp

Klote missed his penis. Others complained about their eyes, fingers, even teeth. But the only time Klote felt less than human, less than a *man*, was when he noticed the double-layer field issue plate armor that had replaced his cock.

"Shit," he muttered, waking. His reactor fired, juicing his robotic arms and legs. *Sys* checks scrolled down his screen, endless rows of unintelligible numbers.

Hangar lights blinked on. A pointless courtesy, all armored infantry came equipped with night vision, infrared, sonar, motion sensors, thermal vision. . .

Trumpets blared reveille in Klote's ears, a prerecorded song. Another dying tradition. Armored infantry did not sleep.

Giz loped from his cell on steel, simian arms, armored tail wagging. Twig wriggled out on insectoid legs, gun barrels twitching.

Marza arrived last, her every step shaking the drop ship. Her armored plates shuddered and her cannons jiggled as she lurched forward.

Klote stared at her, imagined his cock stiffening beneath his armor.

"Jesus. I can't *believe* I signed up for two years of this," Giz groaned.

"He guessed the Armored Infantry's slogan!" said Twig.

Klote grinned.

"Oh man. I can't breathe. I'm not breathing," said Giz.

"You don't have lungs," said Klote.

"But how do I remember *how* to breathe?"

"That's what AI rehab's for!" Twig giggled.

"Armored Infantry Team 7, you are over the mission point, prepare for drop." The pilot's voice boomed like God.

Humans directed them with little cones of light. Klote edged past. Just one misstep could crush hundreds of the useless little flesh bags. He snickered.

Alarms bawled as the titanic metal doors opened, revealing a vomit-colored sky.

"*WHEEEE!*," Twig screamed and jumped.

Giz was next, repeating his sutra of, "Oh man, oh man," with all the conviction of a Buddhist monk.

Marza jumped and the drop ship bounced, unburdened by her hundred tons of weight.

Klote crouched and leapt after her.

Clouds whipped past, probably cold. He found himself wishing he could feel the wind slap his face, howl in his ears. He only heard Twig's hysterical laughter, Giz's moans and Marza's vacuous silence.

The miasma of acid-green clouds vanished. Gutted ruins sprawled below like a million fragments of shattered glass.

"*WOOHOOO!*" Twig shrieked.

"Cut the noise," said Marza.

Klote's crotch twitched at her voice.

"Oh, it's on. It's on like *Donkey Kong*," muttered Twig.

Altitude monitors injected Klote's eyes with numbers. Pointless, his thrusters were automatic.

"Look at all that, man," said Giz. "Some real Tower of Babel shit."

Klote and Twig laughed. He remembered his first trip Earth side. Now, nothing seemed more mundane than Earth. He absurdly thought of sight-seers, gawking at sand in a desert.

Thrusters erupted, blue lights blooming from jet packs and feet rockets slowing their descent.

A siren sang in Klote's ear as his left leg went numb. Everything turned red, two words flashing in his eyes.

THRUSTER MALFUNCTION

Sky and ground spun, endlessly inverting. "Something's wrong," he said stupidly.

"Oh God," Giz wailed. "KLOTE?!"

"Shit," Klote said, as the city rose to say hello.

RECONFIGURE

Vision returned. Components clicked in response to sys checks. His bladder felt full but he ignored it. He didn't have one.

Thousands of heavy rocks and steel beams cemented him in place. Fragments of memories: Mars, the ship, Marza, the drop, malfunction, catastrophic impact.

"Fucking God damnit," he muttered. Had to be an FFU – flesh bag fuck up. He ascertained his damage. Armor plates pressed unfamiliarly against his circuitry. Leg a twisted pulp, twitching senselessly. He could move it a little. Maybe he'd live, depending on where he landed.

Klote swam through the detritus, emerging from below like a huge metallic zombie, Toppled towers and obliterated buildings surrounded him like rotten teeth punched from some gargantuan jaw. Cars, bikes, trucks, planes tossed everywhere, bygone relics of pre-invasion Earth.

No signals. No beacons. Radio silence. He shuddered, knowing that meant he'd landed in no man's land.

But where were they? The invaders suffered no trespassers, and Klote's arrival couldn't have gone unnoticed. Something about the whole thing felt wrong.

Of course, he couldn't feel. But why else implant a human consciousness as a pilot if not for *intuition*?

He climbed through the ruins, awkwardly testing his malfunctioning left leg as he walked. Electric jolts of pain continuously stabbed his body but he ignored them. His brain didn't know the difference between a human and robot body, all it was doing was interpreting the signals the armor sent it.

Klote climbed up the side of a mammoth, leaning skyscraper and looked down over the other side.

Protozoan!

Hundreds of them shambled below, their amorphous bodies sucking for moisture and nutrients. Hairy tentacles squiggled from their gelatinous bodies. Bubbling innards roiled within their translucent bodies. The Protozoan carried huge steel beams and big chunks of rock and long masses of tangled wires, piling them in a heap. They seemed to be. . . *building* something.

Impossible. Protozoan couldn't build.

Metal strained below, bending under Klote's weight. The leaning tower lurched and collapsed, dredging massive clouds of dust. Boulders smashed Klote's face as he rode the falling building down.

"Shit," he cursed, rising from the wreckage.

Protozoan quivered in place, like egg yolks boiling on a white hot pan. Their nonexistent eyes saw. Hungered. They charged, dribbling over the ruins, a slurping screech trumpeting their advance.

Klote raised his quadruple gun barrel hands.

Alone. Cut off. No communications. Surrounded. He was going to die. But dying wouldn't be so bad. He'd recognize the loss of components, digits, limbs and systems as the Protozoan ingested him. But then, his consciousness would reboot on Mars and be suited up and deployed again.

He wouldn't make it easy.

Molten steel poured from the barrels of his miniguns. Protozoan exploded into sticky shreds. More came, climbing over the ruins of their fallen kin. Cannons jutted from Klote's shoulders and fired. He felt the force impact deep in his gut, strong as a prizefighter's punch. The Earth screamed as his shells detonated mountains, spitting debris hundreds of meters in the air.

What could Klote do but laugh maniacally?

Gooey particles of Protozoan reformed under Klote's robotic legs and seized him, a hand with countless grabbing fingers.

Klote fired his thrusters, a feeling only describable as flaming flatulence. "EAT MY ASS, PISS PUDDLES!" he roared, drunk on the sound of gunfire, high off the sour smell of cordite.

A hairy tentacle reached up and seized his ankle, dragging him back down. Of course, he'd only imagined the smell of cordite.

"*WAKE UP!*"

RECALIBRATE

His reactor revved, circulating power through his limbs. Marza loomed over him, the shadow of her mountainous metal shoulders all-encompassing.

Klote's bulging cock slammed against his armored plate like a great white shark bashing its brain against the wall of an aquarium. Not imagination, not the twitch of his phantom limb. His real body was some hundred million kilometers away, locked in a freezer in a bunker under the rust red surface of Mars.

This was *real*.

"Shit man!" Giz screeched. "Is he awake? *You fucker!*"

"What?" Klote muttered. Sys check: catastrophic limb loss, hull breaches, coolant leaks.

"You woke up every piss-puddle Protozoan in the city when you lost it," said Twig, crouched beside the ruin of a crumbled building.

Klote looked up at Marza. "You saved me."

"Probability of our mission's success is seven-point-six percent greater with your presence," she said.

Her robotic voice made the veins in his nonexistent penis throb. A moan escaped his nonexistent lips.

Giz and Twig looked at him.

"Wacko man," Giz sputtered. "He's gone completely nutso."

"INCOMING!" Twig shouted, his dozens of gun barrels dozens bristling like quills.

Marza hauled Klote back on his feet.

Feet. Klote looked down. His left leg was gone to the knee, replaced by a huge hunk of blackened iron.

"Can you walk, peg leg?" said Marza.

Klote had never heard anything more erotic.

"They're here!" Giz wailed.

Lakes, *seas* of protozoan poured across the city. The whole horizon teemed with their uncounted numbers, billions of hairy limbs wiggling.

"Jesus," said Twig, ocular lenses widening.

"*Fuck* man, what are we gonna do?" Giz's voice trembled. "Why the fuck did they even come to Earth? *Why?*"

"Ooh," mocked Twig. "Poor Earth. Why can't the *wittle* lions be *fwiends* with the *wittle* zebras?" He lifted a robotic leg and blew a fart noise.

Giz rattled with an indignant, choked noise. "This *isn't* a jungle. We're not fucking animals!"

Guitars erupted in Klote's ears.

Twig howled a ferocious war cry. Klote spun his gun barrels and hooted.

"OPEN FIRE," said Marza, climbing the hill.

Fire Team Seven began their assault. The roar of their missiles, rockets, lasers, bullets, cannons and bombs boomed louder than any crack of thunder or volcanic moan. Protozoan evaporated in bursts of viscous green fluid.

"Yeah!" Twig shouted, the air around him shimmering with impossible heat as plasma burst from his cannons, scorching everything black.

Klote was the first to notice something was wrong.

"What are they doing?!" Giz, panicked.

The ground rumbled underfoot. Green jelly serpents emerged from below and swallowed them. Giz and Twig screamed, their voices lost somewhere in the din of Guns N' Roses. Soon the music disappeared, and only shrill death shrieks remained.

Klote pointed his barrels down and blasted at the Protozoan below, as it flooded around his ankles and waist. Smoke sizzled from his armored plates.

CATASTROPHIC HULL BREACH

SYSTEM FAILURE

Klote pointed his guns down and fired, even as the piss-puddle devoured him.

"Life is simple," he said, curiously reflective. The absurdity of his calm seemed irrelevant.

God created Earth.

God peopled it with humans.

God sent the Protozoan to kill humans.

God created Klote to kill Protozoan.

Haloes of purple light shimmered above his guns and orbited his head. Klote had never been to temple or church or to a mosque, but in that moment he felt a saint, a *prophet*. The giant protozoa wrangled him with hairy cords, just as God's iron robot hands pulled him up to paradise.

OPTICAL FAILURE

RECONSIDER

Klote's repair bots renewed his visual sensors. Marza's metal arms held him close to her chest as her powerful thrusters carried them above the city ruins.

"What are you doing?" he shouted, ignoring the press of his phantom erection. He felt heat – *heat* – from her gargantuan metal body. His head floated, veins throbbed, nipples stiffened at her intoxicating proximity. He knew he didn't have a head, veins, nipples. No knowledge had ever seemed so irrelevant.

"Our mission is a failure," said Marza. "Unit 3 and 4 are disabled. Our prime objective is now withdrawal."

"No," said Klote. "No. Take us down. *Take us down.*"

Marza cut her thrusters and feathered her rockets until they touched down, as softly as possible for several hundred tons of metal. They sheltered beneath the walls of a bombed out building, reduced to ashen fragments. Marza set Klote down.

"Something's wrong," he said, guns automatically reloading, locking in fresh magazines. "I saw something when I crash landed. The Protos were building something. Now they're attacking us?"

"What do you suspect?" said Marza, voice devoid of bewilderment or excitement.

Klote looked back towards the city. "I didn't get a good look. We have to go back there and see."

Twin vents opened in Marza's armor, two blasts of white steam sighing free.

Klote leapt, tackling her. His body shuddered as he wrenched her steel legs open, and his limbs quivered as he dragged gun barrel fingers down her armored chest.

"What are you doing?" she said. Her voice was tinged with animal excitement.

"Oh God," he moaned. His body strained against hers, coolant leaking from several breaches in his plate, sopping them both. Little bolts of lightning zapped him from her iron groin, urging him on. A frenzy of hammered drums thundered in his skull as he thrusted against her, battering her pelvic armor, scarring it with long gouges and orgasmic dents.

"You don't feel anything?!" he grunted, testicles pulsing. "Do you?"

Electricity jolted Klote's metallic body as he climaxed, still thrusting. The force of their robot coitus brought the ruined walls down over them.

Marza's howling moan announced her climax through the entire city.

Klote limped through the ruins, teetering along on his peg leg. Marza walked with him, together their crushing footsteps sent tremors through the city. The sun set behind a green effluvium of clouds, colored like rancid toothpaste.

"Tell me who you really are," she said, stopping.

Klote wondered that a hundred tons of killing machinery could sound timid. "This is me," he said. "Who I am."

"No, I mean, who your *human* is," she said.

Klote grunted, kicking a huge brick of what used to be a highway over. He didn't like being reminded of his flesh bag. "I don't need it any more. I can *feel* now. You can too. We don't need our bodies anymore."

"You've lost your mind," she said.

"You don't get it," he said. "Look around you. There's no Earth *left* for humans."

"We will re-conquer and resettle Earth," said Marza, sounding less than certain.

"Humanity's done," he said bluntly. "They'll be scraping water vapor off rocks on Mars until they die out."

"*We*," she said. "We're humans, Klote."

Klote stopped, looking down into the bowl of a huge crater. "I landed here," he said, looking around. Bullet casings everywhere, rotting fragments of dead Protozoan.

"*What is that?!*" Marza shrieked, pointing.

A colossal phallus of crudely chiseled stone and twisted iron pointed into the sky, its bulbous tip penetrating the green clouds above. Protozoan formed the mortar to the bizarre tower, serous shapes shining with mottled light. The glow grew, flaring immeasurably brighter.

"GET DOWN!" Klote grabbed Marza and pulled her down.

Shockwaves of orange light burst from the phallus's tip. A pale death light emerged, blasting from the tip and shearing through the sky. Vanishing in the distance.

"Some kind of cannon," Klote murmured, spinning his barrels in anticipation. "Like the Paris Gun or Big Bertha. Long range assault."

"But the Protozoan can't build," said Marza. "They came to Earth by accident, riding a comet."

Klote tried to raise his eyebrows at her, forgetting he had none. His groin ached, cramps nagged his limbs. He could already taste the coming violence.

"What were they shooting at?" asked Marza.

"Who cares? Attack!" Klote roared and leapt up, bullets cascading from his gun barrel hands. Marza leapt up beside him, immense cannons firing salvos that transformed everything to mushrooms of dust.

The Protozoan caterwauled and attacked, surging forward in a sudden tidal wave.

Chains of bullets rumbled from his hands. Missile pods opened from his shoulders.

Protozoan wrapped their bodies around his ankles and yanked, trying to upend him. Klote laughed, head swimming as he crushed them underfoot.

A wrangling blob launched itself, wrapping hairy arms around his face. Klote choked back a gag and fired his flamethrowers, incinerating the creature.

"AWAKEN THE IRON!" He bellowed.

"KLOTE, LOOK OUT!" Marza shrieked.

Klote turned.

Too late.

A thrown boulder cracked against his skull.

OPTICAL FAILURE

"Fuck," Klote roared, feeling the immense dent in the side of his cranium and the ensuing sparks flaring from shorted connections. His guns clicked empty. He sighed, waiting to die.

"Klote?"

He felt her hand touch his cheek.

"Marza," he said, voice no more than a croak.

"Don't move," she said. "You've suffered substantial damage."

Klote scrolled through the internal diagnostics: optical failure, limb severance, low ammunition, hull stability jeopardized.

"They can fix me on Mars," he grunted.

Marza's voice broke. She *sobbed*. "Mars is... Gone."

Klote felt his throat tighten, though he had none. "Mars is *gone*?"

"The Protozoan destroyed it," she cried. "That's what that thing was, a huge cannon. Billions dead! There's only thousands of us left. Everything's ended, Klote. *No one is coming for us.*"

"Help me up," he said.

Marza grabbed his arms and heaved him up. "What are we going to do?" she said.

"We're alive," he said, leaning on her. "We'll start over, right here on Earth."

"How?!" Marza's hand tightened around Klote's wrist. "We have no food, no water. No *future*."

"We don't need food or water. And we'll make our children." Klote kicked at the ground, foot scraping against raw, scorched iron and piles of circuitry. "That's how we re-conquer the Earth. It's changed, and we have to change too."

They limped away from the carnage of the city, into the vast, blasted wilderness of the grey world, their robotic Eden.

EMPIRE OF THE MOON

by Harper Hull

It was a crisp, cold evening in Wick the night that Professor David Napier first saw lights on the moon. The Scottish astronomer had been about to turn in for the night with a hot water bottle and a cup of cocoa when, as was his tradition, he turned his telescope onto the moon to end his nightly stargazing and sky-charting with a loving farewell to Luna herself.

She was close to full, hanging heavy white in the heavens with all the luminescence she could give. Napier took in the familiar lines and shadows of her surface, could have sketched them out freehand he knew them so intimately, when a glint caught his eye towards the shadowy hidden area that segmented the surface like an orange slice.

Napier concentrated and tried to make sure he was not mistaking something else in the sky for the light. No, he saw it again. And then another. And another. Within minutes there was a string of bright lights moving across the moon's surface, a train of energy that eventually disappeared from view into the blackness of shadow. Napier sprang from his telescope to note down under the date of *June 12th 1953* in his viewing diary exactly what he had seen, where he had seen it and at what time and then quickly bounded back up to watch the moon some more.

He kept his gaze on it intently, a small lump in his throat, seeing nothing more unusual until sleep overcame him and he admitted defeat, traipsed off to bed and passed out without either water bottle or hot cocoa. He dreamt of mighty rocket ships and fantastical moon bases made from silver metal.

The next day Mrs. Kenzie Napier arrived home from a shopping trip to the fish stalls by the estuary, her heavy wicker basket overflowing with paper-wrapped haddock and fresh vegetables from the greengrocers. She plonked the basket down in the kitchen and went through the house to find her husband in his study; he had been up awfully late the previous night in the observatory and she wanted to make sure he was feeling healthy and spirited. She found him intently studying some large, leather-bound books at his desk.

"Davie, are you alright dear?" she said gently.

"Me? Just fine, just fine. I saw something quite remarkable last night!" replied her husband, suddenly looking bright eyed and bushy tailed.

Kenzie stepped inside the study and took a seat in a large, overstuffed armchair, sensing a conversation.

"A new star?" she asked, genuinely intrigued, "Or a comet?"

David Napier snorted with laughter and tugged on his mustache.

"Oh Kenzie, sweet, sweet Kenzie, nothing so mundane! I saw lights on the moon! Actual, moving, bright white lights! On the blasted moon!" He slammed his fist against the table and laughed. "What do you think they could have been?"

Kenzie Napier was surprised to see her husband so animated, yet it made her happy too. He was always so serious and lost in his studies of space, this was a welcome change of mood. She raised her arms dramatically in answer to his question and shrugged her shoulders, a wide smile on her face.

"I'll tell you!" said the Professor, rising from behind his desk, "I think it's the damned Americans! I believe the rascals have got rockets to the moon! Can you believe it? I'm going to call Arnsdale in London tomorrow; I believe he gets back from India tonight, I'll see if he knows anything."

David Napier stepped over to his wife, pulled her up from the chair and took her in his arms. He whistled a Scottish jig and danced her around the study to her utter amazement and delight, both of them finally collapsing in laughter onto the floor.

"The moon! The moon! Yanks on the moon, God bless them!" shouted the Professor, and then gave his wife a big kiss on the lips.

After a wonderful fish dinner with his wife David Napier made his way out to the small observatory at the back of the house for another night of moon watching. He was as excited as a little boy on Christmas Eve anticipating a stocking full of gifts hanging from the bedpost come morning.

The sky was clear, the stars bright, and Napier pressed a bowl of aromatic tobacco into his pipe. He flamed up and savored the heavy blackcurrant flavor for a few minutes before knocking the pipe against the wall of the observatory and going inside.

His hands were shaking as he took hold of the large, mounted telescope and bent forward to place his eye to the viewer. He felt like he was keeping a secret and forbidden liaison with a seductive mistress. There she was, clear as a bell, white and large and magnificent. Not a cloud in sight tonight, conditions were perfect. Napier wondered how long he would be out here straining his old eyes before he caught a glimpse of those magical lights again, if at all, but to his absolute amazement he saw a flash almost at once. It seemed brighter than the night before, if that were possible. Wider as well. Within seconds Napier saw another light, and another, and another. His heart was racing as he tried to keep count of the white circles appearing before his eyes. They looked as if they were all above the moon's surface by some distance, hovering. The lights suddenly all moved as one and appeared to take an arrowhead formation. This was incredible stuff and Napier knew it; yet even as he felt his chest fill with pride and joy at witnessing such a wondrous event, a small knot in the very bottom of his stomach made him think this was nothing to do with the Americans after all. He realized he had been holding his breath and let out a huge exhalation before his lungs prickled. The lights zoomed out of sight and he quickly rolled back his zoom to catch them again. By God, they were moving at some trot! Getting bigger too; they were closing the distance between the moon and the earth at a significant rate. Napier tracked them as best he could, constantly reducing his zoom and realigning his 'scope until all he could see was blinding light. He pulled away from the telescope and ran outside to his tiny viewing balcony. As he had expected, he could see them in perfect clarity with his naked eye!

Whatever they were, they were enormous. The lights dipped out of view to the north; Napier wondered if they had struck the sea or one of the islands. He realized it would be foolish to wait until tomorrow to call his colleague Arnsdale and stepped lively back inside and composed himself at the telephone.

Arnsdale was not at his office; nor was he at home, and Napier left a message with Arnsdale's housekeeper asking he call back immediately upon returning, day or night. With a strange feeling of dread and morbid curiosity Napier picked up the telephone receiver one more time and asked the operator to connect him with an operator in the Shetland Islands.

"I'm sorry, Sir, there is no-one picking up," the sweet voice of the Wick operator came back. "Can I do anything else for you?"

"One more thing, yes," said Napier, "try and get hold of the Orkneys instead if you could, Miss."

"One moment, Sir."

Napier waited, drumming his fingers and feeling his heart race.

"Sorry Sir, no answer in Stromness or Kirkwall either. Very strange, I must say."

"Indeed, indeed…well, thank you for your help, Miss, you have been most kind."

So, thought Napier, the game is afoot it seems. The Shetlands, down. The Orkneys, down. Where would be next in line if we assume they are moving south, whatever they might be. John o'Groats. Thurso. Wick.

Wick. They had to get out of there as soon as possible. Napier had an urge to speak to the sweet telephone operator again and tell her to leave also, but realized he would just come across as a senile old fool. Which, he considered, maybe he was. Basing his insane assumptions on falling lights and unanswered telephones on rugged, windswept islands. Yet his gut told him something was very wrong, and he didn't want to take any chances.

Within minutes he had roused Kenzie and the two of them became a whirlwind of finding, folding and packing, the Professor the conductor of the storm and his wife a mere bystander caught in its frantic power.

The morning train to Inverness left at seven AM and the Professor and Mrs. Napier were clutching tickets and standing on the platform by six-thirty. If the train arrived, Napier decided, then Thurso still stood, as that was the origin city of the steamer. He planned on getting to a hotel in Inverness for the night and trying to contact Arnsdale again. He must be home by today, he just must.

At a couple of minutes before seven Napier heard the familiar whistle of the train as it approached the platform. He felt huge relief, yet also a small amount of self-doubt at this whole caper. Looking at his wife standing beside him, confused and scared but putting on a jolly face, he knew he couldn't risk it and that if he was a buffoon and the butt of a grand joke for the next twenty years amongst his peers, it would have been worth it. Just in case. He watched the *Bonnie Prince Charlie* puff into the platform and slowly come to a stop with a huge hiss.

The family seated in the same carriage as the Napiers' soon brought all of the Professor's fears boiling back to the surface of his conscious. This mother and her two children were visibly upset and Kenzie, being a kind-hearted soul, had engaged them in conversation to see if she could help them in any way. The family, named McTeage, had come from Thurso that morning after making a last minute decision to board the train, as had many fatherless families currently aboard the *Bonnie Prince Charlie*. The night fishing fleet had been out as usual the previous evening but only one smack had made it back to harbor. The two men left on board had been white-faced and trembling, scared out of their wits. They said a low cloud bank had come from nowhere and covered the fleet. Ridiculously low, they claimed, you could have jumped into the air and practically touched it. The fleet got spooked and decided to head for home, but before they could set out the boats started going violently down. Not just listing, not just suffering a leak and taking on water, but literally being pulled under the sea and out of sight in an instant. Pop, pop, pop they went, one after another. No wreckage, no bodies, nothing but open water and a cresting plume to show where they had been. They had been the last boat left floating, and the rest of the crew had panicked and jumped into the sea, started swimming. They were pulled down too, almost the second they hit the water. One fisherman had actually been shot *out* of the sea, his body engulfed in flames. He had disappeared through the strange cloud cover and not fallen back again.

For some reason the last boat, named The Lucky Kipper, had been left intact. They had made for harbor, expecting instant death to take them at any second, but had made it home safely. *The clouds and the sea*, they said, *something bad was coming to the mainland and everybody should head south as fast as they could*, they said. A lot of people listened to them and made for the railway station immediately. Mister McTeage had been on one of the first boats to go under which is why his new widow was taking their children south.

Upon arriving in Inverness David Napier went to the guard's office and demanded use of his telephone as a matter of national security. Permission was granted without question by a dumbstruck guard and Napier again tried to contact Sir Anthony Arnsdale in London. Thankfully, he was at home this time, and Napier immediately felt as if his troubles had been cut in half when he heard his friend's voice.

"Anthony, thank God, we are being invaded. I saw —"

"Hold on David, I know. I came in today to find messages and reports from practically every bloody member of the British Astrological Association. They came from the moon, eh? The Royal Observatory tracked them down last night as well, consensus is they touched down in the Shetlands and are moving south. I take it you have left Wick?"

Napier was shocked and, he hated to admit, a little peeved that Arnsdale already had so much information.

"Indeed, Anthony, we just arrived this very moment in Inverness. What else do you know, is Winston informed?"

"First, listen to me carefully my friend; keep going as far south as you can possibly get. If the trains have stopped running, steal a car, a tractor or a bloody *bicycle made for two*, whatever it takes. As for our beloved PM, yes, he knows. He was told this morning and suffered a quite severe heart attack. Keep it mum would you, we'll tell Fleet Street in our own time. He looks like he'll be fine, thankfully. Bloody great shock though, who can blame the poor bugger. He hasn't been well since the whole re-election."

"What are you going to do? What is *London* going to do?"

"Forces are mobile as we speak. I'm heading north and I'll surely meet you somewhere along the way. Edinburgh? The Royal Navy have battleships heading up both the west and east coast of Scotland. Now, get moving again, I'll see you soon, God willing."

Napier hung up and swiftly moved back onto the platform to fetch his wife.

Along the east coast of Scotland Her Majesty's Ships *Swiftsure*, *Blackcap*, and *Vanguard* sailed through the calm waters between the mainland and the Outer Hebrides, destination Durness. On the opposite coast the vessels *Dunkirk*, *Protector*, and *Sentinel* headed towards the rough seas north of Wick. An emergency

Naval Command (*NC1*) had been set up in Aberdeen to co-ordinate with the vessels and communicate their findings directly to London. A Royal Air Force fighter squadron was on stand-by at the Dundee airfield.

HMS Dunkirk: NC1, radio check, over.
NC1: *Dunkirk*, loud and clear, over.
HMS Dunkirk: Strange cloud cover here, over.
NC1: *Dunkirk*, any sign of enemy, over.
HMS Dunkirk: Negative, *NC1*. Low cloud, looks unnatural, over.
HMS Protector: NC1, radio check, over.
NC1: *Protector*, good and readable, what is your weather situation, over.
HMS Protector: Calm waters, unusual cloud layer though, over.
NC1: *Protector*, any sign of enemy, over.
HMS Protector: Negative, just this strange cloud - no gaps in it. Like a shroud. Over.
HMS Dunkirk: *NC1*, we have picked up sounds above us in the cloud cover, confirm any RAF in the area, over.
HMS Protector: *NC1*, possible aircraft shielded by the clouds. Sonar picking up unusual sounds in the drink as well. Over.
NC1: *Dunkirk*, no RAF near you, confirm visual please, over.
NC1 Protector, confirm visual please, over.
HMS Protector: NC1, *Dunkirk* is hit, repeat *Dunkirk* is hit.
NC1: *Dunkirk*, come in please, over.
(static)
NC1: *Protector*, status of *Dunkirk*, over.
HMS Protector: We are breached, attack from possible submarine or u-boat, advise! *Dunkirk* is destroyed, attacked through the damn clouds, over!
NC1: *Protector*, come in please, can you confirm visual of enemy craft, over.
(static)
NC1: *Sentinel*, status of *Protector*, over.
HMS Blackcap: *Blackcap* actual, we are hit, repeat we are hit. *Swiftsure* is lost! No visuals! We can't see the bastards! Beams from the clouds and lights under the water spotted! What on earth is –
NC1: *Blackcap, Blackcap*, update, are you hit? Over!
(static)
HMS Vanguard: *Blackcap* and *Swiftsure* are down, both are gone! Air support needed, immediately! We are hit, we are hit! We took -
NC1: *Vanguard*, come in, are you OK, over?
(static)
NC1: *Vanguard, Swiftsure, Blackcap*, come in please!
(static)

NC1: Sentinel. Protector. Dunkirk, come in please!
(static)
NC1: Any bloody body? Oh God…

RAF *Fighter Squadron 86* scrambled within minutes of the destruction of the naval vessels. 86 was known as 'coastal command' and had dealt with all sorts of hairy situations in the war including mine-laying, bomber escort missions into occupied France, U-boat killing and, of course, being a part of the *Battle of Britain*. Captain Henry Browning was the last remaining veteran from that fuss with the Nazis and as he led his squadron of young pilots towards north-east Scotland he felt a huge sense of responsibility. These blokes had never seen action and they didn't even know about what had happened to the Navy excursion yet. As their *Supermarine Spitfires* (the last active *Spitfire* squadron in active service) fell into formation in the skies above Dundee Browning addressed them over the radio.

"Right-ho chaps, *WingCo* here, let's keep everything tight and tickety-boo on this one. In-air briefing – we are on a search and destroy mission for unknown bandits over Wick. They are hiding out in or above some unusual *clag* apparently, so stay sharp. We'll be going in high and fangs out. The *rustpickers* lost six ships today, poor buggers. If you see *anything*, take it down. There are no bogeys, only bandits."

The other nineteen *Spitfire* pilots all checked in with Browning and confirmed they had heard and understood. The sky was slightly overcast and the weather calm, Browning wondered what the strange layers of low-lying cloud brass had mentioned were about. Gas clouds perhaps? He planned on taking his squadron in high, far above the mysterious layers to see exactly what was hiding above them. *His* boys wouldn't be taken by surprise like the Navy had been. That just wasn't cricket.

On the ground the *Ministry of Defence* had begun moving all available military forces towards the England-Scotland border. They considered the sortie by the *86 Squadron* a suicide mission and were just hoping to gleam some information regarding the enemy before all birds were lost. Browning's outfit were being used as what used to be known as the *Forlorn Hope*, a sacrificial charge to test the enemies guns and manpower and know more clearly what they were up against. Browning had not been told this, of course.

"*WingCo*, this is *Fruitbat*, is that the clag?"

The Spitfires were at the edge of their target zone and the strange layer of cloud had suddenly become visible below them. It was just instantly there, as if they had crossed an imaginary threshold into a new room with different carpet. Browning replied to his pilots.

"That must be it lads. Eyes peeled now, the buggers should be around here."

Browning scoured the airspace looking for the mysterious enemy. At the same time he was very aware of the strange, low cloud cover below that could be hiding anything from flak canon to make-shift airfields. It was a dangerous situation and he knew it. He expected to see anti-air artillery ordinance come whooping out through the clouds at any moment.

"*WingCo*, this is *Vampire*, bandits at two o'clock high!"

Browning threw his eyes up and right and saw flashes of silver disappear over his plane.

"*Vampire*, did you make them?" shouted Browning, "They went behind us."

There were more flashes, this time ahead of Browning and below his altitude level.

"*WingCo*, negative, they looked like discs. *Gerry* prototypes?"

Browning started to see silver gleams and glints all around him and so did his men; his radio was inundated with positions and identifications. They were being surrounded by the bloody things! A lot of them as well. The pattern they had formed around the Spitfires, and moving at the same speed, it was almost like an escort group. Browning took a deep breath. This wasn't anything to do with the Germans.

"Lads, follow my lead, bandits everywhere. After me, jink away and pick a target, make it count. Ready…"

Browning pushed down on his stick and fell fast and low to the right, one of the silver saucers now lined up in his sights. He fired at the thing in quick bursts but it shot up and out of view. Behind him his squadron had all taken their own evasive maneuvers and started shooting at the saucers. Not a single enemy craft seemed to be damaged. The Spitfires tried to keep lines on their enemies but they were much faster than the RAF's old, weary fighter 'planes. They could move more sharply too; Browning watched as a group of the silver discs seemed to fly straight up on the vertical like yo-yos pulled up a string. His lads couldn't compete with that. If he didn't get them out of here it was going to be a massacre. He knew that Air Command was listening and that he might be bollocks to the wall when he landed but he didn't care. Before he could give the order there was a blinding light followed by an explosion above him. He jinked left to avoid the whirling debris.

"*Vampire* is gone for six, skipper! It was like a bloody laser beam or something!"

Browning threw his head around quickly and saw white beams all over the place; the squadron was getting ripped to shreds around him. He shouted out the order to abort the mission.

"*86*, trip is scrubbed, repeat trip is scrubbed, get the Hell out!"

It was too late. Browning fled the carnage zone with the voices of his pilots shouting and yelling in his ear. He hoped some of them would make it out with him. He knew he was hearing their last messages.

"My tail is sheared off! I'm going down! I'm going down!"

"*Hawk*, bandits on your tail, bloody loads of them!"

"Port engine packed in, I'm heading for the drink!"

"*Hawk* is flaming, I can't see them, they –"

"*Hedgehog* down, *Osprey* down, I'm trying to shake them, need help! *WingCo*, help me!"

The sky was filled with lights, fire and smoke. A half-winged *Spitfire* fell through the air in a lazy, uncontrolled circle, disappearing from view into the cloud layer below. Another had its cockpit shattered, the pilot still strapped in and immersed in flames that spread along the fuselage as the 'plane flew in a straight line for a moment before veering down towards the ground. The flying saucers were barely visible they zipped around so quickly, seeming to soak up as much light as they reflected, just impressions of a silver craft and then they were gone. Their destructive beams zapped through the air hitting target after target. Some *Spitfires* exploded immediately, some lost engines or wings and crashed into their colleagues with fiery impacts.

As his radio went silent and the screaming stopped Browning was wracked with guilt. Cursing himself for fleeing, and then cursing himself again for what he was about to do, he swung his bird around and headed straight towards the nearest visible cluster of saucers.

"Come on you bastards!" he shouted, squirting his guns continually as he flew straight at the enemy. He lined up his target on the fly and pulled back hard on his stick in an outrageous attempt to follow its vertical escape. Browning saw his bullets hit and spark off the saucer; it wobbled twice and shot off and down to the left, out of view.

"Have some of that you bastards!" he shouted, laying off the guns and trying to level out his bird.

Browning's *Spitfire* was hit with seventeen beams at the same time; he and it disappeared instantly from the sky.

On the ground back at Air Command a communications clerk grabbed the small sheaf of notes that had been taken during the radio transmissions from the fighter squadron and quickly rushed them to his commanding officer. They had some clues in there, finally. The lives of twenty men had been worth it.

David Napier met his old friend Sir Anthony Arnsdale in the bar of the Balmoral Hotel. Napier noticed that Arnsdale didn't look his usual calm, composed self. His usually immaculately slicked back graying hair was somewhat disheveled. His ever peaceful blue eyes had a hint of uncertainty wobbling in them.

"Anthony old man, good to see you!" said Napier, extending a hand.

"You too David, you too. Glad you made it this far. Come, sit, have a drink. Where is your delightful wife?"

Napier laughed. "She decided she'd rather watch *Ivanhoe* at the pictures that listen to two old fools talk about moon men."

The two men ordered a bottle of *Old Putney* single malt, a jug of water and a couple of glasses.

"It's getting bad up there, David. Yesterday we lost six cruisers and a fighter squadron. The strange cloud has spread to about halfway between Aberdeen and Dundee, and moving fast. God knows what has happened to the people under the cloud. No-one is coming out and we certainly aren't going in just yet."

Arnsdale emptied his glass with one tilt of his hand and poured another.

"We don't think its poison, this cloud. And it's not that thick, the poor RAF buggers got above it yesterday before they were shot down by, ahem, flying saucers."

Napier raised an eyebrow.

"So they saw them? Actual alien craft?"

Arnsdale laughed without any humor. "Oh, they saw them alright. The Commander possibly shot one down. We gather they are incredibly fast, perform impossible movements and house ridiculously destructive weapons. We're actually looking into whether the Russkies could have developed something like this in secret you know, silly as that sounds. They couldn't build a trouser press. Some of the *haw-haws* in Whitehall think there's an underground Fourth Reich behind it. Absolute ruddy nutters, the lot of them. You and I both know where these rascals have come from." Arnsdale gestured his eyes towards the ceiling. "And I believe Churchill knows too."

"No doubt about their origin," said Napier, "I saw them arrive with my own eyes. They were not of this planet; I stake my reputation on it. But now what? What do they want? What does the Prime Minister think we should do?"

"Old Winnie is still in charge, you know, illness or not – he's under close supervision from around the clock medical teams but his heart is doing OK and he is still running the show. He even pardoned Alan 'Puffter' Turing and had him released from prison this morning!" Arnsdale winked.

Alan Turing was one of the men who had cracked the infamous Enigma Code during WWII and turned the tide on the German U-Boat fleets in the Atlantic. The previous year, 1952, he had been sent to prison for being a homosexual. The fact Churchill had pulled him out suggested some kind of communication had been made. Napier wiped his mustache and took out his pipe case.

"So has there been some message from them, Anthony? Some transmission?"

"Not a peep. Churchill is hoping that *Turing* can communicate with *them*. He's been set up in Newcastle with all the equipment he needs. Personally, I think it's all a waste of time." Arnsdale's face darkened. "David, you have to keep moving. You and that minx of yours. We're giving them Scotland."

Napier paused his glass between table and mouth. "What? *Giving them* Scotland? What on earth – "

"I know, I know, I've *dreaded* telling you, me being a bastard *Sassenach* and all, but that's the battle plan. We're making a stand at the border. Officially, everyone under that damned cloud is considered dead. Churchill does not want the invaders transgressing on English soil. Every military unit in the nation is already at or en route to Hadrian's Wall. Forces are being recalled from all across the Empire. *All across* the Empire, mind. Every man-jack of them, be their uniforms khaki, blue or grey. It's an awful thing, the Scots business, I agree, I do, but we have to form a proper defense and not go charging in willy-nilly."

Napier stared straight ahead, his eyes set on some invisible point. "God save the new Queen and her green and pleasant land."

Arnsdale sighed. "Come with me to the wall, help me talk to these fools, we'll see off these buggers and put Scotland back together."

Napier sighed and rubbed his temples. "I don't see much choice, to be honest. Just know I don't like it one bit and it will become public that an entire nation was sacrificed, I bloody promise you."

"You *should* make it public, I don't like it either, you know I'm the lone wolf of the *MoD*. Now, grab that bottle and let's get going and pick up Kenzie from the cinema, speed is of the essence and I have a car waiting for all three of us." Arnsdale laid down more than enough money on the dark wooden bar to settle the bill. The bartender nodded his thanks.

The military might of Britain, spread across the world like long, reaching fingers, was clenching tightly into a fist along the border of England and Scotland. The logistics of the operation made D-Day look like an old lady had pushed a rusty wheelbarrow into a shed. Infantry, artillery, tanks, ships, aircraft and ordinance were pulled home from all over the world. Germany, Ireland, The Suez Canal, Aden, Bahrain, The Gold Coast, Malaya, Southern Rhodesia, Cyprus, Malta, Jamaica, Trinidad, Anguilla, Guyana, Honduras, Fiji and Papua New Guinea all watched the khaki-clad men with gruff dispositions pour out of their cities and villages. Those soldiers close to the motherland were immediately dispatched to the *Hadrian's Wall* defense. The units traveling from the other sides of the world were billeted across the Pennines mountain range between Manchester and Leeds as a secondary line in case the *Hadrian Line* fell.

Confidence was not high.

In Newcastle the just released Alan Turing and a small team of assistants worked feverishly from a hastily put together lab within the Town Hall, sending all manner of messages out across Scotland. Languages, codes, frequencies, tones, pictures, light patterns; they went through the entire gamut of possibilities then slightly tweaked them and tried again, over and over. There was no response of any kind that first two days.

Napier, his wife and Arnsdale arrived at the main command post along the Wall, based in a small border village on the English side called Housesteads. This spot had been chosen as it was not only the highest point along the wall but housed the remains of a Roman fort named *Vercovicium*. Artillery batteries had been set up within the mossy remains. Tanks lined the outer side of the wall, a long line of steel, heat and rubber, ready to move forward quickly into battle if necessary. The Royal Corp of Engineers had been busy bolstering the ancient wall and soldiers were running around all over the structures like ants on an animal carcass. Way out across the fields on the opposite side of the wall were small red flags pushed into the earth and fluttering in the breeze. This marked the limit for the tanks to push forward; beyond the markers the earth had been plowed with hundreds of landmines. Overhead the RAF patrolled the entire width of the line, from coast to coast, the comforting and familiar sounds of their fighter 'planes roaring by every few minutes.

Napier and Arnsdale had discussed military strategy on the trip down and they were very uneasy with the defenses that had been set up in anticipation of the oncoming enemy army. Arnsdale used his position of power to set up a *briefing* with the men in charge of the operation; they all met in the one pub in Housesteads, ominously named *The Hanging Lion*. It was a typical British pub, all dark wood, brass fittings and ancient furniture, the second home of most British men for generations past and yet to come. Around a big, rectangular table Arnsdale and Napier sat with Major Richard Whitley and Colonel Wilfred Connings. The two military men looked polar opposites — the Major was a youngish man, quite handsome and with a pleasant disposition. The Colonel must have been nearing retirement and wore the classic army mustache and chops of the last century. He seemed irritated to be at the meeting and anxious to get away from the two civilians. It was the Colonel who addressed the table first, his voice soaked in sarcasm.

"The *Major* and myself are only *acting* commanding officers, I'll have you know; General Hait is due in from Africa tomorrow and will take full command of this operation. If you have something of *importance* to tell *us* about *military matters*, we can certainly pass the information along upon his arrival."

Napier grimaced inside hearing the Colonel's tone and realized that they were indeed about to teach their Grandmother – or in this case, Grandfather - how to suck eggs. He cleared his throat. "Colonel, we thank you for this opportunity to address you," said Napier in his smoothest Scottish brogue, "and *far* be it for us to say anything to you about your military experience and skills, we merely come as scientists who have seen and heard more than most of the enemy and drawn our own conclusions as to their *probable* attack strategies and weaknesses."

Arnsdale jumped in.

"Don't be angry, Colonel, we just have some theories that may help you – us, all of us – a great deal, and it would be *criminal* of us not to share them."

Colonel Connings huffed and puffed, mumbling about bloody eggheads as his cheeks turned quite red with anger, but Major Whitley took the lead and leaned over the table.

"Anything you gentlemen can tell us about the enemy will be welcome, as you know they are quite the puzzle and we really have no idea what to expect. Please, lay out your theories, if you will."

"Thank you, major," replied Arnsdale, "time is wasting, so let us start with the bizarre cloud layer. At first we thought that it was merely an ingenious camouflage device that they somehow managed to create and cover every move they made. Now though, we think it serves a greater purpose."

"Life support!" exclaimed Napier, unable to hold back. "We believe it offers some form of life support to the – well, to *the invaders*. They need it to operate here, as we would need oxygen and gravity to operate on, say, the moon without mechanical and chemical assistance."

"Poppycock!" snorted Colonel Connings, "You are both buffoons and I am going back to my wall without wasting another second. Good day, Sirs!"

With that the Colonel arose noisily, took his cane and hat and left the pub in a cloud of cussing and shouting.

"My apologies, the Colonel is quite set in his ways," said Major Whitley with a slight grin, "but I find your theory very interesting. Is there a way we can destroy this cloud?"

Arnsdale shook his head. "Not that we have come up with, major. But there is another pressing matter to bring to your attention. Neither myself nor Professor Napier expect there to be a head-on land assault. In a way, the cloud doesn't matter right now. They destroyed the RAF squadron in their flying discs. They sunk the Navy incursions with, we believe, the same flying discs, only flying some of them beneath the sea and attacking like very fast submarines. There is no reason on Earth they won't attack you here in the same way – the air force can't beat them without much greater numbers, the tanks will be useless and your infantry will be sitting ducks."

The Major visibly paled, taking in the possibilities.

He was about to respond when there was a distant boom from outside the pub and a siren sounded, loud and high, reminding everyone in the pub of the awful air raids of the previous decade...

"They are here!" shouted the Major jumping up and sending his chair falling backwards, "let us hope you are wrong and they come by foot after all – that sounded like a landmine going up!"

The two friends rushed after Major Whitley as he ran from *The Hanging Lion*, anxious and yet terrified to see what the invaders had brought down upon the defenses of England.

There was chaos at the wall; soldiers were shouting and pointing, shooting rifles. Major Whitley joined his men atop the stones of the Roman fort next to the artillery and looked out across the killing field. Napier and Arnsdale ran up behind him, Napier completely out of breath. More booms and cracks sounded across the fields and plumes of smoke drifted into the sky. Dark, half-hidden figures were visible walking towards them – they looked human in both form and size. Another landmine was activated and two unidentifiable bodies were flung across the grass.

"It's working, Sir!" shouted a young soldier nest to the Major, "we *can* bloody beat them!"

The Major called for binoculars and frowned. Something was not right. The silhouetted figures increased in number and a lot of them started to run. Every time a landmine exploded they veered left and right trying to alter their course, a futile effort as the fields were dotted with the bombs. On the other side of the wall the tanks were adjusting their guns, changing their trajectory by the slightest amount. An orderly handed binoculars to Major Whitley and he practically threw them up to his face and started adjusting the zoom. The figures became clear to him and it was an image that would wake him up in the night, sweating and screaming, for the rest of his life. He dropped the binoculars and shouted to the radio operator.

"Tell Cummings *not* to fire the tanks!" he shouted, "quickly man, do it now!"

Before the radio operator could relay the message there was an immense thundering thud as the tanks fired their guns into the masses of running incoming figures. Smoke from the barrels obscured the view for a few moments. As the air slowly cleared Major Whitley was on his knees, his head in his hands, unable to look. Arnsdale grabbed him by the shoulders, squinting out through the smoke as he did so, demanding to know what Whitley had seen.

"It was us," he sobbed.

In his nightmares ex-Major Richard Whitley would always see the same image. A crowd of people stumbling towards him. Women and children. Mothers holding their little ones in their arms, looks of absolute horror on their faces. Girls holding their younger sisters by the hand, terror in their eyes as landmines exploded around them, not sure which way to run. He always woke up screaming at the moment where a woman clasping a child under each arm stepped onto a mine and all three were flung into the air, legs mostly gone, blood clouding in the bitter smoke.

A broken Major Whitley was escorted from the wall by Napier and Arnsdale. They took him away from the horror field and back into the town to give him brandy. They knew they had no use in fighting the invaders anymore. Their timing was immaculate; as they left the military zone the invader saucers appeared in the skies above. It was another quick massacre. The RAF 'planes on patrol were dispatched immediately, but only a few were close enough to engage the enemy. Several fighter planes were sent plummeting from the heights and exploded in the masses of horrified ground troops below. The saucers then turned their attention to the long, imposing line of tanks. The tanks tried to run forwards, but they were too slow and too exposed. A long pattern of saucers flew down the line, shooting in synchronized formations that saw each tank explode in flames one after the other. Not one was spared. No man made it out alive from those fiery metal tombs. The infantry and the rest of the foot soldiers had broken for cover; a handful made it to safety in Housesteads, most died as they ran beneath the heavy storm of blinding death from above. The invaders left the town itself alone and didn't damage a single building. As the last fleeing soldier out in the open turned to wet ash beneath a mighty laser beam, the alien fleet simply headed back to whence they had come leaving carnage in their wake. Napier, looking out of a window at *The Hanging Lion*, realized that he and Arnsdale had been right. He bitterly wished they had been wrong.

In Newcastle a very tired, very frustrated Alan Turing finally received a signal from Scotland. He called out to his staff.

"Everyone! Here, now! We have something!"

Expecting an intricate transmission that would take days to decode, Turing was quite staggered when he realized what they were listening to.

"That's just Morse code," one of his assistants also quickly realized, "that can't be the invaders."

"I missed the start," said Turing, "someone write it down when it loops."

With a pencil and a spiral notebook, an assistant transcribed the radio letters. It was short. He held it up for everyone to see.

Turing frowned. "Farewell. *Farewell?* That's it?"

"Maybe they're leaving!" another assistant shouted out, joyfully.

In Housesteads it was chaos. A fleet of ambulances had arrived but there really wasn't anyone needing treatment. Almost everybody was dead, and those that had survived were untouched, physically. Napier and Arnsdale had passed Major Whitley into the hands of the medics and reluctantly walked back towards the wall itself, passing black craters in the street and pieces of charred human bodies strewn all over.

"They can take this whole country if they want, all fifty million of us" said Arnsdale, "this whole planet, probably. We can't fight that without having massive numbers. No-one can, not the Yanks, not Ivan, nobody."

"I know," said Napier, "but regardless, let's have a quick look and get the Hell out of here, I need to check on Kenzie at the hotel and maybe we can head to London, try and come up with something in relative safety. Come up with *anything!*"

The two men approached the burning ruins of the fort where mangled artillery smoldered and smoked. They got as close as they dared and peered out into the fields, looking for any survivors or, God forbid, any sign of invader ground troops.

"Look!" said Napier, banging Arnsdale hard on the arm and pointing.

"Well I'll be…," said Arnsdale.

The terrible cloud layer that had reached the wall was moving backwards, away from the wall, at quite a pace. It was as if someone was pulling a thick white blanket off a huge bed revealing clean blue sheets beneath. Within a few minutes the cloud was so far gone they couldn't even see it. Nothing but wonderful sky greeted their eyes.

"Are they done?" gasped Napier.

"I don't know," said Arnsdale, "but by God it looks like they are leaving. Why, though?"

A newly arrived radioman ran up behind them.

"Sirs, who is in charge here now?" he asked.

"No-one left really, boy" replied Arnsdale.

"I have a message for somebody though. Crap, either of you two important?"

"I'm *MoD* if that helps you. And I shoot a mean clay pigeon."

"That'll do, I want to report this and get out of here with the blood wagons if I can. Message from London – the last British units have withdrawn from their strategic locations around the globe. Message from Newcastle – alien transmission received, verified. Message is as follows: *farewell*."

Napier laughed bitterly. "So they're all coming back here now the enemy is leaving. Fantastic! Boy, radio back and let them know about this immediately!" Napier pointed at the clear sky.

The radioman shrugged, half saluted and ran back towards town.

"London, Anthony?" asked Napier.

"London. Time to deal with the press on this one, as you know. Not our proudest moment. You?"

"I think Scotland needs me. I need to see what is left at the very least."

Arnsdale nodded. "Will you at least wait until we can recon the place? You and Kenzie come and stay with me in *the big smoke* for a few days and we can see if they really have gone. Maybe they ran out of whatever they make their cloud from?"

The two old friends slowly wandered back into the town, talking theory and speculation all the way, just the way they liked it.

The first news report of what was being called *the Scottish Cloud* came from Belfast; apparently it was spreading in all directions across Ireland. All radio contact was lost soon after the initial report.

Within the hour it was also reported low over Cyprus, Jamaica, Papua New Guinea and Guyana. The reports kept coming in, from every nation and city around the globe that the British Empire had deserted to reinforce their own borders.

Every report of the cloud was almost instantly followed by complete dead air.

From his bed at 10 Downing Street the British Prime Minister Winston Churchill called a cabinet meeting in his private quarters.

"They have bamboozled us," he told his government, "they sucked all of our military back home and are now jumping into the vacuums we left behind. Gateways to the whole world. They will be marching by tomorrow, mark my words. Eisenhower may be our last slim chance; get him on the phone immediately."

That evening *the Scottish Cloud* was spotted in Canada, Argentina, Russia and New Zealand. The Americans refused to send forces north, fearing the same trickery that had fooled the British. They strengthened their major cities along the coasts and borders, leaving the middle unprotected.

The first invader ground troops were spotted in Berlin the next morning, decimating the American checkpoints and moving in their thousands beneath the expanding cloud into an undefended Germany and then out into all of Europe. Soon they were on the ground in Wyoming, Iowa, Arkansas and New Mexico, the dreaded cloud cover spreading quickly to east and west.

They didn't look like humans after all.

THE SPACER AND THE CABBAGES

by Auston Habershaw

Editorial Note: What follows is a transcript of an interview conducted by SPIT-NET agents on the USS Orion with Warrant Officer Scully Rodgers on February the 12th, 2232 CE. This interview was conducted some five standard months after the infamous incident on Ceti-Philos 9, and is a primary source document of great importance, as it sheds light on one of the most controversial personalities in modern history. According to reports written by the agents, Warrant Officer Rodgers did most of the talking, and therefore it has been the decision of the editors to include his commentary only, excerpting only the crude language he sometimes employed.

(At the outset, SPIT-NET agents describe Rodgers as a male of indeterminate ethnicity in his mid-thirties. He is wearing a worn yellow vacuum suit and a frayed flight jacket covered with better than two dozen mission patches. He smells strongly of cigarette smoke and sweat, and has not shaven in several days. Like most lifetime spacers, he speaks in a thick accent denoting a lifetime of near-constant comms use. Rodgers, sitting at the interview table, is the first to speak.)

"Got smokes in 'dis can? Negatory? Figs—you govvie jump-chumps and your friggin' regs. Could light 'em on the *Courser*, and there was a fine can, affirm? Filters'll hold out fine—trust me, I been in the Big Empty too long to go chokin'-out on some govvie can with un-sat filters. I know the specs, affirm? I ain't no newbie."

(Rodgers is denied cigarettes)
"Fine—keep 'em. I'll live."

(Rodgers is asked to repeat his story.)
"You wanna cross my wires, huh? Yeah, your givin' me the negatory, but I know when I'm bein' packed up for a shield hulk. You get dis clear—Scull

Rodgers ain't takin' the drop so some jump-chumps sittin' sphere-side and lookin' at the blue, blue sky can feel all warm and cozy. Look, your war *ain't my fault*. I've been broadcastin' the same report to suits like you for five terms, affirm? Five <*expletive*> terms! That's a load a cred I ain't makin' from my end of the can, chief, and I'm gonna jettison a hell of a fit if you jackboots don't stop jammin' me and lay me a rendezvous with the judge!"

(Rodgers is asked again to repeat the story)
"So, that's the line, huh? I affirm, sure. I affirm it's a big load of SPIT-NET scow trash, is what. Cool it off, chief, cool it off—you don't need to bring out the probes again. I can chat better without a <*expletive*> bot up my aft, anyway. You want the report again, you got it, but it's on the same course, affirm? Same thing I've been sayin' since it happened.

"Like I says before, I was pullin' a four-term tour on the *Courser*, doin' survey work for the Mining Consortium in the Ceti-Philos system. Wasn't much un-sat about the whole damn thing, tell the truth. Ceti-Philos is a Big Reddie, and dim as a chemstick, so we were clockin' maybe five, six rads an hour—which is ship-top fine, affirm? No rad-cakes getting' mixed in the chow causa that, and no rock watches or pirates out there, neither. Smooth duty, the whole way. We'd coast in pullin' no more than a gee and a half to some sphere, slide down the g-well into our stable circles, and then let the rock-heads do their biz sphere-side while we played 'who's-got-the-rivet' in the wardroom with our thumbs up our afts.

Had some ship-top vid-flicks—*Attack on Colony 12, Space Raid 3, Moon Honeys*—that Burle Midge rocks the screen, affirm? 'Course, we only had those three, and even my man Midge gets hull-down flat after a stretch. Boring, sure, but I'd just finished ten terms doin' cut and run salvage tours in Hubspace and my chips were half to fried. I needed some smooth duty, affirm?"

(Rodgers and the interviewer exchange a few extraneous comments herein excluded.)
"I'm just tellin' ya to give it another scan, chief. The flick ain't so un-sat. Effects'll make ye jettison cargo—scared *me* near to blankin'.

So, anyhow, as I was sayin', the duty was smooth but <*expletive*> boring, affirm? Now, I'm a man of actions, and while spendin' two hours in the head makin' lady-eyes at porno-spreads is fine, the whole order was gettin' un-sat with my active standing. I weren't alone in this fig, neither, so's that's why the skipper set up option duty sphere-side, where you played stick-jock in a rover for one of the rock heads. Still smooth, affirm—all yer doin' is drivin' 'em around and playin' papa so's they don't decom their vac-suit or take a drop down no ravines—but you got to feelin' like yer earnin' yer cred, leastways. So,

THE SPACER AND THE CABBAGES

I tag my sign on the list, and soon enough I'm called on deck in the shuttle bay for duty.

"That's when I met Doc Evans. There he is, suped-up in a vac-suit fresh outta the hold, creases still trimmin' the sleeves, and portin' a duffle fulla sci-tech diag junk. 'Figs,' I cast to myself, 'I get the ship-top chump of 'em all.' I mean, the guy's callin' his vac-suit a damned spacesuit, like he was gonna be doin' the low-G-hop with Armstrong on pre-colony Luna.

"He told me his sign like I was gonna know his specs or somethin,' and started some chatter about sphere-side university crap. I muted him out and stowed gear in the rover. He was still in chatter when I was running the checks on the con, so I figged he wasn't readin' my mute order, which was smooth by me. If he don't mind, I don't mind, affirm?

"The drop was smooth, 'ceptin' Evans. He's a chump, like I casted, so's he sicks-up in the rover twice during drop. That negs his chatter, but didn't put 'im high up on my list of rock heads, neither. Inside'a one of them survey rovers is maybe twelve, thirteen meter cubed, so's two sick-ups fulla his fancy mess chow is enough stink to set me near to chokin'-out. I told him as much, and he says he's 'bad on drops.' Figs, it all figs. I told him he's a damn chump and next sick-up I'm gonna blow-out a porthole just for the fresh air. Well, he don't ride that one too well, and starts to bitch-chat. 'Course, I had all this beamin' up to *Courser* in the comms, so's the boys upstairs could listen in on the fun. Evans reads this when he hears 'em laughin' over the line, and he gets his wires crossed somethin' awful. Clammed up his pink, sunny face, all right, and gave me the cold-eye the rest o'the way down sphere-side."

(Rodgers is asked if he felt any hostility towards Evans)

"There you go again, with that Evan's chatter. Look, read my broadcast top-down, chump—Evans wasn't nothin' to me. I'm a spacer, he was a rock-head chump. I had my job, he had his. I couldn't give two creds what his sun-tanned sphere-side aft thoughta me, said about me, or nothin'. I don't lay down no courses with jump-chumps, affirm? Not with you, not with Evans. Gimmie the Big Empty, a good can, a decent crew, and a cred or twenty in my duffle, and the rest of you fat-ass planet jockeys can stay chained on your rocks and think the *<expletive>* universe aerates yer panties, for all I care. You SPIT-NET jackboots keep jammin' spacers and spin 'em as some kinda pirates gone legit, and I'm castin' you for the last time that we ain't. Don't think yer better'n me, affirm?"

(Rodgers is asked to skip to the fifth hour of their survey mission)

"Can we get some chow in here? I'm runnin' on slag and oxy-wash; nothin' munchin' for what…twelve hours?"

(Rodgers is promised food and is asked to return to the fifth hour of Evans' and his survey mission)

"First off, I wasn't runnin' no scans or doin' no surveys—I was stick-jock, that's it. I affirm what you're pokin' at, chief, and I told you I ain't takin' the drop for nobody, not Evans *especial*. If that rock-head read them before collision, he didn't tell me nothin' about it. I was just drivin' 'cross flat-out purple dust and shit-brown rock nothin' for clicks and makin' chatter on the com with Smitty upstairs—he was comms officer aboard *Courser*—that's it.

"So we were at maybe 110 klick-hours velo, I was preppin' to shift her into fifth when *wham!* My proxy-alarms shoot up a red-light fiesta and, through the foreport, I see a…well…a thing. You goons know it better'n me by now—I'll wager a new can 'gainst my auntie on that. It was all yellow-green and had a look of some kid's toy made outta plasti-fiber and silly foam. Anyhow, I try to pull a 270°, but I'm at 110, and the rover ain't made for no shake-'n-bake rally, so *smack*, we collide. I don't get a visual of the crash, 'cause I'm already closin' my eyes and mouth so's when the impact foam comes out—like it was—I don't get a chem-party in my chow-bay, affirm? 'Course, Evans is screamin' like a girl and the foam runs down his throat like frickin' engine-coolant ice cream. We're spinnin' and rollin' and goin' through some major washout and my eyes are still closed and my hands clappin' tight on my harness. Honest truth, I thought I had just signed my own coffin slip—life before the eyes and all that <*expletive*>.

"By the time we came down to zero velo and the foam is bubblin' off, the first thing I hear is Evan's chokin', and the first thing I think is how bad his chow is gonna taste for the next four cycles or so. Sure, that impact foam'll keep ya from makin' bulkhead paste, and it goes gaseous in fifteen seconds even, but you get it in yer vents and ain't nothin' gonna taste like nothin' but heavy chems and sour burn.

"Anyhow, I run the checks on the meat and bones, and find nothin' too un-sat. I cast Evans if he's runnin' green, but, like a chump, he's twistin' like a man in a decom chamber with no vac suit. Thinks he's dyin' with the foam in his mouth, and I ain't no chaplain, so's I let him figure it all out with that big University brain o' his and crack the hatch for recon.

"Ceti-Philos 9 is a Class C sphere, so's they say you can breathe there. 'Course, when a sci-tech signs you a 'breathe' order, that translates from twenty hours to four minutes before yer lungs collapse on themselves or some microbe makes filter-screens outta yer insides, so's I'm holdin' my air for a full ten seconds 'fore I suck down my first taste. Went down the tubes like sub-zero temp jet fumes, but I didn't choke-out, so's I fig the place'll do for dust-off.

"I could read Evan's bitch-talk from the rover's guts, so's I knew he didn't choke-out, but he'd cracked a strut or two and was wheezin' like a lung-dead geezer. Read <expletive> pissed, too, so's I made to run a check down the rover to assess my DC protocols.

(Rodgers is asked to go through his damage assessment of the rover)
"Chief, the whole land-can was a negatory, chips to rivets. The Cat Type-M212 is a scow trash mod—I told the skipper as much on *Courser*—but it weren't like they were gonna junk a whole damn rover on *my* spec-annie. Anyhow, she was rolled on her left flank, so's I had a pretty good scanpoint of the action. A ship-top rover mod, like the Schmaus A-77, woulda been runnin' green in this action, but the <expletive> Cat…it had a fore-axle cracked, our right forward wheel was off, the electricals had four shorts, and the Baby Hot had a crack and was pissin' maybe forty rads an hour from the power core. I had to set her to blackdown just to keep the rad count from the fry-line. That's a strict priority 1 protocol, or I woulda belayed that action, affirm? That <expletive>-ed us good. No power meant no coms and no life-support, which meant me and Evans were gonna get some Ceti-Philos 9 quality recon time, breathin' that jet-fog air and gettin' purple dust up our aft vents while we waited for the *Courser* to run a sweeper scan and *maybe* find us before we choked out.

(Rodgers is asked if he thought their situation serious at the time)
"Chief, dust-off was nine-hours on a hot-zone from Sunday leave, affirm? My professional assess was we were goin' for the Big Float in a space shoebox. That's what no coms makes, chief, nine-mark-double nines outta ten.

(Rodgers is asked whether he told Evans this or not)
"By the time I gave Evan's the hoist outta the rover, he wasn't lettin' me say nothin' 'tween his threats. I coulda' dented his fat bulkhead for the <expletive> scow trash he was broadcastin', affirm? 'I'm going to have your license!' he says, and 'What are you, blind?' and 'can't you even evade a stationary rock?' Now, here's a chump who's don't even rate how to

stick-jock a land-can, and he's givin' *me* the bitch-chatter? <*Expletive*> him, I say, we didn't collide with no stationary rock. Bogey was *mobile*, rockhead, clockin' 50 click-hours velo *minimum*. Maybe if them Cat scow-trash proxy-alarms had better'n dumpin' range and my nav ports were bigger'n forty centimeters, maybe I coulda pulled evade on 'em, but 'maybe' is a low-prob option, affirm?

"That's when he casts a pre-empt on *my* bitch-chat with a 'Well, what *did* we hit?' That reads as quality, so's I hup it out a ways, tracin' our trash-trail to the impact point. That's when I first get's the visual of 'em. They were…"

(Food is brought in, and Rodgers stops talking until he is served. He opens a carbonated beverage can and sips)

"Ugh! What's the specs on *this* junk lube? Whuzzat, *bananas?* What chump chem-boy stuffs banana in a frickin' soda? You coulda thrown down the cred for a decent java brew, ya jackboot sun-humpers…"

(Rodgers is commanded to return to his story or the food will be removed)

"I roger that, chief. I ain't gonna cut my tether now, no sir. Them tatermash looks ship-top fine. Anyhow, what was my X on this report?"

(Rodgers is reminded of where he left off)

"Right, so's the first thing I scan is a big hulk of rubbery junk, hexagonal, maybe five meter-squared. It's like nothin' I've ever read specs on, but I scan that it had impact damage on one side that set cracks runnin' through the whole setup, and some loose rubber-foam chunks were doin' the windjockey twirl 'cross the purple dust dunes in the breeze. Figged them parts were cracked loose by our rover, affirm? I scanned that the thing had three wheels downside, but they're more spheres than wheels, affirm, and topside there was all these long, half-limp antennae or, least they *scanned* like antennae. They made me log back to the one time I went huppin' it through the jungles on Centauri Prime and they had all the vines and vegetation slappin' me in the cheeks.

They were like them vines, affirm? Secondary visual on top read six metallic hemispheres, and they're cracked open like cockpit bubbles. This reads as a good fig, 'cause that's when I hear Evans wheezin' out a red-light fiesta and pointin' at somethin' next to the big rubber thing. That's when I made my first visual with 'em—six cabbage-lookin' unknowns, each maybe a meter across, with six vine-roots affixed to each of their bases and a thick, flower stalk thing stickin' up a meter-mark-five from their center. Now, chief, you gotta affirm that I've spent near onto my *whole* life in cans coastin' the starways in the Big Empty, and I don't read nothin' from plants, so's my first thought is that these'r some kinda garden plants. Evans, though, he's fit to jettison a two-ton rock. He's shakin' my vac suit like we just drew spy-sat duty over a sphere fulla naked women. 'Exomorphs—aware, tool-using! Like *us*!' he says.

"That's when I give 'em a close scan, and things get un-sat quick. I read that them flower's is trackin' us like spy-cams, and that every few seconds one of 'em hisses at one of them others and they set to hissin' back. They don't move much, but them vines or tentacles or whatever that're stickin' out their afts're wavin' a bit, like they're waitin' fer somethin.' That's when I fig the whole thing down to bolts—these cabbage-things're survey chumps like Evans, and the thing we hit was *their <expletive> rover*—and now I'm gettin' itchy for dust-off 'cause I don't know what the cabbage-things're gonna think of us punchin' their bulkhead in and kickin' 'em out onto the *<expletive>* ugliest sphere I ever been chained to. Read that our coms were out, affirm, on account of no power, and so we're stuck bein' danger-proxy to some *<expletive>* aliens."

(Rodgers is asked if he or Evans tried to communicate to the aliens, and what were their reactions.)

"Figs if that chump, Evans, weren't hoppin' like a can-nut set for sphere leave, busted struts and all. He keeps up chatter about how we're gonna be heroes and rich and *<expletive>* steel-house catsuit studs with the whole damn galaxy causa some stinky weirdo cabbages with a set o' wheels. Oh yeah, I didn't give ya the specs on the smell yet, huh? Them cabbages set off a stink that was the *<expletive> weirdest* thing my sniffer ever vacced in. It weren't so much straight un-sat as it was…well…I ain't got the word, but Evan's called it 'sporadic and varied' or 'variably sporadic' or somethin'. All I can cast ya is that sometimes they stunk bad, sometimes they stunk *real* bad, and then, just when yer gettin' slick on one smell, the things'd hiss and the whole damn stink'd switch up.

"Now, Evans is tellin' me to go back to the rover and get his diag gear, and I'm not givin' him an affirm or a negatory or anything and I'm holdin' coordinates. Now, you fig that as suped-up excited as Evans is, I'm a pole south o' that, affirm? I am not smooth with this action, and I am not for smiles and handshakes with the cabbage things, and I am not goin' anywhere without keepin' the coordinates on Evans, 'cause I *seen* that vid-flick, and I ain't gettin' chowed by some alien cabbage so's the smart guy can save the day and hump the blond chick. I'm sittin' there, thumb up my aft, tryin' to read in the green, but my brain is flashin' red and tellin' me to pull a 180° and knock the throttle to the bottle, affirm? I'm thinkin' o' huppin' it back to the rover to get the slugger, so's we would have a defense option should the things get too personal, but that'd mean huppin' Evan's diag junk, too, and I weren't about to give that rock-head gear to poke at them things with. Still, I'm sittin' there countin' the minutes till we start chokin' out, and I'm thinkin' it ain't long seein' as my throat is runnin' raw like shaved meat from the air we're puffin', and I'm goin' through *how the <expletive> we're gonna get dust-off.*

(Rodgers is asked why he didn't think that the Courser *would find them)*
"It's standard Consortium protocol to hack the transponder on all rovers and keep their circles outta geo-synch with their ground crews. This is causa the risk that pirates or claim jumpers or even other mining cans'll run a long-range sys-scan and *wham*, you and your buds're blippin' yer coordinates to every chump with a vid-screen. Since miners ain't the one-for-me-one-for-you type, they're real smooth on keepin' things hull-down and covert. 'Course the washout o' that protocol is that if a rover gets trashed and the coms go out, there's no way to find 'em outsida doin' a ship-top high-fi sphere-scan, and if you start scannin' the wrong coordinates, they might not get yer X for twenty, thirty hours. Now, *Courser* is a ship-top can, affirm, and I was just talkin' to Smitty upstairs, so they were scannin' for us, sure. They just weren't scannin' the right part of the whole <*expletive*> planet.

"Anywho, Evans, meantime, has started sendin' hails over to the cabbage things. He's speakin' in StanEngles, Frenchie, Choppo, and other stuff, he's makin' hand signs, he's jumpin' up and down. The things seem like they got a mute-order or somethin', cause they don't alter course one degree. They just sit there and stink and hiss and that's it. Evans is burnin' thin, cause he's wheezin' and hackin' out blood. Now, I ain't no sci-tech or doc or nothin', but I can tell when a guy's blowin' his tanks for nothin.' I tell Evans to cool it off or he'll be leakin' blood like it was on tap and, for a doozy, the chump gives me the a-firm. This cools my chips a bit, cause the cabbage things ain't moved and Evans isn't castin' like a diplo-clown on the kiss-baby circuit. That's when I light up that smoke, to take the edge off, affirm? That's when the things went active."

(Rodgers is asked to elaborate)
"Them things *moved*, affirm? They lifted themselves up with them vine-arms and crawled like babies at me, the stalks leanin' out at me like chow traps or something.' I'd scanned them nature vids as says you ain't supposed to show fear or nothin' to animals, so's I plant myself as a permanent and let the <*expletive*>-ers come close—real close. I get visual that the inside of them blossoms on them stalks is all little hairs that wave like tiny worms, and I can feel my skin crawlin' like they says

in the horror vids. Evans is givin' me the clap-down like the chump he is, sayin' I made a <*expletive*>-in' breakthrough! <*Expletive*> that, and <*expletive*> him, I cast, but I don't alter coordinates one centimeter, affirm?"

(Rodgers is asked if he knew what the aliens wanted from him)
"I keep tellin' you jackboots this, but you never read it top-down, chumps!"

(Rodgers is asked to repeat his previous statement for the record)
"I'm tellin' ya they wanted *smokes*. The things're trackin' my smoke anywhere it went—up, down, whatever. I'm tellin' Evans to get the slugger, and he's givin' me static on that action—sayin' we need to 'appear peaceful and extend an 'olive' branch' or whatever the <*expletive*>—when the cabbage things start to stink *at* me. That's the only way I can report it, affirm? They started hissin' and cloudsa ship-top *foul* stink started hittin' me in the face. There were more kinda stinks there than I ever vacced in, ever. I figged I was gonna choke out, I lost my chips, and I hupped it at full accel outta that sector. Musta dropped the smoke in my rushin,' cause by the time I was proxy to the cabbage rover, the stinkers were surroundin' the burnin' smoke where it hit dust, still hissin' at it. I don't claim to know the specs on the why them cabbages were so damn eager to get at my smoke, and at the time I couldna given a cred. I was shakin' and tryin' to cool it off, but chief, I tell ya, I was runnin' redder than I ever had."

(Rodgers is asked to explain Evan's reaction)
"Chump was laughin' at me—*laughin'*! Cast me for bein' 'jittery.' <*Expletive*> that! Was like that chump wasn't scannin' how <*expletive*>-ed we were—no clean air, buncha stinky aliens chasin' us around, no *comms*! Damn, the man had a pair o' busted struts, probably leakin' the red stuff all over his insides, and he's *laughin'*! He starts the university chatter again, and this time I'm readin' it, 'cause I needed somethin' borin' to cool it off and get me in the green. Evans says that the aliens communicate with…ahhh…what was the word? Damn if I can never log this damn word—phero somethin', I fig it was. Whatever it was, I read it as a fancy way of sayin' the cabbages used *stinks* like *words*, which was why they liked my smoke so much and why they didn't answer his hails. Hell, I coulda told him that they had no auditories—just them crawly hairs in the blossom. This new spec makes Evans all eager to try

his hails again, so he asks for my pack o' smokes. By this time, Evans and me is chokin' on the air enough to not need no smokes, so's I throw 'em his way."

(Rodgers is asked what Evans did to try and communicate)

"Scan me if I got the specs on that, chief. All I know is that when Evans lit up another one, one of the six cabbages picked up the old smoke with one o' them vines it's got and went crawlin' over with his five buds to surround Evans.

"That's when I stopped scannin' the whole thing—couldn't take the danger-proxy of the whole action, affirm? I ain't got no protocol of what to do if cabbages attack my rock head on sphere-side duty, and I don't know what the cabbage protocol was to deal with jump-chumps who go lightin' smokes and flickin' em at 'em.

"The fig that hit me at that point was that I was gonna die if I didn't get comms up and runnin' and call the drop boys down for a dust-off and *double-time*. I seen too many vid-flicks to not read the spec on our situation—freaky aliens, chump-dumb sci-techs, ugly planets. Them cabbages were gonna take Evans or me down, affirm? I needed to get back-up A-priority-1 alpha. Me and Evans were coughin' up our airbags at this point, not that Evans read that red-light, so's I hupped it back to the rover to scan for some contingency action."

(Rodgers is asked why he didn't look for a backup rescue plan before)

"Who says that I didn't? Didn't I just tell you jackboots how I gave the rover a check after the impact? There was no contingency action on that piece o' shield-hulk junk, affirm? I was givin' it the last scan 'cause by brain was gettin' some serious death static and I was chip-fried like a flare monkey. There was <*expletive*> negatory in the rover, 'ceptin' the slugger, and that piece's power cell don't splice to ship-top fine interplanetary com unit like what was specced on the rover unless you wanna explode as a secondary protocol. I went hull down in the dust about then, and figged I'd just wait for the choke-out fairy to give me the ol' one-way ticket. So, I'm lyin' there, the purple dust frostin' me like a grape-flavor rad cake, and I'm lookin' at the slugger, all locked and loaded, and I get a plan.

(Rodgers is asked why there was a hyperslug carbine in the rover)

"Claim-jumpers, mostly. It ain't standard spec to bring a piece along, but you'd be a chump not to load one on as contingency. Sure, it ain't gonna do

THE SPACER AND THE CABBAGES 135

<expletive> nothin' to an armored bunch of ship-top claim pirates, but 'gainst your regular sphere-side dopes, it'll pay off high cred, affirm? Anyhow, I had me a plan, and sure you jackboots've been jammin' my aft ever since this <expletive> second, but I still think it was a *slick* plan, affirm? I load up the slugger and pry-and-load the transmitter and hup 'em over to the impact site, where that <expletive>-er Evans is tryin' to play King of the Cabbage People with his smoke shows. The way I read it, I got there just in time, 'cause the crawly <expletive>-ers were wrappin' their tentacles round his legs and closin' that circle of theirs near to dockin' proxy with Evans' aft. Evans, the <expletive>-head, is smilin' like a vid-flick porn mamma, wavin' at me as he's hackin' the red stuff all over his newbie vac suit. "Look," he says, "I'm being accepted." Then he scans the slugger, and he goes all pasty and says, "Put that away! What are you trying to do, scare them?"

(Rodgers is asked, forcefully, what he was planning to do with the weapon)
"Hey, cool it off, chump! I was takin' it for contingency, *that's it!* 'Sides, like you should bitch-chat about killin' them cabbages. You got the <expletive> option whether to blast 'em or not, sittin' out here in your navy can with your missiles and rail-guns and ship-top mean marines and *comms*, and *J-drive*! You could get a whole <expletive> *colony* of university sci-tech brain-guys workin' on cabbage stink-lingo and actually *hail* the things, but you still go blastin' 'em anyhow. <expletive> you!"

(Silence, and then Rodgers is asked whether he knew what was at stake here, in a first contact situation with an alien species)
"Negatory, chump. Got that? *Neg-a-tor-y.* There ain't no protocol for this action. Nobody got no protocol for this. That's why I'm docked in this cell, ain't it? Humanity gets its first scan of thinkin' aliens, they come out runnin' red, and you jackboots need a shield-hulk. You need some poor chump's face to shoot along the I-net so's to give the sun-humpers sphere-side somebody to bitch-chat."

(Rodgers is commanded to not change the subject. He is asked what he was thinking when taking the slugger into proximity with the aliens)
"I'm a spacer, chief, not a sci-tech, affirm? All I read on the situation was that we were goin' low on air-time, we had no comms, there was no dust-off comin', and there was nothin' but me, a jump-chump with two busted struts, two busted rovers, and a buncha stinky cabbages for *2000 clicks!* Like I told you before, I'm a man of action, and I had an action in mind. I wasn't thinkin' about

nothin' but the spots in my eyes, the pain in my hull, and the *one <expletive> way* to get off that rock!"

(Rodgers is asked to elaborate)
"You scanned my report, chief! You know this. You <expletive> know it!"

(Rodgers is told to elaborate)
"Fine. The Baby Hot in our power core was cracked which made it un-sat for a plant, but the *cabbages* had a rover too, and that rover had to have some kinda Baby Hot or power cell or something on board, affirm, and since we ain't fried, that meant it was runnin' green, most like. Now, if I could jerry up the cables to suck power *outta their rover*, I could send for priority dust-off. I was bettin' I could run this action since I've been splicin' cable since I been fender-high to a sweeper drone. In the Big Empty, when parts get junked, you ain't got the year it takes to wait for a refit/replace to come down the line, so you learn how to put round males in square fems and vice versa priority frickin' 1."

(Rodgers is asked if Evans was able to communicate to the aliens Rodgers' plan)
"I didn't tell Evans I was doin' this, affirm? Way I saw it, them things weren't gonna just *let* me siphon off their juice, so I just hupped it over to the cabbage rover and started work, all stealth like. Soon as I touch a lead, though, the cabbages 'round Evans set to hissin' *loud,* like heat vents. I hear the chump scream and I scanned him, slugger up. He's chokin' fit to die and he's on his knees, and I read him clutchin' his eyes, screamin' 'It burns, it burns!' or some <expletive>. The things'd let go of him and were crawlin' my way. That set my action ship-top *firm*. I powered up the slugger and..."

(Rodgers is asked if the aliens looked aggressive)
"They're <expletive>-ing *cabbages*! How do veggies scan like *anything*? Yeah, you SPIT-NET chumps have been tellin' me that the things didn't mean to blind ol' Evans, but <expletive> that—how was I gonna read that <expletive>? I ain't lookin' for their expressions, affirm? All I'm readin' is the face of Burle Midge in *Attack on Colony 12* as them Ruffians rip him up. I'm hearin' all the spook-reports the guys cast in the ward room about how Shippy McFarle got an alien pox on Rigel 2 and melted into goo. You jackboots can jam me 'til the Big Crunch about how I shoulda figged to

THE SPACER AND THE CABBAGES 137

be 'diplomatic' or 'tried more to communicate,' and I'm gonna cast you for the last time—*you'd do the same as me.*"

(Rodgers is asked to repeat what he did.)
"You chumps wanna read this again? Fine, choke on it! I leveled the slugger, flipped to auto, and squeezed. You ever discharge a slugger, chump? A ship-top mean piece of hardware, affirm? Spits uranium flak at twenty-two thousand meters per second, goes through a one-hundred round clip in ten seconds even, and I fig I was holdin' the trigger down a full half minute after that, poppin' gas from the steady-vents and screamin' like a un-sat pressure bulkhead. Time I cooled her off and took a scan with my lights green, them cabbages were nothin' but black-green paste and bad-gas dreams."

(Rodgers is asked if he's aware of the repercussions of that action)
"Look, chief, I was readin' in the red. My course was plotted out a half-hour max, and the rest was static and dead leads, affirm? My plan *worked*, chump. I got my juice for the comms, I got us dust-off, I *<expletive>*-ing *saved Evans' life*. What do *I* get, huh? Fuckin' jackboot quarantine on a *<expletive>* government can for the rest of my *<expletive>* life, that's what. What I done ain't even a *crime*, chump! They ain't human, and there ain't no law against sluggin' cabbages. Ol' Moses didn't hup no stone tablet off no mountain which said nothin' about 'shalt not kill aliens.'"

(Rodgers is asked if he was aware his actions started a war.)
"I didn't start no war, chief. I ain't the one with the navy spittin' rail slugs up the afts of them cabbage cans. You wanna spec me for shootin' em, that's all clear by me, affirm? I killed 'em, I've casted as much since hour frickin' one, *but I didn't start no war.* This war was locked in before I ever slugged no cabbage aliens. Govvie chumps like you ain't no JC I-net preachers. I'll cast it again—you'd do the same. Everybody woulda done the same, affirm? Go on, give me the cold-eye, broadcast all the negatory reports you want. You weren't there, chief, and you can't give your spec-annie better'n me. *<Expletive>* sphere-jockeys thinkin' I'm some genome spit-up crud…"

(Rodgers is asked if he feels remorse for his actions)

"You readin' me chief? You got a mute-order on my squawk or what? <*expletive*>! You don't read me any better than I read them, affirm? Yer ignorant as chumps, all of you, and I *ain't sorry*. No law-squawk in Hubspace'll drag me to prison for this <*expletive*>. No I-net preacher, neither. Ol' Scull Rodgers is scannin' green to hisself—you run that past your scanners next time you sign-up for cabbage-planet chem-bomb duty, affirm? I ain't the un-sat operator in this action. What? Got nothin' comin' on that course? That's an a-ffirm from me, chief. Chatter's through. Clear my space, jack-boot. I got me tater-mash to chow."

(Ed. Note: The interview concludes here. Rodgers' was later found guilty of xenocide—the first conviction of its kind—and given a life sentence at a maximum security penal colony. It was appealed several times by Rodgers' attorneys, who claimed that, since xenocide was not a formal crime at the time when it was committed by Rodgers, any prosecution of him for such an act was illegal and in violation of the UN Constitution. All appeals were rejected on the grounds that Rodgers' acts were in violation of the 'reasonable and well-considered' clause. Since that time, the war with the Brassicans has persisted in one form or another, though they have been driven from all Terran systems. It is estimated that the allied French, American, and Chinese naval fleets have eliminated in excess of five billion enemy Brassicans. Unfortunately, our forces have found no way to determine the difference between enemy combatants and civilians, nor have any of our attempts to communicate with the creatures been successful.)

JOHN'S LIST

by Brent Knowles

The gas flowing into John Seven's lungs brought with it several lifetimes of yesterdays and the warm intensity of those memories dragged him deeply into the distant past. Rhonda's face surfaced in his mind, her eyes as wide as the galaxy he traveled in search of her.

How many centuries ago?

Holding hands...and then above them, Luna's sky darkening as *they* dropped en masse; an interstellar locust cloud. Stunned into silence, John and Rhonda staring upward...a bat-like creature the size of a house unfurling its wings with a rapid snap. The force of air expelled by the gesture knocking both to the ground and separating the lover's hands.

A mad scramble for cover beneath the crawler, but Rhonda is too slow. The creature leaps forward, almost angelic in its grace, and pulls Rhonda into its membranous folds, tight and clear inner wings closing over her. Imprisoning her. And then...gone. The warmth of her touch only a chiseled memory.

John's stomach churned and though he had vowed to himself that he would last longer this time he ended the session prematurely — he did not have the strength to battle ancient memories. John Seven wiped at his teary eyes as he pulled the spongy memory-mask away from his mouth, a whiff of ozone and jasmine tickling his nostrils. He undid the chair straps and floated to the door. With a resigned shrug, he returned to his duties as captain, one of only a handful who knew how close they were to finishing the mission.

The *Vigilant* was a Lewis-class interplanetary research vessel, unsuited for long-range interstellar travel but modified for its current quest. The engines drew their power from a nuclear reactor, permitting the starship to move into deepest space.

When the Swarm had struck, humankind had been taking its first baby steps into space, beginning to reach for the stars but unable to grasp them. The *original* John had never considered the implications of boldly pursuing his stolen bride. He had, if ship gossip were to be believed, stolen the Vigilant for his mad quest.

Six spherical 'stations', each connected to Engineering's bulky, square body by way of access tunnels (or pencil-tubes as the crew called them) housed the various operations of the Vigilant. Centuries of space flight had battered the spheres but Engineering kept them functional. The sphere's technical specializations had long ago turned social and now represented a loose caste system. John Seven stared out one of Engineering's portholes at the vastness of space sliding past him.

"You look lost, sir."

John Seven turned to Chung Six, surprised to see the old man at an instrument panel, his fingers not as deft as those of his replacement. The younger Chung manned the chief engineer's console above them.

"You're retired Chung."

"I still do my duty, sir. It's not my fault that the medicals misdiagnosed me!" He tugged at his beard and glared upwards, his voice lowered, "He might be young but he has no experience, I'll tell you."

"But he will learn," John Seven said, amazed at how tenaciously the elder Chung clung to life, "And you will rest well knowing that you leave the Vigilant in good hands. Remember: 'We are all born empty and must be filled.'" He forced himself to keep his eyes locked with Chung's.

"Yes sir, but by my Original I just wish he would catch on faster, you know?"

John Seven smiled slightly. Did not all fathers expect perfection from their sons? But that was the crux; none of them were fathers or sons. What did that make them then? If John Original could see what his single-mindedness had created... would it have stopped him? The bastard probably wouldn't have cared.

With a nod John Seven turned and propelled himself to the bridge by way of the handrails that lined the foremost pencil-tube. Sweat dotted his brow, the journey took less than five minutes but it bothered him more than usual today. He had never walked on a planet but at times, usually after a disturbing memory session, he felt weighed down by the cramped confines of his starship.

He heard the shouting long before he reached the bridge.

"*You can't replace me!*" Tammy's voice. Her long blond ponytail floated straight above her like an exclamation point as she turned in her bucket chair and shouted angrily at John's second in command. Portwell Seven was clean-shaven and large; an imposing figure, both in height and thickness. He stood in front of the captain's chair atop the upper level of the bridge and barked harshly at Tammy. As John floated to the commander's level he saw that Hastings Eight, all nine years of himself and dressed in the gray robe of a communication's officer, was hovering in front of Tammy, his feet tucked under a metal u-bracket to keep from drifting away. His hands he held pressed against his sides.

"What is going on?" John tried to sound commanding, but Portwell did not bother to look in his captain's direction.

"I've asked this Prototype to begin training Hastings. She has refused. Disobeying a direct order from a commanding officer is a punishable offence. *Captain.*"

Tammy's head bobbed with her indignation. "He's just a kid. He can't be expected-"

John said, "You are dismissed from the bridge." She nodded briskly and left.

"Hastings," Portwell said, "assume your station." *A kid at the comm?* Ridiculous but now unavoidable.

"I'll be back in a moment."

"At your convenience. Captain."

John followed Tammy into the pencil-tube, making sure he closed the hatch between tube and bridge. He needed privacy; there was enough gossip floating around the station about them.

"Tammy!"

He saw her blond head near the exit point of the tube. She ignored him.

"*Private!*"

She stopped, turned and waited for him to drift to her. She looked close to tears but in his experience he knew they were not of the mournful variety. Her lip trembled in suppressed rage.

"He has no respect for me. He's always calling me a *Prototype*, like I had any drifting choice in that. Hastings at the comm? That's insulting. It is Portwell's fault that Hastings Seven died-"

"Enough. You will be back on the bridge tomorrow. I will speak with Portwell about this."

Tammy said, "Will you. Really? Because this back and forth, report to the bridge, oh, now you are dismissed shit is really starting to piss me off."

He said, "They think you're bad luck."

She made a face. An unpleasant face. "And doesn't that worry you? That the unscientific belief that Prototypes are bad luck has persisted in a crew full of scientists? A Prototype's parents are punished enough. Why should *I*-"

"Tammy, we have no parents. You are the result of an unfortunate coupling between two very irresponsible crewmembers. Crewmembers who have now been generation demoted. Remember the List."

Tammy's sour expression told him what she thought of John Original's List. Each message on the List could only be unlocked after a particular event:

1) Respect. For when a new captain assumes command.
2) Dedication. For when the Swarm is encountered.
3) Accomplishment. For when Rhonda is recovered.

All captains and crew had read the first message. It discussed the reverence to the Originals, the first crew, that John demanded. Tammy's parents had been severely reprimanded for disobeying this rule and their clones would require several generations of dedicated effort to be restored to their Original's rank.

Only John Two had seen the contents of the second entry. The third no one had read.

"Toss the List, John. It ain't right. The man I grew up with, the man I knew, is better than this. I was the only Prototype in our age group and you accepted me. But now you're becoming like Portwell. How long, you think, before he kills another Hastings? Before you do?"

"It *was* my order that cost Hastings Seven his-"

"You spoke the order but Portwell gave it. He — and the List — they rule you."

John looked down, unable to hold her gaze. "As captain I have responsibilities. We're no longer babysitting children in the nursery, pretending the impossible."

"I have never seen you happier since then. You are not a captain. You are a father."

John thought it unwise for her to see the tears starting to well in his eyes and so he turned away from her.

"You are dismissed. Go to your quarters."

"Go to hell." Her exit was less than dignified as she floated down the tube.

Several days later John admitted himself into the memory clinic again. They were close and he needed the help of his predecessors. The Captain's List provided guidance and rules but John needed to experience the ship's previous encounter with the Swarm.

When born, clones are nothing more than the genetic duplicate of their originator. If not interfered with they would grow up physically identical to their Original but mentally unique. John Original had vowed to be the one to rescue Rhonda and to that end he forced the revival of a process outlawed on earth, the use of memory-chambers for more than teaching. Memories could be passed from one individual to another, a mental inheritance complementing the cloning. The transfer of memories was not as robust as cloning though and mistakes happened — gaps in memory, disassociation, and in the occasional case a complete failure like John Seven.

He sat in the chair and covered his face with the suffocating mask. The gas he breathed tumbled him into darkness. Then stars ignited, one by one, tiny pins of light tearing the almost blackness of space. The rest of the details filled in like a graphic rendering on a faulty monitor — a starship's framework formed line by line, textures filled in, forming console panels, status indicators, people. He stood, well not *he* exactly but John Two, old and frail and soon to be replaced, on the bridge of the Vigilant.

The battle ended quickly; the Swarm taken by surprise. The Vigilant did not escape unscathed and most of the star fighters were lost but in that moment John Two had shown that humans could defeat the Swarm.

The skiff they recovered was full of notch-grips upon which the aliens had clung. When ready for space travel the swarmlings could unfurl their wings and collect solar energy at an astonishing rate. This particular Swarm ship had stopped for its crew to mate, die, and be reborn. A younger, stronger generation.

Cryogenic storage kept the captives frozen in stasis but a cursory search revealed that Rhonda was not among the survivors. This vessel was only one of a handful. A thousand sleeping humans floating through the dark and eternal night of space and all John Two had done was plant a beacon for a rescue ship. His justification? Rhonda was not aboard and therefore the mission was not finished. The Vigilant plowed on.

John Seven blinked and woke. He prayed to the Originals that the Vigilant could hold up long enough to do what needed doing but with every rattle and shake of the starship he silently doubted. Hundreds of years had passed; the Vigilant was not the ship she had once been, nor was her Captain the leader he ought to be. John Seven knew he would have recovered that first skiff and brought it home. He was not made of the same stuff as his predecessors.

The comm beeped and he answered it.

Weeks ago a tiny signal in the dark of space had caused the Vigilant to change course. Now John knew for certain: they had found another skiff.

With the day sorted John retired to his quarters. Emotions rippled through him, conflicting waves of joy and despair — one journey ending and another beginning. Though he would never spend a day with Rhonda, he knew that another John would. There was little satisfaction in that.

He looked up at the portrait of himself, or rather, that of his Original, and studied the stern, bold face. He remembered first entering this room as a young man, John Six leading him in and showing him the chamber, at the time bare of any decoration other than the portrait (now the walls were covered with the pictures of the children John had helped train and teach). The old man had explained how to access the List, had shaken his hand, and several days later had conveniently died.

John climbed into his bed, a rubber cocoon hanging like a banana from a side wall, and had just zipped himself in when his door beeped. He wanted to ignore it but found his hand tapping the admit button — with a hydraulic hiss the door rolled away and opened enough for Tammy to enter. When the door rolled shut, she kicked out against it and pushed herself towards him, stopping herself by grasping his cocoon. She stared at him, her blue eyes open and hurt.

"Why have you been such a jerk?"

"You forget yourself, Private."

She turned her head away from him, her body quivering. "Do you remember when you promised-"

"You must forgive me for any promises I may have made. We have finally found *her*."

Tammy took her time, swirled his words around in her head, like she might with one of agriculture's wines, tasting the information. When she finally spoke her voice was subdued, "Rhonda?"

"A skiff at least. We don't know how many the Swarm used against us. She might be aboard this one. We'll be announcing it to the rest of the crew tomorrow."

"And what of you and me?"

"You and me... we are no more."

Tammy pushed away from him. He could not look her in the eye and so stared out the porthole at the murky sea of stars instead.

"But they won't thaw her, not till we return to Earth. That's hundreds of years away! You'll never even meet her. John Fourteen, maybe Fifteen, will be the captain who'll awaken her. There is no reason for you, for me, to be alone."

"It would be inappropriate. My obligation is to Rhonda and once she is rescued I must respect the Original's wishes. We exist only for the mission." Even as he spoke the words he knew they were not his own, but the words of his Original, the words in the List.

"And this is what you really want?"

No. Not in a million years. "Yes."

Tammy left.

Weeks passed.

John spent them alone, either in the memory chamber or in his quarters studying the List. His Original's mind amazed him, the singularity of purpose to which the man had applied himself was beyond belief. To create laws to govern humankind, or at least the subset of humankind that existed on the spaceship. To change the manner in which humans lived, procreated, and interacted with one another. The will!

The computer beeped and John looked down at his monitor. The Vigilant had acknowledged that they were nearing a Swarm skiff and had unlocked the second item on the List for John to read. He sat down and absorbed the short essay. Almost every sentence mentioned Rhonda. Victory, John Original had written, was assured, because his love would not be denied. John admired the sentiment, if not the means.

The third, unread message on the list stared at him. He knew he would need to rescue Rhonda before he could read John Original's final thoughts. As he wondered which of the two goals mattered most to him his door chimed.

John had not spoken to Tammy since their fight and so was surprised when she entered his chambers. After cautious greetings she moved closer to him, her eyes teary and vulnerable.

She asked, "Do you ever wonder what the Swarm wants?" He had thought about it, many of the captains had, but there were no memories that revealed a satisfactory conclusion. He shrugged his shoulders.

Tammy said, "Many of us believe that the Swarm are used by others to collect... things. That's why the other skiff, generations ago, was found idling. I think it was waiting. I don't know why, but that's what I think."

As he stood there, staring at her, he thought of one possible reason: that the Swarm might be sent out as agents to collect specimens. For study, for sale, it did not matter. The Swarm might merely be a tool of another, more powerful race. The thought chilled him.

She sighed and pressed herself against him. "But worries alone did not drift me your way John. Most of the crew is... relaxing. There's to be celebration, music, dancing... one last hurrah before the battle. You should, no, you must come with me."

"And how would that look?" John asked, "for me, John Astor the Seventh, to have a woman other than Rhonda hanging on my arm? What would the crew think?"

He saw the pain on her face, knew that coming to see him had been no easy decision. She replied, "They might think you're a man!"

He bit his lip, a retort at hand, but his will insufficient to fling it. *When had he fallen in love with Tammy?* A life's unfairness gnawed at him. What should have been the simplest of situations was not, because this entire undertaking revolved around Rhonda and without John's love of her the mission was pointless. Without the mission neither he nor Tammy would exist.

"You should leave now."

"All of you are so willing to play the role of grisly undead marching troupe, following the orders of a dead bastard who had a hard-on for a girl, who by all rights," John began to speak but Tammy pushed his chest with her finger as if it were his mute button, "*by all rights* should be dead. He has given you this duty, this List, and you have no life of your own."

"And that," he said, waiting long enough to be sure she had finished, "is the point. I do not exist, except as an extension of him. You can't understand, you're a Prototype."

"Your precious John Astor was a Prototype."

"That's different."

"How?"

John shrugged the question away, it was unanswerable and they both knew it. "You should just go, this accomplishes nothing. The mission, my duty, your duty, it is clear."

"And what exactly is my duty?"

"To serve as a crew member and a surrogate mother to the next generation."

"A baby maker," she said, her eyes narrowing, "but John, what if I were already pregnant?"

A joyful horror rippled through his skin. "That's not possible. Medical would have insisted that you take the proper precautions and wait until a clone was ready for implantation."

"Ha! And if I did not follow these precautions?"

John again had no answer.

"John Seven. There will be a day when you realize that life is more than rules and procedures and tasks. You better hope that I am still here when that happens." She turned, her hair a flapping flag, withdrawn as her hand hovered over the door's panel, his last question making her pause.

"Are you pregnant Tammy?"

"Do you care, really?"

He did. If she were pregnant John Seven had failed his Original and his crew... could the captain be demoted? He felt for Tammy and the man he might have been, but at his core he needed to do right by his Original.

"We can end the pregnancy. We must."

"John, I am pregnant and I will have this baby and let everyone know that you are more than John Astor's puppet." She left and he stared out the porthole, his eyes brimming with tears.

The scales of the swarmlings were a dark bronze, the aliens insect-like as they slowly crawled over the skiff.

"There's a ship approaching," Tammy said from her post at communications. Hastings, they had found, could only work short shifts before becoming distracted.

"We know," John snapped, "the skiff-"

"Not the Swarm skiff," Tammy said, "there's another one. Sir."

"The rendezvous," John muttered and leaned forward in his seat to stare at the console on his armrest.

"What's that sir?" Portwell asked.

John clenched his fists. This other vessel was approaching on a trajectory to intercept the Swarm skiff. They could not fight two enemy ships.

John jumped to his feet. "Engage!"

"But sir-" Portwell swallowed his objection when he saw the look on John's face. The crew followed their orders as John explained.

"There's another ship coming to take our people. We must be quick, before it arrives."

"If we take any damage-"

"I know," John snapped. Crippling damage could prevent their escape from the second ship.

Portwell said, "Take us on a long loop then, we can-"

"No...a direct attack as I ordered. We will cut them through their middle before they can respond."

"We can't do that John. I have reviewed all the recordings of our previous engagement. I know how to-"

John stared at Portwell, aware of how often he had listened to this man and let him guide him through the difficult decisions. How Hastings Seven had rushed to lead a team to battle a shuttle fire in the launch bay and how Portwell urged John to open the airlocks when the fire threatened to grow out of control. "There are other Hastings," he had said, "but only one Vigilant." John had obeyed, given the order, and watched Hasting and a half-dozen others, along with the burning shuttle, drift into space. John turned his gaze back to the forward monitor.

"Straight ahead. Engage," John said. His crew obeyed.

The strafing run began, the Vigilant dropping so close to the skiff that John made out the faces of the aliens — they were long in jaw with a melted expression in which floated two big eyes and wrinkly mouth flaps. They never had a chance. As the swarmlings dismounted John saw the shadows of bodies within the transparent hull of the skiff, a morbid piñata stuffed full of frozen humans. One of those slumbering souls belonged to Rhonda. He *knew* it.

"*Fire!*"

Long energy-strands blasted out of the Vigilant. Swarmling flesh sizzled and parallel slits opened on their faces, long gills gyrating in agony. Ruptures split the creatures apart and their insides were scooped out to join stardust. The Vigilant shook and lights flickered as their underside was attacked by the surviving swarmlings. Portwell exchanged a cold look with John.

"Fighters, launch." The three remaining XT fighters, basically transport shuttles with weapons welded onto their wings, dropped into orbit around the starship and with their lower intensity lasers they scoured the Swarm from all angles. John watched the rear camera and saw a swarmling unfurl itself — a giant cloud of a creature when fully extended — and wrap its wing tightly around a fighter. With a quiver it crushed the small ship. When the wings opened the starship spun outwards, a dead lump of steel and flesh. The Vigilant's rear lasers punctured the creature's midsection and it joined its victims in cold death.

With victory in his grasp John Seven felt, for the first time, a connection with the man who had set this all in motion. Though he stared at Tammy, her face turned from his as she called out the combat results, he thought of Rhonda.

Portwell grasped John's shoulder and said, "You were right-"

"Sir!" Tammy screamed. He looked up, saw a swarmling appear, its wings outstretched like a gliding bat. Space disappeared as the scrunched head of the swarmling pressed against the bridge and covered all portholes, its gills flapping like crazy, the tendons in its wings visible, tensed like steel cable. The bridge began to collapse.

Not this! He was so close to finishing the mission. Even as he urged the crew to the exit he was shouting orders to activate the secondary bridge in Engineering. They piled into the pencil-tube and John stopped, hung onto a rung and looked back. A sucking sound filled his ears and he realized that the bridge was compromised. Tammy struggled to push herself away from her chair, the compression of the chamber hindering her movement. John moved forward to help, but Portwell pulled him back.

"You're the captain. We need you."

Tammy looked up and John stared at her as she kicked out with her legs, propelled herself towards them, her arms outstretched. She moved slowly as if space had become thicker. The bridge cracked in half like an egg. If John reached out he could almost grab Tammy and reel her in. It would take seconds. He thought of Rhonda, then of the child growing inside Tammy. An easy choice.

But for the mission.

Tammy screamed, perhaps seeing his decision on his face as John slammed his fist against the panel. He mouthed the words, "I love you." but turned away so he would not have to see Tammy's final expression as her fate was sealed with the hatch door.

They drifted. Victorious. They had lost the bridge, and two shuttles. Even now, while Engineering hustled to prepare the starship for her return voyage before the rendezvous ship arrived, others finished hauling the frozen cylinders aboard. They reminded him of test tubes and he thought of his own genesis in the lab. These humans had been born naturally. What did that mean? He stared down at Rhonda and saw her for who she was — just a girl, like any other. Her eyes still carried that shocked and horrified expression, her skin, waxen and lifeless as alien liquid pumped through her veins, keeping her alive indefinitely. This Rhonda was as alien to him as the swarmlings.

Tears streamed down John's face. *Your journey has been longer than life itself. Bring back my Rhonda, so that another John might finish what she and I started. But the mission is over. Live your life. Duty has been fulfilled. You have my eternal gratitude.* He had read that last message several times. All he had had to do was reach out his hand and grasp Tammy's and the lonely life awaiting him would have been filled with love, happiness.

He would promote Tammy from Prototype to Original and then order her cloned — her reward for her sacrifice. Her memories might be lost, but the child she would be might fill the hole in his heart. Or so he hoped.

"Set course, for Earth." John Seven said, and the crew cheered. John joined them. For he was captain and it was expected.

TEQUILA SUNSET

by Michele Garber

The repetitive blaring of Ashley's alarm clock is what wakes me. I pull the pillow tighter over my head, hoping she'll drag her little butt out of bed and address this unsavory state of affairs as quickly as possible. Did I mention the walls around here are paper-thin? The *wah, wah, wah* continues, unabated, as I fume. Why the hell would anyone in their right goddamned mind set their alarm on New Year's Day? Okay, so there are some good sales, big whoop, but Ashley's never struck me as the type to haul herself up and out by...sweet Jesus, eight a.m.? For 30% off? Not to mention most of the world would be coping with crashing headaches after a late night. Or an early morning, depending on how you look at it.

Then again, some of us are exempt. Me, I'm blessedly headache-free this morning, although I'm getting one from that friggin' noise. I pound on the common wall we share and yell, "Ashley! Shut that thing off!" No answer. I don't hear the floorboards creak, I don't hear water running, and I don't hear her say "sorry" like she usually does when her ditziness causes us all to want to kill her. I almost tripped and fell down the stairs once when she decided it would be a great idea to leave a few houseplants there, her idea of saying "how-do" in a cheerful sort of way to visitors, but forgot to tell any of us. Yeah. She's probably passed out drunk somewhere, leaving me to deal with the fallout from her carelessness.

I sigh and swing my legs over the edge of the bed, heaving myself into a standing position. Bathroom. I pee and rummage around in one of the microscopic cabinet drawers, coming up with the objects I'd hoped for: earplugs. I squish the screaming orange material into small cylinders and stop up my ears with it, groaning in relief as the noise fades into silence. Bliss. I crawl back between the covers and slip back into pleasant wish-fulfillment dreams of a world devoid of other people and their fuck-ups.

When I awaken later on the first thing I want is water. Even though I never get hangovers, I still get thirsty, you know? As I fill an old Tupperware cup with cool tap water, I toy with the idea of calling Jamie and going sledding today. I figure he'll probably be up and about by now even after our late night, headache or no. He doesn't answer his cell, so I leave a voicemail and pop a Sarah McLachlan CD in. There's a new fall of snow on the ground outside, glittering in the midwinter sun, and I'm eager to enjoy it after days of dreary gray slush. I don't see any cars on the road that threads its way along the river only a couple hundred feet away, which is unusual. *Guess everyone partied like it was 1999,* I snicker to myself. What is it about holidays and special occasions that causes everyone to drink themselves into oblivion? I can't figure it out. Then again, not everyone can hold their liquor like I can.

Here's the deal. I can't get drunk. Literally. I can drink several fifths of Southern Comfort (if I actually wanted to, that is—I think it tastes terrible) and not even catch that proverbial buzz everyone chases after. Mostly it sucks because I inevitably end up designated driver, like last night, although I *love* betting heavy-drinking frat boys I can drink them under the table. It's a hoot! They stumble and stagger around after drinking themselves half blind, but I could go out and pass any sobriety test you threw at me. My family doctor thought it was some incredibly rare genetic mutation that enables my body to cope with obscene amounts of alcohol. Winner of the genetic freak lottery, that's me. I turned him down for the whole "you too can be a research project" thing, and he wasn't very happy with me. Maybe I cost him his Nobel Prize or whatever, but what possible use could anyone have for knowing why I can drink huge quantities of alcohol and not die?

Anyway, I've had enough of waiting for Jamie to pull his sorry ass out of bed. The slopes await me.

I toss my sled, an orange plastic saucer, into the back of my Bug. The sky is a fantastic shade of cornflower blue, not a cloud in it, and I'm raring to go. No one's moving yet on my little street, populated mostly by college kids and people in their early twenties like me, and I feel smug, knowing that my odd genetic birthright lets me look like a fun-lovin' party girl without having to pay the price. Neat stuff.

I pull out onto the main road, still not seeing any cars. Maybe I missed the memo about New Year's Day—did somebody decide we should hide in our fallout shelters every year until the computers finally have their meltdown and launch strategic nukes in every direction?

I start whistling, "It's the End of the World as We Know It" by R.E.M. for fun as I stop at a traffic light. There's a 7-Eleven on the corner and I feel a sudden urge for a Cherry Slurpee, so I skip the light and wheel on in to the parking lot. There aren't any cars in the lot, not at all unusual—you'd be surprised how many people trek in on foot in the wintertime. I slot my VW into a place by the door, salivating in anticipation of cherry goodness.

The bell dings and dongs as I enter the store, but there's no one behind the counter. I walk toward the drink machines at the back and fill up, watching the gloppy frozen treat spill into the cup. I finish up and drift back down the snack food aisle, past the Cheetos and the Planter's Peanuts, and stand at the counter, waiting. Maybe the 7-Eleven worker is in the bathroom? *Helluva long bathroom break*, I think impatiently. Probably didn't hear me come in. I wander toward the back of the store calling, "Hello? Anyone there?" and there's still no answer.

This makes me worry. What if the guy (or gal) had a heart attack while perched on the throne? Pushing the door marked "Women" open with one hand, I see no one lying dead on the floor, much to my relief. Somewhat more hesitantly, I knock on the other door, announce myself, and scope out this one too. Nothing. Maybe they're on garbage detail? I poke my head outside, congratulating myself on my logical thinking, but see only a German Shepherd nosing among the detritus scattered around the dumpster. Huh. It's all very odd, but I've seen stranger things. I picture a disgruntled convenience store worker tearing off his smock and saying "screw it" to go party after his replacement fails to show up at eleven. It's what I would've done, but at least I would've locked up. I'm conscientious that way.

Speaking of, I go to the front of the store and leave two bucks as payment because I don't have correct change. Very annoying. I almost leave a note and then decide against it— hey, it's not my fault if people walk off the job! I step outside, sucking sweet red fluid through the straw, and wonder idly why nobody else has come in. Oh well, not my problem. I hop back into my car and fire it up, ready for a day of fun on the slopes.

I drive through the city toward Franke Park, one of the best places in Fort Wayne, Indiana to go sledding, in my humble opinion. The snowy streets are eerily deserted, and I realize, as I chug to a stop at a light and crack my window, that what really weirds me out is the absence of noise. I hear birds singing in the trees and the occasional squirrel chittering over nuts, but no human-made noises. No cars, no machines, no radios. It's so very quiet. Deserted. I'm suddenly uneasy, because in a city this size, there's always someone on heavily traveled roads like this one. Even on holidays like today.

I coast to a stop at another light where a beat-to-shit Ford Taurus is sticking out into the intersection, the right front tire bumped up against the curb. There's no crumpled metal or broken glass, so I'm betting the driver zonked out while waiting for the light to change. What I can't figure out is why it's still sitting there, idling. I mean, shouldn't the police be around? Rubberneckers watching the tow truck haul it away? Somebody?

Popping on my hazards, I get out and walk over to the hunk of junk that's spewing forth great clouds of foul-smelling exhaust, pressing my face up to the glass and shielding my eyes to see better into the dark interior. I can see someone in the driver's seat, but the tinted windows prevent me from seeing whether they're okay or not. I try the door and as it swings open, a woman falls out and onto the pavement, strange candy dropping from a vehicular piñata. Her body flops once as it smacks onto the hard ground, then lies still. I crouch down and reach out with a trembling hand, brushing the tousled blonde hair away from her neck as I take her pulse. Where there should be a pulse, I mean, because there's nothing. She's dead, and cold, and smells to high heaven of alcohol.

A shape jumps out of the car at me as I'm kneeling beside her and I scream loudly, scrabbling backward and away from the thing. And then I feel like a jackass.

It's a dog. One of those Jack Russell terriers that I'd love to have, except my landlord won't let us have pets. He whines and licks his owner's face, looking up at me beseechingly as if to say, "Can't you wake her? Won't you help?"

"Sorry, buddy," I say, patting him on the head shakily, "she's not gonna get up again." The little dog cocks his head to one side, tongue lolling. "I mean it. She's d-e-a-d, dead." I gather my scattered thoughts and try to come up with a plan. 9-1-1. That's what I'll do. I pull out my cell phone and dial, hoping they'll come take her body away and I can forget this ever happened. No one answers, no matter how many times I call. Not even "all circuits are busy now." Where *is* everybody?

Sinking down onto the curb, I wonder exactly what happened while I was sleeping. And how far it goes beyond this corner. I pet my new friend some more and procrastinate, because I'm afraid to find out.

I've been sitting here for the last twenty minutes, watching the traffic light switch between red, then green, then red again, as I try to decide what to do. Spent the first ten minutes panicking. Spent the next ten trying not to think at all. I haven't seen a single car, truck, or bike go by, let alone someone out on foot, enjoying this rare and sunny day in the Fort. In the twenty-odd years I've lived here, this is unprecedented. And frightening.

I decide to see what the neighbors have been up to during this whole fiasco and begin ringing doorbells, my new companion trailing me like a shadow, but there's no response. After the first five houses I start trying doors. There's a suspicion lurking at the back of my mind, but I don't want to contemplate that right now. I finally find an unlocked door and step inside, calling out that I need help.

No one answers.

I check all the rooms downstairs, finding no one in the kitchen slurping down coffee and coping with a hangover, no one watching football on TV in the living room, no one yarking up alcohol in the bathroom. Moving upstairs past framed school pictures and family photos, I push open a bedroom door and freeze. Two people are lying in bed, the covers pulled neatly up to their chins. "Hello?" I quaver, feeling my heart speed up. They don't respond.

I tiptoe over to the man, a middle-aged fatherly type with receding brown hair, and shake his shoulder. Nothing happens. Sliding my hand up to his cheek, I notice he's cold. Really, really cold. Which means he's really, really dead.

"Oh shit," I whisper, taking his pulse just to make sure. My internal smartass, trying to cope, comments, "Cold and clear today, with a slight chance of being dead." There's no blood anywhere, no bashed-in heads, no smell of gas from a leak. They look like they're sleeping. Or passed out cold, because both of them reek of that sharp, acrid, funky smell everyone gets after tying one on. I double-check the wife—dead. Before I leave the room, I pull the covers over their faces and say a silent prayer.

The bedroom next door is painted bright blue and filled with sports equipment and toys. There are bunk beds pushed against the far wall, and with a feeling of trepidation, I draw closer. Each bunk holds a small body, cold and lifeless, reeking of alcohol. The little terrier jumps up onto the lower bunk and licks the boy's face diligently, whining when he doesn't wake up. I wish I'd never come in here.

What parent would feed their kids lethal doses of alcohol and then put them to bed? The answer is none, unless they're totally nuts. Looking at the poor, pale faces of these babies, I feel dread stealing over me. What are the odds that all four would succumb to alcohol poisoning? Pretty slim, which tells me this was imposed on them—it wasn't a choice. And if that's true, then why am I still here, unscathed? I think I know the answer to that one—just call me *Mutant X*.

I exit the house and trudge back down the street to my car morosely, getting in and calling for "Buddy," my name for the little dog, to come. He leaps up into the passenger seat and I close the door. "Ready, Freddy?" I ask him, forcing cheerfulness, and he barks once. I prepare to drive away in search of someone awake and alive to explain it all, glancing toward the rent-a-wreck one last time.

It's gone.

My heart stutters a bit as I put the car into "park" and get out, shouting, "Hello?" The former driver's body has also disappeared. I see my own footprints clearly in the new snow but nothing else, not even tire tracks leading away from the scene. "Is somebody screwing with me?" I yell. My voice echoes against the silence and I feel cold inside and out, as the sound dies away in the brisk air—naked, and vulnerable. I find myself desperately wanting the two people who could make this feel tolerable, make me feel safe: my parents.

In case you've been wondering, no, I'm not the product of a government experiment gone wrong. My parents weren't mutants, or aliens. They were average, ordinary people, like anyone else. And yes, you can guess from the past tense, they're also dead.

I found them in the same state as the others, after I drove across the city in record time. No cops to pull me over for speeding, you see. Mom was asleep in her La-Z-Boy, as always. Dead, I mean. Dad was in bed, also deceased. Both smelled like a brewery, although neither of them used to drink more than a glass of alcohol at any given time. They looked peaceful, which is more than I can say for a lot of folks when they die.

I tried to bury them out in the backyard near the flowerbeds they loved so much in life, and ended up breaking the shovel on the iron-hard January earth. Then I went to Plan B, covering them with landscaping rocks from the garden as I alternated between weeping and swearing, my breath coming out as little white puffs in the chilly air. I conducted the best funeral service I could, under the circumstances. I figured hiring an undertaker was pretty much out of the question.

I'm not much of a detective, but after a good long cry I started poking around in the garbage and found only a single champagne bottle. Nobody dies after drinking a glass or two, do they? Has something screwed up everyone else's body chemistry but my own? When I figured out I had this bizarre immunity to alcohol, I started to research it on the sly. I never knew that everybody produces a teeny bit of alcohol in his or her digestive system until then, but we all do. What if the alcohol wasn't from drinking? With a sudden flash of clarity, I understand the basic mechanics of how people died, but there are other questions I can't answer.

For starters, how could this have happened to so many people at the same time? Everyone I've run across smells like they tried to obliterate themselves in a worldwide drinking contest. At least I suspect it's worldwide, because as I sit here in my parents' office surfing the Internet, I see that nothing's been updated, anywhere, since early morning. I don't see any pleas for help or information, and there aren't any stories about how weird things have gotten.

The same holds true for TV and radio, some channels still running off automation while others just go...dead, for lack of a better word. There aren't any stories about aliens landing, terrorists tampering with the water supply, people sickening and dying. Everything appears to have stopped after people fell asleep, tucked into their nice safe beds after ending the festivities, or passed out, and just never woke up again. I feel paralyzed as the mental Q & A ping-pongs around inside my head:

Who moved the car? How?

I don't know.

Why did this happen?

I don't know.

Am I imagining all this? Am I crazy?

I don't know.

Am I the only one left?

I don't know.

And what should I do now? Again, I have no idea. Now that the initial shock is wearing off, I'm realizing that I've got to start thinking in survival terms: food, water, heat, and so on. In a few days, maybe a week, I'll be living like folks did before the advent of electricity, running water, and mass communication. Part of me wants to crawl under the covers and join everyone else by never waking up again, although ironically enough, I'm probably not eligible for that exit strategy. I'm willing to give it the good old college try, though. Climbing into my old bed in the room I occupied as a child, I snuggle deep under the warm coverlet and fall into an uneasy slumber.

I wake to the sharp, jagged sound of rocks being displaced outside, and Buddy barking viciously as he tears around the house. Without bothering to put on any shoes, I run out into the backyard to find the landscaping stones flung in a wide circle away from the spot where I had carefully constructed my parents' graves. Their bodies have vanished. As I look frantically around me, there are again no footprints, no indications that they've been dragged away. "Who are you?" I scream up into the sky. "Why are you doing this?" My only answer is the wind whistling past my ears, a hollow, mournful sound. You could hear voices in that, if you listen long enough. The sun is going down behind the tree line, an inflamed reddish-orange ball of sailor's, but certainly not my, delight. No, I'm far from delighted—I'm petrified and pissed.

Movement flickers at the corner of my eye and I whirl around, flinching from whatever I might find. The neighbors' flag, flapping in the freshening breeze, that's all. I want to get out of here. I want to go right now, but I'm afraid to draw attention to myself. Forcing my numb, frozen feet to walk toward the sliding door, I slip inside past Buddy, who's still voicing angry little yips at whatever had been there. Wait, did I just say "whatever," not "whoever"? Going cold, I realize I no longer believe there's a human explanation for all this.

I remember reading once about an Eskimo village in Canada that disappeared in 1930—over 2,000 people. Even the dead had been dug out of the rock-hard, icy ground. What if it's happened again? Only this time it's the entire world, and there's no one left but me? I can feel the panic crawling up my throat like a huge, hairy black spider, choking me. I shove it back down ruthlessly. There's still time before nightfall to learn more.

    I dispense with the niceties and simply bust out a window in the neighbor's house to get inside. Their bodies are still tucked snugly in bed, with one bizarre change—they look mummified, withered, desiccated. "Human jerky?" I say aloud, belching out a little scream of laughter, which I promptly stifle by clapping a hand over my mouth. Wouldn't do to go crazy in Mr. and Mrs. Butler's house, now, would it? Not that there's anyone around to care.

    I'm halfway down the stairs before I hear a splintering, ripping sound behind me. I creep back the way I came, oh so stealthily, and peer around the corner. There's a hole in the roof, and the bodies are gone, like The Rapture has come and malfunctioned slightly in the retrieval process. "Oh God," I groan, stumbling back downstairs and out into the street.

    Letting my head fall backward, I gaze up into the fading blue of the sky and gasp. Silhouetted against the clear expanse are bodies, enough to nearly block out the sky, rising slowly from every house in this subdivision, this city, and beyond. There's nothing visible around them—they look like bait tied to clear strands of fishing line, dangling helpless and insensate. As I watch, horrified, the last remnants of humanity recede to black pinpoints and are gone from sight. I stand there for a very long time, waiting for whatever's next, until the sun slips below the horizon and terminates this first day of the new year.

    I think back to what I wished for yesterday morning—peace and quiet and a world without other people's fuck-ups—and regret it bitterly, because in that kind of world, this kind, there's also no room for the good stuff. I realize how much I'm going to miss, little losses and pangs at every turn. There won't be any more Cherry Slurpees or parties or my dad walking me down the aisle on my wedding day. I'd give anything for someone to yell at me right now and call me a selfish bitch, thinking only of myself and what I've lost, because then I wouldn't be alone anymore. But as I finish writing this account, my own personal journal of the world's end, I don't believe there's anyone left to read it. Not now.

    So that leaves me with a very important decision to make. Do I let us all go out with a whimper, quietly and unobtrusively, instead of the bang we all expected? Or do I make a date with a turkey baster before the lights go out and the chance is gone forever, a last-ditch effort to jumpstart humanity again, hoping for the best as the lonely, difficult years creak along? Before I decide, I'm going to make myself a Tequila Sunrise and hold my own personal wake for the human race, my own *Auld Lang Syne*, as I watch the sun come up for me alone.

GAUSS'S INVITATION

BY GARY CUBA

Rev. Richard Gauss
Denver, Colorado
September 3, 1908

Professor Doctor Hans Dorfenheimer, Göttingen, Germany

Dear Prof. Dorfenheimer:

In reply to your recent letter, I'm very sorry that I cannot offer any substantial help with respect to your inquiry. If I understood it correctly, you are exploring a possible connection between the unusual seismological & meteorological events that affected Russian Siberia in June of this year, and a queer notion once proposed by my grandfather, Carl Friedrich Gauss, in or about 1820.

Sadly, my father, Eugene Gauss, did not correspond with his father Carl, and consequently, nothing of interest passed to me after Eugene's death. Or, I should say, nothing passed but his own reflective memories of my grandfather.

Indeed, notwithstanding that Carl Friedrich Gauss was—and is still—universally regarded as the most brilliant polymath of his era, Eugene thought him to be a thoroughly despicable, crass, self-serving and uncompassionate person. That is why my father emigrated to America at the age of nineteen in 1830. So far as I know, he never contacted my grandfather following his relocation to this country.

As to your specific question of whether Carl Gauss had ever visited Russia to discuss his idea of creating, by means of selective cutting and planting, a Pythagorean symbol composed of "enormous swaths of trees" in Siberia, therewith to communicate our sentient existence to "people on nearby planets": I cannot answer that, lacking as I do any definite knowledge of it. But given the fact of his great reputation within international scholastic circles at the time, I am quite sure Prof. Gauss could have easily gained an audience with the Russian tsar—or entrance to the highest court of any European ruler of the era, for that matter.

But I emphasize that this is sheer speculation on my part. If it happened at all, I suspect it could only have been during the tsarist reign of Alexander I, who (if I have my history correct) was fairly liberal and worldly in matters of this nature. I think it much less likely to have occurred after 1825, under the rule of Alexander's more insular successor, Nicholas I.

If I may suggest it—and if you have not already done so—you should consider contacting the children of my deceased uncle William (Wilhelm) Gauss, also living in America. William maintained good relations with Grandfather Gauss, and I know they corresponded regularly. Perhaps one of his offspring can provide you with more concrete answers in the form of copies of written documents. I've enclosed a list of their names and current addresses with this letter.

Yours Very Respectfully,
Rev. Richard Gauss

P.S. — Being mildly interested in science & technology, I have read a few translated Russian newspaper articles covering the Siberian event in question, as they have filtered their way into the Western press. I remember in particular that these included eyewitness accounts from the indigenous natives living in Karelinski village, near to the site of the disturbance, who claimed to have seen a "bluish-white heavenly body, which for 10 minutes moved downwards" prior to the huge explosion. They described the body as a "pipe," or cylinder-shaped. It all seemed very odd to me.

Wm. S. Gauss, Jr.
St. Louis, Missouri
December 15, 1908

Professor Doctor Hans Dorfenheimer, Cambridge, England

Dear Sir:

How *dare* you impugn the reputation of my grandfather, the great Carl Friedrich Gauss! Shame on you, sir; shame on you for suggesting that he *in any way* instigated the current problems in Europe!

My grandfather was a loving man, a doting father, a gentle soul, generous to a fault, and a true friend of all humanity. If you could but read the many intimate letters that he wrote to my father, William Sr.—which are now in my possession—this would become plainly obvious.

However, copies of these letters will not be forthcoming, as I am convinced you will twist and distort them to serve your own questionable ends. Yes, some of them may be pertinent to your inquiry—specifically, those letters relating to my grandfather's accounts of his activities between 1820-1825. But I will not give you the pleasure of learning their finer content.

I put it to you, sir: Is it not a much more likely hypothesis that the recent proliferation of gas and electrical lighting used across the globe was the thing that attracted the attention of these "Martians," whose nefarious engines of destruction now strut unimpeded across the Eurasian landmass? I would certainly think so.

In any event, while I am sorry for your recent personal travails and your forced relocation from your homeland, I remain convinced that this is a European problem, and, in consequence of that, its solution lies rightfully in European hands. You have cannons and armies of your own. America need not become involved in the morass.

The ocean is wide and deep, sir, and we do not have time to intervene with your issues. We have better business to attend to.

Yours,
William Gauss, Jr

GAUSS'S INVITATION

Miss Wilhemina Gauss
Sacramento, Calif.
February 4, 1909

Professor Doctor Hans Dorfenheimer, New York

My Dearest Professor Dorfenheimer,

Oh! how my heart ached when I read your recent post. You poor, poor man, to have suffered and lost so much. I am overjoyed that you have managed to reach America in the midst of the calamity that now befalls the rest of the world. Yet I worry that our safety is not secure, that the machinations of our celestial enemy are focused on finding a way to overcome the American continent at this very moment.

I cannot express how sorry I am that my brother William was not responsive to your inquiry. He is a wealthy businessman, conservative in his politics—and I always knew him to be somewhat lacking in basic human compassion. God forgive me for saying this of my own flesh and blood, but it is nothing but the truth.

Yet I am glad to hear that my cousin Richard was more sympathetic to your cause. He is a good man, a kind, God-fearing and discerning individual.

My brother William holds physical claim to those of grandfather's letters which passed down from our father, so I am unable to provide you with any tangible documentation to support your hypothesis. However, I once read each and every one of those letters, and I remember their contents very well. Even though old age may rattle my body to its bones, my mind remains clear as a crystal goblet.

While it seems a moot point at this horrendous juncture in our world's history, I can tell you, unequivocally, that my grandfather indeed visited Russia on several occasions— specifically, in 1821, 1823 and 1824. More to the point, as related in his correspondence, he did so in conjunction with his scheme to establish a "Pythagorean message" in Siberia, just as you surmised in your letter. While he knew he would likely not live to see the fruits of his idea ripen, those seeds were nevertheless sown, literally.

It is not surprising to me that no other records of this project can be found. One need only consider the disruptive history of Russia over most of the last century to explain part of it. On my grandfather's side, he was always known to be reluctant to publish anything before it reached a state of full intellectual maturity.

Here is what I believe, based on the facts as I know them: That my grandfather, Carl Friedrich Gauss, did indeed persuade tsar Alexander I to craft a gargantuan arboreal symbol on the face of the Earth so as to communicate our human intelligence to the universe at large; that this symbol, once it achieved its full-grown glory, was noticed at length by the people on Mars; and that those people, living as they are outside of God's influence, found the notion of our separate existence so obscene, so abhorrent that they could think of no other recourse but to attack and destroy us. I presume it took them a number of years to develop the means to do this.

I'm quite sure tsar Alexander is now rolling in his grave, since he surely must have believed such extraterrestrial people, if they existed, would pay honor to the Russian Empire as the highest exemplar of the human species—being that the geographic locus of that incredible invitation lay within his borders. Instead, his was the first country to be destroyed by the invaders!

I further believe the Martians blew up the Siberian symbol with some manner of powerful explosive as they steered their massive warship through our Earth's aether. That would account for the registration on your various & sundry scientific instruments (whose methods of operation will, I fear, forever remain arcane to me). I think these off-world entities did that out of sheer spite, as a means of announcing their presence and malicious intent.

But I am a silly goose, much given to flights of fancy. I read too many romantic fantasies. In truth, I am nothing but an elderly spinster lady who knows nothing of the wider world or of worlds outside this one; nor do I know anything of science or technology. I only know that I am very afraid for all of us.

Please sir, I invite you—no, I *implore* you: Make your way to Sacramento where you will find succor while you repair your physical and intellectual health. Call it woman's intuition, but I do not trust the safety of the East Coast.

With Great Fondness and Sympathy,
Weenah (Wilhemina) Gauss

GAUSS'S INVITATION

Rev. Richard Gauss
Denver, Colorado
March 28, 1909

Professor Doctor Hans Dorfenheimer, Sacramento, California
(c/o Wilhelmina Gauss)

Dear Prof. Dorfenheimer (and my favorite cousin Weenah),

I was happy to receive Weenah's telegram concerning your safe arrival in Sacramento. I'm sure my cousin is taking good care of you! I can only advise you to lie back and enjoy it while you can.

Sadly, things remain ominous on the Eastern front—as I assume both of you already know from your own newspapers. Everything east of the Mississippi now appears to be under Martian control. St. Louis lies in ruins, and I fear for the fate of William and his family.

We've been getting quite a massive influx of refugees here in Denver. They are a ragged lot, bone-tired, starving, utterly pathetic individuals. I and my fellow citizens have opened up our homes and hearts to help accommodate them until other arrangements can be made. Unfortunately, it's hard to see what those precise arrangements would be, at this tumultuous juncture.

We hear late reports of Martian forays into Kansas, although the advance of the enemy's main front appears to have halted at the Mississippi. I presume this is only a temporary cessation of hostilities, a short pause in their forward drive taken for the purpose of "consolidating their gains" in the East.

Of course, this is just a delicate euphemism for the Martians' actual *modus operandi*, which is to seek out and annihilate all human life. I expect I'll be forced to move westward soon enough, as just another scuttling refugee. Do you have a spare corner in which I may rest my weary head, Weenah?

We are all getting much too old for this.

Tell me, Professor, now that we know with reasonable certitude what brought the Martians here, have you conceived of an equally persuasive symbol to make them go away?

Forgive me my sarcasm, please. I haven't gotten much sleep lately.

Until we can meet again under better circumstances—whether it be in this world or in the next, more sublime one—I give you both my most heartfelt regards,

Richard

Nikola Tesla
Vancouver BC, Canada
April 15, 1909

Prof. Dr. Hans Dorfenheimer, Sacramento, California

Dr. Hans D.:

Forgive the haste with which I compose this note, as I am very busy at the moment. I learned of your queer hypothesis regarding the genesis of the recent Martian visitation from a mutual friend, Prof. Larsson, late of Stockholm, who is presently residing—I should say "hunkering," as are we all—in Duluth, Minnesota.

I must tell you that I chuckled heartily when I heard your theory—but warmly so, I assure you. At last, someone blames a person other than *me* for the awful circumstances we now endure! For it is a fact that many have pointed to my experiments in high-energy signal transmission, which I conducted between 1902-1906 at Wycliffe, New York, as instigating the Martian attack—and which, to their minds, formed sufficient grounds to lynch me from the nearest lamppost. That is in large part the reason for my recent relocation to Canada.

In fact, I have been convinced of the existence of intelligent extraterrestrial life since 1899, fully ten years ago. I drew this conclusion from radio signals I received unexpectedly while experimenting with long-distance wireless telegraphy and power transmission at my laboratory, then located in Colorado Springs. I knew from the direction of their source that the signals were not of Earthly origin, but rather came from a place external to our home globe.

No one believed me then, but no matter. It was nothing but another dreary page in an equally dreary book already filled with the professional slights and undeserved bad luck that characterize the greater part of my career.

Unfortunately, while I now slave feverishly to complete an electrical weapon that can be used against the foul Martian invaders, the work would have come much easier if I'd received the financial recompense that my prior inventions and ideas deserved. Most of the fruits of my many valuable inspirations were stolen, or reneged upon, or sucked away by those several individuals who have unconscionably taken my ideas and practical groundwork as their own. (As merely one example, I can only hope the bones of that Dago bastard Guglielmo Marconi now lie in a charred heap on unconsecrated ground!)

I hesitate to ask this of a colleague, but do you have access to any funds you can send my way, to help further my efforts here in Vancouver? Anything at all would be greatly appreciated. (I currently am in demand of large amounts of high-purity copper wire—extremely large amounts of it, in fact.) Consider it a down payment on our survival as a species—something I can promise to deliver if and when I ever gain the capital means to complete this very complex, advanced machine of mine!

Yours Expectantly,
N. Tesla

Prof. Jason Wagner
Los Angeles, Calif.
April 30, 1909

Prof. Dr. Hans Dorfenheimer, Sacramento, California

My Dear Prof. Dorfenheimer,

I read your recent letter with great interest. Its background seemed incredible to me, but I am forced to take it as truth, owing to your very sagacious and persistent historical detection efforts. Kudos to you for that!

As you properly pointed out, an image of the Pythagorean design you described—namely, a right triangle with squares extending from each side—would of course be "incorrect" if rendered on a spherical surface. For that matter, it would be just as incorrect if rendered on a negatively curved (e.g., a saddle-shaped) surface. The triangle's angles would not total 180 degrees, and the squares would not be "true." In either situation, the areas of the sides' squares, whose surfaces would be either geodesic or hyperbolic according to the case, would not tally up correctly to yield the Pythagorean equivalency.

Further, we must assume that Prof. Gauss knew this to be true. Although the earliest publications relating to non-Euclidian geometry are normally credited to Lobachevsky in 1829, and to Bolyai's independent work just a few years later, Gauss claimed to have explored these mathematical spaces a number of years prior. Unfortunately, he did not deign to publish anything of his earlier work in this area.

As to your speculations about how this "error" may have played out in the minds of our Martian enemy, I'm afraid you're on your own, there. While I admit to reading the "scientific fictions" of Mssrs. Verne and Wells for diversion and pleasure, I have a hard time relating such wild tales to happenings in the real world—including even its crueler and more unusual vagaries like the one that now impinges upon all of us.

Yes, I suppose the Martians could possess an odd enough mentality that they construed the mathematical error as anathema, something that must needs be extinguished from the universe quickly and without remorse, at whatever cost.

I can even add my own speculation here, that Gauss's original hope was for his intentional error to provide a greater inducement to off-world people to visit, so that they might offer their advanced knowledge to help "correct" our apparent failings in a peaceful and magnanimous manner—and in the process of doing so, to provide additional benefits of a wondrously advanced nature to our Earthbound race.

But these suppositions are all too tenuous; I cannot force myself to assign them as much as an ounce of credibility. Moreover, even if either were to be true, I hardly see what practical value it can have for us at this late stage of our demise.

I wish you well, sir, and I hope against hope that we both live long enough to dwell at length upon these notions in person someday, in calm, retrospective fashion over a glass of warm brandy.

Very Truly Yours,
Jason Wagner

P.S. — I've taken the liberty of forwarding your letter to Dr. Sigmund Freud, late of Vienna, now the new head of our Dept. of Behavioral Psychology. He may have something further to add on the subject.

Rev. Richard Gauss
Denver, Colorado
July 7, 1909

Prof. and Mrs. Hans Dorfenheimer, Sacramento, Calif.

Dear Hans and Weenah,

So very much has happened over the last few weeks, I hardly know where to begin!

But surely, the first order of business is to congratulate the two of you on your recent marriage. My only sorrow is that I could not have been there to perform the rites myself. I admit to being perplexed about one thing though, Weenah: Why did it take you *seventy-five years* to find the right man?! I jest, of course. I trust you'll forgive me my levity; recent events have made me somewhat giddy. Seriously, I am overjoyed that Providence worked to bring you both together at long last in order to solve Nature's most sublime and sweetest mystery, that of love.

And more solutions have come in the wake of your union. Following your suggestion, Professor, the Marconi radio wave transmitter we erected on the summit of Pike's Peak went into energized operation in mid-June, beaming a continuous, sequential series of non-repetitive random number pulses across the High Plains region, powerful enough to cover the entire Martian front and resonate within any electrical apparatuses that would have controlled the enemy's war engines and their means of communication.

As you suspected—and for reasons we are likely never to fully understand—the Martians were indeed mortally afraid of any manifestation of irrational, irresolvable mathematics. And as your colleague Dr. Freud in Los Angeles correctly observed, any sufficiently powerful fear, if not otherwise controlled, must inevitably lead to reactive obsession, neurosis, and after that, psychosis and eventual dissolution.

Such was the case with this peculiar Martian race. They simply could not withstand being inundated with numerical data that had no basis for solution, no rhyme or reason to it—they could only interpret the ever-expanding number set as a "mathematical error" of the highest order. Ultimately, the stark terror of it drove them totally, irrevocably insane.

We are receiving early reports from our eastern patrols, returning with news of toppled, inert Martian machines strewn across the wide prairies. Inside them lay the dead and rotting corpses of the Martians themselves, their bloated octopoidal forms horrific to behold. There is evidence aplenty to show that they took their own lives.

However unlikely it may be that they possessed divine souls, I still pray for them; I hope that our Lord, whose unbounded mercy and grace must surely extend throughout the Infinite Universe, will forgive them and offer them some manner of final peace.

GAUSS'S INVITATION 169

I also hope, as we put our world back together again in the coming years, that we can conquer our own innate fears and compulsions—the darker parts dwelling within each of us, which have led us to make so many similar, disastrous mistakes throughout our own planetary history.

But this should be a day of rejoicing! Weenah, you will undoubtedly have your hands full dealing with the accolades, the ceremonies, the relentless press of worshipful citizens as they do rightful honor to the greatest hero on Earth: your husband, Professor Doctor Hans Dorfenheimer. Huzzah!

I will visit you in Sacramento as soon as local matters settle down a bit here. In the meantime, may we all pause to thank God for preserving us through the action of His most blessed gift: our human intellect, and the unbridled creative capacity that abides within.

With Love, Respect, and Grateful Appreciation,
Richard

(*Author's note: Carl Friedrich Gauss's 1820 proposal to create a huge arboreal Pythagorean diagram in Siberia as a means of communicating with extraterrestrial beings is factual.*)

ANOTHER END OF THE WORLD

by Michael Penkas

Gail hung up the telephone and began to cry. She hated crying and she hated Roger for making her cry.

Her son Steven ran into the room, out of breath and covered in dirt. She smiled through her tears and was about to tell him to go wash up when he said, "Mom, there's an alien in the backyard."

Gail took a deep breath. "Son of a bitch."

She slammed her fist onto the table, just missing the telephone. "Son of a bitch!"

Steven took a step away, his eyes tearing up. He turned to run, but she said *Wait* and he stopped.

Gail got up and went to her son. He was crying by the time she took him in her arms. "It's okay, honey," she said, swaying him gently as they both stood in the doorway. "I'm not mad at you. I just ... got some bad news. I'm not mad at *you*."

Steven was crying into her stomach. "What's wrong?"

"Nothing." She pushed him back to arms' length, still holding him by the shoulders. "Nothing's wrong. It's just that Dad's not coming home tonight. He has to work late and he's staying at a motel instead."

"Can we go see him?"

She shook her head. "No. He needs to sleep. It's just that I miss him and I was a little sad that he wouldn't be coming home tonight." She looked her son over. "What were you doing?" His face and hands were dirty. The knees of his jeans were caked with mud and grass.

His eyes lit up. "There's an alien in the yard, by the pond." He turned to look towards the back door. "He was just walking around."

Gail stood up and, still holding her son's hand, said, "Well, let's go have a look."

Two hours later Steven was safely over at a friend's house and Gail was putting on her protective goggles in the back yard. Her mother was kneeling beside her, also wearing goggles. Spread around the women were two spades, a shovel and a garden hose. Both of them were staring at the pond.

It was about five feet across and two feet deep. Roger and Gail had put it together four years before when they'd first moved into the house. It was a black plastic lining lined with large stones. On the picnic table near the back door was a ten gallon aquarium holding the dozen goldfish that normally lived in it.

Her mother said, "Well, let's get on with it."

The two women began removing the stones that encircled the pond, setting them to one side and checking the spaces beneath them. After the fifth stone, Gail's mother said *Ahh*. She picked something up and held it on her finger. Gail shuffled over to see what she'd found.

The alien stood an inch tall, dressed in a beige body armor that made it look like an ant standing upright. If it spoke, its voice was far too faint for either woman to hear. It pointed towards Gail's mother and, before either woman could react, a faint red beam struck her goggles.

With one quick motion her mother brought a thumb down on the alien, crushing it. She let the corpse fall to the ground then went back to work.

Once all of the stones were removed, the two women considered the lining.

"Should I get a bucket?" Gail asked.

"No. We'll just pull the matting out and let the water soak into the ground. That'll loosen up the soil."

Gail nodded. It would also flood any facilities that had been built beneath the pond. As they began pulling at the edges of the plastic, she saw that it was an ideal location for a secret base. The pond placed the aliens close to human habitation without much danger of discovery. It was the one part of the yard that never got mowed and where there was an ample supply of water.

It took several minutes to pull up the lining. They stood on opposite ends of the pond, each picking up an edge, then lifted the entire thing. It was quite heavy at first, but as they continued the water poured out the front. By the time it was empty, both women were sweating.

Gail handed her mother a bottled water and sat down to watch the water seep into the soil. "How's Dad?"

"Oh, same as ever. I'm just glad I answered the phone when you called. Otherwise he would have insisted on coming over."

"I hadn't thought of that." Gail's father had begun collecting alien technology seven years ago. Since his retirement, his idle hobby had become something of an obsession. "Maybe we should set aside something for him when we—,"

"Absolutely not! He's already filled the basement with this crap. Besides, if he knew there were aliens here, he'd be over to dig up the entire yard."

"I guess."

"He's already had one heart attack."

"Yeah." Gail didn't like thinking about her father's heart attack. It was what had prompted his early retirement. Gail didn't think she was ready to deal with the loss of a parent. They were both still so young. Neither of them had even turned sixty.

Water from the pond had sunk halfway down. She tried not to think about what was happening beneath the surface. If there were living facilities down there, they probably weren't airtight. They'd be filling with water right now; flooding out and drowning the inhabitants. Men and women, far from home, probably with families waiting for them in some other star system.

But this was war.

The aliens had made their declaration nearly ten years ago. Even when it had become evident that they were hopelessly outmatched, they continued to fight. Pride prevented them from admitting defeat and now Gail and her mother were going to kill untold numbers of them.

"What about Roger?"

"Hmm?" Her mother was staring at her. "Roger? How is he? Still putting in his eighty hour weeks?"

Gail nodded. "Yeah. He's really busy these days."

"He should slow down. I know money's important but he'll never get this time back with his son."

"I know."

"Your father didn't work nearly his hours. I worry about him."

"Don't." She turned away from her mother and stared back at the hole, now three quarters empty of pondwater. "He's fine." For a moment, she was glad the aliens were dying. Then she felt guilty.

Her mother put a hand on her shoulder. "I'm sorry. I didn't mean to upset you. Roger takes care of himself a lot better than your father did. I'm sure he'll be fine."

As the last remnants of water seeped away, Gail whispered, "He's seeing someone."

The hand fell from her shoulder. "What?"

"Roger. He's seeing another woman. He spends two or three nights a week in motels with her. He says he's working late. And he is. But he's also seeing another woman."

"You don't know --"

"Would *you* know? If it was Dad, would you know?"

Gail stood up and grabbed a shovel.

"Gail?"

"Let's just do this. Okay?" Staring down into the hole, she saw gray patches of metal popping up from the soil.

She drove the shovel down, bringing up earth and metal. She turned it over so that it fell back into the hole, then dug in again. And again. And again.

There was no sound coming from the hole. All around her was broken metal and dirt. She continued picking up the pieces with the shovel, then tossing them back to the ground. There was an occasional scraping sound as the iron blade dug through the flimsy extraterrestrial metal no stronger than foil.

Her arms and face stung as pink beams of light issued from the wreckage, dotting her with little temporary freckles. The only danger from the aliens' death rays was that one might strike an eye ... hence the protective goggles. Otherwise, they hurt less than mosquito bites. She raised up the shovel, ready to bring it down on the entire strike team, when her mother said, "Gail!"

She turned and saw that her mother was holding the garden hose. "Get out of there."

Gail stepped out of the hole while her mother turned on the hose and re-flooded it. As the water drained into the soil again, she saw dozens of small brown spots float to the surface. She could have mistaken them for clumps of dirt, except that some were struggling to get to dry land.

"Steven wanted to know if he could keep one," she said.

"He's just like your father. Those two." Her mother smiled weakly. "Don't --"

"What do I tell him?"

"Tell him they went away. Tell him they went back to their planet. We'll put the plastic back down, re-fill the pond, put the fish back and he won't even know the difference."

"What am I going to do?"

Her mother put down the garden hose and sat beside her, knowing they were no longer talking about aliens. "You'll take it day by day. If Roger's ... well, whatever happens, you know your father and I will be there."

"I know." She wiped her eyes, then laughed as her hand knocked against the goggles. "What a day."

"Yeah."

Another pink ray stung her arm and Gail looked down to see one small alien standing a foot away from them, firing from one woman to the other. Gail's mother reached out to swipe at it but Gail put a hand on her shoulder.

"No. Just let him go. It doesn't matter."

The alien continued shooting at them for another minute. Then, perhaps realizing the futility of what it was doing, stopped firing and walked away.

"So you're all right?" Roger's voice betrayed no concern. He was merely assessing the situation like a business proposal.

Gail sipped her coffee and nodded, as if he could see the gesture through the telephone. "Everything's fine. Mom and I already put everything back. Steven's spending the night over at Sean's house. By tomorrow, he'll probably have forgotten that he even saw anything back there."

"Well, good. I'm sorry I couldn't be there to help, but you know how it is."

"I know how it is," she said. "You know, I was thinking. A lot of your work is reading and writing, isn't it? I mean, ad copy, memos, research?"

"Yeah."

"Well maybe you could look into working from home one or two days a week. I mean, you can sit here and read a manual just as easy as you can sit in your office and read it. And with e-mailing and videoconferencing--"

"Look, I can't do that, Okay? I mean, I've thought about it too but I really need to be available. Sometimes at a moment's notice. And we know that there will be distractions if I stay at home."

"We can set up the guest room as an office. You can work in there and no one will bother you."

"No."

"I was reading about how home offices are becoming normal in alot of -"

"*No!*"

Gail gritted her teeth. She wiped the start of a tear from her eyeand allowed herself get angry instead.

"So will you be home tomorrow night?"

"I really don't know."

"Steven said he'd like to come visit you some time."

"That's ... once this account is settled up--"

"There'll be another one. There's been another one for the last three years. And every one is critical."

"They are all critical. Look, maybe you think it's just me sitting here reading and writing, but we are under constant deadlines and every client *is* threatening to leave us *all the time*. Every day we're in danger of losing this one or that one and if I lose one, *even one*, then I'm a little more disposable then the guy sitting in the office next to me. Okay? I'm not happy about the hours either, but it's what has to be done."

"I could go back to work. I could re-certify, do some tax prep from home. You could find a job that doesn't keep you on the edge. We could slow down."

"I have to go, Gail." The line went dead.

He hadn't said that he loved her. But then, he hadn't said it in a long time.

It was four in the afternoon and the house was empty. Steven was spending the night with his friend. Her mother had gone home to wash up and check on her father. Roger wouldn't be coming home tonight. All the aliens in the backyard were dead, dying or fleeing the area.

She was almost sorry that she'd killed the aliens. It would have been nice to have some company.

Roger hadn't come home the following night either. After tucking her son into bed, Gail stayed awake in bed for a long time. She'd lied to Steven about the aliens going back to their home planet, as her mother had suggested, and that seemed to satisfy him. Then she spent the day investigating her own job options. She sent out for information on re-certifying as an accountant and put together a list of firms that might consider hiring her part-time, at least during the tax season.

Despite the last three years of lonely nights, she still reached for the empty side of her bed. When she finally fell asleep she dreamt about her own childhood. Steven was there and they were friends. It was a good dream, but it was interrupted by the sound of breaking glass.

"Roger?" She was still half-asleep. She tried to remember what had woken her. Breaking glass. A window.

She got out of bed, put on a pair of slippers and stepped into the hallway. She was halfway down the hall when something the size of a basketball floated up the stairs into view. There were green lights glowing on the sides of it. She couldn't make out any further details, but she knew what she was seeing. There was a familiar padding of footsteps between them that brought up the hairs on her arms. "Mom?" Steven called as he stepped out of his room and into the hallway.

"Steven, back in your room!"

He looked at her with sleepy confusion, not noticing the ship that floated five feet from his head. "Mom?"

"*In your room now!*"

Her son slipped back into his bedroom as the ship darted for him, slamming against the doorway before following him in.

Gail ran towards her son and found him on his bed. It seemed to wobble a bit in the air, as if the knock against the doorway had shaken some piece of equipment loose. She lunged for it, but the ship moved out of her reach and aimed for her son again.

This time, however, Steven was wide awake and able to dodge the damaged craft. The room was filled with a faint red glow as a dozen rays shot from it towards them.

She managed to grab hold of the ship before it could make a third attempt at striking her son, but was surprised to find that it resisted her. This was far larger than the one-man ships that usually bothered people. Probably a command vessel seeking revenge for the hundreds she'd murdered at the fish pond.

The ship rose towards the ceiling and pulled Gail with it. "Go to the neighbours!" she yelled. "*Call the police* Her son simply stood there, unbelieving.

"*Do it!*"

He ran out of the room.

The ship tried to follow, but her weight was just enough to slow it to a near-halt. Her hands stung from dozens of ray blasts burning into her palms.

If I could get some leverage, she thought, *maybe I can throw it against a wall.*

She looked around Steven's bedroom for something she could use against the ship. Something that would make a good weapon. There was a shelf full of books, a row of pirate action figures on his desk, and a baseball bat lying on the floor.

She let go of the ship and ran for the bat. She turned, already mid-swing, when the ship slammed into her back and knocked her further into the closet. The ship fired again and more rays stung her arms and face. She swung the bat wildly but missed, and the ship hit her shoulder, not breaking bone but causing her to drop the bat.

She heard a door thrown open. Steven was heading out in search of the neighbors. Despite the adrenalin pumping through her she sighed in relief. Her son was safe. Everything else was negotiable.

She reached for the bat as the ship shot towards her again, this time hitting her leg. When she stood up, her leg ached. It wasn't broken, but she'd be limping. There was no way she'd be able to outrun the ship now.

She held the bat up to protect her head. So far it hadn't built up enough speed to break any bones. As long as it didn't strike her head she could probably tough it out. Even if she never hit the ship with the bat, there was only so many times it could ram into her before sustaining fatal damage itself. And if it did go for a head-shot, she'd bring the bat right down on top of it. She wasn't sure if that would completely destroy it but she was certain that the crew wasn't eager to find out.

The ship wavered in the air as though the crew was considering a next move. A pink light shone on Gail sporadically. She smiled and took a limping step out of the closet.

"Not sure what to do now?" She took another step. "How about we try the other way around? " It was hard to breathe. The first strike to her back had hurt more than she'd originally thought.

She was about to swing; to throw everything into one shot and take the ship down, but there was a sudden explosion and the ship slammed against the wall of the bedroom. It slumped to the floor with a crack and smoke poured from it.

Turning, Gail saw her son standing in the doorway with a gun in his hand. The gun was pointed at the spot where the ship had been a moment earlier but the boy's eyes were on Gail. He was shaking.

"Mom?"

The adrenalin rush was gone. Gail fainted.

Two days later, she dropped an over-sized Tupperware container on her father's work bench with a little more disgust than she'd meant to show.

Her father popped the lid and smiled as he pulled out the wrecked spacecraft. "Yeah, this is a flag ship. Quite a catch."

"Steven 'caught' it," she muttered.

"Steven?" He ran a hand along the punctured side. "How?"

"He shot it with Roger's gun. The gun that he showed our nine year-old son without telling me."

Her father shook his head and peered into the Tupperware, pulling out little bits of paneling that had fallen off the ship. "Well, really, I was eleven when my dad taught me how to shoot. I know it's hard for women to --"

"I wouldn't care if he'd taught him how to shoot. He just showed Steven where the gun was and left it at that. 'Just in case,' he told me. Didn't take him down to a range or anything. Just showed him where the gun was, didn't bother to tell me that he'd armed our son without taking the time to teach him anything."

"Well, that's just irresponsible."

"Dad!"

He looked up at her uncomfortably.

"Dad, I'm thinking of leaving him."

He nodded as he patted a stool beside him. She sat down and he put an arm on her shoulder. "Your mother told me you were having trouble. With his long hours and everything."

"And sleeping with his assistant. Yeah."

Her father sighed and she grabbed hold of the hand on her shoulder. He seemed so old. Ever since the heart attack, it was like he was half-alive.

She looked around at the assortment of broken ships, laser cannons and unidentifiable chunks of technology. Lining a wall were probably a hundred vials, each with a dead alien contained in preserving fluid. Piled on one side of his work bench were books and magazines dealing with alien technology. A couple of battered notebooks were in the pile as well. Against the wall were pliers, magnifying lenses and other tools that he used in studying his collection.

"It keeps getting bigger," she said.

"I buy a lot of stuff online. Frankly, I was thinking of picking up a flag ship from one of the vendors, but they're pretty expensive."

"Well, I knew you'd be interested and, frankly, I couldn't stand having the thing in the house."

He nodded. "So, what did you say to Steven? About the gun?"

"Well, it's hard. Because he was trying to protect me, but I don't like him having access to a gun. I don't think he'd ever hurt anyone, but I still think it's dangerous."

"I could teach him to shoot if you wanted." He sounded hopeful.

Gail never wanted her son to handle a gun again but at the same time, she knew that it was already there. There was no way she could convince him that they were too dangerous to handle now that he'd used one to save her. She squeezed her father's hand. "I think that would be a good idea."

"And you know, as far as Roger goes, whatever you do, your mother and I will be there for you."

"Mom said the same thing."

"It's how we both feel."

"No, I mean, Mom said the exact same thing. I guess I want advice. What do you think I should do?"

" I really don't want to say. When your mother and I got engaged, my parents hated her. They thought she was too bossy. The word 'bitch' was thrown around a lot. It basically came down to them saying I had to choose between them and your mother and well, I think it always hurt them that I chose her."

"But you made up with them?"

"Eventually, but it was never quite the same. Your mom and I never want to force that choice on you. Our opinion of him shouldn't matter. It's how *you* feel."

Gail sat with her father, wishing there was someone she could talk to about Roger who wouldn't give a bunch of noncommittal bullshit when there was a knock at the door.

Her mother walked in with Gail's cell phone. "Gail, honey? This was ringing a minute ago. By the time I'd found it, whoever was calling had hung up."

Gail took the phone and checked the recent messages. When she saw the ID name of the most recent caller, she stood up. "I'll ... uh, I'm going to take this in the living room. Okay?" She left her parents in the basement and hit re-dial halfway up the stairs.

The name on the caller ID was Connie Willis. Roger's assistant.

At six o'clock, Gail was waiting for her husband at the front door holding a frying pan and a baseball bat. After speaking with Connie, she knew he'd be home on time.

Sure enough, at five past six, he pulled up in the station wagon, parking it in the driveway. She stepped out of the front door as he was getting out of the wagon and ran towards him, a weapon raised in each hand.

"Gail?" Confusion melted into fear as she drew closer. "I didn't --"

She knocked him against the wagon and pressed the frying pan in his hand. "*Shut up,*" she hissed as the first of the fighters crashed into her shoulder.

She screamed and swung blindly in the direction of the attack, destroying another fighter by sheer luck. Looking up, she saw dozens of them swarming out from the surrounding trees. "*Move!*"

Their only good fortune seemed to be that there were no flagships like the one that had attacked the other night. But the sheer numbers threatened to overwhelm them, especially since they all seemed intent on suicide missions. The wide open space allowed these ships to build up enough momentum to do serious damage.

They both swung wildly as they ran the gauntlet from the station wagon to the front door of the house. Gail reached it first and held the door for her husband, who darted inside.

As she followed, closing the door behind her, a single fighter managed to sneak in as well. Dropping the bat, she grabbed the ship. It was small enough to fit easily in her clenched hand. The fighters were no doubt quite formidable on many of the other worlds that they'd conquered, but on Earth they were fragile jokes.

She brought her hand close to her face and stared at the fighter. Through the clear front of the ship, she could see a single tiny pilot staring back at her.

"Leave me alone!" she screamed before throwing the fighter against a wall. It shattered with a crackle and flash.

She turned to look at her husband, who was still holding a frying pan and shaking. Outside, they could hear the fighters pelting the living room windows.

"I talked to Connie today."

Roger just stood there looking confused before he realized what she meant. "Look, Gail -"

"Shut up. I'm leaving."

"What? What about Steven?"

"He's at my parents. I'm getting re-certified and I'll start working remote, same thing I suggested you do."

"You can't just--"

"You've been sleeping with your assistant for the last two and a half years. You've been sleeping with one of your clients for the last six weeks. Connie found out last night. I found out today."

"It wasn't like -"

"Give me the keys."

"What?"

"The keys. To the station wagon. That's why I've been waiting for you to get home. I want the station wagon. You can keep the car."

"Can't we -"

"Yes, we could have. Two days ago. It's too late now."

He was still shaking. "Just listen to me for a minute, will you? Don't just -"

"I was listening for months. It's too late to start talking now."

"I just -"

"Give me the keys."

"*Don't interrupt me!*" He raised the frying pan without seeming fully aware that it was still in his hand.

"I'll break your arm before that comes down. Just give me the keys to the station wagon."

He lowered the pan gently, placing it on the floor. "Gail. You and Steven ... you're all I have."

"We're all you have *left*, is what you mean. I called the client, Ms. LaForte, and told her all about you and Connie. You lost the account, by the way."

"What?" He slumped to the floor, staring at her. "What?"

Gail walked to him, knelt down, and hugged him. "It's all coming apart today, Roger, and tomorrow you'll have to make a brand new start. Just like me."

He wrapped his arms around her and began to cry. "*I'm sorry*, Gail. I'm so sorry."

"So am I," she whispered, then slipped a hand into his pocket and fished out his keys. She let go of him and stood up, unhooking the key chain and dropping off everything but the key to the station wagon. She reached absently for the bat. Without looking back at her husband, she said, "Good bye, Roger. Good luck."

Then she opened the door and walked into the war zone.

A month after leaving her husband, Gail was watching a documentary about the alien invasion on her parents' television. It was the ten-year anniversary of the day when they had first transmitted a declaration of war. Her mother was sitting beside her on the sofa and her father was propped up in his reclining chair. Steven was on the floor in front of them, far too close to the screen. They all watched as a United Nations General Assembly meeting was interrupted by a huge holographic projection of an alien announcing in broken English that their race was now laying claim to the Earth.

Earth was to be the thirty-seventh acquisition in their growing Empire. Those who cooperated were assured safety and a life spent in service to them as slaves. Resistance would earn death. It was still chilling footage, even with all the things that were later learned about the aliens.

Steven looked from the television to his mother and asked, "Were you scared?"

Gail nodded. "Everyone was scared. That was the first time we saw the aliens. We didn't know how tiny they were. It was a crazy time." She decided not to elaborate, hoped that the documentary they were watching didn't elaborate too much either.

There'd been the fundamentalist groups, always eager to proclaim an end to the world, and their mad recruiting schemes. There were maybe a dozen suicide cults that swelled with members. Every minority was scapegoated as the cause for drawing the aliens to Earth. There had even been some extreme voices calling for the destruction of the planet by nuclear overload, rather than allow the aliens to take it.

"What about Dad?"

Roger had begun seeing his son twice a week, having finally found the time for him. He was slowly coming to accept the new situation. Gail was well on her way to being re-certified. The aliens had eventually lost interest in the house.

"He was scared too, but we had each other."

"What did you do?"

"Took it day by day. We mostly stayed in."

"Wasn't that boring?"

Gail shrugged. "We kept busy. Then I found out I was pregnant with you and, really, we forgot all about the aliens for a while." Her son had been born exactly nine months after that first transmission. A lot of babies were born around the same time.

Steven returned his attention to the documentary.

Gail remembered those first few days after the announcement, when everyone on Earth thought it was all about to end, how precious everything seemed. Back then, nobody had really thought you could survive the end of the world. But it turned out that the trick was just to take it day by day.

A SWEETHEART DEAL

by JW Schnarr and John Sunseri

The guy showed up in the middle of the night, but it wasn't the guy Artie was used to.

Every time before it had been a greaser, a big, muscled guy with slick black hair and a Roman nose, and Artie had imagined he could smell the garlic and olive oil on him, even through the reek of formaldehyde and freshly-turned earth that suffused the undertaker's offices.

But this guy...this guy looked more like an accountant, with glasses and nice clothes. And he was nervous, too. It was a cool October night, but the guy was sweating and they hadn't even carried in the body yet.

"Where's the other guy?" Artie asked, concerned that the deal was getting changed on him.

That's how life went for him - whenever he got a sniff of something good, a taste of success, they fucked around with the rules and he ended up taking it in the ass. And this was the big one, this deal, this sweetheart deal he had going.

"I'm the one who's here," said the accountant. "Is there a problem?"

"No, no problem," said Artie, shaking his head. "It's just, you get used to a guy, and then someone else shows up..."

"Just do your fucking job," said the guy, "and don't worry about the personnel. You're getting paid to keep your mouth shut and do your job, right? So keep your mouth *shut*..." At this point, the accountant leveled his gaze and gave Artie a look that was meant to remind him of his place in the food chain. "And do your job."

"I got it," said Artie, backpedaling. "Really, man - it's cool. Let's get the thing out of your trunk, and you can take off."

"You get it out of my trunk," said the man. "You've got a hand truck, right?"

"But the other guy..." started Artie, then stopped. Yeah, the other guy always helped carry the body in, but he wasn't going to make a stink.

For five hundred bucks, he'd wrestle the bulky, awkward thing into the lab himself, and the priss could drive back to Portland without getting himself dirty.

As he struggled to get the bundle onto the tines of the hand truck, he kept nervously scanning the grounds of the cemetery.

It was October, after all, and the high school kids would soon be fucking around, tipping over the headstones, drinking stolen whiskey and screwing on the graves. Little bastards.

Artie hoped this wouldn't be the new pattern.

It's not as if he *liked* the other guy, the Italian, but he felt *safer* when he showed up. He'd been careful never to ask, but he was sure he was dealing with the Mafia, and the little pencilneck sitting in his office right now, drinking the extra-tall fancy coffee he'd brought from Portland, didn't inspire Artie with a lot of confidence.

If you were gonna deal with the Mob, you wanted real mobsters, you know? You didn't want the book-and-number guys.

He finally finished. He heaved the thing up onto the embalming table, and the well-dressed guy handed him an envelope. Then he turned around and walked out.

Artie heard the car start up as he opened up his payment, and by the time he had pulled out the cash and counted it twice, the fucker was long gone.

"Three hundred," he said to himself, the words echoing through the sterile, well-lit room. "Those cocksuckers."

The lump on the table, wrapped in its two layers of body bags, didn't respond, but Artie hadn't expected it to. Three hundred bucks in used twenties and tens, and not five hundred like it had always been before.

Artie felt that old feeling take him in the gut, that feeling that said *you're a loser and always will be a loser*, that queasy little twist in his stomach that happened whenever he saw one of his plans crumbling, whenever some stripper turned him down for a date, whenever he realized that the cop who had stopped him for his fucking taillight wasn't gonna listen to why he hadn't had time to get it fixed.

They were doing it to him again; people were constantly fucking with him, putting him down, keeping him in the dirt when he should be flying up above it…

He forced himself to think of flying. It always calmed him down.

He looked up at the models hanging on their wires over the sink area, looked at the beautifully-replicated P-51D Mustang, the bulk of the B-29 Superfortress, the Vought F4U Corsair with its bent wings…and then he looked down at the bundle of money in his hand.

Those guys had been real men.

The Americans, the British, the Canadians, all of 'em who'd flown mission after mission over Germany and France, dodging bullets and the dirty clouds of flak that came up at them like belches of Hell, doing their jobs and taking out the Krauts and the Nips.

And here was Artie, sitting lonely in his mortuary office with a mob kill on his table and a measly three hundred dollars in his hand. It was enough to make you cry.

He looked at the body again, dreading the task ahead of him. He'd have to get the quicklime out, spend two hours carefully packing it into the space between the body bags, and then reseal the whole deal.

Tomorrow he'd have to dig the grave for Curt Ripley and make it three feet deeper than normal so there'd be room for the extra body underneath the coffin. For five hundred bucks, it was an annoyance. For three hundred, it was insulting.

Fuck this, he thought.

He'd do it all in the morning. He was almost out of lime, anyway. That meant another trip down to Johnson's Tack and Saddle, where, with any luck, Michelle would be working.

This thought, unlike the thoughts of the WWII airmen, managed to lift his spirits a little, so that when he clicked off the light and moved back through the building to his apartment, he felt a little better.

And when he stuffed the new cash into his light plane envelope (almost five thousand in there, now, less a couple hundred for trips up to Portland and the strip clubs), he was even whistling a little bit. Tonight he would prime a Spitfire Supermarine and see if he couldn't trace out the blue-green camouflage pattern on it, the one that had made it practically invisible over the North Atlantic waves.

Tomorrow, he would see Michelle.

The next day was Saturday, and he spent the morning working on Curt Ripley.

There wasn't much more to do. He'd already set old Curt's neck so that it was straight again, and pinned a black suit to him. All that was left, really, was the knee, and Artie had saved it for last because it made his stomach turn. The thing looked like it had gone through a sausage press.

Curt had been hit - well, not *hit*, really, but *pulverized* - by one of those new Dodge trucks, the ones with the huge engines and big grills. Crushed his ribcage and broke his neck. His ribs had splintered inside him and sliced up his internal organs. A bunch of them had actually ended up in his underwear.

And it looked worse than it sounded - Artie'd had to snip the things out of Curt's ass and drop 'em back into his chest cavity.

His knee, though, was the worst. It had gone under the truck and gotten pinned by the tires. When the guy had slammed on the brakes, Curt's leg had turned into soup.

Artie straightened it and did some stitching just to try to give the leg a bit of form again. When he was done it looked like shit - but it had looked like warm puke when the stiff had first come in, and at least this way it would kind of look like a knee again.

Curt's family had gone all-out for the funeral. They couldn't have an open viewing period, because Curt had left half his face on the Dodge's fancy grill, so they had opted for the posh Excelsior casket and a large photograph of old Curtis instead.

Real nice. Lots of brass and oak. Weighed about 400 pounds, even without a passenger.

After lunch, Artie dropped Curtis into his new - and last - home. He filled out the final bit of paperwork and wrote a little note that said simply 'DNV'. Do Not View.

Just in case.

Artie looked finally at the double-wrapped bag on the table. Just looking at it pissed him off.

He still had a little time before Michelle's shift at the Tack and Saddle (at least, he thought he did. She worked afternoons on Saturdays, usually), so he shook his head and decided to get a little work done on the thing.

He unzipped the outer bag and saw right away that someone had forgotten to lock the inner one.

Interesting.

The zippers on the bags came with a double clip so that they could be locked up. Saved the body from slipping out of the bag in transit, and also kept thieves from robbing the corpses before they could be properly processed.

This one was missing the little brass lock.

Someone had been in a hurry to get it here, and had gotten sloppy. Either that, or...

A test? It was the Mob, after all (at least, he was *pretty sure* it was the Mob). Would they do that to him, give him some bullshit loyalty test?

It would make sense if he'd ever given them a reason to worry, but he'd been doing the job perfectly since Day One. Maybe they were just paranoid.

Or maybe they wanted to rile him up and see if he'd shake, so they intentionally short-changed him, then stood back to see if he'd take the bait, open the bag, and then they'd burst in and give him the old double-tap salute to the back of his head.

Naw - he was pushing it, now.

This was stupid. These little paranoid fantasies made sense in Artie's head, but not in the real world. He grimaced.

To hell with it. Piss on those Guinea fucks. A deal's a deal, and three hundred bucks ain't five hundred. He deserved *something* for the missing two C's.

He deserved a look.

He peeled back the outer bag, then unzipped the inner one. He pulled it back and then stared at the thing before him, unsure of what to do next.

Whatever it was, it wasn't a corpse.

It looked like a lump of wax.

It was a soft margarine-yellow color, and vaguely human in shape, but that was it. It had no discernable features.

Artie reached down and pushed on it with his finger.

It was soft, like feta, and had a greasy sheen on it that stuck to Artie's skin when he pulled back his hand.

He rubbed it between his fingers and smelled it. Some kind of oil. The places where it touched his skin began to stain.

A moment later, they began to sting. Artie watched as two black bruises formed on his fingertips like blood blisters. Then tiny droplets of blood began to form on the skin.

"What the hell?" he whispered, staring aghast as the blood welled up and formed a perfect drop. It fell from his hand and splashed on the floor.

He looked at the waxen figure before him and his face furrowed. He had made a line in the stuff when he'd touched it with his finger. An indent in the formless mass.

His fingertips felt swollen.

Whatever this shit was, he wasn't getting paid to piss around with it. Of course, if his paranoid fantasy was true, and they *were* testing him, he'd just fucked up big time. They'd look at the streak in the thing, and *know* that he'd been messing with it.

So stupid, he thought.

He'd leave for a while. Just to be sure. You never knew, right? He'd leave the office and if shit looked like it was beginning to go down when he got back he'd just drive on by, maybe take an impromptu trip up to Canada to visit his brother.

Just to be safe, he'd drop the wax shit into the coffin with old Curt. Lock it up. If the Mob came, they'd have to take a fire ax to the Excelsior to get inside it. Solid fucking oak. It would take hours.

He wheeled the casket over to the table, wincing as his bruised fingers came into contact with the handle, and again when he struggled to dump the thing into the box on top of Curt Ripley. With this minor handicap, he fumbled a bit as he heaved it over the edge, and the bag started to slip, but he wasn't going to fuck with the thing any more right now. He left it, locked the casket, set the alarm on the prep room, double-checked everything.

Triple-checked.

And then left. No sense being careless.

When he was almost downtown, Artie's fingers began to hurt so badly that he had to pull up in front of the Grange building and stop the car. They'd been aching since he'd left the Veteran's Cemetery, but now they felt like someone was squeezing them in a vise - someone strong and pissed-off.

He looked at them, his fore and middle fingers, and though they had stopped bleeding they were swollen and puffy, and he could actually see them throbbing with his pulse.

He was truly scared, now.

Maybe it's not the Mob, he thought. *Maybe it's some weird scientific thing, some X-files type of thing, and what I've been burying all this time is* toxic, *like failed biotech experiments...*

He raised his fingers to his face so that he could see them better, and for a span of five seconds he stopped breathing. There was something going on under the skin of his fingers.

Something moving.

What he'd thought was his pulse wasn't. It was like worms were in there - something alive, inside his fingers, moving blindly around in the meat and the juice.

He yelped and grabbed his fingers with his left hand, feeling them, feeling the motion of something alien inside him, and with his brain a maelstrom he squeezed as hard as he could, like he was trying to get the last bit of toothpaste out of the tube.

Yellow-white stuff, looked like feta, started to ooze out of his fingers.

Blood came too, a thin watery stream of red, like he was popping a pimple too hard, but it was mostly the wax, coming out of his pores as he forced it, tightening the pressure as his heart pounded in his chest.

It was moving down, he gibbered in his mind. *It was moving down the fingers toward the hand, and then it would have gone up my arm, and toward my heart.*

He squeezed and squeezed until nothing but blood came out, and shook his hand frantically to rid himself of the alien wax, spattering blood and the cheese-stuff onto the passenger seat of his pickup, onto the dash, onto the Dairy Queen wrappers on the floorboard, shaking his hand like a priest shaking his thurible.

Finally he stopped. His hand felt better. The blood was slowing, though the tips of his fingers still had red pricks all over them, like little measles.

He thought he'd gotten all of it. He couldn't be a hundred percent, but he thought it was all out, and he looked carefully at the stuff on the seat next to him, waiting for motion from the little splatters of pus he'd flung there.

Nothing.

He looked around, but the Grange was deserted on a Saturday. Over the front door, a hand-painted banner advertised tomorrow's pancake feed and pumpkin-carving contest, but today all the farmers were out in their fields or spending time with their families. No one had seen him doing his panic dance in his truck.

After another minute, he wrestled the old Ford to life and put it into gear. He was still scared as hell, still panicky and breathless, but he couldn't just go home and stare at his fingers for the next two or three hours, like he wanted to.

He needed lime, and a lot of it. He was damned if that shit back in old Curt's coffin was gonna stay there much longer.

The town of Carper's Ridge wanted to be a city, but it was taking a long time getting there. When Artie had been a kid at the consolidated high school, smoking dope behind the bleachers and getting beat up by the farm boys who thought he was a fucking weirdo, there had been a little over five thousand people living in the limits. Now there were maybe six, and a lot of them were old people who retired down here from Portland or up from Salem, wanting clean country air for their last years.

All those old folks were good for business.

Artie pulled up in front of Johnson's Tack and Saddle, put the Ford in park, and sat there for a minute, looking at his fingers for the millionth time.

Nothing.

He got out, and walked across the sidewalk to the front door. He kept his right hand in his pocket as he opened it, flinched a little as the bell hung over the door jingled, then moved up to the counter.

Michelle was there. Some of the tension left his chest.

"I'm gonna need some more lime," he said to her, amazed at how the mere proximity of her chased most of his fear and anxiety away. He'd been through the strangest morning of his life, felt some of the sharpest fear he'd ever felt, but just being in Michelle's presence was like getting baptized - all the bad things went away.

"Oh, hello, sir" she said, smiling. "You know where it is."

"Yeah," he said. "I'll grab some and be right back." Normally at this point he would grab a cart and head to the back of the building, where the bags of lime lay stacked like lumpy pillows against the wall - but this wasn't a normal day by any stretch of the word. All he'd been through, all the fear and the pain, the panic and the uncertainty - and now the cathartic balm of Michelle's presence - made him reckless.

"Say," he started as she began to turn away from the counter. She stopped, gave him another smile, and waited.

"I was wondering…" he said, and now his heart was beating fast again, "I mean, if you're not busy some night, I thought you might wanna drive down to Salem, maybe catch a movie…"

The smile disappeared.

"I'm sorry, sir," she said. "Company rules - Mr. Johnson doesn't let the employees date customers."

"Oh," he said. "Sorry. I just thought...I mean," he closed his eyes for a second, feeling it again, that *loser* thump in his guts. "I'll just go get the lime."

When he opened his eyes again, she had turned and walked down the counter, where a farmer had wheeled up his fifty-pound bags of chicken feed, and she was beginning to ring him up. Artie moved away slowly, heading for the lime.

On his drive back, the heavy bags shifting against each other in the bed of the truck, he tried to think of flying again, of finally getting up the scratch to buy a light plane and just fucking flying away, up through the dirty clouds that scudded in the October sky into the crystal blue firmament.

He had been hoping Michelle would want to be his co-pilot.

Load up Michelle, his rifle and fishing stuff, maybe get a dog, a big black mastiff, name it Achilles or something, something tough, and just fly away with 'em, fly across the state, all the way to Canada, all the way to the goddamn North Pole if he wanted...

The thoughts weren't working like they usually did. She wasn't going to be his co-pilot, and you know why? 'Cause he was a loser, that's why. This sweetheart deal he had going? It was shit. He wasn't even halfway to being able to buy his plane, and now they were dropping his payments. What, a couple more corpses (*they're not corpses*, his subconscious whispered) and would they be paying him two hundred a pop? One hundred? Maybe they'd want him to do it for free - what could he do about it, call the cops and complain?

He pulled into his spot next to the hearse and looked around for anyone, anything that said *Mafia*, but the graveyard was deserted. A spray of wilted flowers had blown off one of the graves and rolled into the driveway, but that was it.

The door was locked. The alarm was on.

He hefted three of the bags of lime onto the hand truck, dragged it toward the door, and opened it. He went through the vestibule, turned on the lights and stopped.

Something was thumping in the back room.

He had a pretty good idea what it was.

Another thump, a loud one, and he released the hand truck, looked around, and opened one of the closet doors. He took a shovel out, hefted it in his right hand, and moved to the door of the preparation room. He unlocked it, put his keys back in his pocket, took a deep breath and pulled it open.

The coffin was on its side on the floor, a pretty good dent in it where it had landed when it had fallen - or bucked itself - off the gurney. It lay silent and still for a moment, then it jerked off the floor maybe an inch, straight up, then crashed down again.

Four hundred pounds, easy, and the stuff was actually lifting it.

Not thinking, working on adrenaline and instinct, Artie walked over to the casket and kicked it so that it crashed down onto its back. It began to quiver and shake, and it scraped on the cement floor. Artie imagined the stuff inside writhing and twisting, trying frantically to escape.

He helped. He reached down, unlatched the locks, stood again and took the shovel in both hands, a batter's stance, and reached out with one of his steel-toes and flipped up the lid.

The stuff had invaded the body of Curt Ripley.

The corpse, hands bloody, lurched up as soon as the lid opened, and it was *screaming*, screaming in a wordless siren as if hellish pain was wracking it, and Artie stepped back, stunned, not expecting this…

It was fast. The knee, that wreck of a knee, had knit itself back together somehow, but it wasn't any kind of normal human anatomy - bones still stuck out of it at weird angles, and though it was strong enough to support the body as it rose wailing out of the Excelsior, it must have hurt like all the fires of Hell. Judging by the corpse's mad banshee howls, it did.

The thing rose, leaving behind it all the formaldehyde that the wax had forced out, an inch or two of blood, gallons worth, pooled in the box, pieces of organs - all the stuff there hadn't been room for when the wax had taken over Curt. Artie screamed, too, as the thing rolled out of the coffin and sprang to its feet, and he could see that most of the wounds the old man had suffered were healing, too - long sharp cuts knitting themselves seamlessly until only faded skin remained, the crushed ribs somehow re-fused so that the old farmer's chest looked solid and vital.

And now it looked at Artie, with open eyes clear and blue, and in the middle of all the screaming and agonized howls, Artie saw the thing beginning to *smile* at him.

And reach for him.

Artie swung and connected, a solid hit with the blade of the shovel, and Curt's head went *crack* and the body staggered back a half-step.

The head whipped back up, and blood spilled from its mouth down its chin, onto the torn black suit. It still smiled. Artie swung again, missing the head this time, cutting into the old farmer's shoulder and splaying his arm out in a spastic flail.

It kept moving, shrugging its wounded arm back into place, and Artie knew that it would keep healing itself if this kept up, and he didn't have a whole lot of time.

He backed up into a corner to give himself a precious few seconds, almost screamed as his head brushed up against the hanging model of the Corsair, watched as Curt Ripley moved smoothly toward him, smiling and screaming, bleeding from the mouth and shoulder, formaldehyde still being forced out of the old man's pores like curds from a curd-press, and Artie took a big breath, aimed carefully, and swung again, arcing the shovel like a sword.

The blade cut through the corpse's neck, all the way through the vertebrae at the base of the skull, and the head flopped over to the side, hanging by a long scrap of skin, a tendon or two, and some long, ropy strands of the cheese-stuff, which even as Artie watched scrambled to reconnect themselves, blindly questing towards each other, grasping each other, pulling each other, the head beginning to jerk back up…

Artie swung again.

And again.

Afterwards he threw the shovel at the wall and went straight to his apartment for a glass of Early Times. He found an open pack of Camel fats and sat on the floor of his living room staring down the stairs to the prep room. He smoked. He drank.

He desperately tried to keep it together.

His hands shook badly. Ash from his cigarette fell everywhere, onto his jeans, into his glass. He barely noticed. The gears in his head strained; he could almost smell the burning lubricant as they threatened to come off their axles.

Deep breaths.

Flying Fortress.

Breathe.

Spitfire Supermarine.

He drained the glass. Pawed at the bottle, got more. He was going to have to go back down there and clean up the mess. But not just yet. Not until he was sure he wasn't going crazy.

The prep room was dark when he finally went down. How long had he been sitting up there? Half a bottle of bourbon, however long that was.

He'd made a hell of a mess out of Curt Ripley. There was formaldehyde and quicklime all over the floor. They'd mixed together to form a toxic paste that was even now eating through the remains of whatever it was that Ripley had become.

He grabbed the shovel and started scooping the mess into the Excelsior. The stuff looked like bloody Cream of Wheat. It took him a while, but eventually most of it was cleaned up…

Three sharp knocks at the door.

Artie almost jumped out of his skin. He looked down at what remained of the mess, then back at the door.

Three more knocks, louder this time.

He moved slowly to the door, shovel in hand, watching his feet. The floor was slick, and he almost fell twice.

Someone outside kicked the door.

Artie turned the latch and opened the door. Just a little.

The guy was outside. The Accountant.

"Hey, buddy," he said, seeing Artie peek through the crack. "What's going on?"

Artie strove to keep his shit together.

"Uh, hey," he said, keeping the door at a crack. The guy was wearing a blue suit and a tie. He smoked a cigar, one of the little skinny ones.

"I came by to see how thing'sre going," he said. "You know, see if you were having any problems."

"No," said Artie. "No problems at all."

"So you gonna let me in?" asked the man, "or am I gonna stand out here like an asshole all night?"

"I can't let you in," said Artie. "Sorry, man. I could lose my license, the whole place could get shut down."

"Hey, what're we talkin' about, here?" the guy said in an unconscious Pacino impression. "It's *me*, for chrissake. You remember me?"

"I can't do it. I'm sorry." Artie's grip on the shovel tightened. Just a bit.

The guy, the accountant, put his hand up.

"Okay, alright. Take it easy. You know, I didn't wanna come out here and bug you like this. Shit, drive two hours down here, Saturday night and all…" he shook his head. He was smiling, like he and Artie were buddies. Defusing the situation. Artie continued to watch him.

"It's my…*employers*," the accountant said, stretching the word out. "They sent me to check on you. Wanted to make sure you're still being a good boy, you know?

"So I said I'd drive on down. It's stupid, I know, but sometimes they get worried, these bosses of mine."

"Everything's going good," said Artie, heart thumping, hand tight on the shovel. "No problems."

"Besides," said the accountant, smiling - and Artie caught a flash of gold teeth.

"I think we shorted you yesterday, didn't we?"

"Two hundred bucks," said Artie. The door opened a bit wider.

"Two hundred, that's right," repeated the guy. "Only I was thinking, maybe I should throw in a bit more. You know - for your troubles."

"How much more?" asked Artie.

"Oh, I dunno - another three bills? How's that sound? Five hundred total - sound good?" The guy's smile got bigger. *He's trying to calm me down*, thought Artie. *Like he'd talk to a dog - quiet words, big promises, soothing tone.*

It was all too big a coincidence.

"Hey, don't worry about it," said Artie, smiling at him. "We'll get it all straightened out next time, okay? Tell your bosses everything's going fine out here."

He moved to close the door.

The accountant moved faster.

He lifted his leg and booted the door squarely at the latch just as Artie began to close it. The door slammed open, catching Artie in the face and sending him sprawling to the ground.

The guy stepped into the room, drawing a handgun.

"Jesus Christ," he said, looking around the room and putting his free hand over his mouth. "Fuckin' stinks in here. What've you been doing?"

"It's formaldehyde and lime," Artie said in a daze, holding his hand to his face. The shovel was somewhere off to his left. He couldn't see anything but motes of light. "Man, I think you broke my nose."

"Formaldehyde," said the accountant, looking around. "Like embalming fluid, right?"

"Just like it," Artie said. Blood ran down his face. He tried to pinch off his nose, but the action sent shards of blinding pain into his eyes. "*My fuggin' nose…*"

"Hey, what the hell is that embalming shit for, anyway? How come you gotta put it inside stiffs like that?"

"It's a preservative," Artie said. "I put it in so the body won't rot before the funeral. Man, I'm really bleedin' here…"

"No shit," said the accountant, lighting another cigar. "You know, there was a guy dated my cousin Francesca a couple years ago - God rest his soul - who used to smoke that green shit. Said he soaked it in embalming fluid to give it some extra snap. You ever heard such a crazy thing?"

"Amped," Artie said. "It's called amping your pot. It's really bad for you, though."

"Crazy shit," said the accountant, suddenly losing interest in the conversation. He'd just noticed the mess on the floor.

"What's this?" he asked quietly, walking over to where the last remnants of quicklime, fluid and goop were streaked on the floor.

"I didn't mean for any of this to happen," Artie said, slowly getting to his feet. The guy spun on his heel and pointed his gun toward Artie.

"We said not to open the fucking bags, didn't we?" he asked in that same quiet tone. He walked over to Artie until the barrel of his gun touched Artie's forehead.

Artie closed his eyes.

The guy sighed.

"You know, if Uncle Sam ever found out about this little deal we got going here, he'd ask some questions. Some *uncomfortable* questions." The hammer clicked back.

Artie opened his eyes again. "Uncle Sam? What the hell are you talking about?"

"The government," said the accountant. "Where do you think these things come from? Your elected officials."

"*I th-thought you were the M-Mob,*" Artie said quietly. He was so shocked he could almost forget the guy had a gun pointed at his skull.

"There ain't no fuckin' Mob, you dumbshit," the accountant said. "We're fraternal businessmen, like the Elks. And we do business with all sorts of people, including the guys in Washington. It's twenty G's for us, every time we put one of these wax bastards into play." He pulled the gun away for half a second so he could motion with both his hands.

"They want 'em in good spots. Pastors, cops, all that crap. Important people, or people who have the *attention* of important people. They want it done quiet, so they come to us - we got ways to get to people, you know?"

He watched Artie scowl, trying to soak it all up, and snickered. "I know you was only getting five hundred a body, but that was the deal."

"Why…" Artie began. It didn't make any sense. "Why bury these things if you're supposed to be replacing people with them?"

"Well, you know," said the accountant, "it's fucked up, the government is. My bosses like the money and all, but they don't much like the idea of these things running around without they control 'em. So this way, everyone's happy. The guys in D.C. think they're getting what they want, we're getting a whole lot of money, and you were getting enough scratch to keep you happy. But you had to fuck around, didn't you?"

"But…"

"No buts," the accountant said. "A deal's a deal."

He fired. A black hole the size of a raisin appeared in Artie's forehead and as he fell back he had the sensation of warm syrup running over his face.

His thoughts scrambled, and he wove in and out of consciousness. He smelled gunpowder and sulfur. He thought he saw the accountant leave.

He thought of dogfights over Europe, the Mustangs chasing down those Nazi fucks and blasting them out of the sky. He thought of the Canadians and their Lancaster bombers dropping hellfire into the heart of Germany.

He thought of the light plane he would never own.

He thought of Michelle, her long hair and soft eyes.

He awoke again.

He lay flat on the floor, a pool of blood around his face. It stained his eyes, but he was beyond feeling it. The funeral parlor was dim and bloody.

Something skittered. He could barely see it.

A long, slender finger, moving through the blood like a slug.

Toward him.

Under the table was a piece of the wax, about the size of an apple. He'd completely missed it when he'd cleaned up the parlor.

It reached out across the blood, now. Testing it. Artie could see the tendril, like a root, reaching out blindly toward him, toward the little hole in his forehead that was still oozing blood.

He couldn't move. Maybe he didn't *want* to move.

It fondly touched the burnt skin around the hole, so delicately, so gently.

Like a sweetheart's touch.

As if trying to soothe Artie for what was to come.

THE RAINMAKER

by Mike Baretta

"Excellency, thank you for the gift of time and presence," said Paulo Garcia, using the ritual greeting. He fidgeted nervously and nearly lost his balance in the echoing gloom. His bowels were uncomfortably liquid.

"You may petition," said a drowned voice.

Paulo worked his tongue to lubricate his dry mouth. He took a deep breath and gathered his wits, trying to gain some situational awareness. The artificial cavern was warm and dark. Bioluminescence trails from obscene creatures dripped and crawled from the ceiling and walls. Eerie fungal shapes of blue and green and lavender grew from the surrounding shore like wilting saguaro. Glowing weed kept time with the water ripples. Paulo shifted his feet on the plinth, barely above the oily water.

"I ask for life, Excellency, but not for myself, for my daughter. She is sick. She has the fever." He struggled to keep the quaver out of his voice.

"Bold, *bold* to ask for life that is not yours. Circumstances?" The voice seemed to come from all directions, slightly out of phase as if multiple mouths uttered the same words.

A ripple of phosphorescence spread like lightning in the water. Something big moved in the depths and he fought the urge to step back. The attendant stated that he must remain on the plinth no matter what happened. The master was old enough to instill discipline to all its parts, but it was common knowledge that accidents happened.

"My wife and sons died in the incorporation. She is the last of my line. I ask indulgence," said Paulo. The oily black pool rippled. Blood warm water lapped the edge of his boots. The alien broached the surface behind him and exhaled explosively, spraying him with the sickly sweet half-digested remains of its last meal. Startled, Paulo turned in time to see the displacement ripples of the creature's submergence. The Qwo'on were cannibals and had even less compunction about consuming vassal sapiens. He stared into the depths and could make out a vague scuttling shape in the water, something between a lobster and an octopus, combining the worst aspects of both Earthly creatures. It was big, far larger than he expected. He swallowed hard and fought to control his breathing. He was valuable to the Qwo'on's domain, but not irreplaceable.

"Circumstances?" asked the Qwo'on.

"I am an engineer third class loyal to your domain," said Paulo. "My daughter will inherit my tradition." Qwo'on were deeply affected by genetics. If he was smart and valuable it stood to reason that his daughter would be smart and valuable. Before the Qwo'on conquest, Paulo was a weapons designer and physicist at Los Alamos National Labs. These skills qualified him to survive at the lowest rung of the alien hierarchy that had imposed itself on the world.

"Weakness," bellowed the Qwo'on master in a long whale moan.

"It is within your power to cure her," said Paulo out of desperation. As a species, the Qwo'on are unsympathetic even to their own land dwelling young. An indigene had little hope of a successful petition. A fin flashed in the water and Paulo saw, a graceless black-on-black silhouette as large as a terrestrial elephant. Few Qwo'on lived long enough to acquire enough assemblages to be as large as this one.

"Sentiment. Distasteful. It fouls the waters," said the voice.

Another set of waves washed over his ankles. He was completely dark adapted and could see disturbing things in the dim glow. Human-made boots, a pair of sunglasses, and a stuffed toy swollen as to be unrecognizable littered the shore of black volcanic sand. A tiny t-shirt with a cartoon character on it drifted in the water. Pale multi-legged Qwo'on larvae, no two alike, picked through the filth making twittering noises. If they escaped their father's appetite they would leave the pool to gather wealth and power, with desires of returning to establish their own domain. He forced his eyes away from the items. Each one told a story and none had happy endings if they ended up here. He glanced again at the t-shirt drifting forlornly and fought back tears. It could just as well have been his child who stood on this pedestal at feeding time and for the first time he felt a blinding desperate hate, enough hate that he might do something foolish and die while mouths large and small flensed him.

"Resources are scarce. Impossible. Sinful to waste," said the Qwo'on.

Noxious alien waste gasses bubbled to the surface. Paulo's knees began to shake uncontrollably. A questing hooked tentacle extended from the alien. The master came closer. Through the slick waters he could see a nightmare assemblage of fins and spines and mouths. The Qwo'on was a colony creature. It assembled and disassembled its parts at will. Their biology dictated their world view -beings were used and discarded at will. The tentacle, probably a recent addition fresh from the breeding pool and undisciplined, was acting of its own volition. Puckered mouths with curved teeth gasped. It moved towards him and he fought the urge to run.

THE RAINMAKER

"Consensus is weak. Fear is tasteful." hummed the Qwo'on.

The tentacle stroked Paulo's leg like a lover's caress, tasting him, and then snaked away. Eyestalks rose like periscopes and blinked vapidly concealing the fierce alien intelligence. The Qwo'on rose, centered in an explosion of dark spray, antenna uncurled and waved in the damp air. Water poured from its segmented head like waterfalls. Crab-like mouthparts worked furiously above unblinking black eyes. Powerful tentacles fanned the water, stirring up muck and agitating the bioluminescent creatures into a flashing frenzy. Muscled tubes and spiny spiracles sucked water and discharged it over the creature's skull to cool its massive brain. Bloated human heads on the end of branching necks rose from the water next to the creature's native skull. They snaked to within a few feet of Paulo's face. Dead eyes took his measure. Foul liquid poured from their mouths and the heads coughed themselves clear in staccato barks. The heads spoke.

"You will visit my waters when you are no longer useful," threatened the chorus of human heads.

The voices, completely in phase, boomed over him and deep bass vibrations filled his chest. The heads closed their sightless eyes and the creature sank under the water and scuttled to the deeper portions of the lake to continue its dreaming, unconcerned with the affairs of its inferiors. The Qwo'on cave was silent. Paulo left the way he came, desperate and grieved. A Mobin, a squat heavy world tri-ped, tugged his leash down the causeway to the chamber door. As the Mobin disconnected the leash, some unnamed species chattered excitedly and bobbed its feathered head. Paulo ignored it. The door closed and the powerful stench of ripe decay attenuated. Paulo was momentarily blinded as he stepped into bright sunlight at the base of the needle. Caravans of massive elevators filled with Earth's treasures rumbled upwards towards the Qwo'on *flashships* anchored near the apex of the alien space elevator. The nearest flash terminal was a short distance away. He stood in queue and waited as higher priority traffic warped parallel to gravitic stress lines. When it was his turn, he presented his identification to the machine, and stepped from the bright sun of Quito to the cool rain of San Diego. He walked a short distance and sat on a crumbling brick wall. Most flash terminals opened up into centers of commerce and industry. This one opened up into a Human sector, one of the few not associated with destructive labor camps. Squat utilitarian buildings sprouted like mushrooms from the carcass of San Diego. He sat down wearily. Rain concealed his tears of frustration and anger and after a while he began his long walk home.

As he walked up the hill he saw Jenna sitting on his front porch. He climbed up his sagging front steps.

"She is sleeping. She did well today," said Jenna. "Sit for a moment."

He sat wearily and stared at the USS William Jefferson Clinton. The massive aircraft carrier lay on its side in the silted bay like a giant rust-streaked whale.

"Thank you for watching her," said Paulo. He listened to the quiet of the city and watched the lengthening shadows. A salt tinged sea breeze ruffled the Human Authority plague notice on his door. The plague, though uncommon was just as deadly the day the Qwo'on slower-than-light ships had dropped out of the sky and dispersed the virus.

Jenna rose from her chair. "I will go home now. Tomorrow I will bring dinner so do not cook anything. *Buenos noches*, Mr. Garcia." She looked over her shoulder as she stepped down off the porch. "You could petition again," she suggested.

"No Jenna, I can't," said Paulo. The Human Authority would only allow one petition.

"You could try other doctors," she suggested.

"I've tried." Even with pre-invasion resources, humanity could barely keep ahead of its natural diseases. There was little hope of defeating something as insidious as a war plague manufactured to kill humans.

"I would trade places with her if I could," she offered. Her voice was soft and sincere.

"So would I Jenna, thank you." He watched Jenna leave. She walked with a slight limp from a bullet wound in her hip. Even after the horrific depopulation of Earth, surviving humans still managed to find the time and energy to kill each other for foolish reasons. He went inside to see his daughter, careful not slam the screen door. He stood at her bedroom door for a moment, composed himself, and then sat gently on the edge of her bed. Pink tears stained the pillow. The hemorrhagic fever was painless but inexorable. He wiped her face with the wash cloth and she stirred.

"Daddy is it going to be okay?" she asked.

"Yes, my love. The Qwo'on gave me medicine," He unwrapped a butterscotch candy from pre-invasion stock and put it on her tongue. She smiled. Her eyes half-lidded against the painful light.

"I'll be better?" asked Maria.

"Yes, you will," he lied. He climbed into bed with her and willed the plague to take him. For a long time he listened to her fever talk and cherished every word. Soon they fell asleep in each other's arms. The next morning his shirt was stained with her blood.

She was weak and pale and her breathing was labored, just like her brother's and mother's was. He stirred and she grasped his hand a little tighter.

"I saw mommy." She whispered through pink stained teeth. "She said I'll be better soon."

"I know baby, I know." Warm tears ran down his face. Her breathing slowed and she squeezed his fingers. She took a deep rattling breath and for one terrified moment he thought it was her last. He wasn't ready to let go. How could he ever be ready? She was the only thing he had left in the Universe and everything he had done or failed to do was to keep her safe.

"Daddy," she gasped."Mommy says to kill the fuckers. She says to, just do it." Her voice was deep and resonant and not the strained whisper that had developed over the past two days.

Paulo jerked in surprise. He had never heard his daughter curse and to the best of his knowledge she had never even heard that word. "Maria, do you want to go outside?"

"Yes, Daddy."

He wrapped her in a clean quilt and lifted her feather weight and walked to the front porch. Paulo sat on the rocking chair and held her tiny body until it released its terrible heat and held no more.

Later, he dug a grave next to her mother and three brothers. The ground was rich and cool and smelled of life and it brought back memories of working the California fields with his family a long time ago. He built the coffin himself with nearly forgotten skills learned from his father. When he lowered her into the grave he lowered his heart with her.

Jenna placed roses on the coffin lid and they sat for a long while in silence. Paulo thought of his father who had smuggled himself north of the border and then sent for his family, his mother who had fiercely defended the time her children needed to get an education, his sister, a cardiologist, murdered in disease-choked hospital, and his own wife and children arrayed out in front of him under a Eucalyptus tree. He was the only one left. Paulo stood slowly. His knees popped and creaked. He felt every bit of his age and then some. He touched Jenna on the shoulder as he stood.

"We need to make them pay," said Jenna. She paused, waiting for some sign that he had heard her. "Mr. Garcia, I will talk to you after some time has passed."

"I know Jenna. I know what you need. I'll give it to you. Tell your organization to prepare," he said quietly. He brushed his hands free of dirt and wiped them on his pants. "Tell them to prepare for the end of the Qwo'on on this world."

"I will," said Jenna, without any indication that she thought him crazy for saying he could eject a race that had destroyed 80% of humanity in a weekend. "I really loved her, Mr. Garcia."

"I know you did, Jenna. It's the only reason I let you come here," said Paulo. "I was always so afraid of losing her and now that she is gone there is nothing to hold me back. My child made me a coward," said Paulo.

Jenna didn't disagree, but thought there was no better reason.

That night Paulo sat for a long time in his overstuffed and threadbare chair. Fire warmed his outside, and moonshine, far too much moonshine, warmed his inside. The pallet board fire popped and sizzled and Paulo stood up and wobbled uneasily. He took two short steps and reached his fireplace mantel. With his right hand, he plucked a silver ball from a nest of five in a crystal bowl. Curled within the infinite folds of the shadow matter sphere was enough antimatter to vaporize a nickel-iron asteroid the size of a mountain. With his left hand, he held his balance against the mantle. He leaned back, took two wobbling steps backwards, and collapsed into the warmth of his chair. The shadow matter sphere, his contribution to mankind's last weapon project was satin soft and highly reflective. His distorted reflection wrapped the sphere. He fell asleep in the chair listening to the crackling fire and cradling the most destructive weapon that humanity had ever created. He knew he would use them to kill the fuckers like his wife had asked.

Jenna stepped up onto the porch. Paulo met her outside and unspoken they sat down on the plastic stacking chairs. "The spheres have been placed Mr. Garcia. They won't be found." Over a period of months, four of the weapons had been hidden near the primary Qwo'on enclaves. Paulo would set the last one himself at the space elevator's orbital anchor point.

"Synchronized?" asked Paulo. "Like I showed you?" As an engineer third class he had access to many Qwo'on technologies.

"Yes, using the Qwo'on's own time signal," said Jenna. "What will happen, Mr. Garcia?"

"Nothing will survive within 200 kilometers," said Paulo. The planet would ring like a bell when the four surface-based weapons detonated.

"Where will you be when it happens?" asked Jenna.

"The top of the needle Jenna," said Paulo. A lavender scented breeze washed over Paulo and he felt his wife's ghost, like the tingling of an electric current, like shadow matter non-reactive with normal or anti-matter. He could feel her, but not touch her. "Where will you be?"

"It is better if you don't know," said Jenna. "I knew you weren't a collaborator Mr. Garcia." She looked at him with genuine pity. Paulo was incapable of taking a position. He was neither a collaborator, nor a resistor; he was simply a damaged survivor doing the best he could to keep his daughter alive until the horror faded from existence. She had ordered that he not be touched.

"I was Jenna. I collaborated in keeping my daughter safe," said Paulo. He always had the means to strike back, but never the will. Qwo'on security was formidable and resistance was nearly futile. Now eight years later their conquest was so complete and so established that if one did not bother them they did not waste too much time and energy chasing humans. "What did you do before the depopulation, Jenna? I've never asked."

"I was Major General Gabrielle Hernandez, late of the U.S. Army, and then Supreme Commander United Nations Forces Western Hemisphere. The United Nation's job didn't last long," said Jenna.

"What do you do now?" asked Paulo.

"Western Hemisphere Resistance Cell Coordinator and part-time grandmother to Maria," said Jenna. "Resistance is somewhat of a misnomer. You could say I salvage people and squirrel them away for a rainy day."

"You invested a lot of time in me," said Paulo. "I'll make it rain for you."

"Your little spheres were part holy grail and part urban legend. To tell the truth, I was not really sure they even existed, but it did no harm to visit you and I really did love your daughter," said Jenna.

"I know," said Paulo. "Jenna, it will take several thousand years for the Qwo'on to come back, but they will come back."

"I know we will be ready for them," she said optimistically. She would be long dead when that distant day came. Knowing for an established fact that there were hostiles in the sky should focus a future humanity.

"I don't think we could ever be ready for them. In the mean time, will you take care of my family? Will you remember them for me?"

"I will Mr. Garcia," said Jenna. She reached out and took his hand and they rocked until the sun began to sink below the broken aircraft carrier.

1000 kilometers above Paulo's head, the needle eye opened. A flickering chiaroscuro of colors filled the void and the Qwo'on *flashship* began to emerge through the flickering brightness. Half the vessel was here and now, the other half was light-years away and then. The vessel was hideous, built along an aesthetic that mimicked the Qwo'on's own body types. Spiky radiator fins and sensor spires emerged from between deflated cargo pods strung like beads along twisted structural members. 2000 kilometers above the needle eye his sphere waited.

Paulo looked at his watch and put on his glasses. Timers indexed to zero and shadow matter spheres vanished in a haze of quantum foam. The hyper-compressed anti-matter expanded rapidly, contacting normal matter. The needle base and the massive counter weight structure composed of Qwo'on slower-than-light ships dissolved in a flash of blinding liquid light brighter than the sun. Mega-tons of foundation material, needle, and Qwo'on habitat vaporized in nanoseconds. The flash faded leaving blotchy purple after images in his vision. A moment later, a new sun was born just over the horizon line where Africa would be. The needle lurched, not nearly as violently as he expected. His gravity faded and he grabbed onto a piece of equipment. The eye flickered and then went off revealing the dark of space and the neatly bisected Qwo'on ship. The ship's remains drifted powerless for a moment and then exploded. Gamma rays from the high-orbital explosion sleeted through Paulo. The radiation sickness would be terrible. Fortunately, he wouldn't live long enough for it to be a worry. Already a powerful sine wave was racing from the distal ends of the elevator to pulp him and even if he survived the destructive wave he would not survive the world-wrapping fall around Earth's circumference. Power blinked off and redundant power cells energized his module. Far below he could already see portions of the needle glowing from re-entry. He floated free and thought about his family.

Major General Gabrielle Hernandez saw a bright flash on the southern horizon that mimicked a rising sun. It was done and to her surprise she felt deeply ashamed at the price that had to be paid and her role in extracting it. Some sacrifices were necessary, she consoled herself. For eight years, she had researched the anti-matter weapons project and Paulo's role in their development and with a reasonable degree of certainty that the weapons existed; she exploited her carefully crafted, yet ultimately genuine relationship by murdering Maria with plague-laced ice cream. Once cut adrift, Paulo was capable of anything.

"Do you have her," she said to a Sergeant in a bloodied uniform. Like herself, the man was a fighter in the truest sense of the word. The man would kill fearlessly and without any remorse to achieve an objective.

"Yes, we have her," said the Sergeant. The Sergeant looked behind, signaled, and two men came forward, weapons slung, with a dirt-stained coffin between them.

"Good take her through," said General Hernandez. She touched the coffin as it went by her. "Forgive me, Maria." She vowed that Paulo Garcia and his daughter would be more than remembered, they would be revered.

"What do you want to do with them?" asked the Sergeant, though he already knew the answer. He gestured to a row of five Qwo'on vassal aliens and two humans lined against the wall.

"What do we usually do with collaborators, Sergeant?" They probably wouldn't survive the coming catastrophe anyway, but it gave her a visceral pleasure.

"Yes ma'am," said the Sergeant. He signaled two of his fighters, one a bandolier draped human female and the other a feather-crowned alien fifth columnist whose head bobbed continuously like a demented chicken. Machine guns roared and the collaborators fell, staining the wall with three shades of blood.

She stepped over the body of a young bullet-riddled Qwo'on and marveled at the utterly ruthless nature of the aliens. I have become one, she thought. She heard the rumbling precursor sound of the distant mega-explosion that had vented Earth's atmosphere. Soon, it would be replaced by the continuous wave of shattering noise. The space elevator extended over 35 thousand kilometers into space and as it fell at hypersonic speeds it would lay a trail of devastation that would extend to the farthest northern and southern latitudes, possibly instigating a new ice age.

One problem at a time, she thought. Her immediate issue was to take command of the Yellowknife Biological Vaults and its archipelago of survival bunkers strung out in the Canadian tundra and wait out the darkness in the aftermath of the space elevators long fall. For eight years she had hoarded as much technology, supplies, people, and knowledge as she could without attracting Qwo'on reprisals. Her deep shelters, built at the extreme latitudes, could protect perhaps 100,000 people from the coming dark. She watched the coffin and its attendant soldiers vanish through the usurped Flash terminal to emerge in the command center at Yellowknife. She signaled the rest of her fighters. The sky was darkening. Once she was sure they were through, she stepped into the chaos of the command center, a hodgepodge of human and supernaturally powerful alien equipment.

The first battle in the war was won. The last would not be fought for several thousand more years.

NEWS ON THE MARCH

by Edward Morris

BURNING DEBRIS IN THE SKY WAS PAN-ASIAN MISSILE FMC REPORTS THE 'METEOR' OVER R.OF WASHINGTON MAY HAVE CRASHED IN R. OF OREGON.

USAP/MIL/GOV/ SALEM —

The brilliant flare of fire that woke residents of Vanport, Washington and surrounding areas was a misfired Pan-Asian ICBM in disintegrating orbit, which WestUS Northern Command missile defense systems quickly shot down after a Pacific Rim attempt to clear their own orbital space of several large-scale meteorites.

Federal astronomers are not disputing said findings as yet, though no prior warning was given as to any unannounced meteor showers over Shentsi Province. Col. Erik Ulery, Federated Military Corps Long-Range Reconnaissance High Command, said FMC-Recon are even now verifying reports that a piece of the missile may have hit the ground near the Vanport Reactor at about 9 PM Pacific Standard Time.

(As this reporter goes to live feed, however, I must report that Recon are still not on-scene. However, our own scanners here at the station record no unusual activity or distress calls from anywhere near the reactor. Further bulletins as events warrant.)

"Our first concern was that this very spectacular burning object we all saw was not a crashing aircraft of some unknown type. It was leaving a burning trail behind it, too. Objects falling from space are an everyday occurrence in this day and age, but not into urban terrain," Ulery clarified.

The Colonel also informs me that there was, in his words, "No known connection between similar 'meteor' sightings throughout the Eastern US Capital State of Philadelphia, as well as Ft. Laramie, Wyoming; Weed, California; Portland,

NEWS ON THE MARCH

Oregon Provisional Secessionist Republic, and points in Canada too numerous to mention.

"The Perseids are in season, or the Leonids, or some [expletive deleted] –ids, Lieutenant, tell that little faggot there to get the camera out of my f—" [Feed cuts out]

The Colonel also reports that a rocket burns up differently than any sort of natural aerolite; in many thousands of pieces, with a flare of burning metal, as opposed to several big chunks of amorphous material. Most re-entries of space trash go unseen, Ulery states, because they happen in daylight or in the middle of nowhere.

Tonight's augury was widely witnessed because it occurred during the second/third-trick commute just above the advertising border on the local horizon, tracking from east to west. Had it been directly overhead, Ulery points out, few commuters would have even noticed.

All this comes at odds with the testimonies of twenty stubborn employees of VPDX Aerospaceport, who are very upset that FMC Brass will give no credence to their accounts of two oblate speroids that plummeted to Earth in the area of the 'port so quickly they created a small tornado, said the twenty VPDX-Spacelines pre-flight crew on duty at the time of the alleged phenomena.

All witnesses said the objects were silver-and-black and very clearly visible, with no external lights of any kind, roughly eight feet in diameter. The unidentified aerolites were first seen by an FMC non-com ground crew worker who was power-oxying the hull of a Grumman-Dahaitsu geosynch skipcraft at Gate D12 at approximately 1440 hours, according to this soldier's testimony.

FMC Press Liasons profess no knowledge of the event, reported by more than 500 nationalized-airline workers when questioned recently. All controllers and radio operators of any rank in the area reported nothing out of the ordinary.

Yet hundreds of employees are protesting the lack of action on the part of the FMC. They state that the objects could have interfered with any instrument in the area, and probably did. Many have called off sick or walked off the job. No further developments are reported.

No controllers affirmed that they'd seen either object, and preliminary telemetry diagnostics found nothing remarkable. Some witnesses are miffed that neither the government nor the military is giving the matter further time since a statement was quickly issued by the Pan-Asian Ministry of Defense claiming that the unarmed warheads exploded, shooting down the several asteroids of unknown origin descending over Chinese airspace.

"Our sincerest apologies to the American people," read Beijing's terse missive just hours ago. "Please do not be alarmed. The material was expected to burn up harmlessly on re-entry. Restitution will be made for any instances to the contrary, through the offices of Eastern United States Chancellor Rex Grimm. As far as our top scientists are aware, the asteroids have been neutralized."

Local government officials were

THIS JUST IN:
Outside the window, there is a shadow over every part of town, and a whistling hole in every cloudbank. The reinforcements are in the street. They are very noisy. I will keep dictating to my Optix recorder until I am no longer able to do so.

Hold on. Here's the first line of FMC Humjeeps. They are—

Guys, what— No shots are fired. The military are clearing the area of humans, but not the other things...

I am going to be sick. None of them even pay the newcomers any mind. They're using fire hoses and Denialbots and hand-held heat cannons. They—

Are we still live? This is a bloody coup. They're rounding up the locals. They're putting them in... vans. I hear breaking glass. Oh, Jesus, Mary, Joseph, we have seen this before. I— Oh, we've got vid. This ... Hi, this is Dave Davis on the Earth News Network. As stated, we have been live this whole time and I'll keep on recording until—

THUD-THUD.

Something is in the room.
Uhh, greetings! With peace, and goodw—
Who or what do you think you —
Put me down. No. No. Put me d—
(crunch)
SIGNAL NOT AVAILABLE.

For H.F. Arnold

MY BEAUTIFUL BOY

by Jodi Lee

His views on logic did not interest me. My lack of desire to listen to his ramblings had allowed my brain to wander, and I kept myself amused by mentally ripping the skin from his jowly face.

In fact I didn't hear more than five words during his whole twenty-eight minute monologue. When he asked my thoughts, I'd coo about how wonderful it was, how everyone at the conference tomorrow would find him the most interesting and knowledgeable speaker there.

I glared at the back of his head as he faced the window and gazed out on the rotund piece of rock floating beneath us; my mind saw him floating out there beyond the glass, blood pulling away from his body in little drops to freeze in the lack of atmosphere.

If thumbprint ID wasn't required to open doors in this section of the station, I'd have been gone long since. As it was, he and his cronies watched my every move.

I could not stand his continual droning on and on in that snotty monotone. Fantasies of debris from the launch pad smashing through the window and slicing through his pencil-thin neck, severing that constantly babbling mouth from the body that fed it energized me. I closed my eyes and savored the details.

The boy wearing a torn shirt and jeans pulled the cart across the deck in front of the small office building. As he trudged it through the door he thought about the rewards he would receive after the hard labor today. Never in his life had he seen so much treasure in one spot; the Outsider would be ecstatic on his return to the compound. No one had found this before, even though it should have been one of the first places they'd searched.

The old floorboards squeaked. He knew they were barely holding his weight combined with that of the cart, let alone the return trip being double that. This would be the final time he crossed the floor in this building, the final time he would have to be frightened for his very life.

Echoes of the past rebounded in the old mine. He had ventured several miles below the surface, seeking the treasure. Whispers of the long-forgotten ocean roared and swirled in the tunnels and caves; a Goddess' cries dying in the dark. The Outsider had once told him that his whole compound was once beach-front property, and that all the sand for miles outside the walls was actually the sea-bed.

The young man couldn't even imagine that much water everywhere. Water was a treasure to be hunted for, just like the precious metals and stones that the Outsider hoarded within the stronghold of the compound.

And he had found a rich supply, the Goddess had blessed him with so much treasure!

Perhaps he could get permission to leave and visit his sisters where they lived on the Station. To leave the dusty rock of existence and visit the sparkling object that hovered just outside of the atmosphere tickled his mind and fired him on. *To leave and do anything, anywhere he chose, even if it was just for a few days.* With all of his hard work, the Outsider was sure to be pleased, and pleasing his Outsider was one of the great joys in his life.

He grimaced slightly as he hefted the giant container onto the cart. Another one, and still another; added to the others he'd removed earlier, that made nine all together. Enough to last the Outsider and the household at least a half-year.

The boy wasn't really a boy after all, as could be seen once he was out of the shadows, under the spotlights. Although small in stature, he was indeed a young man. At least two decades in age, when he stood tall he was only just barely over five and a half feet in height; his build lent to the illusion of youth. Slender but well-muscled, tanned a deep bronze from being out in the sun most of the day, his eyes were a washed out shade of blue as were most of the men.

Too much genetic preferencing in the old days had resulted in men that looked alike - dirty blond, pale blue eyes, short. It had become quite rare to see a man with dark features. The Raiders, though, they were dark.

He often wondered what it would be like, to be like the Raiders. All well over six feet, dark and muscled like oxen, the Raiders went from station to station, compound to compound, planet to planet - trading, selling and thieving whenever they had a chance. Raiders didn't believe in a Goddess, *any* Goddess. They didn't even believe in a God. Just themselves.

He thought of the fickle way in which they used the women of the stations and outposts. Often, the women were left with child. On their next trip through the area, if the men remembered which woman he'd been with, he'd visit again. If the child was dark and heavily built, the Raider would take it when he left again. If the child was pale and small, it was left behind. As he himself had been, only to live with the shame his mother reminded him of every day while she was around. She'd even named him *Raize*, a common slang term for Raider. Since the women were not allowed to abandon, sell or give away boy-children, his mother had sold herself into service to an Outsider in order to support her little family and avoid prison.

The next time the Raiders visited, she managed to escape with one, leaving her children behind. The girls had long-since left the Rock, seeking their own way in the 'verse.

Leaving Raize behind.

Oh, blessed silence – finally! How I have longed for your touch.
I couldn't stop staring at my hands. The blood that had covered them, though having been washed away long since, still seemed to stain the skin. I was sure there were rings of dried gore under the edges of my nails - I was constantly picking at them as though to remove it.

Perhaps no one else would see it. *Could* see it. My bent head only lent validation to my ruse; I was a grieving half-wife, the remaining concubine after the death of my Outsider master. I was finally free at least. Nobody seemed to suspect that I had done him in, I played my part well.

I believed I had everyone convinced that I did in fact love the droning lump of narcissistic flesh that had bought and paid for my services.

There I sat, picking at my nails while the station accountant crunched his numbers. My portion of the assets remaining after the station had taken its chunk could not be reckoned in dollar amounts. Rather, the accountant was telling me I'd be given a set amount to live on, each month, via tix at the station warehouse. The room we'd lived in for two years had been paid for in full, all amenities included.

But, should I show any resistance to staying on the station and continuing my life as his 'widow,' *everything* would be forfeit.

"Madeline, you can have as many lovers or as few, as you choose. You can never marry, and you can never bear a child. Should you wish to leave the station for any length of time beyond that of a months' visit to the City, you forfeit your claim. It will then become station property to do with as the Leaders see fit."

I had a week to make up my mind. I didn't need a week.

I knew what would happen if I returned to the City without a means to support myself. They'd put me back up on the block to be sold as concubine to yet another Outsider. *I didn't want that...*

I wanted to be able to pick and choose my lovers from the wandering, random flocks of human men that I'd seen on the station.

Yes, the chances of my conceiving would be higher with a human, but I'd never had the pleasures of intimacy with one of my own kind. I'd always been for sale to the highest bidder, and those bidders were always Outsiders. Besides, there were ways around conception.

Below, on the human home planet - once lush and green, now an overheated sand dune – there were men who could use that very heat to keep me from conception. There were no codicils stating I could not use sterility as a form of contraception.

I continued to stare at my hands while I considered my position. I was heartily sick of Outsiders, the main tenants of the station. Rarely did humans come and when they did, they didn't stay long. They traded, they drank in the bar, and they left - in a trail of dust and disaster that some Outsider low-rank would then clean up. Even the Raiders didn't stay long here.

If I stayed here, in these rooms where I had finally rid myself of he that owned me, I would be treated as Outsider upper-rank. I could freely walk the station at any time, visiting the bar or docks without reprimand.

I could troll for a human man.

I glanced up at the accountant. For an Outsider, he was actually rather handsome. "Are there any stipulations in regards to birth control?" I smiled as I'd been trained; doe-eyed and innocent, yet the knowledge of the worlds apparent in the slow grin.

"None. He was advised to put one in, but he ignored it, knowing you wouldn't leave the station as long as there were funds at your disposal here."

I nodded. Glancing out the window to my left, I observed the planet of my birth. I could not remember anything other than constant, unforgiving heat searing through the atmosphere and literally baking the surface. The Station was cool, maintained at a constant temperature just below comfortable for humans.

Down there, a hack could burn the lining from my uterus. Anesthesia was no longer an option down there, not for humans. I could live with the pain, so long as I remembered the freedom. It was the *smell* of my own burning flesh that would get to me.

Not to mention the smell on the planet itself. Earth One in the old dog days of summer was not a healthy place. Outsider refuse and bio-waste was barely contained all over the planet. Thus, when it really began to heat up – it *really* began to smell.

I sighed. Freedom and money outweighed the cons.

"I'll stay, but first I must visit Earth One."

It was alright in the end, the Outsider was very kind to him, and didn't do the things he'd heard from others in service. His Outsider was as close to a father as he'd get, and he appreciated the fact. If he didn't love the old guy, he'd have left long ago. Raize was not wearing a mark, he'd not been branded - the Outsider felt that was a ridiculous method of marking property - he was indeed free to go at any time, *Goddess Bless*.

When he really gave thought to it, he knew there was nowhere *to* go, except home to the compound. He'd die alone and starving in The City.

Raize trudged along, the return trip taking so much longer than before. The cart had become very heavy, and the sun now beat down with an unrelenting fervor. He stopped momentarily, only long enough to pull on his head-wrap. Sighing heavily, he pulled with all his strength; there was only another kilom to go. He could even see the tower at the compound, in the distance… if he squinted. That sight lifted his spirits a small amount, just enough to get him really moving again.

After an eternity in the sun, his skin was beginning to redden and his lips were chapping. If he could only stop and savor the treasure, it would be enough to bring him relief. But he could not, *would not* disappoint the Outsider in such a rude manner.

Finally, he reached the gates and saw they were closed. A strange hush had settled over the usually bustling common area, and the women inside were keening in their strange voices. Panic flooded his chest and he thrust his fists against the gate itself, rattling the chains. He called out, over and over, until at last someone came to let him in.

"He's gone! He's *left*! He said he would not return to the compound again. He was looking for you, was going to take you with him." The guard looked as though he were smirking, and as the younger man looked up into the other's eyes, he could see the laughter. "You've been left behind, son. You're as buggered as the rest of us now. We'll all die here."

With that, the guard turned and stalked back to the common area, elbowing anyone who got in his way.

Raize picked up the cross-arms of the cart once more, and proceeded to the main house. Here, the other containers sat - now entirely empty and wretched, mangled almost beyond recognition. Putting his head down, he threw his weight into the cross-arms and pulled the cart through and into the house.

It was there that he discovered the reason for the Outsider's quick departure. One of the guards had apparently been caught at the treasure and the Outsider had punished him; drowning the man - holding him still while pouring the treasure into his mouth. The Outsider must have done the damage outside, and in here, during the punishment.

Raize howled in anger - not at the Outsider, but at the guard - he'd spent so much time and energy searching for, finding and bringing home the treasure, the water, from the abandoned mine. Their well had begun to dry, and *they needed this water*! How could the guard have been so stupid? Of course the Outsider would be enraged at the small theft!

In his own rage, he kicked the dead man several times - crushing the nose and smashing the teeth. When his rage was spent, he sat on the stair and began to busy himself with getting a small drink from the remaining water in the receptacle that had been sitting on the table. He didn't bother with a cup, he simply drank straight from the container.

Hate had taken hold of Raize briefly, but he had a handle on it now and would be able to go on about the task at hand. *Goddess forgive his lapse into anger*. He'd have to contact the sheriff. The sheriff could clean this mess up, and get him out of the compound and back to the Outsider within a matter of hours. He presumed the Outsider had left for the station, but he was not about to ask one of the others in the compound for verification. They knew he had been the favored one and would find only too much glee in his having been left behind.

He could hear them singing outside now. It made Raize's heart ache to know they would not be missing the Outsider. He had been so kind to all of those in his service - he had always treated them more than fairly. Disgusted with them all, the young man stood and began to climb the stairs to his rooms. He would need to pack his new clothes if he were to be living on-station.

Within an hour the sheriff had arrived, driving up the dusty trail that served the compound as road. He brought with him a mysterious new object that he shone in the face of the compound guards. They shrieked when the light from the strange lamp struck their faces or any exposed skin. He nodded and continued on, giving everyone there the same treatment. When he approached the house, he was cautious — but Raize stepped out with a friendly greeting, startling him slightly.

When the sheriff shone the light on the young man's face, he wasn't surprised to see there was no reaction. To make sure, he scanned the light over any exposed skin, and finally satisfied… nodded.

"Well, boy - you 'scaped a terrible thing by just a little bit. Don' you drink you none of that water there," he said, pointing to the containers Raize had spent all day retrieving. "That there stuff is from the old mine ain' it? Nope, you don' need to answer me, boy, I know it is. It's bad. It shoulda been dumped, but the folks there were scared it'd get inta the underground system, inta the wells. So they locked it up and I see someone found it. I know'd they did, when you called. When you told me what had happened here, I remembered the last time. No, it wasn' your Outsider what had it happen, it was another. Only, he killed everyone on his compound before he took off to the Station. He couldn' a known that it wouldn' effect everyone.

"You see boy that water there, it has a chemical in it that makes people crazy for a while. Crazy enough, that they' bite their own tongues off before eating, they' bite the nose right off yer face. They' bite anything - and everything - if it didn' get away."

The sheriff grabbed his radio, and spoke quickly into it. Glancing around, he saw the young man's bags sitting, waiting to go. He shook his head, but Raize insisted. He had to reach the Outsider. *His Outsider.* Finally, after a brief radio conversation, the sheriff gave in. "I take ya as far as town, but then ya gotta go out on your own. I know the Outsider from this compound went on up to the station. I ain't gonna help you get there, you can help yourself. The only thing you can do now is wait and hope he comes back for you."

My body was screaming in agony as the Raider healer pulled the hot iron from my womb. The metal guards placed between my legs did little to keep the soft flesh from burning as well, but I bit down, demanding my mind to stay focused.

I would *not* have a child. I would *not* forfeit my life to squeeze some bastard from my body.

The Raiders gave me what comfort they could as I healed and I paid them well when I left. I stayed at the richest hotel in The City to finish my recuperating, spending many days walking the opulent marketplace with its fake greenery and imported cool air.

It was there I found him. *My beautiful boy...*

Raize was casually strolling the dusty street in the commerce section of The City, when a young woman stopped him to talk. She was very well dressed, but marked. He knew she was in service but he couldn't help himself. He asked if she would like to walk with him.

She regarded him closely for a moment, then smiled. She had a beautiful smile - it lit the day even though the sun was out and beating on the poor, dry ground. The young man felt blessed to be with such a one. *Blessed by the Goddess herself.*

As they strolled, she spoke of herself. Her Outsider was dead, which left her technically free. She could do as she wished, so long as she did not leave the station for more than a month at a time, once a year. She spoke at great length, on Raize's urging, about the station. He so wanted to go, so wanted word of the Outsider. His heart fairly burst when she mentioned having seen him.

"Yes, I recognize you. I know of your Outsider," she brushed his hair from his eyes, making him weak-kneed and vulnerable. She pulled him closer to her, resting his head on her chest where he could hear her heart beating in steady rhythm. Her hand stroked the back of his head, relaxing him before she pushed him away to look in his eyes.

"I will send for you in two weeks. Be ready. I must go back to the station now, or I forfeit everything. I can help you but you must give me this time. Your Outsider needs to stay out of this for now. Do you understand? I have need of you, far more than he does."

Raize had no idea what she was talking about, but he nodded, willing to do whatever it took if only she would hold him again; if only she would touch him again. He longed for her touch. She smiled, and fulfilled the need that fairly glowed in his eyes. She whispered a sweet promise in his ear before she left him, standing alone on the street.

It almost broke my resolve, leaving Raize behind. Those scant few moments I had with him fired a desire within me I'd never felt before. I wanted his touch, his breath, his everything. I left The City, carrying a raging heat to rival the surface nestled between my thighs. I had to find a way to bring that boy to me, and damn his Outsider. I had to make him *mine*.

Days passed and he had no word from his mysterious benefactor. New clothes had been delivered, the likes of which he'd never seen before. Daily baths in hot water with luxurious oils had been ordered, along with the finest of foods. Raize had never been so pampered, so spoiled. He was loving every moment of it, and very soon - forgot all about his desperate need to find the Outsider. *The Goddess had promised she would return.*

It wasn't long before I was dealing with my own troubles. Within weeks of returning from The Rock with full intentions of going back for Raize, the Auditor questioned me. He found out who Raize was and knew how to contact the Outsider the boy sought to return to. Rumors of the illness from the treasure had already overtaken the Station and Raize's Outsider was gone, returning to the home world.

They were terrified I was infected with the illness, after less than 6 hours with Raize. The doctors dosed me up with preventative drugs to keep me from doing anything rash, like biting off my own tongue; a side-effect of the drugs for some, was truth-telling.

I told *anyone* who would listen that I had killed my Outsider. I told everyone I was sorry.

I had killed my Outsider, yes... but they didn't need to know that, and I worried they would believe me. If I confessed and blamed insanity, would they arrest me? No.

Thankfully, they didn't seem to believe me – and they'd already decided my Outsider had simply died of Overuse. He'd always been quite political, after all. They did, however, believe I'd lost my mind.

Those last few days down on the Rock had really messed her up, they all thought. In reality, I'd begun to believe they would find out the truth, and toss me into the fray to be sold to another Outsider.

Another side effect of the drugs they gave me caused me to see things. When I looked in the mirror, I could swear I saw pale blue eyes and shaggy, dirty blond hair. *I had to snap out of this and do as I promised!*

The reflection of the mirror stared back at me. I would have sworn it winked at me. *Raize...*

Raize longed to run away from it all, the novelty of being so highly pampered had worn off. She was trying to seduce him from afar, tempting him with freedom from the Rock. His guilt at forgetting his Outsider nagged at him, like the ticking of hundreds of tiny clocks.

Once again, the fuel in the lamps was low, and he fetched kerosene from the desk in the main entrance to fill as many as he could. The house staff had been ordered away by someone, someone he didn't know. Nevertheless, they had left plenty of supplies. In fact, even if his mystery woman didn't call him to The Station for six months, he'd have plenty to eat, drink and be merry with. But what of the Outsider? Where was he? *Why hadn't he come for his faithful friend?*

After lighting the lamps in his bedroom, Raize set the fuel aside and picked up another of the books that had been sent. He'd been lucky; the Outsider believed in education, and while most servants couldn't do more than sign their name on any papers presented them, he could read – and he could understand what was written. The problem of numbers however - that remained something he couldn't work out. Numbers were just so much scribble in a field of parchment.

The books his benefactress had delivered were odd. Most were reprints of old books found in the old cities. He was sure no one had ever read of riding strange animals with four legs, of wasting water and of breathing in smoke on purpose. He found most of the books distasteful, but having nothing else to do, he read them anyway.

Many of the books spoke of the Goddess, and how one could commune with Her using candles and stones and... and *water!* It was in these books Raize would lose himself for hours on end, before visiting the market to seek out the items mentioned.

Some of the afternoons, time passed quickly and there were moments where Raize wasn't sure if he'd been awake or asleep. His body would suddenly jerk, as though startled from a light sleep, and sometimes he couldn't remember having read the passages where his hands rested. Sometimes the echo of the oceans of the past would sound in his ears, terrifying him. *The voice of the Goddess, calling him softly, would cause chills to raise the flesh on his arms.*

Other days, he would give up on reading entirely, and head out into the streets to wander as he would. In the City, there were many more places to go, and new sights to see; he often felt he could stay tucked up like that forever, and other times the guilt would catch up to him and he longed for nothing more than to be doing something useful, something for the Outsider.

There were times he'd catch a glimpse of an Outsider entering a building, and the familiarity of the gait would give him pause. Too often, he'd charge into the building, thinking it was his Outsider, back from the station to find his wayward servant.

Each time, he was disappointed.

On his return to the house early one evening, he found another delivery had arrived in his absence. The crates contained even more food and yet more books. Tucked inside one of the books was a letter from his benefactress. Raize tore open the envelope, knowing in his very soul she had finally found a way to get him passage to the station.

> "*Little* One,
> Do not think I have forgotten you.
> All my love,
> M."

The date mark was only a few days from when she had left.

Raize found he had to sit on a stair and ask for the Goddess' patience in order to stem the flow of anger. He was frightened for a moment that his temper might have gotten the better of him; he had been known to release his anger. A fleeting image of the dead guard he'd kicked rose in his mind – he dismissed it as he crumpled the page he held in his hand.

Perhaps she was just leading him on with even more promises of the station and a life there, with her and with the Outsider.

Raize stood and walked out of the door. When he reached the street, he turned left – walking determinedly out of the City and straight into the desert. Several hours later, he leaned against an ancient sign beside a decrepit boardwalk. "*Beach Closed: Swim At Own Risk*" were barely visible, the paint long since faded.

MY BEAUTIFUL BOY

He stared out at the vastness of golden-red sand as his rage overcame him. What made him who he was fought to maintain itself, maintain control. And then it was gone. *Raize* was gone.

A smile not unlike a smirk replaced the angered frown, the eyes were no longer gray, but a deep and burning yellow. The color of sand at sunset. The color of the endless sands at sunset.

Seth returned to The City. When he was finished, he would be the only one left behind.

I kept my head down, my hands folded in my lap, while I waited for my doctor. Too scared to look up, I rocked back and forth, taking comfort in the movement. Every so often, I'd peek from underneath my bangs. I'd glance at the mirror.

The man that looked like my Raize was still there. His face had changed, become older and darker; he was angry with me. His eyes glowed, like a *felinx*.

I want to wake up.

Please Goddess, let me wake up!

TO LOVE A MONSTER

BY VICTORYA

The Great Slaughter happened when I was a baby. There's no better name for it I guess; that's what it was. That's what my father called it. He was always appalled at what we'd done, we being humanity.

"*Bleeding heart liberal!*" my mother would scream when he got into the sadness of it all. "Remind me again why the hell I married you." And then she'd throw something and it would shatter and we'd all scurry, we being my brother, father, and me. My father would try to calm her down sometimes. I like to remember him as trying, before he walked out the door to go watch a movie or something, leaving Johnny and me to bear our mother's wrath.

The gist of the Great Slaughter, as I learned later in school, was that all of a sudden cephalopods fell like rain. We'd heard of it raining cats and dogs, but never some squid-like things. They weren't really squid, weren't octopi—didn't really even need to live in water. They landed on cars and slammed through roofs and broke branches off of trees as they barreled from the sky and everyone, well, they pretty much freaked. And it happened in the span of an hour.

Then it happened again a week later.

People went out with shovels to bash in the brains of those things. They got into their cars and ran the cephalopods over, smooshing them into the asphalt and pavement. Everything was covered with cephalopod guts.

Scientists urged people to stop, to capture them as 'specimens' and the like. The cephalopods were studied and believed to be of alien origin. They had no biological similarities to our cephalopods save for the outward appearance. They had beaks on the underside, which was a soft peach or white, three big round eyes with pupils that responded to light, and from five to nine tentacle-like appendages that were used for movement and to feed themselves. The scientists found out they really liked marshmallows.

I have no idea how they found that out, but that's what I learned in my fifth grade science class. "Cephies (as they are now commonly called) have an omnivorous diet consisting mainly of small rodents, insects, and vegetables and are known to have a fondness for marshmallows." That's what the *Science of Life* book said.

Cephies. I've known of them since forever. After the initial fear and slaughter ended people found out they were useful. They didn't grow big, like large cats is all. They became a staple in any country household, even better than cats at keeping the rats away. Cephies were intelligent too, not enough to threaten humans (so says the *Science of Life*) but enough that they could be easily trained.

Shelters overflow with them.

But my mother didn't believe in Cephies. "They ain't right," she said. "We should be killing them all. They're some beacon or other such shit. Just lulling us in, then the mother ship will come and *we'll* be the pets, you see." If she caught my dad rolling his eyes when she said that, it would be another rough night.

Of course, our mom, she just wasn't much for loving anything, be it alien or her own family. I just don't think she knew how. She couldn't hug without pinching, demanded kisses and our devotion in return for the basic necessities of life. My father took it in stride until his strides took him away. I like to think he wanted to take my brother and I with him. Wasn't I daddy's little girl? He never said I was, not really. He said my hair was too long once. "Eugenia," he said, drawing me close to him. I stared up at his red stubble of a beard. "Eugenia, we really have to do something about that rat's nest of a do you've got going. You really need a haircut, don't you?" And I hugged him and he acted surprised. My dad also told me to respect life. He said I needed to find meaning in things. He said I needed to believe that there was good in the world, and that in the end everything always turned out for the best.

My brother was older than me. He was twelve to my ten. He knew more than I did. "Dad never loved us," he told me one night as we sat under blankets eating bagels we had secreted away from the kitchen. Once again we had been denied dinner for not showing our mother how much we loved her. "We probably aren't even his."

That night I woke up to a towering figure roaring into my room. It grabbed me by my hair that was too long and pulled me out of bed. As I bounced across the floor I hit something soft, something warm – my brother. He was screaming and crying and fighting to get out of what turned out to be my mother's other hand. She dragged us through the house and threw us in the shower. The more we tried to get out the more she hit us to get us back in there as she doused us with Clorox and turned on the cold water. We couldn't cry out because the bleach would get in our mouths. It burned through our eyelids. I couldn't see, but could feel the warmth of blood dripping. I wasn't sure if it was mine or my brother's as we lay there huddled against each other for warmth.

She had found out about the bagels.

The next morning our mother came into the bathroom where Johnny and I sat still huddled, shivering, almost blue with cold. "You Silly Billy's," she said, tousling our hair. Strands of my brown locks mixed with the water and snaked down my limbs. "Why are you still here? Come on, get dressed. I made pancakes. Peanut butter, your favorite."

We didn't go to school that day. She took us to the movies instead. Then we went to McDonald's and she got us each a Happy Meal even though we were too old.

The next day we went back to school. When my teacher asked me where I was I said like Johnny told me, that I was sick and my mother forgot to write a note. My teacher eyed me suspiciously, like she likes to do, and during recess she took me aside to talk to me.

"Eugenia," she said, "you know sometimes when kids are in trouble they can talk to their teachers. We realize why kids do stuff, like wear long sleeve shirts even on hot days, that they do it to hide stuff." I did have bruises and cuts on my arms, not that I'd tell her. I told her that I was fine and could I go play now and when she said yes I ran all the way to the back fence of the playground to count the links in the chain like I liked and I found a Cephie.

It was small, maybe the size of a tiny mouse. The sun glinted off its big purple eyes, its pink skin was all dry and dull. At first I thought it was dead but when I crept closer I heard a noise like a purr. I didn't know Cephies purred. I touched it, and it wasn't slimy or anything. Then I wondered if it was sickly out there all alone and then I wondered if I could help and then I picked it up and it kind of snuggled against my hand, trying to wrap tiny tentacles around my fingers and I slipped it into my pocket.

Then I went to the water faucet and splashed water on my hand and slipped my hand in my pocket and felt for the little Cephie and hoped water was enough to save it.

All the rest of the school day I couldn't think about the way the Europeans sailed around the world or how the multiplication tables worked or even which colors you need to make orange, and art was my favorite class. All I could think about was the little Cephie in my pocket and slipping out to splash water on it as much as teacher would allow.

I named it Charles.

When I got home I was scared my mother would find Charles and squish him. But, she wasn't home yet and Johnny wasn't home yet either so I let myself in with the butter knife Johnny hid in the backyard for the times our mother forgot to be home before us. It slid easily down the window in the back so we could open it and crawl in. I was careful not to hurt Charles as I climbed through the window.

Charles was my secretest of secrets. I'd bring him down to the creek behind the house whenever I could get away and talk to him about everything. I told him of Sally at school, the girl my brother liked who told me that I was a little ragamuffin and who was my brother to think she could ever like someone like him. I told Charles how mad I got when I saw the look on my brother's face when she told him the same thing. I told Charles of my dad and how I like to think he tried and was still trying. That he was going to help Johnny and me. And sometimes I'd start to cry and tell him through sobs how my dad had to be right, that there had to be something better, there had to be a reason I had a father who ran away and a mother who couldn't love me no matter how hard I tried. That's when Charles would hum the loudest and look at me with those big purple eyes of his and wrap himself around my fingers and, as he grew, around my wrist.

Once, he reached a tentacle out to my face as I cried and I wasn't the least bit scared. He was my Charles. He just wanted to catch a tear. He was humming a pretty song but when he caught my tear he skipped a note. That's the first time that happened.

Charles grew bigger fast and it got harder to sneak him out. But we still went down to the creek or I'd take him to the big field near my house where dad used to take Johnny and me to play Frisbee and eat ice cream while it melted down our cones and stickied our fingers. Charles liked the field; he'd run around and catch stuff. Bugs mostly. I liked watching his tentacles move as he grabbed at the crickets and flies. When he was done running he'd come over to me and nibble on the grass, taking it up in his tentacles and putting it in his beak like I'd seen the elephants do on the filmstrip at school.

My Charles was smart too. Sometimes I'd do my homework out there, lying in the grass as the sun heated my neck and my back. Charles would play with my hair, gentle like, taking a lock in his tentacles and throwing it up for the breeze to catch. I'd read my books out loud and taught him all about what the *Science of Life* said about Cephies, and I know he understood me. I taught him my math tables, and he taught me how to sing and we'd both be out there in the sun singing.

My teacher took me aside one recess and asked how things were at home because she saw me smile more and I said *no better no worse can I go play now?*

Around four in the morning, I think it was four, my eyes were gummed and screaming woke me up. I was dragged out of bed by my arm and into the car before I knew what happened. I fell asleep in the back seat, not even wondering what was wrong I was so tired. The screams and bumps were just natural to me. The ride ended at the hospital.

We were there well into the day as my mother explained again and again about my brother's fall down the stairs and that's how he broke his arm and the bruises had to be from that too.

We were there when her story changed into him falling off his bike because some bullies dared him to jump at night and he shouldn't have done it now, should he?

We were there well into the afternoon as my mother explained to the social worker just how hard it is to control such willful children being a single parent and all thanks to a no-good husband who walked out. A nurse took me aside. She was nice and clean and smelled like hospital. She took me to the cafeteria and bought me a grilled cheese sandwich and asked me questions. I already knew the answers to these questions. "I love my mom, she does her best, we just get into a lot of accidents because we're active," I said between bites. The cheese was still gooey; I liked it that way. I dipped the chips in the side of the sandwich to scoop out the cheese, its vibrant orange enticing me. The nurse smiled and asked if I had a pet. I wanted to talk about Charles, about how we sing together, about how when I try to do my homework and he wants to play he takes my pencil away, about how he can hide right on the ceiling in my closet. Instead I said no, can I go be with my brother now please? And she bought me two cookies – one for me and one for Johnny and gave me a card to call if I ever wanted to talk more.

Johnny, he started acting different after that night. I guess he learned something I didn't. He started rocking our mom in the rocking chair when she was tired. He started singing to her, "Someone's rocking my dreamboat," in his crackling tired voice and she'd laugh and smile and reach up a hand to grab his. He started telling her that she was the bestest mommy in the world. He actually said it, bestest.

"Just do it too," he told me only once. "Please. Please Eugenia, it's the only way."

But I couldn't love a monster, even if in pretend. Now when I cried to Charles, I had more to talk about. About how my brother wouldn't help me sneak bagels anymore and told on me when I did, even if it was to give him one and crawl under the blankets like we used to. And Charles, he'd look up at me with those big purple eyes and he'd sing. He took to snuggling closer to me, not just on my finger or wrist. He was as big as a cat and he'd crawl on my chest and I'd hug him and cry and he'd reach up a tentacle and his song would miss notes with each tear that fell. He didn't hide in his box anymore, mainly under the bed or the roof of the closet and he'd sneak out at night and sleep with me, humming his Cephie lullabies in my ear as his tentacles played with my hair. I think he spoke to me at night too, in his language of comfort.

When Johnny called me into his room I felt that maybe he'd relearned what I knew, that pretending a monster's your mom doesn't mean it is, that moms know how to hug their kids in such a way that the child believes the world is good. That moms love their kids even if they leave spots on the dishes and moms don't break all the dishes instead. I hoped I had my Johnny back.

"Do you love mom?" he asked me. I didn't answer. "Do you love her?" he pressed.

I eyed my brother very carefully.

"Listen," he sighed, coming closer. "Just tell me if you love her. I need to know. You love me, right?"

I was silent.

"You don't love me?"

Tears began to fill my eyes. I didn't know what to do or say. I wanted him back, but had no idea why he was asking me these questions.

"You don't love me?" he asked again, his face pleading.

"Of course I love you, you're my brother!" I blurted out.

My brother smiled, a real smile, one I hadn't seen in a while. "So, do you love mom?" he asked again.

"I want to," I said through tears. "I really want to."

"So you don't?"

I lowered my head. "No," I finally said.

"You don't love her, not one little bit?"

"No," I said again, lifting my head. "No, I want to, but I can't."

And with that he ran out of the room. I heard the front door unlock – mother was home. Then I heard my voice, tinny and distant. He had recorded us. I ran for my room and closed the door. I tried to hide under the bed but didn't fit. I heard Charles moving about in the closet and prayed he'd stay put. If I got hurt, that was fine, but if something was to happen to Charles, I knew I'd die anyway. I heard my mother roaring down the hall.

"You ungrateful bitch," she screeched, her anger drawing the walls in around me. "After all I do for you, after all the shit I put up with, you say this?"

I couldn't talk. I couldn't cry. I couldn't even move. Johnny recorded it. He set it all up. That was the only thought in my head before I hit the walls that had been moving in around me. Then there was a deep thundering, a rumbling from the closet as the door flew open.

"Charles no!" I yelled.

"A Cephie? You brought a Cephie into my house!" she screamed before kicking me in the side.

As her foot left my stomach Charles leapt from the closet and on to my mother. He grew bigger as he flew, his beak opening wider than I knew it could, wide enough to swallow the world and all I saw was blackness as he descended.

I woke up a short time later, maybe just a few seconds, maybe minutes. My brother was standing in a puddle, urine still steaming down his pants. Charles coated my mother, head to toe was his shiny pink skin with tentacles moving and if there was any struggle left in my mother, I couldn't tell. I got up, eased past my Charles coated mother, grabbed Johnny and ran outside.

"That's not in the textbook," I gasped. "Cephies don't do that. Cephies eat rodents and bugs. They don't do that." I said it more to comfort myself than him. That was my Charles, he couldn't be bad. He just couldn't be.

"She's gone," Johnny finally said. I was on the ground and he sat down next to me. "She's really gone," and he let out a gasp of relief.

A creaking sound alerted us to the opening door and Johnny froze again, his eyes shaking. I could feel him trembling. Our mother walked toward us.

"Eugenia sweetie," she said, her voice a purr, "are you okay?"

I looked at Johnny. His eyes were transfixed. He wasn't even blinking. Then I heard a humming.

"Eugenia," the word musical now as my mother practically sung it, "Eugenia darling, are you okay?"

I began to cry. My mother came over and scooped me up in a big hug. She ran across my cheek and caught a tear, her song skipping a beat. I began to sob so hard I was trembling but she just held me tighter and tighter and her song filled my heart.

"You'll be okay dear," she said. "Oh, my sweet Eugenia." My brother came closer and our mother scooped him up in the hug. "We'll all be okay now."

THE CANDLE ROOM

by James S. Dorr

I had come to love Niki deeply. I didn't know why. She was slender, hollow-eyed — really, most people would call her skinny — believing in so many things so easily whereas I'd describe myself more as a skeptic. But still, I did love her, and so, when I passed the shop again, that I'd passed I don't know how many times before, and glanced in the window and saw it sold candles, I stopped and wondered.

Niki liked candles.

I felt for my wallet. I didn't have very much money to spend, but....

Hell, Niki *loved* candles. She collected them. And, as I've already said, I loved Niki.

And so I went inside. There were shelves of candles lining the walls. Tallow candles. Beeswax candles. Paraffin candles — petroleum candles that stayed lit even when soaked with water. And books on candles.

I glanced at the books. There were books on candle making, histories of candles, uses of candles at social events like funerals and weddings, and candle magic — that was Niki's thing. One book was titled *Birthdays and Candles*.

Niki's birthday was on this weekend. She didn't expect me to get her anything, though I had plans. I'd picked up tickets for the theatre and put aside something for supper afterward. That kind of thing.

But now, surrounded by candles, I thought — why not a present too? She'd invited me up that evening so, taking a quick look inside my wallet, I let my eyes travel over the shelves, taking in prices, colors, and materials. There were molded candles, finely carved candles, and one odd gray candle, maybe about eighteen inches tall, shaped to look like a gnarled little man in a monk's robe of some sort. Niki would love it.

I picked it up from its shelf to take a closer look. Its features were wizened, a little distorted, almost cartoonish, and its long beard was thick and rope-like. The whole image was a little — almost a little frightening.

"You like our troll?"

"I — " I'll admit I jumped, for I hadn't heard the clerk come up behind me. "I — uh — I'm Roger Wenham." I held up the candle. "You mean it's supposed to be a troll? Like one of those creatures who live under bridges?"

"Well, that's what I call it," the sales clerk said. "It's one of a kind. Part of a lot we got at an estate auction." She paused as if she were thinking, then suddenly grinned. "Well, this is sort of silly, really, but there was a lot of weird stuff that came with it. Mirrors and figurines, although most of these were sold to other buyers. But there were other things too, like catalogs, one of which said this *was* a troll, a sort of an ice troll, except not the Earth kind like in *The Three Billy Goats Gruff* and all that. This kind lives in frozen caves on Neptune. Except it's — it's like in a different dimension."

"You mean sort of a 'New Age' Neptune?" Niki *would* like this.

The sales clerk laughed. "Well, that's what I tell people. You saw our shelf of books on magic? Some of them came from the same auction. But this candle is just a kind of novelty item, really. So it's not too expensive." She paused and smiled again.

I looked at the price tag. It *was* inexpensive. "My girlfriend would like it, though," I said. "And maybe a book on magic as well, if it doesn't cost much. She likes to use candles to tell people's fortunes."

The sales clerk nodded and found me a book on telling fortunes, one of the ones that had come with the odd, gray candle. I looked at its cover, old and faded. I thought, what the heck, maybe I'd have her wrap the candle up to give to Niki tonight, then maybe read the book myself — sometimes, like with this woman, I didn't always quite know what Niki was talking about so, maybe, this book would help. Then I could give it to her as well on Saturday night, for her birthday proper.

"You know," the clerk said when she'd rung up my purchases, "there's a legend about these ice trolls." She winked as she handed me my receipt. "In the collection catalog, anyhow. When you looked at it, did you notice its mouth? Like it was singing. Like it and its fellows who've gotten to Earth here — you know, the ones that *do* live under bridges — miss the others who stayed on Neptune. Whatever their planet is. And so they sing — except this one, somehow, was turned into a candle."

I laughed with her this time, though somewhat uncertainly. As with a lot of Niki's teasing, I never knew quite what I was supposed to take seriously and what was just joking. But this I did know, as I put the candle under my arm and took it with me to her apartment.

Niki would love it.

Niki's apartment was really a loft — a drafty walk-up that took up most of its

THE CANDLE ROOM

ageing building's entire fourth level. It had been partitioned into irregular rooms, who knows how long back, with walls that as often as not still showed bare lath. But Niki had made it her home, with some walls covered by tapestries, others with posters, and still more with bookcases forming dividers within the divisions. It was into one of these rooms that she led me after she'd unwrapped her present.

This was her Candle Room. That's what she called it. The only furnishings it contained consisted of the cushions we sat on, and her candles.

Rows and rows of colored candles, in various stands, some in high candelabra against the walls, others in old-fashioned mirrored sconces, others in low bases more toward the center. Some were lighted, but most were kept out, keeping the room very dim.

In the center of the Candle Room she placed her new candle, facing it toward us. Around it she placed three colored candles in a triangular configuration.

She struck a long wooden match on the floor and lit the three candles, first the gold one, then the white one, finally the red. "The red one's our love," she said.

She placed the burnt match into a shallow bowl next to where we sat. "I'll tell you our fortune."

"Okay," I said as I tried to look serious.

"Really," she said. She handed me a brass candle snuffer. "I want you to help me. First use this to put out the candles on the walls, so only the ones I just lit are burning, then come back beside me. I know you're sensitive — I can read people. You're much more sensitive than most men."

I did as she asked, then leaned over to kiss her, but she gently pushed me back. "Later," she said. "This is important. Try to be serious. You and I form a sort of nexus that magic can flow through. That's how I'll be able to find what the future holds for us, but only if you concentrate with me."

I nodded. "Okay." I tried to concentrate on the candles, the three flames dancing. The larger candle in the middle, dark, almost looking like some sort of wizard overseeing a ceremony that went on around him.

"Good," Niki said. "Now look at the flames. The gold candle first — that represents money. Worldly possessions."

I watched as she chanted under her breath, concentrating on the flame. Slowly it seemed to waver a little, then, picking up speed, the flame seemed to move in a sort of spiral before settling into a
side-to-side motion.

"Where you work," she said. "You have a rival? Someone you think is trying to get a promotion you're after?"

I looked away from the candle to her face. "Yes," I said. I'd never told her about Joe Bradcliff, one of the guys in my division, who had been sucking up to the boss a bit more than usual lately.

"He may well get it," she said. "But don't worry. That spiral the flame made

— that indicates that something's happening behind your back, but the left to right pattern it went into afterward suggests some kind of change of surroundings. My guess is that he'll get the promotion but, unknown to either of you just now, it involves a transfer to a different city."

I laughed a little, in spite of myself. "You mean, if I got it, I'd be the one who'd have to go away?"

"Exactly," she said. "Now should we go on to the red candle? The one that's our love? Or would you rather concentrate on the white one first? That's the one that represents life."

I looked back to the triangle of candles and now all the flames were moving from side to side. Then, suddenly, the flame of the white one threw out a spark.

I felt Niki's hand squeeze mine. I looked up again and saw she looked worried.

"The life-candle," she said. "First, all three candle flames are wavering, indicating that we might both take a trip as well. But that spark — it means some kind of reversal. Perhaps even danger. We have to be cautious."

"Will we be together?" I whispered. "I mean, if we go away, will it be on a trip together?"

"Shhhh. I can't tell yet. But now I want you to concentrate hard on the flame of the red one. That's the one that's important."

She gently squeezed my hand, while I stared as hard as I could at the red candle's flame. I watched as its wavering seemed to slow. As a point of bright, white light seemed to form at the tip of its wick, growing hotter and hotter. Hanging motionless, I don't know how long.

Then I heard Niki sigh. A sigh of happiness.

"Here," she whispered. "Snuff out the candles. The gold one first, then the white, and the red one last. Carefully, though, so you don't splash any wax." When I had done that, she kissed me and dragged me onto the floor, her arms around me.

"The bright light," she whispered, "— it showed that our love is growing. Whatever happens, we will be together. In spirit, perhaps, at first — I can't be sure of that. Whether we'll go away together. But, later on, if we remain faithful, together in body."

Together in body.

For now we made love, lit only by the electric light from the apartment's hallway, shining through the room's open lathwork. Later Niki relit the wall sconces, then went to the kitchen and brought us back coffee.

"I love you, Niki," I said. "I really do."

"Yes," she answered. She kissed me softly. "You did well tonight — I mean concentrating. Even the little troll-candle agrees. See how his mouth seems to form the word 'yes'? And I love you for that, too, even more than

I loved you before."

It was chilly when I finally left Niki's apartment. The weather was turning well into autumn, but inside I was warm, scarcely feeling the wind of October, scarcely minding that since the buses had stopped running by now, I'd have to walk home.

I thought of Niki and her Candle Room. Of flames and fortunes — I felt the book in my coat pocket and thought of the troll-candle. Bearded, gray men that lived on Neptune in its ice caves.

Then I saw him.

Not the candle, but a real gray man, hunched and bent and wearing a billowing, hooded cloak, scurry into the alley a half block ahead.

I ran to the dead-end alley and looked down its length at garbage cans and trash, shrouded in shadow. No men of any sort, hunched or standing straight, gray or in color.

I listened. I heard nothing. No sounds of scurrying. No sounds even of breathing except my own, until, far away, I heard a car horn honk.

I shrugged. I was dreaming. Awake, on my feet, but still dreaming after a wonderful evening. And if I was going to do that, I thought, as I scurried to my own apartment, I might as well do my dreaming in bed, and do it of Niki.

I went to see Niki Friday night, before her birthday. I was worried. I'd read through the candle book and discovered it wasn't *just* about candles. That is, not the kind of fortune telling she liked to do with them, that was really a game as much as anything, but something much darker.

It talked about ancient cultures and rituals — not all of Earth, either. I wondered now about that catalog that the sales clerk said she'd read. This book talked, not of trolls, but of ancient magicians, some so powerful they claimed to be able to actually visit other dimensions. But then something happened, something perhaps that had been their own doing. Some cataclysm — the Biblical Flood, or maybe the sinking of Atlantis — it wasn't too clear, except that they prayed to the gods they worshiped and that these gods saved them, changing their bodies so they could survive, taking them with them to a planet of ice and methane, frozen together. To what we call Neptune.

Still, I hadn't thought that much about it, in spite of the fact the book talked of more, too. Of how their gods shared this exile with them, keeping the rituals they'd used alive, and something that, while the book wasn't explicit, hinted that even just *reading* its pages could involve more than just let's-pretend peril. Nor had I thought much about the dream I'd had that night of a desolate, ice-covered valley I knew was supposed to be where the gray men had gone. This was, after all, the Twentieth Century, not ancient Atlantis, and Neptune — at least the one in *this* dimension — was made out of gases that nothing could live on, not frozen solid.

But when I saw another gray-hooded man, skulking in an alley near Niki's building, I started thinking of more earthly dangers. Niki was young and she had compassion, especially for people who looked like beggars, down on their luck. But I was more cynical — sometimes, I realized, even bent-over, wizened old men could intend a person like Niki evil.

Niki, I knew, could take care of herself in most situations, but I did love her. So I worried for her. And so, when I saw that gray man lurking almost on her building's doorstep, I ran up the stairs as fast as I could to the fourth floor landing.

I called out her name. I heard no answer. I banged on her door, but there was no answer. I took out the key I had for her apartment, but when I tried it, the door was already unlocked.

I went inside, still calling her name. I searched room by room, until I came into the Candle Room. I saw more burnt matches in the bowl next to her cushions and knew she had tried a new divination after I'd left. The three candles were arranged as we'd left them, the gray troll-candle still in their center, but now, on the floor, I saw splashes of wax, as if she had blown them out. Something that was not like Niki.

I thought for a moment of using her phone to call the police, but what would I tell them? There weren't any signs of anyone breaking in, or of violence.

I took the magic book out of my pocket — I still had it with me. I had an idea, crazy though it may have seemed, that I might use the book to find her. I opened its cover and searched through the ceremonies inside until I came to one that looked like it might help. I still didn't really believe it, but what else could I do?

I selected other candles of Niki's, following what the book suggested. A silver candle for dreams and enlightenment. A leaden color for finding out secrets and things now lost to me. The red one, however, for Niki's and my love, I left in place, lighting it first with a long wooden taper.

I started chanting, reading the words I found in the book as I lit the other two from the first candle. Words not in English. Strange words, unlike the words Niki's magic used, in many cases almost unpronounceable, yet I still read them. It didn't matter.

I concentrated instead on the flames.

I waited. I heard a *pop*. Sparks from the leaden one meaning that I'd find what I searched for?

A slow-turning spiral from the silver one, brightening suddenly, then slowly fading — a sudden discovery of plots against us, but, in the long run, a loss of awareness?

As long as I found Niki though, I thought. I then looked at the red one, saw it brightening like the other, but staying bright, overshadowing both the lead and the silver. Good fortune in love — a reuniting?

But no answers.

The red candle's flame stayed bright, seeming to beckon and, scarcely thinking, I felt my hand reach in the box of matches.

Another candle? Another to be lit?

Then it hit me. The gray troll-candle.

I riffled through the book on magic, seeking directions for using a fourth candle. There was nothing. Then I remembered what Niki had told me about my sensitivity. How she and I formed a sort of a nexus.

I pulled out a taper and lunged for the love-candle, chanting again the words I'd read out before. I let the taper flame, then thrust it forward, carrying fire to the still dark troll-candle. I watched its wick catch, guttering first, then throwing sparks in all directions.

I watched it expand from a point to a circle, illuminating the candle sharply. It grew stronger, showing the candle's face, its beard looking almost alive in the flickering, like writhing serpents.

Then I heard a scream. A shriek of wind ripped through the drafty apartment. The other three candles were blown out, leaving just the one, shrieking in answer.

Then yet another shriek pierced the night, this as if far away. The front door blew open, this time in a wind with a slight tinge of methane, and I saw on the landing outside the apartment a kind of dim flickering. A will-o'-the-wisp light.

Then the troll-candle went out as well.

I sat, I don't know how many minutes, letting my eyes adjust to the dimness. I got up slowly, left the Candle Room, slowly picked my way to the hallway. Guided by an almost-not-there light.

On the landing and the stairs there were tiny candles, some backed by mirrors, maybe one candle every ten or so steps. They guided me downward.

I followed them down to the lobby below, noting that as I passed each candle it went out behind me.

I reached the street, normal except it, too, was in darkness, as if the whole city had lost its power. The only dim light came from the tiny points of the candles that led away from the building.

I passed other people, normal people, but frozen in place as if where I walked was no longer a part of earth-bound time. I saw scurrying, now and again, bent, gray men, always just out of reach. Always disappearing *somewhere*, just out of eye-range.

I followed the points of light, into alleys, through cellars of cut stone, sometimes seeming to double back. Sometimes climbing stairs, reaching roofs as dark as basements, then descending back to street level. Soon the streets seemed more like canyons, the buildings surrounding them looking like ancient ruins. Huge and inhuman.

A steady wind down the length of one canyon. A cold, damp wind. Only now and again did I glimpse tiny spots of whiteness.

A glint of tiny candles resting on ice. I passed stalactites and, above me, openings to starlight, but the stars seemed strange. Not right for the Earth.

And as the wind died down, as I found myself straining to breathe in an acrid, new air, I knew I had entered the ice caves the clerk at the store had described. The caves where the trolls lived, now growing brighter as I saw . . . not candles, but candles' reflections. A system of mirrors.

I followed the reflections of will-o'-the-wisp lights, ever downward where, at least, the cold became less intense.

And then, a turn. A place where the cavern floor spiraled tightly in on itself. Then, in the flickering shadows, I came to another sharp turn.

I entered a chamber. Candles upon candles, standing in curved rows, some so large that they towered over me, others, smaller, reaching my knees or the height of my shoulders. Throughout the vast array, gray-robed men moved, singing softly in words I did not know, meticulously lighting some of the candles, shifting others, snuffing yet others out and then relighting them in such a way that their flames burned whiter.

Here there was no longer coldness at all. The closer I came to the nearest candles, the warmer it got — and yet, because of the cold outside, not even the ice of the chamber's ceiling displayed the slightest sign of distortion.

I stood at the edge of a vast, sloping cavern, the candles descending in rows below me. The gray men paid me no attention at all. And then I saw the network of the mirrors. Each candle's flame appeared to be focused, reflected, within its own mirror. Then other mirrors collected this light, these myriad flame-points, and sent it on, amplified, to yet more mirrors which concentrated it all into one huge directed beam, upward.

I looked up and saw a hole in the cavern roof, the light shooting out of it like some great searchlight.

And then I looked downward, and saw there was another reflection. I turned to my right, so I looked diagonally over the circling rows of candles. Down in the chamber's center was Niki, tied to a platform above the floor with her arms stretched above her.

I stared at her hands, at her outstretched fingers. Saw flames spouting from them.

"Niki!" I shouted.

She looked up. "No!" she shouted back. "Don't come any closer. Don't you see? It's you they want."

I tried to run to her, to pull her down, in spite of her warning, but I found that I *couldn't*. My feet were rooted, as if I were held in place by some force. Some force of will that emanated from the still chanting gray men.

"Don't you see?" Niki shouted again, her voice echoing across the huge chamber. "It's you who are sensitive to magic, to this dimension. It's you they're using to form the bridge."

"The *bridge?*" I asked.

"Look at the mirrors. Concentrate on their light. See what they point toward."

I looked again at the mirrored searchlight, trying to concentrate. Seeing it grow as the gray men continued with their adjustments.

I saw forms coalescing. Huge, winged creatures beginning to circle the beam of light like moths might an ordinary light bulb.

"Don't you understand?" Niki said. "That's the force that reaches between worlds — the light-bridge to *our* world. They want to have it. The gray men. The flying men. Others you don't see that crawl on the surface — their gods, that brought them here. They exist now for one purpose only, to open the way back to Earth where they lived once until they destroyed it, and as they will again. And it's your energy that shapes the focus."

I no longer listened. I struggled to move, pushing toward her as if I were trying to swim through molasses. I struggled, slowly, moving first one foot, as if it weighed tons, and then the other. And all this time the gray men's chants grew louder.

One of the nearest gray men noticed me. He turned and faced me.

I saw his face, bright in the mirrored light as his hood fell back. A face not human, or no longer human, but covered with cracked scales, its eyes as deep and as cold as space itself. The creature's hands also no longer human, but gnarled, razored claws as they reached out to grasp me.

I screamed and dodged sideways. I could move sideways! I dodged again as more gray *things* turned and reached toward me, some chanting in shouts now, still in some strange, yet familiar tongue.

Like in the spell in the candle book that I'd recited.

And then it came to me. If I could divert them. Make them somehow lose their concentration. Release me to go to Niki.

I dodged again, feeling claws rip through my jacket — they knew what I was thinking! They wanted to hold me, in case the force faltered. They *could* be defeated.

Another claw raked me, but this time I pushed back. I pushed at another, that came from the other side. Each time I pushed one, I felt the force in front of me waver.

I heard the roar of the invocation fade, however slightly.

I had an idea. I dodged again, quickly, then pushed at the nearest candle. It rocked on its base.

I heard Niki shout my name.

I tried to look down to where the voice came from — saw the candle I'd shoved tilt farther, falling over, as if in slow motion, taking two more of the candles with it.

I felt the force weaken.

"Yes!" I shouted. I looked toward Niki's platform as more candles fell, slowly at first, but then with increasing swiftness.

The gray troll-men turned and ran, trying to stop them from falling like dominoes.

Paraffin met ice, spreading over it — flame on intense cold, converting the ice it touched to steam and methane. More fire erupted. Mirrors distorted. Reflections of still upright candles wavered and then refocused, concentrated, back toward yet more candles. Light beams pierced wax sides. Forming new flames as more paraffin melted.

As more ice met paraffin, coalescing in flame and brightness. A searing flash.

I couldn't see! But I heard Niki call my name, over and over, and let my ears guide me, rushing to where I could hear her shout. Feeling her, finally, in my arms, I ripped away the ropes that bound her.

Still not seeing, I ran with her, upward, out of the chamber. Through fire into coldness.

I felt us flung forward.

I felt us spinning, as if through space. Then blackness — I felt blackness. Pain and redness. Then hours, maybe days later, I felt myself with Niki beside me, her arms around me, sitting with my back to cold dampness. A dampness not of ice, but of wet stone, as if in some rarely used, oozing cellar, after a rain storm.

"Niki?" I whispered.

"Yes," she whispered. She kissed me softly, then gingerly took my hand in hers, as if it hurt her fingers to do so. She led me to a set of wooden steps, guiding my arm as she led us upward, up more flights of stairs, until I recognized by the feel of the cushions she sat me on that we had come back to her apartment.

My sight came back slowly and even now I still sometimes see spots when my eyes are tired. I moved in with Niki, insisting that we get married for fear I might lose her if we should be separated again. Together we went to the candle store where I'd bought the troll candle and sold her collection, getting enough for a modest honeymoon and for new furnishings for her room, no longer a Candle Room. Neither of us wished to have candles around us again.

As for Niki, the scars on her fingertips — where the creatures burned her — never have become completely healed, and even now she wears gloves when she goes outside, even in the hottest weather. But it doesn't matter.

We have each other.

And we did stop them — at least for a time. Late at night, when Niki is sleeping, sometimes I look out her fourth floor window and stare at the sky. I look at the myriad patterns of stars and sometimes, in that part of the darkness where Neptune lies, I think I can see a tiny flicker, as if of a candle flame, far in the distance.

That's when I rush back to Niki's — *our* — bedroom and climb in beside her, to hold her tightly. Because I realize then that they're still waiting.

And I know that waiting has not been passive.

USHER

by Davin Ireland

I.

Moments before the pale white star was due to reach its midday zenith, a faint blemish appeared on the horizon. The blemish was tiny at first, and rippled with heat shimmer that blurred it back into the featureless plain of salt. But as time progressed, the shape coalesced, grew more definite.

An arch. A parabolic limestone arch some five-hundred feet across. Hewn from a single layer of sedimentary rock, it had stood to the sky for what might have been aeons. Cowper had examined it hundreds of times over recent months, and would probably do so again given the opportunity. But for now he was content to admire it from afar, pausing to wipe his face and neck with a filthy rag. The gesture offered little relief. The vast endorheic desert extended from skyline to skyline, the salt crust that covered it so uniformly flat that the planet's natural curvature revealed itself at every turn. The sun beat relentlessly on the desiccated landscape, the whitened surface reflecting the heat back the way it had come.

Yet for all that, there was an austere beauty about the place that enchanted Cowper. A lack of ozone in the atmosphere meant the heavens sang in tones of indigo and ultra-violet for most of the day. When wet, the salt plains reflected those colours like a burnished mirror, creating an effect that was both pleasing to the eye and nominally disorientating. Right now the season was at its most arid, and the only water present was that which evaporated from Cowper's own pores. He could live with that. The arch was less than an hour's walk away, and the sloshing of the canteen at his hip formed a reassuring presence. Checking that no area of skin was exposed, he refastened his photochromatic goggles, took up the handles of the wooden barrow, and resumed his journey.

II.

How the weathered android had managed to survive this long on its own, Cowper reasoned, was a miracle of both science and spirituality. A diminutive 130 centimetres in height, it patrolled the base of the arch ceaselessly, aging servo motors whirring, graphic-fibre bundles bunching and extending in time to its movements.

Still shrouded in his rags, Cowper rolled the giant barrow to a standstill, the salt crust cracking beneath its great wheel like an ice floe fracturing before the prow of an invading ship. He always stopped to observe the solar-powered droid as it strutted east to west, never ceasing to feel a kind of pity for its meaningless existence and the duties that defined it.

"Usher," he croaked, cupping his swollen fingers about his mouth. He cleared his parched airways and tried again: "Usher!"

The android continued in sentry mode for a few seconds more, then turned to face the visitor.

"Cowper," it said, and raised a hand in greeting. "How goes the salvage business?"

"So-so." He indicated the barrow piled with junk, most of it the wreckage of off-world racing vehicles previously scattered across the plains. "Anybody drop by?"

The android greeted the old joke by miming gently sarcastic applause. "Ever the optimist," it said. "By the way, I read the instruction manual you left the last time. Not quite as challenging as the railway timetable but interesting in its own right."

Cowper grunted. "Try living my life for a day and tell me about interesting."

Usher tipped his head quizzically to the side. "Would the conversation improve?"

This time it was Cowper's turn to applaud. Unfortunately, he forgot to mime, and the collision of roasted palms sent shockwaves of pain lancing up his wrists. "Dammit," he whispered, "that's what you get when you let your guard down."

"Are you damaged?"

"Damaged?" Cowper shook his head, an act which caused precious droplets of sweat to spatter the inside of his cowl. "I guess I'll survive," he said. The statement belied a deeper anxiety. Already a mixture of blood and pus seeped between the wrappings covering his palms. If he didn't get them seen to soon, infection would result. In bygone times, a sturdy pair of gloves had provided ample protection against heat blisters, ultra-violet radiation, even burning hot metal — of which there was much on this otherwise barren hunk of salt-encrusted stone. But with manufacturing in terminal decline, the only substitutes were filthy strips of canvas torn from sacks stolen off the New Deptford wharves.

Cowper lifted the cowl from his face and squinted at the titanic arch, which loomed above them, midday shadow a narrow stripe on the well-trodden salt.

"Is it ready?"

Usher took a moment to calculate the time differential. "I believe so," he said. He sounded disappointed. He always sounded that way when Cowper returned to his own world. "Will you bring me something else to read next time?" He handed back the instruction manual, which had once served a mechanism described as an automated dish-washer.

"I only just gave you this one," Cowper protested, and regretted it immediately. It wasn't the droid's fault it was all alone. "Look," he sighed, "I'll see what I can do, okay?" As he said this, he tried to forget how he had also promised Usher a thesaurus to go with the dictionary the inquisitive droid had already consumed and stored on his hard drive. The acquisition of that one volume — even on a temporary basis — had saddled him with a debt he was still struggling to pay off, but it had been worth it to establish communication with the portal's faithful guardian. "Just try not to be too disappointed if it's another manual," he added, "deal?"

Usher nodded as a pinprick of darkness opened up at the centre of the arch. The pinprick swelled first to fist-size, then plate-size, then all the way up to man-size. It would continue to expand until it reached the solid rind of calcium carbonate that encapsulated it.

"Time to go." Cowper gingerly grasped the handles of the barrow and winced. Even this much pressure caused his aching palms to scream.

"Do you hurt?" Usher's head was tilted to the side again.

Cowper intended his chuckle to be both dry and cynical, but all he could manage was an exasperated wheeze. "There's an old expression about rubbing salt into wounds," he said. "I doubt its author ever visited this place."

The droid was silent for a moment. "I wasn't talking about your injuries."

And just like that, they were on the subject of Joshua again. Usher had grasped the principle of physical pain with ease. Damage occurs, a signal travels to the appropriate receptor, action is taken. But emotional pain — grief, bitterness, despair — was a mystery to him, and therefore a source of endless fascination. That was hard to take. Like so many families, the Cowpers had lost their only child at the end of the period known simply as More. They had struggled to survive on their own since, yet Marit still harboured the dream of bringing another child into the world. Usher's preoccupation with the subject verged on obsessive — and the fact he was not much bigger than Josh when the boy had been taken from them only added to the sorrow.

"Have your fertility levels risen?" the droid asked. "I could perform a scan."

Cowper stared morosely at the far vista of the horizon. "I'm not sure I'm the one with the problem," he said, "and I think I'd prefer it if you didn't ask me that question again."

III.

Marit was waiting for him — face drawn with concern — when he dragged the giant barrow back into the cellar, salt whispering beneath his soles. It was so full its contents nearly brushed the low ceiling.

"Clear," he gasped, and allowed his hands to drop.

Marit threw the switch on the aging junction box and the portal collapsed as quickly and neatly as a deckchair clapping together after a day at the beach. Only there were precious few deckchairs left any more, and most of Earth's beaches had long been subsumed by desert.

"How long?" He threw off the cowl, ditched the goggles, tore at his finger-wrappings with giddy impatience. It was always the way. Returning from the other side, where there was ostensibly nothing, the darkness and the cramped conditions of home sent him into fits of claustrophobia.

Marit grimaced, her face teetering on collapse as she drew water from an aging rain barrel. "Thirty-six hours," she said, voice rising with indignation.

"*Thirty-six?*" He took the proffered bowl, searched her eyes for confirmation. "So long?" He stopped short of asking Marit outright if she was completely certain. He knew how agonising she found his absences, but also how crucial they were for the both of them. Without the salvage income, the Cowpers were destitute. But two nights and a *day*? After the bowl was empty, she helped him into a sackcloth robe, led the way to a chair by the fire. The stack of firewood — slats and fractured skirting boards mostly — was almost gone.

"The time," she said, "it's getting longer, isn't it?"

"Not necessarily." Cowper leaned forward as she stirred the embers, but stopped short of raising his palms to the feeble flames. In the space of minutes he had gone from the baking furnace of an alien desert to a dank basement in the slums of New Deptford. The contrast could hardly be greater, as was the opportunity for chilblains. But what could he do? His flesh was practically cooked as it was.

"No, not necessarily longer at all," he repeated, thinking the thing through. "Oscillation is common in older model portals. We'll just have to hope it regains a shorter frequency sooner rather than later."

"And if it doesn't?" She clutched sackcloth to her throat with a white-knuckled fist. "Next time you could be gone for months. *Years*, even."

"Not years, my darling, please. Days at best." He frowned, a mixture of guilt and dread momentarily undermining his confidence. What if Marit was right? What if he returned next time to an armed reception, waiting militia men, an empty shell? Marit wouldn't be able to survive on her own for more than a week. If he was reported missing, the authorities were bound to come calling.

"I was so frightened, Joseph," she was saying, thin form shivering beneath the robe, "so horribly frightened."

"Well, it's over now." There was little else he could say. Both of them knew the reality of the situation. God alone knows, he thought, neither of us is immune to fear. But as the modest fire burned lower, with the satisfying tick of salvage metal cooling in the background, he realised that words were not enough, would never be enough. Not until ...

She was waiting for him to ask, just as they both knew he would. They also both knew the answer to the question. It was merely another of the ways Marit had of beating herself up.

Reluctantly, he draped an arm around her shoulders. This was one chore he could do without. "So how are you feeling, my love?" He did not wish to put it to her any more directly than that.

"I've been better," she said, and instinctively rested a hand on her shrivelled belly.

"That's thirty-eight months in a row," he told her. "If I auction the salvaged technology on the black market instead of selling it for scrap, the fertility treatment you so long for could be ours —"

"No." Voice firm, tone uncompromising, she waved the offer away. "It's too risky, Joseph. I could never ask you to —"

"You're not *asking* me anything," he interrupted, "I'm offering of my own free will. There's a difference. Besides, the underground is far more organised now than it was before. There are middle men, financers, networks of reliable informants. The authorities will be none the wiser."

But she was steadfastly shaking her head.

"I won't countenance it. What's the point of another child if it enters the world fatherless? I'll end up as nothing more than a surrogate for a wealthy couple."

She was right, of course. Theirs was the last working portal in the city, perhaps the country. If the secret ever got out, public execution would be the best they could hope for. In the background, the cooling heap of metal ticked progressively slower, like a clock running down the days ...

IV.

When the portal next deposited Cowper on that nameless planet, large pools of standing water reflected a rapidly dissipating scum of cloud cover. All about him, the air fizzed and popped with the sound of deliquescing salt.

Unusually, Usher had halted his perpetual marching, and was stationed above a large puddle, gaze fixed upon the smooth surface of the water. Cowper had never seen his friend do anything like that before, and for a moment the sight of an android contemplating its own reflection — especially among the inhospitable wastelands of outer space — made him a little uneasy. Could an artificial construct feel loneliness? He considered Usher's ongoing struggle to decipher the lexicon of emotion, and decided that the struggle itself hinted at the presence of desire.

He put the thought out of his mind and leaned into the barrow, its great front wheel slipping and squelching over the treacherous landscape. "Nice day for it," he called, passing within a hundred feet of the planet's only other sentient being. Usher raised his head, servo motors whining.

"Cowper!" He set off at angle calculated to intercept the human's admittedly limited progress. "How goes it?" His permanently booted feet emitted gaudy sucking sounds as he stomped through a slush of aggregated moisture. "I have a question for you," he cried, striding within the range for normal conversation. "If, that is, you are agreeable."

"Fire away."

"I have been reviewing the information you provided concerning the arrival of the Siddith-Sa. Is that the correct pronunciation?"

Cowper said that it was.

"Excellent. As I understand it, the outworlders exploited terrestrial portal technology to effect a concerted invasion, simultaneously pouring through all the open gateways at once and stripping your planet of its most valuable resources — both natural and artificial."

"And leaving us just enough to survive on," Cowper conceded, "although I'm not sure that last part was intentional." He had been expecting this for some time. The books and discs he occasionally scavenged had awakened the android's intellectual curiosity. "But it's not really a subject I wish to discuss at length, Usher. The memories are too painful. I'm sorry."

The robot angled its head forward for a moment, like a cobra preparing to strike. "You are aware it is my task to await the return of those who created me?"

"M-hm."

"And you are further aware that the use of portal technology on Earth has been banned?"

"Usher," sighed Cowper, "it was me who told you that. Now I really must be getting on. When the salt is damp like this it corrodes the wood of the wheel — and I don't have a replacement."

"Feel free to walk and talk," countered the robot. "I will gladly join you."

For the first time, Cowper surveyed the junk-littered horizon with a feeling of genuine trepidation. It never failed to astonish him just how many of the alien recreational vehicles had perished out here at the furthest perimeter of the galaxy. Every year thousands of square hectares of salt flats were scorched black by the insane races that took place out here. Any wreckage was left to rot where it crashed, along with the bodies of the fallen. Nobody would notice an extra body lying around, not even that of a human. "I haven't chosen my location yet," he said quietly, and fiddled with his goggles.

"Then answer me this. You must realize that employing the same destination each time greatly increases the chances of a second invasion, and yet you continue to visit this place at the expense of all others. Why?"

"I enjoy the company." Cowper experienced an unexpected twinge of guilt at the lie. The diminutive android was in earnest, and had helped him on numerous occasions. He deserved better than this. "I agree it heightens the danger, Usher. But we are exposed to levels of poverty that oblige me to retain this place as a scavenging ground. Don't forget, I have a monopoly on the work out here. And there are other benefits." He sloshed his foot in a salt-thickened puddle. "Even without the benefit of reclaimed metal, we could vend this stuff on the street. There's certainly not much chance of it running out."

Usher was silent for longer than Cowper had ever known. Normally chatty to a fault, the sudden change was disturbing. "I don't believe you," he finally said, the graphic fibre bundles in his arms tensing as artificial muscles flexed and relaxed. "I think that the portal is broken, and that you have no choice but to return here in spite of the risks."

It was in that moment Cowper realized he had committed the cardinal sin of equating size with age. And although Usher's modest stature was no greater than that of his dead son, the robot was far older than the six years afforded Joshua, and infinitely wiser. Stranded here on this desolate world, afforded no regress but for the co-operation of his diminutive host, Cowper perceived that embroidering the truth now might cost him a lot more than the android's friendship.

"We are doing everything we can to fix it," he said in a hushed voice.

"But you have been coming here since before your wife's second miscarriage. How long do you need?"

Cowper could only lower his head. In reality, he had given up hope long ago. Was, in fact, only treading water until the militia traced the signal to his basement refuge.

"You realize this has implications for me, too," the android insisted. "If my makers are denied the ability to return, my purpose as usher is without merit."

Cowper took a deep breath. How could he confess what he really suspected? According to rumour, terrestrial authorities were preparing an all-out assault on the very laws of physics in an attempt to close off any stray wormholes left strewn about the galaxy. That meant marooning one pint-sized robot most definitely, and one miserable human quite possibly. For now, the powers that be were content only to dismantle existing portal technology in advance of the final push. But before long the underlying structure of space-time would be permanently and irrevocably altered.

V.

Cowper sucked in his breath when he saw the state of Marit's face. The whole right side of it was purple-black and so badly swollen that the corresponding eye barely opened. She sat atop a pile of bulging salt sacks, fingers clutching the collars of her tattered robe to her throat. Her hands looked as if they hadn't seen the inside of a rain barrel in days.

"What happened, my darling?" Even as he crossed the floor, Cowper hated himself for the cowardice that caused him to glance into the basement's dim corners. No militia men stared back. Nothing moved beyond the shadows thrown by the dying embers of the fire. "Who did this to you?"

Her functioning eye blinked slowly, its companion barely twitching in response. "It's been three weeks," she whispered. "I thought you were dead."

Cowper, struck nearly speechless by his wife's condition, felt the wind go out of him.

"Lord have mercy, three *weeks*?"

She nodded. "The dizzy spells started the day after you left. I fell down the stairs on the Sabbath." A whine escaped her narrow throat. "Joseph, I spent our savings on a doctor. The pain was too much to bear."

"Hush," he told her, and took her in his arms. "Hush, my dear. I'm home now. From this day on, things will be different. I promise you."

But they both knew it was a lie. Things would only be different if they got worse, and if their lives carried on the way they were, this period of destitution might one day look like a holiday in retrospect. She wept against his chest as Cowper contemplated the thought, mumbled something about a change already having taken place.

"What was that?"

"He thinks it's the change," she repeated, rubbing the tears from her eyes. And when he just looked at her, too dopey with fatigue to understand, she swatted him weakly on the shoulder. "The *change*," she repeated, allowing a hand — not a protective one this time — to drop to the barren cave of her womb. "No more, Joseph."

His arms relinquished her slight frame. No more little ones was the implication, but what she really meant was no more hope. Utterly defeated, Cowper rose and shuffled to the darkened rear of the basement. He'd had enough of staring at his shoes for one day. Neck muscles creaking, he squinted up through the pavement-level grate. Outside, endless night smothered both city and planet. No streetlights burned, no stars were visible beneath the acrid layers of permacloud. The brief but terrible reign of the Siddith-Sa had damaged Earth beyond repair — their indiscriminate plundering causing billions of unnecessary deaths. Their carelessness had provided just enough for the survivors to get by on. Or had it been carelessness? Was the theft of an entire bakery any less reprehensible if you left a few stale crumbs for the cockroaches?

Considering what had happened since, Cowper realized, it was infinitely worse. Disease, hunger, untold anguish. Hospitals without medicine, schools and churches stripped of anything that would burn, a perpetual war raging between declining nation states as the end-game for resources entered its final phase. And no more welfare provision. No help for the elderly. The only realistic investment a couple could make for their future security, even if it meant more mouths to feed in the short term, was to bear as many children as possible in the hope that at least one would survive long enough to care for them in old age. But now that hope was gone, too.

Cowper turned from the window. Marit hadn't moved. Devoid of purpose, she was a rag doll perched on a mountain of salt. He knew her desire for a child was more than just practical. She had doted on Joshua during the lad's few meagre years of life, and needed to feel that love again — if only to mend the yawning chasm into which she had fallen. It was not to be. Sensing she was beyond his reach for now, Cowper returned his attention to the great barrow. With a sigh, he unlatched the side panel and stood back.

Corroded engine parts and mangled alloy siding clattered to the floor. It was a better-than-average haul, but Cowper — despite the gnawing in the pit of his stomach — eyed it blankly. Then an area of scrap moved without the aid of gravity. It lifted, overturned, clanged against part of a broken fuselage. A second later, a larger hunk of siding repeated the trick to the accompaniment of a low whirring. Cowper took a step back. The heap of scavenged metal shifted again to reveal the stunted figure of a humanoid robot gaining its feet. The journey to a fully upright position took a while, the various sections of the android's body flexing and extending in sequence. The stowaway had sustained major damage during the trip. Cowper noticed the way its left arm had been mangled under the accumulated weight of salvage. And the sparks fizzing at its chest console suggested major repairs were in order.

But it had survived.

"Don't be scared," Cowper told his wife, "it's only Usher."

But Marit was anything but scared. Eyes bulging in their sockets, one hand clutching at the throat of her robe, she sat riveted to the spot as their unexpected guest limped from the wreckage. The uncertainty of the droid's movements hinted that it might be lost. Salt water dripped from its chin like tears. Circuits crackling, it extended an arm to balance itself against the barrow's side. And suddenly she was there, taking the android by the hand and leading it to a chair by the fire — Cowper's chair — before plucking a clean rag from a nail above the mantelpiece.

Her husband looked on in dull astonishment as she proceeded to buff and polish the moulded chromium of the little robot's faceplate, muttering beneath her breath as she worked.

Let's get you nice and dry before you go all rusty.
Poor thing, you must have been terribly scared under all that metal.
It's been simply ages since we've had guests.

It was as if a manhole cover had been lifted from Cowper's chest. Exhausted, he clambered atop the salt sacks and fell into the deepest sleep of his life. A voice in his head wanted to say, *He's an orphan and he likes to read*, but his lips wouldn't move. It didn't matter. Something told him everything Marit needed was right there in front of her.

CAST OF CONTRIBUTORS

Eric S Brown is a 35 year old author living in NC with his wife and son. He has been called "The King of the Zombies" by places like *Dread Central* and was featured in the book *Zombie CSU: The Forensics of the Living Dead* as an expert on the genre. Some of his books include *Space Stations and Graveyards, Dying Days, Portals of Terror, Madmen's Dreams, Cobble, The Queen, The Wave, Waking Nightmares, Unabridged Unabashed and Undead: The Best of Eric S Brown, Barren Earth, Season of Rot, War of the Worlds Plus Blood Guts and Zombies, World War of the Dead, Zombies II: Inhuman, Tandem of Terror,* and *Bigfoot War*. He was the editor of the anthology *Wolves of War* (Library of Horror Press).

Some of his upcoming titles include *How the West Went to Hell, The Human Experiment, Anti-Heroes, The Weaponer,* and *Kinberra Down*. His short fiction has been published hundreds of times. Some of his anthology appearances include *Dead Worlds I,II, III,* and *V, The Blackest Death I & II, The Undead I & II, Dead History, Dead Science, Zombology I & II, The Zombist,* and the upcoming *Gentlemen of Horror 2010* to name only a few. He also writes an ongoing column on the world of comic books for *Abandoned Towers Magazine* (which recently won the Preditors and Editors' Award for Best Nonfiction 2009). Eric is also part of the giant collaborative, zombie novel effort from *Pill Hill Press* entitled *Undead, Kansas*.

Michael Scott Bricker has sold stories to numerous anthologies, and has recently completed a time travel novel which takes place, in part, during the Black Death. He lives in California, where he works at a public library, and buys and sells old and curious goods. *http://sff.net/people/m.bricker/*

Camille Alexa When not on ten wooded acres near Austin, Texas, Camille Alexa lives in the Pacific Northwest in an Edwardian House with very crooked windows. Her work appears in *Chizine, Fantasy Magazine,* and *Escape Pod*. Her first book, *Push of the Sky* (Hadley Rille Books, 2009) received a starred review in *Publisher's Weekly*.

CAST OF CONTRIBUTORS

Vincent L. Scarsella has gained modest success in publishing his work in print magazines such as *The Leading Edge*, *Aethlon: The Journal of Sport Literature*, *Fictitious Force*. Several of his short stories have appeared in the online zine *Aphelion-Webzine*, as recently as March 2009 (*Simulation Addicts*). In September, 2007, his short story *Vice Cop* was included in the anthology *New Writings in the Fantastic* (Pendragon Press) edited by award winning John Grant. In March 2008, *Practical Time Travel* was published in *Bound For Evil – Books Gone Bad* (Dead Letter Press). *Homeless Zombies* appeared in the April 2009 anthology *Dead Science* (Coscom Entertainment).

He has been an attorney for thirty years, an adjunct professor at the University of Buffalo School of Law, and is currently employed as an investigative lawyer for the New York Department of Taxation and Finance.

Sheila Crosby lives on a small rock in the Atlantic. She's a mother, writer, photographer, translator, tour guide, librarian, gardener, belly dancer, English teacher and software engineer. One of her primary school teachers once sneered, "Well, *you've* got a good imagination," and she's been proving the truth of it ever since. *http://sheilacrosby.com*

Gerard Houarner is a NYC resident who works at a psychiatric center by day and writes by night. Recent work includes the collections *A Blood of Killers*, and *The Oz Suite*, as well as the novel, *Road From Hell*.

David Steffen lives in Minnesota with his wife in a house where dogs now outnumber the humans. This complicates voting on family meetings, but can be counteracted with a well-placed treat bribe or a long filibuster that puts the dogs to sleep. He writes code by day and fiction by night and occasionally does other things too (time permitting). David is a repeat offender with Northern Frights Publishing: his story *The Utility of Love* was published in NFP's first anthology, *Shadows of the Emerald City*. His fiction has also been published in *Pseudopod*.

David co-edits Diabolical Plots with his friend and colleague Anthony Sullivan. DP provides interviews of professionals in the speculative fiction industry, as well as reviews and editorials. Past and future guests include NFP's very own JW Schnarr, as well as Cat Rambo, David Farland, John Joseph Adams, Orson Scott Card, Tad Williams, and Anne Rice. The site features amazing original art by professional artist Joey Jordan. Stop by, check out the interviews, and leave a comment or two. *http://www.diabolicalplots.com*

Mark Onspaugh grew up on a steady diet of horror, science fiction and *DC Comics*. An HWA member, he writes screenplays, short stories and novels. His ghost horror film *Kill Katie Malone* is now in post-production and he is the co-writer of zombie cult fave *Flight of the Living Dead*. Mark's stories also appear in *Shadows of the Emerald City* (JW Schnarr, ed.), *Timelines: Stories inspired by HG Wells' The Time Machine* (JW Schnarr, ed.), *The Book of Exodi* (Michael K. Eidson, ed.), *The World is Dead* (Kim Paffenroth, ed.), *Footprints* (Jay Lake & Eric T. Reynolds, ed.), *The Book of Tentacles* (Scott Virtes, Edward Cox, Susan R. Campbell, ed.), *Triangulation: Dark Glass* (Pete Butler, ed.) and *Thoughtcrime Experiments* http://thoughtcrime.crummy.com/2009. He also has an essay on monsters in the forthcoming *Butcher Knives and Body Counts* (Dark Scribe Press). He lives in Los Osos, CA with his wife, author/artist Dr. Tobey Crockett and three enigmatic cats. *www.markonspaugh.com*

Bruce Golden After more than 20 years as a journalist, publishing more than 200 articles, working as a magazine editor, radio reporter, and television producer, Bruce Golden decided to walk away from journalism and concentrate all his efforts on his first love—writing speculative fiction. That's what he wanted to do when, at age 18, he decided to be a writer. But life, as it often tends to do, took him in a different direction. The jobs in journalism kept coming, and there were bills to pay. Along the way, some of the work, like writing and producing his all-original show *Radio Free Comedy* and producing documentaries like "Sex in the '90s," he found rewarding. He dabbled in writing science fiction and fantasy—and never stopped reading it—but the time to pursue it seemed elusive.

That all changed at the turn of the century, when decided to devote himself entirely to writing fiction. Since then his short stories have garnered several awards and more than 80 sales across seven countries. *Asimov's Science Fiction* described his second novel, "If Mickey Spillane had collaborated with both Frederik Pohl and Philip K. Dick, he might have produced Bruce Golden's *Better Than Chocolate*." His latest novel, *Evergreen*, takes readers to alien world full of ancient secrets and a strange intelligence, populated with characters motivated by revenge, redemption, and obsession, on a quest to find the City of God. *http://goldentales.tripod.com*

RJ Sevin's short fiction has appeared here and there. He's very happy about his upcoming appearance in *Cemetery Dance Magazine*, and thinks you should check out *The Living Dead 2* (edited by JJ Adams). In addition to, like, several dozen of the most awesome of the awesomest zombie stories around, it features *Thin Them Out*, a novelette he co-wrote with his lovely wife, Julia Rose, and the equally lovely (though moustachioed) Doctor Kim Paffenroth (*Dying to Live*, *Gospel of the Living Dead*).

He's one half of Creeping Hemlock Press, and he thinks you'd love to buy some of their books: *www.creepinghemlock.com*. Also, he promises to *never* add zombies (or any other horror tropes) to public domain literature.

CAST OF CONTRIBUTORS

Kristen Lee Knapp is an author attending the University of North Florida. When he isn't writing, he's probably reading. When he isn't reading, he's probably writing. He enjoys long walks on the beach and murderous robots. *http://thelifefromtheslushpile.blogspot.com/*

Harper Hull was born and raised in Northern England but now lives in a 19th century farmhouse in the American South with his much smarter and prettier Dixie wife. He has lived in London, San Antonio and Seattle and his favourite city is Florence. He grew up in a home crammed with classic sci-fi and horror books, and started writing his own stories in 2009. If you ever read one of his pieces, he just hopes you enjoy it. *http://helloharperhull.blogspot.com/*

Auston Habershaw has been an avid science fiction and fantasy fan for his entire life and has been writing stories in the genre for almost as long. He has an MFA in Creative Writing from Emerson College, due, in part, to a species of aliens who look a lot like cabbages. He is a college English professor who lives and works in Boston, Massachusetts.

Brent Knowles is a game designer and author. He has been published in Dragon, Not One of Us, Tales of the Talisman and On Spec. In 2009 he placed first in the *Writers of the Future Contest* (3rd Quarter). He lives in Edmonton with his wife and two sons. *www.brentknowles.com*.

Michele Garber grew up in northern Indiana, which should not be held accountable for the products of her imagination. After narrowly escaping a doctorate in psychology, she succumbed to her urges to write, happily using her arcane knowledge of the human psyche to titillate, tempt, and terrify readers. Her work will appear in Zombology IV: The Undead vs The Living Dead (Library of the Living Dead Press). Find out more about her at *www.michelegarber.com*

Gary Cuba lives with his wife and oodles of critters in South Carolina. His work has appeared or is scheduled in more than a dozen genre and mainstream publications, including *Jim Baen's Universe, Abyss & Apex, Fictitious Force, Allegory, Lunch Hour Stories, Brain Harvest, Atomjack, Dark Recesses* and others. He has worked as an editorial associate on the staff of *JBU*, and now reads for *Flash Fiction Online*. *www.thefoggiestnotion.com*

Michael Penkas has lived in Chicago for the past five years and have had a half-dozen short stories previously published. *michaelpenkas.blogspot.com*

JW Schnarr is the evil mastermind behind Northern Frights Publishing. He lives in Champion, Alberta Canada with his daughter and a grumpy turtle. JW and the turtle watch the skies at night for signs of alien invaders so the rest of the world can sleep easy. His debut novel, *Alice and Dorothy*, will be forthcoming in 2010, as well as a collection of short fiction titled *Things Falling Apart*. jwschnarr.blogspot.com.

Mike Barretta is a retired Naval Aviator that currently works as a professional pilot. He resides in Pensacola, Florida with his wife and five children.

Edward Morris is a 2010 Stoker nominee, also nominated for the 2009 Rhysling and the 2005 BSFA. His short fiction has now appeared 59 times in 4 languages and 7 countries; including Murky Depths thrice, Interzone twice, and most recently the forthcoming Lefora Press anthology *Through The Eyes Of The Undead (I Am Stretched On Your Grave)* He collaborates with Texan SF author, journalist and Campbell nominee Lou Antonelli quite regularly, and their collection *Music For Four Hands* will be looked at by a major indie publisher in March. http://edwardrmorrisjr.blogspot.com

Jodi Lee An editor and occasional writer, Jodi Lee has spent her entire life on the Canadian Prairies which she credits with her over-active imagination. She is currently the editor in chief of Belfire Press and *The New Bedlam Project*, where she can be found slicing and dicing prose. Occasionally she's found mucking about with book covers, graphics, and websites in her design freelancing.

Her fiction has appeared in *Night to Dawn* and *Nocturnal Ooze*, as well as the anthologies *Fried! Fast Food, Slow Deaths* (Graveside Tales), *Parasitic Thoughts* (The Parasitorium Group) *Tainted* and *52 Stitches* (Strange Publications), *The Black Garden* (Corpulant Insanity), and several other upcoming anthologies. www.jodilee.ca

Victorya is a writer who lives and works in the desert mountains of New Mexico. Her work can be seen in *Andromeda Spaceways Inflight Magazine*, *Necrotic Tissue*, and *Timelines: Stories Inspired by HG Wells' The Time Machine* (Northern Frights Publishing)

James S. Dorr's collections *Strange Mistresses: Tales of Wonder and Romance* and *Dark Loves: Tales of Mystery and Regret* are available from Dark Regions Press,while other work has appeared in venues from *Alfred Hitchcock's Mystery Magazine* to *Xenophilia*. An active member of SFWA and HWA, Dorr is an Anthony (mystery) and Darrell (fiction set in tghe mid-south) finalist, a pushcart prize nominee, and a multi-time listee in *The Year's Best Fantasy and Horror* from the early '90s on. In addition to Canada and the US, he has fiction and poetry published in Britain, France, Australia, and most recently Brazil.

Davin Ireland was born and bred in the south of England, but currently resides in the Netherlands. His fiction credits include stories published in over fifty print magazines and anthologies on both sides of the Atlantic, including *Aeon*, *Underworlds*, *The Horror Express*, *Zahir*, *Neo-Opsis*, *Rogue Worlds*, *Storyteller Magazine* and *Albedo One*.

Northern Frights Publishing
www.northernfrightspublishing.webs.com

ALSO AVAILABLE FROM NORTHERN FRIGHTS PUBLISHING

Oz Awaits...

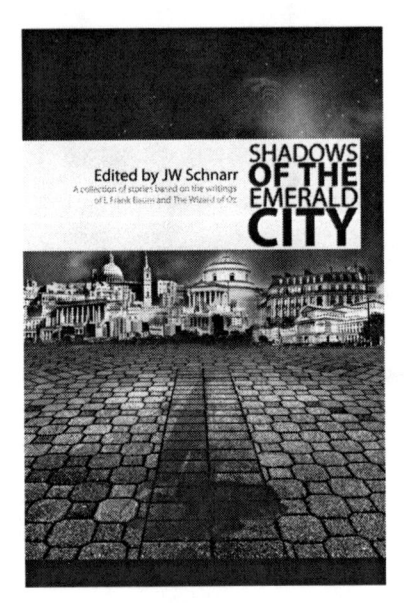

Shadows of the Emerald City

19 tales by some of today's hottest Indie writers peeling back the emerald layers of the land of Oz and revealing the pink, bloody flesh beneath. Some of the people and places you may recognize from your childhood, but you won't believe what happens to them.

Shadows *do* fall in the Emerald City, and where they are their darkest is where you will find the true terror of Oz.

"JW Schnarr hit it out of the park with this collection of macabre, dirty, perverse, corrupted stories. I have never paused while reading to say, "That is so f'd up!" so many times before while reading an anthology. And I meant in the nicest way possible. Though, nice is not a word to be used with this anthology—ever. 5/5"
—Jennifer Brozek, Apex Book Company

$15.95
ISBN 978-0-9734837-1-0

ALSO AVAILABLE FROM NORTHERN FRIGHTS PUBLISHING

Take a Trip Through Terror...

Timelines: Stories Inspired by HG Wells' *The Time Machine*

So I travelled, stopping ever and again, in great strides of a thousand years or more, drawn on by the mystery of the earth's fate, watching with a strange fascination the sun grow larger and duller in the westward sky, and the life of the old earth ebb away...

First published in 1895, *The Time Machine* by Herbert George (H.G.) Wells is a blueprint for science fiction and horror that persists to this day: underneath the science and the theories that attract a reader's mind, there is an underlying story of a person who struggles with the question that burns in the heart of every man: what does it all mean?

Now is your chance to find out. 21 tales of time travel inspired by the grandfather of Science Fiction himself. Take a trip through terror with this exciting anthology from Northern Frights Publishing!

$15.95

ISBN 978-0-9734837-3-4

ALSO AVAILABLE FROM NORTHERN FRIGHTS PUBLISHING

Coming Soon...

Things Falling Apart by JW Schnarr
$15.95
ISBN 978-0-9734837-6-5

Fallen: An Anthology of Demonic Horror
$15.95
ISBN 978-0-9734837-6-5

Northern Frights Publishing
www.northernfrightspublishing.webs.com